TONI BLAKE

LOVE ME IF YOU DARE

A CORAL COVE NOVEL

AVON

An Imprint of HarperCollins*Publishers*

AVON BOOKS
An Imprint of HarperCollins*Publishers*
195 Broadway
New York, New York 10007

Copyright © 2015 by Toni Herzog
ISBN 978-0-06-222953-3
www.avonromance.com

First Avon Books mass market printing: January 2015

Avon Trademark Reg. U.S. Pat. Off. and in Other Countries, Marca Registrada, Hecho en U.S.A.
HarperCollins® is a registered trademark of HarperCollins Publishers.

Printed in the U.S.A.

To my wonderful editor, May Chen,
on the occasion of our tenth book together!
Thank you for so getting me.
You rock!

Acknowledgments

$\mathcal{I}$ sometimes feel that my acknowledgments read like a broken record, because I thank the same people over and over again. However, that's because they are such a help to me—over and over again—and it would be remiss of me not to express my sincere gratitude.

Thank you to Lindsey Faber for her amazing brainstorming and problem-solving abilities, along with the suggestion of using Peter Pan for the quotes and thematic aspects of this one.

Thank you to Renee Norris, not only for always being my wise and helpful first reader when the book is done, but also for sharing her boating and sailing expertise for this particular story.

Thank you to my amazing publishing team: Meg Ruley, Christina Hogrebe, and all the fine folks at the Jane Rotrosen Agency, and May Chen and the whole Avon Books/HarperCollins editorial, marketing, publicity, and sales crew. And thank you to Tom and the art department for yet another gorgeous cover!

It takes a village, and all of you are mine.

His courage was almost appalling.
"Do you want an adventure now?"

J. M. Barrie, *Peter and Wendy*

Chapter 1

CAMILLE THOMPSON tugged her suit jacket into place and smoothed down her skirt. She was over-dressed for the occasion and she knew it. It was by design, a weapon. In her line of work, a woman *needed* weapons, both direct and more subtle, like a crisp red suit that showed confidence and authority before she ever even spoke a word.

She stood before an old fifties-era row motel in a little Florida beach town named Coral Cove. The long, white building sporting a red roof was well kept and tidy, but the parking lot empty. The latter was definitely in her favor—another weapon. And when a glance up at the kitschy sign—of a large, smiling red crab outlined in a tube of red neon—shot a tiny twinge of something like sadness through her veins, she efficiently pushed it right back down from wherever it had sprung.

In her line of work, there was also no room for
sentimentality—or for being the least bit charmed
by a gigantic smiling crab.

She had a job to do—time to get started.

The heels of her black pumps clicked across the
asphalt as she headed for the motel's front office,
and she used the short walk to put on her game
face. Another day, another dollar.

She opened the plate glass door and stepped
inside from the midday tropical heat, ready to face
her opponent, but the only thing that greeted her
was the old song lyric, "Sign, sign, everywhere a
sign," blaring from unseen speakers. It was the
only indication of life in the room that sported
a tall counter, some random wooden cabinets
behind it, and a few large potted palms that had
seen better days. She tapped the old-fashioned
bell on the check-in desk, but when no one came,
she figured the music made it impossible to hear.
"Hello?" she called. "Anyone here? I'm looking for
Reece Donovan. Hello?"

The instant the second hello was leaving her
mouth, the music went silent and a dark-haired
beach bum type appeared in an open doorway
behind the counter. He smiled. And Camille's
chest contracted slightly. She had no idea why.

"Sorry about that," he said, grin still in place.
"Business is a little slow, so afraid you caught me
rockin' out." He ended with a wink that other
people probably found endearing. And he had
that scruffy unshaven thing going—which never
appealed to her since she liked her men well-
groomed, the way *she* was.

"What can I do for you?" he asked. Though that was when she sensed him taking in *her* appearance as well. Realizing that she didn't look like a typical customer at the Happy Crab Motel.

"Reece Donovan?" she inquired.

"One and the same." He still grinned. And she couldn't help noticing his eyes were a rich, deep shade of brown. It was hard not to like him. But maybe that would make this less confrontational than it sometimes was.

And with that in mind, she got straight to the point. "You can sell me your motel," she told him with a smile of her own.

At this, his mouth dropped open slightly and his eyebrows rose into a critical arch.

Since he was clearly now tuning in to where she'd come from, she went on, confirming it. "I'm Camille Thompson and I represent the Vanderhook Company, developer for Windchime Resorts."

"*Oh*," he replied. His tone said, *You again.*

She continued undaunted, though, smile still in place, ready to help him see reason. "I know my associates have approached you with several offers to buy the property on numerous occasions over the past six months, and that you've declined all those offers. Clearly this place means a lot to you—understandable for any business owner." She nodded perfunctorily, letting him know she related. "I'm sure you've put a lot of yourself into this place and I can appreciate its charm. But I'm also sure you'll be pleased to know that Vanderhook is adding an additional one hundred thousand dollars to our offering price. Given that our previous offers were already considerably more than the property is worth, I'm certain you'll agree that accepting this one is the only wise decision you can make."

Reece Donovan cocked his head slightly, an unmistakable glint of self-assurance in his gaze. "On the other hand, I'd say property is worth whatever somebody's willing to pay for it. So it looks like I've got myself quite a valuable little motel here suddenly."

"Touché, Mr. Donovan," she said, admiring his attitude but not looking forward to the work she now knew it would require to wear him down. Even though she *would*. She always *did*. She'd just hoped it might not take a lot of time. Often that was how it went—a property owner was a hard sell, but she showed up, sweetened the pot appreciably, appealed to his or her good senses, and closed the deal verbally in ten minutes or less.

She was Vanderhook's secret weapon and though no one knew exactly what made her so effective, she attributed her many victories to pairing a large sum of money with her sense of confidence and authority. Whatever the secret to her success, though, she'd earned the title of Special Acquisitions Negotiator with years of convincing resistant property owners to sell.

"Of course you're right," she went on, boldly meeting his eyes with hers and still smiling. "It's definitely valuable or I wouldn't be here. But as it stands, you have no business, as sorry as I am to have to point that out. The property isn't being put to best use, and we can *both* rest easy once you allow Vanderhook to change that."

He never broke the gaze. Most people did. Most people found that kind of direct eye contact with a stranger a little unnerving. "Maybe I'd have more business if there wasn't a big 'Windchime Resorts Coming Soon' sign in the lot next door. Kinda makes the motel look closed. And I think you kinda know that." He finished with a short nod.

In fact, she *didn't* know about the sign. But she did know the use of such signs on already acquired adjoining properties was often helpful in the very way he'd stated. "Actually, no—that's a surprise to me," she said.

"Well, here's another surprise. I'm not selling," he told her, his expression still pleasant even if a little arrogant now—he clearly took satisfaction in shooting her down. Then he added, "At *any* price."

Now it was Camille who let her eyebrows rise—in challenge. A part of her was enjoying this, too. Yes, she wanted to close the deal and move on with her life, but she also couldn't help respecting a worthy adversary. "At any price?" came her retort. "That's a very strong statement."

Yet Reece Donovan simply answered with a shrug. In khaki cargo shorts and a faded yellow T-shirt displaying a surfboard emblem, he was clearly a man comfortable in his own body.

But quit noticing that. Stick to work. Time to take a new approach. "You clearly love the business you've built here, and I respect that. However, I'm trying to make you a wealthy man, Mr. Donovan.

With what we're offering, you could buy *five* places like this. Just think, five brand new Happy Crab Motels—smiling crab signs could dot the Gulf Coast. Or . . ." Now she shrugged easily, too. "You could invest—do it smartly and you could live off the income. Regardless of what you do with the money, I'm offering you a future full of options, any of which leaves you far better off than you're starting out." Then she added, "No offense."

"None taken," he answered smoothly. "But you're assuming I don't like where I am. You're assuming I want more than I have. Thing is, I like it just fine. And I don't need five Happy Crabs— just the one I've already got."

In truth, she was a little taken aback. Vanderhook intended to have this property and the amount they were offering was enormous—the kind of money few people would be able to pass up. She couldn't help wondering exactly what made Reece Donovan tick.

But mostly his attitude just made her want to win. So she prepared to barrel forward anyway. Sometimes it was about forcing the issue. And putting the actual dollar signs in front of someone's eyes. Just in case they weren't quite getting the full impact. She lifted her leather briefcase onto the check-in counter and opened it.

"I've already had a contract drawn up with the new terms and amount." She withdrew the document from a manila folder and turned it to face him on the counter. "Look it over. Think about how much we're offering here. That kind of money will go a long way. Perhaps you have someone else you'd like to run the offer past—a wife or significant other? Additional family members?"

He gave his head a short shake as he let his eyes drop coolly to the papers before him. "Nope, not married. I make all my own decisions."

Hmm. Why did that please her? Especially since the input of a spouse would have potentially strengthened her position.

She used the index finger of one well-manicured hand to point to the dollar amount, just to make sure he focused on it. "Surely this is an offer you can't refuse," she suggested.

His eyes held a hint of amusement when he lifted them to her. "Isn't that what the Mafia says? Are you gonna make me sleep with the fishes, too?"

Despite herself, she smiled, still rather liking his sense of fight. It was almost a shame she knew how futile it would ultimately be. "Sign on the dotted line," she told him, "and I'll be happy to take you out to a celebratory dinner at Coral Cove's finest restaurant."

It surprised her when the proposition met with a laugh.

"That would be the Hungry Fisherman next door," he said, giving her another small grin.

"Perfect," she said. "You can *eat* the fish rather than sleep with them."

"But I'm thinking it's not your style," he added. "You're dressed a little too fancy for the seafood buffet. In fact, you're dressed a little too fancy for Coral Cove period." Then he stopped, shifted his weight from one foot to the other, cocked his head to one side, and for the first time looked a little distrustful. "I'm not sure you really get what we're about here."

She remained undisturbed. It was her job, after all. Even if it had been a while since someone put her through her paces. "I'd be happy to go wherever you'd like, overdressed or not, once we close this deal, and then you can tell me exactly what Coral Cove is about over dinner." She used the opportunity to push the document on the counter a little closer to him. "Take a look at the contract, Mr. Donovan. Consider what we're offering here instead of just turning it down out of hand."

"No thanks," he said as comfortably as if she'd asked him to buy a box of Girl Scout cookies. "The Happy Crab isn't for sale. And by the way, you're a little formal for *my* taste, too. Nobody around here calls me Mr. Donovan. I'm Reece."

"Okay," she said pleasantly, but she was only affirming the part about his name, not about the motel. "I should warn you, though, *Reece*, that I don't take no for an answer."

In response, he lowered his chin ever so slightly and pursed his lips, looking like he was trying to figure out how to deal with a misbehaving child. "That's too bad . . . Cami. You don't mind if I call you Cami, do you?"

She let her gaze narrow slightly. The tone between them had begun to change and he was baiting her now—she could feel it. "Actually, I do."

"Your name is too fancy, too," he informed her. "So . . . sorry, Cami, but the answer is still no." Then he hiked his thumb over his shoulder to the right. "But if you want some seafood on your way out of town, the Hungry Fisherman isn't half bad and they could use the business. I'm sure you're all for supporting ailing, locally owned establishments because it's the nice thing to do, right?"

"Touché again, Mr. . . . . *Reece*." She didn't manage to hide her smirk, though—which was a mistake, even if small. It was like revealing a chink in her armor, something she didn't usually let happen. But now he was subtly insulting her, questioning her moral grounds. And she didn't like the way he was shortening her name, trying to minimize her, make her sound like some simpering young girl when she was likely the most capable woman he'd ever met. Not that she'd never been insulted before while doing business. Some property owners were actually much ruder than Reece Donovan had been so far. So why was *this* guy having even an infinitesimal effect on her?

"On the contrary," she went on, "selling your motel to Vanderhook would benefit Coral Cove— including the restaurant next door—far more than hanging on to it ever will. I'm trying to help you take the first step in reviving the part of town that's obviously fallen into decay."

When his whole body stiffened, she could tell that last part hadn't gone over well. "Decay?" he shot back at her. "You're calling my place decayed?"

Her spine went a little more rigid, as well. "No," she said sharply. "I'm saying that when other establishments around you have gone out of business and are left empty, as many have, in real estate and public affairs it's commonly referred to as a state of decay. Don't take anything I say personally, Mr.—" She stopped, blinked—she didn't usually call property owners by their first name and wasn't sure it was a good idea. " . . . Reece. This is business. But make no mistake that *part* of my business is rebuilding areas that need it, and you can't deny that this older part of Coral Cove is in trouble."

"And you think tearing down my place and putting up a generic high-rise resort hotel is gonna fix it all, huh?"

She gave one succinct nod. "I do. Though I promise you that nothing about Windchime Resorts is generic. And I'm sorry that your business has to be the one to go in order to start progress here. But the land has to come from somewhere. And we have indeed already purchased the small lot next door. And as I keep reminding you, you're being more than fairly compensated, and you can do anything you want after that."

He leaned slightly closer over the counter, his gaze sharp and penetrating now. "You're talking as if I've sold you something. I haven't. And I won't."

Her heartbeat kicked up a notch at his very intensity, and without quite planning it, she leaned forward a bit, too, her focus never leaving those big brown eyes of his. "Everyone has a price. Everyone."

As she waited for his reply, she heard the beat of her own heart in her ears now.

"Not me," he said, voice low, bordering on gruff.

Her chest began heaving slightly beneath her suit. "We'll see about that."

She'd never handled a negotiation during which she'd felt so very . . . unsettled. Ugh, did it have something to do with those damn eyes of his? And for some inexplicable reason, her attention returned to that unappealing stubble on his chin. Despite herself, she found herself kind of wanting to . . . touch it.

"Yep, we sure will," he said. "And in the end, you'll be sorry you wasted so much of what I'm sure is your precious time, *Cami*."

She drew in her breath at his use of the shortened name again. She didn't usually suffer that kind of response and she didn't like feeling off her game.

"You can tell the whole Vanderhook Company that it's just not happening," he said, then began shaking his head. "Man, something about that place just *sounds* unscrupulous." After which he snapped his fingers, adding, "I know. It makes me think of Captain Hook. And I guess you think you're some kind of Tinkerbell—you think it's as easy as swooping in here to wave your magic money wand and sprinkle your fairy dust on me—but it's not gonna work, honey."

Inside, she prickled, yet rather than let it show this time, she instead forced a hard smile to say, "First of all, I'm not anybody's honey. And second, I'm a hell of a lot tougher than Tinkerbell ever was."

This produced the first hint of a grin she'd seen from him in a few minutes, even if this one came out looking colder. "I don't doubt that. But I'm still not selling my motel."

Their gazes remained locked. Though now she found herself trying to somehow see behind his eyes, understand what he was about. Because this didn't add up.

She lowered her chin slightly, truly wanting to know the answer when she asked, "Why? Why on earth would any sane man hold on to a dying old motel when selling it will make you rich? What am I missing here?"

Once again, Reece Donovan leaned a little closer, and this time every molecule of her body tightened a bit more as he calmly, deeply replied, "None of your business."

But her unbidden response didn't matter. This was just another typical work day for her. So Camille paused to regroup, take a deep breath. And then she answered just as calmly. "Fine. I'd like a room."

He balked. "You're not serious."

Yet she was. "Look, I flew down here from our corporate offices in Atlanta to meet with you, and I could use a little rest before I fly back."

His eyes bolted open wide. "You flew here? For this? A phone call would have been cheaper."

"Regardless," she said, resisting the urge to roll her eyes, "I have to spend the night *somewhere*. So I'd like to check in."

Reece shot her a glance she'd have deemed critical if she'd cared.

But she didn't. Starting now. Starting now, this

guy had zero effect on her, like every other property owner she'd had to strategize her way around over the years.

"I think the resorts up the road might be more your style," he said. "You know, the resorts like the one you want to build *here*."

"Probably so," she agreed, "but . . . maybe I'd like to see what's so special about this place."

"I never said anything was special," he pointed out, "only that I'm not selling." He narrowed his gaze on her. "Seems to me more like you just want to stick around and get under my skin."

He was right, more or less. But she ignored the accusation, along with the fact that it made her think about his skin. "I'd like a room," she repeated, "and from the look of the parking lot, I'd think you would welcome the business."

As before, the man across from her shifted his weight from one foot to the other, but then he got more agreeable. "You're right," he replied. "You want a room, Cami? You got it. I'm more than happy to take your money in return for the annoyance."

And as she handed over her credit card a few seconds later, their fingers brushing during the exchange, two notable things struck her. That Reece Donovan's business was so archaic he didn't even use a computer to manage it. And that—oh crap—an undeniable ripple fluttered up her arm at the touch.

But what does it matter? Soon enough she'd secure his signature, obtaining the property for Vanderhook, and then she'd never see him again.

CAMILLE unloaded her small roller bag from the trunk of her rental car and pulled it behind her across the blacktop toward the slightly cracked sidewalk that led to her room. Reece was right— the Happy Crab wouldn't be her first choice in accommodations. But she wasn't going back to Atlanta until she figured out how to procure this property from him. She'd never failed in a negotiation and she had no intention of messing up her perfect record now. Occasionally someone played hardball. It only meant she had to stick around a little while, until she beat them at the game.

Given the entire lack of cars in the parking lot other than her own, she was mildly surprised to see an old man ambling up the walk at the other end of the long, narrow, one-story building, but she didn't give him much thought, instead taking in more details about the place than she'd noticed a few minutes ago.

Its tidiness showed her that Reece took good care of the place. The red-and-white color scheme suited the retro feel of the establishment. And though the white paint was beginning to crack and peel in one spot, being baked in relentless Florida sun tended to do that, and given the dearth of customers, she couldn't blame the guy for not wanting to put the money into new paint. Soon enough the building would be bulldozed anyway.

When she reached door number 11, she lifted the old-fashioned key Reece Donovan had given her—and for the first time noticed it was attached to a red plastic keychain shaped like a crab and sporting the same happy face as the big sign out front. It made her smile a little in spite of herself.

When she attempted to slide the key in the lock, however, it stuck. So she pulled it out and tried again, this time getting it in all the way, but it still wouldn't turn.

"Pardon me, miss—can I help with that? All the locks are due for some lubrication—just haven't got to it yet."

She looked up to see the older gentleman she'd spotted a minute ago, now realizing that he carried a bucket. His gray hair could have used a trim, his beard was a little spotty, and his dirty shorts and golf shirt made him the least tidy thing she'd seen here so far—but his eyes were kind and she felt instantly at ease with him. "Are you the maintenance man?" she asked.

He hesitated only slightly. "Somethin' like that. I help Reece out. He's been real good to me." He pointed to the key still jammed in the lock. "May I?"

"Sure."

She stood back from the door and watched as the man lowered his bucket to the concrete and stepped in, jiggling the key a bit, then using his other hand to turn the doorknob—and the lock clicked open.

Withdrawing the key, he pressed it back into her hand. "There ya go, miss. Hope you enjoy your stay. It's a real nice place for sure. And now that

Reece has a guest, I'll put a little graphite in this lock next thing and it'll work like a charm for ya."

Something in his manner warmed her heart, even if his sweet nature left her feeling a little melancholy in a way she couldn't quite understand. "Thank you very much, Mr. . . ."

"Name's Riley, miss," he said, retrieving his bucket.

"Thank you, Mr. Riley."

"Happy to help," he assured her, and as she wheeled her suitcase into the room, she found herself feeling just as curious about him, in ways, as she was about his employer.

The room was much like she would have expected: clean, simple but friendly, a softer pastel beach décor than the exterior of the building. The one surprise was the window in the rear of the room that looked out on the bay.

She'd known a natural bay edged the rear of the property—it was a key component of Windchime's interest, although the waterfront area would probably be reconfigured to suit the resort's needs. But she hadn't expected a room with a view, the small window revealing a planked dock with a few sizable boats tied up to it. The white sails and riggings against a blue, cloud-dotted sky were like a painting come to life.

Were the boats connected to the Happy Crab in any way? Did Reece own one of them? All of them? Seemed unlikely.

But what did she care anyway? Soon they'd all be relocated elsewhere so that progress could march forward in Coral Cove, and she'd be on the road to some other waterside destination to secure the next sale for Vanderhook and Windchime.

The digital clock next to the king size bed informed her it was just past three. Her first order of business: take a shower, put on more comfortable clothes, and start getting Reece Donovan to like her. At this stage of the game, it would be necessary to piece together a plan based on the individual seller, but the one thing she sensed already was that he would need to like her before she'd get anywhere.

And despite her qualms about getting too comfy with a property owner, she had to concede that it was time to bring things down to his level—if he didn't like her formality, she would have to cease being so formal, that simple. So changing into some shorts and a more weather-appropriate top seemed in order. And as it was already over eighty degrees on this spring day, a cool shower sounded nice.

Stripping off her clothes, she tossed her jacket and skirt on the bed, then let her bra and panties drop in a heap next to the pumps she'd taken off. Stepping into the small bathroom naked, she retrieved a pastel green towel from the rack above the toilet to have handy for afterward, then she pushed back the shower curtain—and let out a blood curdling scream at the sight of the monster in her bathtub!

She nearly tripped, stumbling backward as the huge, scaly creature with tiny legs began scrambling around the old porcelain tub. As it scrambled, she screamed some more, even though she couldn't see much of it as she clumsily retreated farther—she could only make out part of its horrible head and a humongous tail now whipping about, slamming into the wall this way and that.

What the hell was it? And God, what if it got out and chased her?

Her first instinct was to flee the room.

But I'm naked.

She still held the towel, so she threw it around her as she moved toward the door.

But I'm still naked.

Then—ugh—she heard the thing scrambling some more! It was clearly on the verge of exiting the tub—so she screamed again, only slightly aware that she'd begun hopping from foot to foot as if it might suddenly be slithering around on the floor beneath her—even though it was in the next room.

But then again, if there was something like that in *there*, how did she know there wasn't another one out *here*, under the bed or something? Oh Lord.

She hopped some more and whimpered.

The bed. Get on the bed.

She leapt up on it, the towel still loosely circling her body, held together in front by one tightly-clenched fist.

That was when the door to her room burst open and Reece Donovan rushed in.

And—uh oh—she was still naked.

... And this, as we shall see, led to mischief.

J. M. Barrie, *Peter and Wendy*

Chapter 2

REECE BALKED, taking in the sight before him. If he'd been drinking, he'd think he was seeing things. But since he was completely sober, he had no choice but to conclude that the stiff, starched, manipulative woman who'd tried to wheedle him out of his motel a few minutes ago was now standing on a bed in Room 11 wearing nothing but a towel and looking a little crazy.

"What the hell's going on in here? Were you screaming? What happened?"

Stark terror shone in her blue eyes as she pointed toward the bathroom. "It's in there!" she said. Which wasn't exactly the helpful explanation he'd been hoping for.

He just blinked his confusion. "What's in where?"

She shook her head nervously, her eyes still filled with fright. "I don't know *what* the hell it is, but it's in my tub! It's—it's . . . a dinosaur or something!"

Reece narrowed his eyes. He was pretty sure there wasn't a dinosaur in her tub. But he strode into the bathroom, glanced down, and—oh, now he understood.

Riley had finished some plumbing work in this room earlier—that was why Reece had given it to her; he'd known nothing would leak or dribble. And apparently Riley had had some company while he worked.

Stepping back out of the bathroom, Reece glanced toward the panicked, naked woman on the bed and gave her a quick grin. "That's not a dinosaur. It's just Fifi."

The naked woman squinted down at him. "Fifi?"

"My giant iguana."

Now it was she who blinked and looked confused. "Your giant what?"

"I-gua-na," he said, enunciating each syllable in case she was hard of hearing or something.

She continued to appear horrified. "You have an iguana? They come that big? Why would you have such a thing?"

He didn't bother hiding his amusement. She didn't seem nearly as tough as she'd claimed back in his office, or even as tough as she'd actually seemed. "Yep. And that's why it's called a giant iguana—because it's giant. And she's a pet."

Despite the clear answers he'd given, she still looked completely perplexed, her mouth open in the shape of a perfect "o." "A pet," she repeated dryly.

"Uh huh."

"Strange pet."

He shrugged. "Different strokes." Then he glanced back into the bathroom. Fifi was agitated, hissing and swishing her tail. No wonder, with all that screaming. He spoke in a soothing voice to say, "It's all right, girl, everything's okay. Nobody's gonna hurt you." After which he glanced back to Cami—a name which, frankly, he thought suited her much more than Camille. Especially when she was naked. "You scared her," he accused.

Cami's eyes flew wide. "*I* scared *her*?" Then she shook her head. "What on earth is it doing in my room?"

This woman was earning no points by calling Fifi "it." "*She* must have gotten locked in when some work was being done in here this morning," he explained. "Happens occasionally and I have to go looking for her. Sorry about that." Though it was hard to keep a straight face for the last part since he wasn't really sorry at all. For a normal guest, he'd have been sorry—but for this one, he actually thought it was pretty damn funny. As long as Fifi didn't end up too traumatized.

"You don't *look* very sorry," Cami pointed out.

"I'm as sorry as I can be," he told her, which was the truth. He just couldn't be very sorry at the moment. Then he raised his eyebrows to add, "You can come down off the bed now."

At which point she started to appear a little more . . . aware of things. Like maybe that she'd blown her tough-business-woman cover. And like maybe that she wasn't wearing any clothes.

The towel covered way more than any bikini, but it was still sexy as hell. And part of him didn't want to think a piranha like her could be sexy—but on the other hand, sexy was sexy and what guy was immune to it?

Back in the office, he'd known she was an attractive, confident woman with a pretty face and a shapely body. But now he was seeing . . . more of her. And not just skin. Now he was seeing that she was . . . human. And human plus attractive . . . somehow he couldn't *stop* seeing the sexiness now. Even if he thought she'd blown the Fifi thing out of proportion.

As she stepped toward the edge of the bed and he held out his hand to help her down, his gaze dropped to the creamy round curves swelling from the top edge of the terrycloth and he couldn't help thinking his seafoam green guest towels had never looked quite so hot before.

After reaching the floor, she clearly realized where he was looking and drew back her hand with a gasp.

He flinched at the move. "You're naked," he said in his defense. "I can't help it."

"But you burst in without even knocking," she accused.

"You screamed. Don't scream if you don't want somebody to burst in."

She let out a small harrumph, apparently conceding the point—or at least unable to invent a comeback.

"I thought there was actually something wrong," he went on, suddenly feeling a little indignant. Given the racket she'd made, he'd been envisioning something like an intruder, or fire.

"Something *was* wrong," she insisted.

"Yeah," he said, not trying to hide his sarcasm, "my dinosaur was in your bathtub." He took a couple of steps back in that direction, glancing toward the iguana to say softly, "Come on, Fifi Girl. Come on outta there and let's go." Then he made the little kissy sound she often responded to and watched as she began to climb slowly out of the tub, calmer now than when he'd first arrived. "Good girl."

Cami took a few tense steps back, wariness filling her gaze, as Fifi followed him out into the room.

"She's harmless," he promised. "For a dinosaur." He quirked an amused grin her way.

She didn't smile back.

He returned his glance to Fifi—admittedly a slow mover—as she followed him toward the door, then spoke to her in a playful voice. "She thought you were a dinosaur, Feefe." Then he looked to Cami and lifted his hands into monster-like claws and said, "*Rawr!*"

She flinched.

And he let out a laugh.

And she made a mean face at him, which he just ignored.

"A shame there *wasn't* a dinosaur in your tub," he mused. "I'd be rich."

"You could be rich anyway if you'd just sell me your—"

"Stop," he said, holding up one hand, palm facing her. "Not gonna happen."

And to his pleasant surprise, she actually stayed quiet. Probably worn out from the big dinosaur scare.

As he and Fifi reached the door, he looked back a final time to say, "Have a nice night, Cami."

"My name is Camille," she pointed out once again.

But he only shrugged. "You say tomato," he replied, then cheerfully whistled the tomato-tomahto song as he waited for Fifi to amble out behind him before shutting the door and walking away.

REECE stood behind the check-in desk, taking a quick look at the weather app on his phone. Sunny and clear. Then he peered out the plate glass window toward the beach across the road.

All those people having fun on their vacation right now, within his very eyesight? Not a one of them was staying at the Happy Crab. And the fact was, other than a few friends, he was mostly alone in the world.

Despite those things, however, he remained laid-back, easygoing—he chose to focus on the good in life instead of the bad. He was a pretty carefree guy most of the time, even when there were plenty of reasons he could be otherwise.

But the one thing he needed in order to *keep* being carefree was this motel. It was just a part of him. And he didn't care if anyone understood that or not—he only wanted his life to stay the way it was. Why was that so hard for this chick to understand?

He glanced absently in the direction of Room 11. Was she taking that shower right now?

Hell, she was probably afraid she'd pick up dinosaur germs from the tub.

But if she *was* in there . . . was her body as gorgeous without a towel wrapped around it as it had looked? Was she running a fresh bar of tiny motel soap over those silky curves? Were there lots of suds? Reece liked lots of suds.

Then he gave his head a brisk shake and glanced to Fifi, now curled comfortably in her favorite corner of the office, behind the desk. "It's been too long since I was with a woman," he informed her.

Because *this* woman was not his type—so why was he thinking about her in the shower? Sure, he'd seen some nice towel cleavage. And who was he kidding—he'd noticed her long, gorgeous legs, too. And when she'd stepped off the bed, the towel had barely covered her and he'd caught a sexy-as-hell glimpse of hip—he'd even seen tan lines. But no matter how sexy she was under that red suit, she still wasn't his type. At all.

And okay, he'd had some fun catching her with her defenses down—it wasn't his fault it had happened, but he'd taken full advantage of the situation. "I still can't believe she thought you were a dinosaur," he said to Fifi. He was used to the Feefster catching guests a little off guard, but having someone call her a dinosaur—that was a new one.

And if Camille Thompson had been anyone else, maybe, just maybe, he'd have thought it was . . . cute. But she *wasn't* anyone else. She was the Vanderhook Company personified. "She's a vulture," he added to Fifi. And he didn't like that she'd scared his iguana, either.

"Doing okay now, girl?" he asked. She couldn't answer, of course, but he still felt the need to soothe her. Iguanas could be a lot more sensitive than they looked, and it didn't take much to frighten his. She'd grown used to being around strangers due to living at a motel, but sudden noises—like a screaming lunatic—tended to upset her. Fortunately, she usually calmed down quickly, too, and Reece knew his presence put her at ease. "Don't worry—we won't let that mean lady in the towel bother you anymore."

Just then the office door opened and Riley stepped in. "That new guest down in room eleven had trouble with her key, so I told her I'd put some graphite in the lock," he said.

"Good idea," Reece told him as Riley walked around the counter toward the maintenance closet behind it.

"She sure is a pretty lady," the older man said.

"Yep." Reece couldn't argue that. Wouldn't even try.

"Was there some trouble in her room? I heard a ruckus when I was workin' in seven. But stuck my head out and saw you go rushin' in, so figured whatever it was, you'd call me if ya needed me."

Reece gave the old man a soft smile. "Fifi was in her tub. She'd never seen a giant iguana before, so it scared her a little."

Riley tossed him a sideways glance. "Sounded like more than a little."

And they both chuckled before Reece said, "She deserved it, though."

Riley had been searching out the graphite on a low shelf, but this drew his gaze back to Reece. "What do you mean? She seemed like a nice lady."

"Afraid not," Reece informed his friend. "She's with the company that keeps trying to buy me out."

Riley's aged eyes darkened at the news. "Well, that's a cryin' shame, that is. But . . . maybe you're judgin' her too quick. She might still be nice."

Yet Reece shook his head in a knowing way. "Nope, she's pushy, manipulative, and refuses to take no for an answer, no matter how many times I give it to her. And everything about that company has struck me as money-grubbing and unscrupulous—and she strikes me the same way. Pretty or not."

When movement outside drew Reece's eyes to the plate glass windows and beyond, Riley's followed and they watched the lady in question cross the parking lot in denim shorts, a fitted tank, and flip-flops. "Huh," he said. Now *he* was the one caught off guard. A little anyway.

"What?" Riley asked.

"Just didn't think she could look so . . . casual." Or . . . cute. But that part he kept to himself.

"She's awful cute," Riley said then, as if on cue.

He gave the older man a quick glance. "I guess. Maybe."

And Riley laughed. "No maybe about it, padre. A shame ya think she's so . . . what'd you call her— unscrupulous? Otherwise, if I was a fella your age, I'd be plantin' Fifi in her room every chance I got and just waitin' to come to her rescue."

Reece couldn't help letting out a good-natured laugh at the idea. But only the idea. In reality, he wanted nothing to do with Vanderhook's little Miss Tinkerbell. Maybe it *was* a shame, but he couldn't change who she was or what she was about.

"Oh well, doesn't matter," he told Riley. "She'll be checking out in the morning and going back to wherever she came from."

Hopefully never to darken his door again.

THE day was waning on Coral Cove Beach by the time Camille took to the sand, her beaded flip-flops dangling from one hand. Families busily packed up to go, tossing towels in beach bags, folding up colorful umbrellas. Still, she found a certain charm in it all that she hadn't quite expected. She was used to spending time at resorts that were lavish but . . . in some ways all alike. She was accustomed to seeing precise rows of matching umbrellas or cabanas lined up like little armies facing the water—and something appealed to her about the scattered, colorful randomness she took in now. A striped umbrella here, a turquoise one there, the wooden red-and-white lifeguard stand in the middle of it all. A young couple flew bright kites near the pier that made crinkly sounds as they twisted and turned and swooped in the wind.

The whole scene made for a nice distraction

from what was really on her mind. She'd embarrassed herself with Reece Donovan.

Dinosaur? She'd really said dinosaur?

But it had looked sort of like one. Or a dragon. Not that saying *that* would have been much better.

And on top of it all, he'd seen her in nothing but a towel. Talk about feeling naked, both figuratively and literally. And then he'd made fun of her.

She'd never been so disarmed in front of a property owner before; she'd never let anyone in her professional realm see her looking or acting any less than sophisticated and in control. Now she felt as if her armor had been stripped away, like Zorro if someone ripped off his mask. Without his mask, Zorro was still Zorro, but . . . without it, it was impossible not to comprehend that he had other sides. And so did she. She was sorry she'd let Reece Donovan see any of them.

She also remained sorry to find him . . . oddly attractive. Odd because she just didn't go for beach bums or anyone who could fall even remotely into that category. And she especially didn't go for one dumb enough to pass up an offer as great as the one Vanderhook had so generously presented to him.

And yet there was something about his cool confidence. And, again, his eyes. And grin. Though maybe the grin had been a little less appealing when he'd been practically laughing at her.

Not many people made her feel vulnerable. Or got to see her feeling weak. But when she'd walked into the bathroom, ready to relax with a nice long shower, and instead she'd seen that . . .

that *thing*, when she'd least expected it, she'd reacted like a little girl.

*But you're not a little girl anymore. Haven't been
one for a very long time, and thank goodness.* She liked
who she was as an adult much more. Or maybe
she just liked the control she possessed over her
life now much more. She'd built a good one for
herself, and she'd worked hard to get where she
was, hard to overcome a past she resented.

*The truth is, screaming at that giant iguana made
you feel just as weak and defenseless as when you were
a kid.*

She sighed, putting one bare foot in front of the
other as she made her way up the shore. *And Reece
Donovan saw you like that.* She shook her head, still
a little put out with herself. She never made mis-
takes on the job. Ever.

But it would be okay. It took more than one
giant iguana and its arrogant owner to keep her
down. Now was the time to regroup.

So what was she going to do to get this guy to
give up that dinky little motel?

What was his attachment to a completely failing business that could make him rich if he simply
let it go? Maybe she needed to dig for that answer.
And in the meantime, she should also start looking for ways around it if she came up empty.

One thing she knew for sure, though, was that
after the bathtub incident she felt even more determined than before to make him sell. Before that, it
had been all about business and succeeding—but
now it was almost a point of pride, too.

Though even if her pride hadn't come into play

here, she still had to figure out a way. It wasn't an *if* for Camille—it was a *how* and a *when*. That simple.

As she'd hoped, a walk on the beach had cleared her head. And was slowly bringing her normal confidence back around. Coming to a halt, she lowered her flip-flops to the sand and reached for the cell phone in her pocket. From it, she sent a text to her administrative assistant, Kate.

NEGOTIATIONS GOING SLOWER THAN EXPECTED ON CORAL COVE, FLORIDA PROPERTY. CANCEL MY CALENDAR FOR THE WEEK—I'M GOING TO NEED TO STAY A FEW DAYS TO GET THIS ONE UNDER WRAPS.

Next order of business: putting her game face back on. Remembering who she was. And what weapons lay in her arsenal. The biggest, hands down, was her unwavering confidence. Which had—okay—wavered just slightly over the last couple of hours. But that was rare, there was a first time for everything, and it was over now. And the next time Reece Donovan saw her, she'd make him forget she'd ever appeared the least bit vulnerable or weak in front of him.

REECE had slept poorly. Visions of an evil Tinkerbell had danced in his head.

But it was a new morning, and a happy one, because Vanderhook's shapely henchman—or hench*woman*, as the case may be—would be checking out of the Happy Crab, leaving the Crab to be happy again, and she'd also be checking out of his life.

And if you want a hot chick—and his reaction to little Miss Cami in a towel told him maybe he wanted a hot chick—*there's a great big beach right across the street, filled with all the people staying at the fancy resorts up the road.* As a man who appreciated a good, no-strings fling, he was living in the perfect place for it. Maybe he'd go for a stroll on the beach today himself, see what was new in bikinis this season.

Getting up, he ran his hand back through his hair in a light effort to tame it a little, tugged the covers up in a light effort to make the bed, and pulled on a pair of gym shorts in a light effort to dress. If there were more guests at the Crab, he'd have been up and at it much earlier, but as it was, he saw no need not to take it easy.

What if the guests never come back?

It was a question that had been flitting around the recesses of his brain lately, but his general solution was just not to worry about it. Some stretches were leaner than others, but he was in good shape on money. And yeah, winter had been unusually slow and business hadn't picked up in early spring like usual, at least partly due to that damn Windchime sign—*but it'll be fine.*

The small lot next door had been home to a snowcone stand for years, but it had closed and the little white hut had sat vacant for months now. In fact, he'd thought if business ever turned around that maybe he'd buy the land himself and improve it some way—sell beach amenities from it or something. Until that Windchime sign had gone up.

He'd be damned if he'd let a high-rise resort be built here. Up the road, outside town, that was one thing—resorts fit well enough there, and the land they occupied had been only marshland until their arrival. But here, right in the heart of Coral Cove with all its old-fashioned one- and two-story businesses, it didn't make sense. And besides, the Happy Crab was more than his business; it was his home.

Meandering through his small apartment and out into the office, he spied a small box of donuts on the counter and knew Riley had gotten them from the Beachside Bakery next door. For a man who had so little, Riley was generous. But then, he suspected Riley would probably say the same thing about him.

Reaching inside, he plucked out something that looked jelly-filled and took a bite. Yep, jelly—yum. Then he glanced through the open door of the small room on the other side of the office, outfitted with heat lamps and other iguana-related comforts, to the giant iguana who rested in the corner. "Morning, Feefster. I'll get your veggies together in a few. Shame you don't like donuts, though—you don't know what you're missing."

That was when he caught a glimpse of the motel pool out the office's back window and was stopped in his tracks—by the sight of a gorgeous woman in a coral-colored bikini stretched out on a lounge chair.

Were his eyes playing tricks on him? Was it really as easy as: wish for a hot girl in a bikini and one magically appears by the pool? And he couldn't *really* tell if she was gorgeous from this distance—but from where he stood, she looked pretty perfect: blond, curvy, scantily clad. All the important stuff.

Still, who the hell could she be? He squinted, looking again. He let friends use the pool when the place was empty, but they always checked with him first. And since no one had checked with him . . .

Forgetting that he'd just rolled out of bed, he pushed through the back door and toward the mystery bikini lady.

And the closer he got, the more he realized she wasn't such a mystery. She was . . . Tinkerbell, damn it. It was after ten A.M. and he'd just assumed she'd be gone by now.

As he moved on bare feet over the concrete toward her, he realized two things: She totally rocked that coral bikini, and the fact that she was still here didn't bode well. At all.

He walked right up to her chair, trying not to appreciate how nicely her breasts filled out the bikini top or how provocative she looked all stretched out that way, her arms flung carelessly over her head, her eyes shut. *And I refuse to get a hard-on.*

"Um, almost checkout time," he announced, knowing he sounded a little too impatient. But all things considered, he didn't much care.

Her eyes fluttered open and she looked sleepy,

sexy—kind of like a woman who'd just had really good sex. *For God's sake, dude, knock it off. She's a vulture.*

"Is it?" she asked lazily. "No matter. I'm not in a hurry. I've decided to take a little vacation, maybe stay few days."

"Tell me you're kidding," Reece begged.

"Can't, because I'm not." Her self-satisfied look edged its way under his skin.

His voice came out brittle. "Lucky me."

"You *are* lucky," she insisted. "You need the business."

Reece forced himself to stay calm. "You're right," he agreed. "Especially with so many dinosaurs running around."

To put it with brutal frankness,
there never was a cockier boy.

J. M. Barrie, *Peter and Wendy*

Chapter 3

𝓕OR THE first time since she'd opened her eyes, Camille found herself giving him a once-over. He looked messy . . . but good. She intended to focus on the messy part. "Is this how you greet all your guests in the morning?"

He shot her a pointed stare. "Usually only the ones I wake up next to. But looks like you got lucky today, too."

Okay, so he was turning things sexual here? Of course, he'd already done that a little when she'd been naked yesterday, but frankly, that had seemed more understandable—and somehow less in-your-face. Or maybe the whole situation had just felt too surreal for her to really process it all correctly.

At any rate, she simply shrugged and replied, "Matter of opinion." And did her level best to look completely unaffected. Even though his gray cotton gym shorts sort of . . . clung to him a little in front.

And even though his chest was nice. Muscular but not he-man muscular, with a nice smattering of hair that she wouldn't have minded touching. What was it with wanting to touch his body hair? And he was tan, too. *Stop noticing already!*

"Well, at least I'm wearing more than a towel." He glanced down at himself and added, "Sort of anyway." And looked smug. Like he was God's gift to women.

And suddenly she imagined waking up next to him, like he'd said. *Oh, for heaven's sake, stop! Seriously! Since when are you so . . . man-hungry?*

Since now, apparently. That just wasn't usually her way, though.

"That's different," she defended herself to him. "I didn't go parading around in it purposely."

"Look," he said, suddenly sounding all practical and as if she were a child to be reasoned with, "what difference does it make? We're at the pool. I'm wearing as much as I would if I were going swimming. And in fact . . ." He stopped to glance down at the empty white lounge chair directly next to hers, one of many. "Maybe I'll just join you out here for a little while. You wouldn't mind that, would you, Cami?"

She tried not to make a face at the annoying nickname, but was pretty sure he could tell he'd struck a nerve anyway. He was ridiculously good at that. But at least she was no longer behaving like the weak, wimpy girl he'd seen in her room yesterday.

"Free country," she tossed off as he took a seat and lay back, clearly getting comfortable. "Although if you think you'll drive me away by forcing me to spend time with you and irritating me, you're wasting your time. I'm sure I can irritate you just as badly."

She saw only the slight quirk of a grin at the edges of his mouth as he looked out over the pool and said, "You already do."

And despite herself, she smiled inside. "Well-played, Mr. Donovan."

At that, however, he slanted her a critical look. "Now that *does* irritate me. How many times do I have to tell you –"

"*Reece*," she said, correcting herself before he could go on about it. "Reece, Reece, Reece. Happy now?"

He shrugged. "I wouldn't go *that* far. But I'm a little less irritated." Then he relaxed back into his chair again.

They stayed silent for a few minutes after that, and Camille worked to get a firmer grip on the situation. After all, this was an entirely different way of pursuing an acquisition than she'd ever put into play before. A part of her questioned the wisdom of it. Lying here next to him in a bikini seemed pretty unprofessional. But then, perhaps that ship had sailed during the whole standing-on-the-bed-in-a-towel-screaming incident. And she had to get him to sell the motel *somehow*.

Maybe you should just relax. Enjoy the sun. It did feel good on her face, on her skin. She didn't often relax and unwind, so maybe she should do what she'd claimed, make this a mini-vacation. During which she would figure out how to get his signature on that contract.

"Mind if I ask you something?" he inquired.

She sent a dry, cautious glance in his direction. "Probably, but go ahead."

He tilted his head, met her gaze, and made her heart beat a little faster, just from that. "What do you really hope to gain by sticking around here? Because when I tell you I'm not selling, I mean it."

"I believe you," she assured him. And she did— she just intended to change that. "But maybe I just like the peace and quiet. After all, I had the whole pool to myself before *you* came along and ruined it."

But as they exchanged looks, and she accidentally let the tiniest glimpse of a smile sneak out, which he then returned, she realized that they were perhaps beginning to settle into a more peaceful sort of battle. It was that whole thing about having a worthy opponent, respecting your adversary. Yes, she would have preferred if he'd just sign on the dotted line and let her call it a day, but since he hadn't . . . well, at least she found him interesting, and challenging. There were worse traits.

But back to business. He'd given her an opening, so she was going to take it—going to start very subtly trying to understand his seemingly unshakable attachment to this place. "And maybe you have me curious about Coral Cove. Maybe I want to learn more about what makes this place tick."

"Just so you can tear it down?" Crisp accusation colored his voice.

She looked back over at him, almost admiring his integrity. But maybe he was still missing the big picture here. And if so, she was willing to spell it out for him. "We don't want to tear down the whole town. Just this motel. So don't worry—I'm not trying to make you think I'm going soft on this, or that I can be convinced the Happy Crab should stay. I can't. It's my job not to. But that doesn't mean I'm not interested in learning about the area."

He returned a bold look and said slowly, thoughtfully, "Cami, has anybody ever told you that you're kind of a hard-ass?"

She flinched—but kept her game face on, despite being taken aback. The word didn't wound her—she was too tough for that—and yet . . . maybe, for some insane reason, she didn't like *him* seeing her that way.

Though she had no idea why, so she was just going to ignore that odd little feeling. "I don't believe so," she replied smoothly. "But I'm going to take it as a compliment—no matter how you meant it."

He replied with only a short, almost indulgent nod that left her feeling a bit empty inside. One more useless emotion to push away.

Back to work. "You seem pretty attached to Coral Cove," she said, "so if you want to show me around, it would give you maximum opportunity to irritate me. But if you'd rather not, I'm perfectly happy to wander around on my own without anyone annoying me."

Next to her, she sensed him thinking it over and then heard him let out a breath. "On the one hand, I've lived here my whole life, so I know the place, and if you're determined to stick around and go investigating, maybe I'd rather do it *with* you than risk letting you terrorize my iguana and possibly everyone else in town. On the other, this would also give *you* maximum opportunity to irritate *me*, too."

"And I would take full advantage of that," she pointed out.

"I don't doubt it," he said. "And you already are."

She sensed his amusement at their continuing repartee more than she actually saw it—just before they exchanged looks. She took in the dark brown of his eyes again, and despite herself, even found something about his messy hair appealing now. Though she asked, "Do they not have barbers or hairdressers in Coral Cove?"

He blinked, clearly confused. "Yeah. Why?"

"You could just use a trim, that's all."

He let out a laugh. "What a hard-ass." Then he rolled his eyes and said, "But now that you're even officially flinging insults, too, I guess I should show you around—even if it's against my better judgment. Just to keep you in line."

She gave a short nod, pleased. But only because it was the next step in her plan to figure out how to get him to sell—not because she actually wanted to spend more time with him. Even if the idea of it made something in her chest feel warm. "That sounds fine," she informed him. "Though bear in mind you bring out the worst in me."

"Likewise," he said. "And my iguana isn't too crazy about you, either."

* * *

As Camille turned over from her stomach to her back on the lounge chair, she experienced an unusual self-awareness. Maybe it was the idea that he was watching her, taking in her every move, taking in details about her body. Or maybe *she* was the one taking in details about her body.

She wore this same bathing suit whenever she traveled or swam, and being in a bikini didn't typically give her sexual thoughts or feelings. Today, though, she was noticing the curves of her own breasts more, and wondering if he was, too. She found herself hoping they looked perky—and she couldn't remember the last time she'd harbored that kind of wish. She was a mature woman whose mind usually dwelled elsewhere—on business, on practical matters, even on lofty issues like the state of the world. Her breasts were not a lofty subject, but suddenly she was aware of them.

Of course, they were *making* it that way by being more sensitive than usual. And as she resituated in her chair, attempting to subtly tug her bottoms into place, a glance down revealed that her nipples were hard. Did he see? Was he watching? And yikes, it was about eighty-five and sunny—there wasn't exactly a chill in the air—so if he saw, did he think he was the reason? And was he, for heaven's sake?

You're thinking too hard, worrying too much. Just let this be.

She reminded herself to relax, that this was simply combining work and a vacation. She supposed she was more accustomed to feeling completely in control of a situation, and Reece Donovan was tampering with that a little. *So maybe you should just see this as a new challenge, a new work environment of sorts.* She bit her lip, though, thinking: *How exactly does working fit in with wondering if he likes how I look in a bikini?*

"Where is it you said you're from?" he asked, still stretched lazily out alongside her in the next chair.

She flinched, because they'd both stayed quiet for a while. Then tried to sound like her usual more cool, mature self as she replied, "Atlanta."

"Not from there originally, though, right?"

She glanced over at him, curious. How did he know that? "I grew up in rural Michigan. Why?"

He tilted his head slightly against the reclined lounge chair. "Not a lot of sun up in Michigan?"

"Sure there is. Why?" she asked again.

"Well, I'd just think anyone who's spent much time in the sun would know you have to wear sunscreen next to the pool. You're burning, Tinkerbell."

She drew back at the name he'd called her. It had been bad enough the first time, in his office yesterday, but . . . "Really?" she snapped. "Cami isn't bad enough? Now I'm Tinkerbell, too? A weak, delicate little fairy?"

He shrugged, looking as arrogant as usual. "You and she might have more in common than you realize. I remember her being pretty conniving." Then he flashed the first full-on smile she'd seen from him today. "And besides, you'd be disappointed if I didn't irritate you."

"Would I?" she challenged him, trying not to feel the added warmth of that sexy grin.

"Regardless," he pointed out, "you need sunscreen."

And Camille couldn't help feeling a little stupid—she'd truly forgotten completely about it. She sometimes spent time in the sun when traveling for work, but everything about this little business trip had gotten skewed in ways she hadn't expected. "I didn't plan to stay," she reminded him. "And so I didn't bring any." She glanced down at herself once more, this time trying to make out any pinkness, but in the bright sunlight, she couldn't tell exactly what she was seeing. "How bad is it?" She used one fingertip to pull aside part of her top to look—and then—crap, realized she was acting like she knew him well enough to do that in front of him. "Sorry," she said quickly as she let the top go back into place.

He didn't seem the least bit bothered as he said, his voice coming out a bit deeper than usual, "I don't mind. I like tan lines."

The words—or maybe it was the unmistakable heat in them—left her tingling in sensitive places.

And it made her uncharacteristically nervous. "Even on a hard-ass?" she asked without quite planning to.

He delivered a sultry smile, eyes half shut. "Even on a hard-ass."

She supposed she'd been trying to diffuse the sexiness between them with that question, but it hadn't worked. Next move: practicality. "Have any sunscreen I could borrow?"

"Sure," he said, somehow infusing even *that* word with a tiny little bit of heat. "Be right back."

She watched as he got up and moved around the pool toward the motel office, just as laid-back and comfortable as he'd first struck her. But now he was sexy, too. She took in the tan on his back, a birthmark on his shoulder. One more thing she suffered the slight urge to touch. *Well, at least we've advanced to something besides hair.* And then she bit her lip once more, as if it might somehow quell the warm need now flowing through her body.

It had been a while since she'd had sex. Tyler, a man she'd dated for two years, had been the last. They'd broken up over a year ago, her choice. And she hadn't particularly minded not having sex since then. She *liked* sex, but she wasn't the kind of woman who really hungered for it or noticed when it was gone. And she'd always been thankful for that. Like most other parts of her adult life, it was a thing that felt easily within her control.

Except, then, what the hell was *this*? This strange attraction to a man more unlike her than any she'd ever felt drawn to before. The very idea of it at once repelled her and . . . well, if she was honest with herself, it also lured her. Because it was mysterious. And something in it felt lush, like a thing to be explored. Maybe because something about him so intrigued her.

Or . . . maybe it was just plain animal magnetism. And maybe that was something she'd never really experienced before. Maybe she'd thought she was above all that, that she just didn't respond to men that way. Yet try as she might to pretend it wasn't happening, she was responding to this one.

But he's so not like you! And he's a client, for God's sake! And a really difficult one, too.

Part of her thought: *Seriously now—you are a seasoned professional; you are a very mature and accomplished thirty-two-year-old woman. You do not let something as minor as sexual attraction make you behave unprofessionally. So maybe you need to just put your business suit back on, hop the next flight back to ATL, and figure out your strategy from a respectable distance.*

But another part of her saw it differently. *Go back without that signature and everything changes. You're no longer invincible. Your record is no longer perfect. Vanderhook's confidence wavers. So does your own, deep down. And . . . what's so wrong with playing this as it lies? Maybe one aspect of being a mature, confident woman was deciding it was okay to follow this path, see where it leads, in business . . . and maybe even in pleasure, too?*

She gave her head a short shake, to clear it. That last bit was going too far. She couldn't quite make that mental leap.

And she had no more time to mull it over at the moment, because that was when Reece exited the office's rear door and padded his way back to her across the concrete on bare feet.

"Isn't it hot?"

He raised his eyebrows at her question, not getting what she was asking. She seldom spoke without thinking first, but that was another thing Reece Donovan seemed to inspire in her.

"Your feet. On the concrete," she clarified.

The corners of his mouth quirked into a grin. "I'm tough," he claimed.

I'm tougher, she affirmed silently.

"You changed," she said then, noticing he'd put on swim trunks while he was gone.

"You seemed uncomfortable with my shorts. And I figured if I went for a swim in them, you'd get even *more* uncomfortable."

He slanted another arrogant look in her direction—so arrogant, in fact, that she decided to just ignore it altogether. That would teach him. Maybe.

When he reached her, he handed down a bottle of old-school suntan lotion—she'd been hoping for the more easily applied spray that didn't have to be rubbed in. But she took it from him with a simple, "Thanks," and as he sat back down beside her, she squirted some into her hand and began to smooth it onto her legs.

She felt him watching. Felt self-conscious. But also . . . a little turned on. His attention made her feel . . . sexy. And maybe she'd almost forgotten what sexy felt like. Or maybe she'd never really even felt it this way before. Something in this was raw, a little feral. It was a silent but visceral thing moving between them. And try as she might, she couldn't quite think like that practical, suit-wearing side of her usually did.

But you need to. If you're going to follow this path, you need to be in it fully, with complete self-assurance, and with a plan. And the only plan that fit with this scenario was: *Don't be ashamed to use your feminine wiles to get what you want.* She was here for a reason. She wasn't going home without what she'd come for. *So put all of this together and make it work for you.*

And something in that resolve snapped her out of the self-consciousness. She wasn't that girl in rural Michigan anymore who let herself be consumed by emotions, and lack of control, and the pressure to succeed. She'd left that part of herself far, far behind. *This . . . is just another way of doing your job.*

And now as she smoothed the coconut-scented lotion over her thighs, rubbing it in with wide circular sweeps of her hand, nervousness changed to confidence. Because it had just become part of winning, convincing him to sell. And that made it easier, less . . . scary. Nothing about her job scared her, after all. If this was just a means to an end, there was no need to question it, no need to worry, no need to think about how much they didn't have in common or how drawn to him she was. This was just business now.

Of course, she still felt it—in her breasts, in her bikini bottoms. As work went, it was . . . well, a little more exciting than usual. His eyes following her hand was exciting. Sensing his silent, growing desire for her was exciting. She wasn't sure how they'd gotten from sniping at each other to this, but here they were, and it was going to lead to her victory with him.

That feminine confidence continued to swell inside her as she applied the creamy sunscreen to her arms, and then her tummy. She made sure to be thorough, spreading the lotion right up to the top edge of her bikini bottoms, letting her fingertips ease just barely inside the elastic to make sure she covered every bit of sensitive skin. Though it felt as if somehow it was actually his *gaze* applying it, caressing her.

"Your back is the worst spot," he pointed out from where he lay propped on one elbow in his nearby lounge. "That's what I first noticed, when you were turning over."

"That's a shame," she said easily, "since I can't reach it myself."

"I guess you want me to do it for you," he said, sounding put out. She was almost grateful for his tone—the preceding silence had grown so heavy and sexual to her.

"Depends," she replied, shooting him a suspicious glance. "I'm afraid you'll leave big hand marks or something as a way of getting back at me."

He tipped his head back slightly. "That's an idea. I'll keep it in mind. But . . ."

"But . . . ?" She raised her eyebrows, met his eyes with hers.

"But . . . you can trust me."

Camille held the gaze, trying to figure out if he was being real or just playing a game. He'd sounded shockingly sincere. Though she didn't know why, or if she should believe it.

Yet, finally, she turned her back toward him and passed him the bottle, saying, "If I have big hand marks later . . ."

"You'll what?" he challenged her.

"Scare your iguana," she answered.

"Uh oh," he said. "Them's fightin' words, Tinkerbell. I love that iguana."

"You're an intriguing man, Reece Donovan," she told him as she faced fully away from him, effectively leaving her skin in his hands.

There can be no denying that it was she who first tempted him.

J. M. Barrie, *Peter and Wendy*

Chapter 4

REECE SEARCHED for a reply as he squeezed lotion into his palm, but he didn't find one. He'd never been called intriguing before. And he kind of liked it. He kind of liked it from her in particular. She was smart, after all, and worldly. But then, maybe she was playing him, just trying to butter him up.

Pressing his hand to her upper back, just below her neck, was like touching fire. Her skin felt warm from the sun, but it was more than that. Chemistry. Magnetism. That thing you couldn't measure but you damn well knew when it was there. The heat seemed to move up through his arms and into his chest, then down through his torso. Hell, he was getting a little hard now. Just from putting sunscreen on her.

She'd piled her long blond hair up on top of her head in some sort of stylish looking knot that allowed him to study the curve of her slender neck, the silky skin of her shoulders. It was sunburnt, as he'd told her, but not as badly as he'd let on. Still, he said, "Does this hurt?" Skin was sensitive, after all.

"No," she said in little more than a whisper. And he began to wonder if this felt as good to her as it did to him.

But what the hell am I doing here? Am I actually putting the moves on her? Reece was no stranger to making a move on an attractive woman—he wasn't fond of big, serious relationships, but he liked spending time with women; he liked playfully seducing women who didn't mind casual fun. Only this was different. Really different.

Just a few hours ago, he'd thought of her as a vulture. And he guessed he still did. But he liked her a little better now. And every instinct he'd had about her body being gorgeous was correct. The parts he could see anyway. Which were, frankly, most of them.

So what's your plan here, dude?

Most of the time, if he'd found himself in this situation, he wouldn't feel he *needed* a plan. He'd just go with the flow, let it happen however it happened. But again, this was extremely different. This woman was trying to cajole him into selling away his business, his life's blood, his home.

Maybe she's entirely capable of casual fun, completely independent of her job. That was a nice thought.

Or . . . maybe she thinks she's gonna get you to change your mind in some weak moment.

But if that was the case, she had another thing

comin'. And maybe it was crazy to be letting himself so thoroughly enjoy the backrub he was giving her now—he kept adding lotion, but really, it had evolved into a backrub, plain and simple.

Though . . . on the other hand, maybe it was the absolute smartest thing he could be doing. Keep your enemies close, right? And if she insisted on spending time here, at the Happy Crab, and in Coral Cove in general, maybe the best move he could make would be to stick to her like glue. As long as he was with her, she couldn't do damage of any kind. Not that he even knew what sort of damage he thought she might try to do if left to her own devices, but why take the chance? And if sticking to her like glue meant getting close to her in other ways, too . . . well, he could just view that as a perk. And a potentially damn nice one.

Just don't let your guard down.

Feeling he'd milked the backrub about as much as he could, he told her, "Your neck is getting a little pink, too," then proceeded to put more sunscreen in his hand and smooth it on higher up, exploring the gentle curve of her neck where it led up to her hairline, taking in a few freckles sprinkled across her right shoulder and a slightly sexy mole. The mole would normally be hidden up under her long hair, and the fact that he was seeing it, touching it, felt almost . . . intimate in a way, because it made him aware that he had to be this close to her to know it was even there.

And he knew she could very easily do her shoulders herself, but he went on, applying the lotion over both of them anyway. She didn't protest and he liked that. He also liked how slick and shiny her sunkissed skin became beneath his touch because something about that was sexy, too.

Still behind her, he eased his hands even a little farther forward, onto the front of her shoulders, glad there was enough lotion left on his fingers for that to make sense. Sort of. Leaning forward so that he could watch his own work, he rubbed it in with firm, sweeping circles on her flesh, his gaze dropping to her breasts. Nice view from this angle, and he went still harder in his trunks as he took in their sweet roundness, as his touch grew gradually but perilously closer to those soft swells held so sweetly aloft in her bikini top.

The real reason he'd changed into trunks was knowing they would hide it better if she had that particular effect on him—and turns out he'd made the switch in the nick of time. The fact that she hadn't stopped him, that neither of them had said a word in a while, added immeasurably to the silent lust moving between them.

It was all he could do not to go further, not to ease his palms down over her. What would she do? Slap him and claim innocence? Or moan and welcome his touch? Either extreme seemed equally likely and he couldn't remember a time when he'd been so tempted to play with fire. Her breasts lay just beyond his fingertips, and he could already feel them in his mind. She'd gone physically tense, but not in a bad way, and he had, too, if he was honest with himself. This was no normal seduction, no normal beach bunny on vacation looking for fun.

And that . . . was what made him finally pull his hands away and move swiftly back to his own chair. "All done," he said, playing it cool, like he wasn't fighting the most intense desire he'd suffered in quite a while.

Then he handed her the bottle of sunscreen he'd abandoned a few minutes earlier and, with his other hand, pointed in the general direction of her boobs, saying, "But you'll want to do those, too. It would be a shame for them to burn."

"Thanks," Camille said softly. *But they already are. With heat and want and other entirely unwise things.*

Except . . . hadn't she decided to play that card with him already? Hadn't she decided that asking to spend time with him, letting their banter turn to flirtation, was all a means to an end? An end she needed to reach?

Yet as she watched him get up, walk to the edge of the pool and smoothly dive in, slicing into the water almost silently to disappear beneath the surface for a few seconds, she had to ask herself some questions. Like where was the line? Where did she draw it? She'd never done this before, so she wasn't sure, but she knew she needed to be careful. For more reasons than one.

She'd never been into casual sex. Even with someone she really clicked with. She just wasn't that good at keeping things "un-serious" once she got that intimate with someone. So . . . how much was she willing to use her sexuality to get what she wanted here?

You have to have limits. And you can't sleep with him. First of all, you don't want a game like this to go that far because that stretched into being smarmy. And second, you sure as hell don't want to get attached to a guy you have nothing in common with, not to mention a guy who you fully intend to conquer on the business front.

Now Reece had emerged up through the sparkling blue water and floated on his back. She watched, thinking it had gotten hotter out and that she wouldn't mind taking a dip, too, but not while he was in the pool. Under the circumstances, she feared only madness that way lay.

So she tried to regroup instead.

You're going to set limits.

You just don't know what they are yet.

You'd better figure them out.

"Hello there."

The voice drew Camille's attention from the man in the pool to a couple approaching through the breezeway next to the office. Both appeared to be in their thirties, the guy sporting a dark ponytail and small beard. The woman carried two swim noodles and both wore beach garb.

"Hi," Camille said, wondering if they'd checked in to the Happy Crab without her knowing.

About that time, Reece stood up in the pool, the water hitting just above his waist, and as it sluiced off his hair and body, he lifted a hand in an easy wave to say, "Hey, guys. Come on in, the water's fine."

Oh, so they weren't customers—they were friends. And on some level, that satisfied her because it meant this place still had no business and that it remained a perfectly good idea to raze it and put something bigger and newer in its spot.

But there were other things capturing her attention, too. Like that more than the water was fine. The man *standing* in the water, a wet lock of dark hair now curving down onto his forehead, was also fine. So fine that it was becoming disconcerting in certain moments, like this one. His fineness, it so happened, was running through her entire body in long, twisting ribbons of electricity she couldn't push down or deny.

"Beautiful day for some sun-worshipping," the ponytail guy said in Camille's direction. His outgoing, friendly nature caught her a little off guard, but she instantly liked him.

"Yes, it's lovely out," she agreed. Only a few puffy white clouds dotted the otherwise bold azure sky.

Then the ponytail guy looked to Reece. "Aren't you going to introduce us to your friend?"

"I'll introduce you, but she's not my friend," Reece said without missing a beat.

Oh, okay then. So his little dip into the water had been about putting some distance between them, and maybe that was indeed a good idea. And if there was a teeny tiny part of her that suffered a smidge of disappointment over it, she refused to acknowledge it. His reply to Ponytail Guy was exactly what she'd needed to help make this completely about business again, all of it. And when she remembered that, she wasn't worried at all—since when it came to business, she had all the confidence in the world. All his fineness and all her ribbons of electricity be damned.

Reece glanced her way then to say, "Cami, these are my friends, Fletcher and Tamra. Fletch and Tamra, this is Cami and she's with the company trying to buy me out even though I keep saying no. I'm pretty sure her current plan is to drive me crazy until I do." Though he'd turned his focus on his friends, now he switched it back to her, complete with a pointing finger. "Which I won't. To make sure we're completely clear on that."

"If you were any clearer," she informed him, "you'd be completely transparent."

Fletcher laughed out loud as she and Reece exchanged looks, his probing. Her words implied she knew something about him, that she could see through him, even though, of course, she didn't and couldn't. But he looked a little concerned, and she liked that.

"My name is actually Camille," she explained to Fletcher and Tamra in her most pleasant tone, "but Reece likes to call me Cami to get on my nerves."

"Does it work?" Fletcher asked speculatively. He wasn't joking—his tone said he was sincerely curious, a student of human nature.

She just smiled. "Yes, but *everything* he does gets on my nerves, so he could just as easily save himself the trouble. And for what it's worth, I'm merely trying to relax in the sun here, and it's him who keeps acting as if I'm constantly pressuring him to sell. I guess he's just hoping that making me look like some kind of ogre will drive me away, but that won't work, either."

As Fletcher glanced back and forth between them, Camille grew still more intrigued with him. He struck her as a guy who didn't miss much. And he proved her right by saying, "There's clearly a lot of tension here. So would it be better if we came swimming another day, or will having other people around help?"

"No tension on my side," Reece claimed. "I'm as easygoing as ever. So stay, swim. It's good to see you guys." He tossed a look to Camille like an afterthought, informing her, "I let friends use the pool when business is slow."

She resisted the urge to reply, *Then I guess they're here all the time*, lest his friends think she was a jerk. The woman, Tamra, hadn't said a single word since arriving and Camille was getting a standoffish vibe. And no wonder, since Reece had already made her out to be some kind of corporate monster.

As Fletcher and Tamra laid out colorful towels on a couple of chairs near a corner of the pool, Reece went on to say, "Fletcher is a tightrope walker and one of the more interesting dudes you're likely to meet. He performs at the Sunset Celebration every night on the beach, next to the pier. You should catch his show while you're here."

"A tightrope walker," Camille said. "That makes you interesting already." And truly, a tightrope walker was the last sort of person she'd expected to find in sleepy Coral Cove.

"Tamra is a local artist. She sells her stained glass and pottery at the pier, too. They live on Sea Shell Lane in the residential part of town at the north end of the beach."

Camille smiled. "Well, how wonderful that your work allows you to spend sunny days like this together."

Though that made Tamra blink in a funny way as she slid off the long, gauzy skirt she wore over her bathing suit, and Fletcher said, "Oh, I think you might have the wrong idea. Tamra and I are neighbors. And friends. Purely platonic. I'm married."

Oh. Feeling a little silly, Camille tried to cover it by saying, "Well, nice that your wife doesn't mind you having female friends. I guess she probably works during the day then?"

And when even that produced an exchange of glances between the other three, she wondered how she'd put her foot in her mouth *this* time—until Fletcher informed her, "My wife is away right now."

And Reece added, "Actually, Fletcher's wife left him a couple of years ago."

Camille tried to hide her shock and confusion, but was pretty sure her eyes had gone wide. Why on earth would Reece just blurt something like that out? And why did Fletcher then still act happily married?

"And it's okay for me to tell you that," Reece added quickly, probably reading her expression, "because Fletcher was about to anyway. He's an upfront kinda guy."

Now it was Camille who blinked, and for perhaps the first time since her arrival here, was left speechless.

"It's all right," Fletcher assured her calmly from

the lounge chair where he'd just settled in his swim trunks. "I promise." Clearly he felt her discomfort and wanted to put her at ease. "Because she's gone right now, but she's coming back. It's just a matter of being patient, that's all."

Still Camille remained stuck on what to say. She'd thought some of her conversations with Reece so far were bizarre, but this surpassed that.

"We worry a little about Fletcher having false hopes," Reece told her, now leaning on the edge of the pool near her, head propped on his arms.

"But I don't, because my hope isn't false," Fletcher replied as certainly as if he were telling her the sun would rise tomorrow. "She'll be back."

"I . . . hope you're right," Camille said then, finally finding her voice.

"I am," he assured her, then added, "These two are just worry warts. And I appreciate their concern—they're good friends. But there's nothing to worry about—it'll all work out fine in the end." And with that same inquisitive tone she'd sensed in him earlier, he now changed the subject—to something with the potential to be just as awkward. "So you're with the developer who's trying to buy the Happy Crab? We thought they'd finally gotten the message that Reece isn't interested in selling—but alas, no, it appears."

"Correct—no." She kept her pleasant voice in place not only because she didn't want to seem like a creep, but because she already liked Fletcher despite the strange discussion they'd just engaged in. In addition to her other observations, he already struck her as a far more reasonable man than Reece. And also because what she was about to say was true. "We understand his attachment to this place, but time and progress marches on, and we truly believe the deal we're offering is not only in his best interest, but also in the best interest of the entire community."

"There are probably other businesses you could purchase in the area instead," Fletcher offered thoughtfully, "whose owners *don't* have such a strong attachment to their property."

Hmm. While it wasn't much, Fletcher's words felt like a hint, a clue. *Exactly what is your attachment to this motel, Reece?*

"So why not shop in greener pastures, so to speak?" Fletcher went on.

"Believe me, I would prefer that," she replied. "But I'm afraid the Happy Crab is in a prime position for Coral Cove's next resort property. And Windchime, in association with Vanderhook, is very determined to build here. We've offered what is, to be blunt, an almost obscene amount of money for the place."

"But still I won't budge," Reece added as if to remind her. "So I'm not sure what she hopes to accomplish by continuing to hang around, but she's at least lowering my vacancy rate. And she seems determined to see what Coral Cove is all about, so I've agreed to show her around—mainly to make sure she's nicer to other people than she's been to me."

The edges of Fletcher's mustache twitched upward, resulting in half a grin. "She doesn't seem so awful. Other than her overall mission, that is."

"Isn't that enough?" Reece asked.

But Fletcher moved on. "So what are you two crazy kids planning on doing tonight to see the town?"

"I'm leaving that up to Reece," Camille replied. "I'm just after a taste of Coral Cove, whatever that brings."

"Well," Reece said, standing upright in the pool again to thoughtfully stroke the stubble on his chin that now actually seemed sexy to her, "I can't think of anything more Coral Cove than dinner at the Hungry Fisherman."

Camille had seen the Hungry Fisherman restaurant next door to the Happy Crab. The large sign out front featured a rather menacing-looking, slicker-wearing fisherman outlined in yellow neon and the parking lot had seen better days. It was the last sort of place she'd normally eat. So . . . why was some part of her actually looking forward to it? "Sounds good," she said easily.

And Fletcher laughed.

"What's funny?" she asked.

He cast a friendly grin her way to reply, "You have no idea what you're in for."

> . . . But he had also a noble sense
> of justice and a lion courage to do
> what seemed right to him . . .
>
> J. M. Barrie, *Peter and Wendy*

Chapter 5

CAMILLE SAT across an old laminate table from Reece in a booth with a tear in the seat. "These booths have been here since the fifties, right?" she asked, at once thinking how horrible that was in some ways but also what a long history they had.

"Believe so," Reece said. "Abner—that's the owner—his uncle built the place back then. And Abner and his wife, Polly, bought him out in the mid-seventies."

Camille glanced at the woman across the room waiting on another table. She wore a rust-colored waitress's dress and the closest thing Camille had seen to a beehive hairdo outside of pictures. "Let me guess—that's Polly."

"Yep."

"And I'm wagering she's been wearing that same uniform since the day she started working here."

A small smile curled the corners of Reece's mouth. "Probably. Certain things don't go out of style around here the way they do other places. We're not always looking for new and better—we appreciate the tried and true, and history, and nostalgia."

Nostalgia. It was a nice word for the way this area of Coral Cove made her feel. If the parking lots weren't pockmarked with holes and the paint jobs a little crisper—and, say, the booths in the Hungry Fisherman a little newer—she could feel as if she'd stepped back in time to the early days of Florida's beach culture. But the problem with that was . . . the parking lots *were* pockmarked, the businesses were empty, and obviously not everyone appreciated nostalgia or the area wouldn't feel so rundown. "I'm not immune to nostalgic charm," she told him. "Just so you'll know I'm not an ogre."

His sexy eyes took on a hint of amusement.

"What?" she asked. "What did I miss?"

"Are you sure?" he asked. "Because I told Fifi something like that just this morning. But wait . . . maybe I said vulture. Or piranha." He gave his head a short shake. "Can't remember. But the point is that I'm probably not quite convinced."

"The bigger point, however," she said sensibly, "is that this particular brand of nostalgia isn't packing the booths. The same way the Happy Crab isn't exactly lighting up the No Vacancy sign. People appreciate it from a distance. But to them, the tried and true is . . . the McDonald's on Route Nineteen. It's Applebee's and TGI Fridays. It's Marriott and Hilton."

"And Windchime Resorts?" he asked, eyebrows lifting.

She gave a short nod. "What's considered tried and true has shifted over time. It's not *my* fault. It's not *anyone's* fault. But when you boil it down, my job is to ultimately give people more of what they consider dependable, tried and true. And while people might be filling their homes with refurbished furniture and decorating in shabby chic these days, for most people, when they travel, newer feels better."

"Just so *you* know," he said, "I get that. I understand what most people want on a vacation and how the travel industry has changed over the years. But that doesn't mean anything to me personally. And it doesn't mean I'm gonna sell my motel."

Just then, the woman she'd identified as Polly came over, order pad in hand. "Evenin', Reece," she said with a smile, then shifted her gaze to Camille. "Who's your lady friend?"

"This is Cami. Cami, Polly. Polly, Cami. But she isn't my friend. She's with Vanderhook, the developer I told you about a couple months ago, the one who wants to buy the Crab."

Camille let out a breath of irritation and leapt into the business of trying to repair her instantly ruined reputation with Polly. This was getting old fast. She smiled up to say, "But I'm not a monster, I promise."

"So she keeps claiming," Reece said with a dry smile he flicked back and forth between the two women.

Poor Polly, thrown unwittingly into the middle

of their animosity, looked more perplexed than uncomfortable. "Well, if she's so awful, Reece, mind if I ask why you're eatin' dinner with her?"

Camille couldn't resist casting a smugly satisfied look to her attractive nemesis across the table since she thought Polly had made a pretty good point.

"Just protecting my interests," he replied, looking completely unruffled, which annoyed her. "If she insists on hanging around town, I figure I should keep an eye on her." And a hint of humor graced his voice for that last part, but only a hint.

"You both havin' the buffet?" Clearly, Polly wanted to get down to business here. Which suited Camille fine.

Yet Camille still glanced to Reece before answering, just to see if that was his recommendation. "Are we having the buffet?"

"Yep, two buffets," he said to Polly.

After she walked away, Camille asked, "Are you going to do that every time you introduce me to someone? Because if you are, I'll just get to know the town on my own, thankyouverymuch."

She'd hoped he'd respond to her pointed look with an expression that at least bordered on contrite, but it didn't happen. Still, when he said, "Okay, you're right—I'll knock it off," she was appeased. For the moment anyway.

When the two of them proceeded to cross the room—a dark, wooded place that seemed designed to feel like an old fishing boat or ship—to the buffet, she realized the man filling his plate opposite them wore a fancy pirate hat, complete with fur trim. With khaki pants and a golf shirt.

And perhaps the weirdest part was that no one seemed to notice but her.

"So . . ." she began after they returned to their torn orange booth, "did you see the guy in the pirate hat, too, or did I just imagine that?"

The question barely made Reece look up from his food. "That's just Abner."

"Abner . . . as in the owner? Polly's husband?" She felt her eyes go wide.

Reece simply gave a short nod while forking a hush puppy into his mouth.

"But . . ."

"He likes hats."

She tried to weigh this, yet still failed to understand. "But . . ."

"Nobody really knows why he wears them, and nobody really questions it anymore. In fact, if anybody has a problem with Abner, it's more that he tends to be a little surly, not that he wears weird hats."

"Hmm," she said, taking that in.

"See," Reece said, "we accept people the way they are here, eccentricities and all. That's why it's a nice place to be."

"That's . . . well, lovely really," she said, meaning it. *But maybe it's also why . . . this town is dying.* Though she kept that part to herself. Eccentricities just didn't play great to the masses, to the vacationers who saved up all year to come to the beach and wanted to know what to expect, wanted places that felt dependable and safe. Tried and true. The *new kind* of tried and true.

"So," she said, when Reece didn't reply to that—

probably refusing to acknowledge she could be nice—"your handyman seemed very pleasant. Much more than the motel's proprietor, I might add." She popped a scallop into her mouth in conclusion, as if that would emphasize her point.

"Riley isn't technically my handyman," he explained. "But you're right—nice as the day is long."

Camille lifted her gaze to him. "What's the deal then, if you don't mind my asking? You can't afford to pay him? So he works for free?" She imagined the old man being retired and bored enough to help Reece out. Though something didn't add up in the thought—maybe it was the way he'd been dressed, in mismatched clothes that seemed dirty. Dirtier than a retiree volunteering a few hours a day as a handyman would wear. Or the fact that Reece seemed to have plenty of time on his hands and could probably do his own handyman work if he couldn't pay someone else to do the job.

"I can afford to pay him," Reece said easily, wiping a napkin across his mouth.

So Camille just squinted her confusion. "Then . . ."

Reece tilted his head, gave her one of his usual critical looks. "You're really nosy."

"Curious," she corrected him pointedly.

He cocked his head back in the other direction and flashed a frank expression. "Okay—this isn't really anyone's business but Riley's, so if I tell you, you have to swear you won't treat him any differently or act weird to him."

What on earth . . . ? "Of course," she said. "I promise. What's the big secret?"

He shrugged. "It's not a secret from most

people—and he probably wouldn't mind me telling you. I just want you to keep being nice to him."

She widened her eyes impatiently. "Of course I will." Then motioned with her hand for him to get on with it.

"Riley's homeless."

Something in Camille's heart shifted, dropped a little.

"So I let him stay at the Crab for free. And he insists on helping me out on handyman stuff— stuff I've always done myself until recently—as a means of paying his way. It's about his pride, so I let him do it. He doesn't have much else, so I figure if it lets him keep his self-respect, why not? And he does good work, as good as I'd do myself."

Camille took all that in but tried not to have a visible reaction.

Because she didn't want to be softened. And maybe she already was in some way, but if that was the case, she sure as hell didn't want to let it show.

Still, how many people would do that? How many people would give a home to an old man who didn't have one? Granted, it wasn't the same as taking someone under your own roof, but still . . . you didn't see Riley living at one of the resorts up the road. And she knew he would never be able to live at a Windchime Resort, either. Because . . . resorts just didn't do that.

"Is . . . that why? Why you won't sell?" It had just hit her. *Now*, to tear down the Happy Crab would be to tear down Riley's only home. It would be tearing down Reece's home, too, but that was different, because it would come with enough cash to live in a beachside mansion if he chose. But Riley obviously didn't have as many options.

"No," he said simply, scooping some macaroni and cheese onto his fork. "That's not it. If I had to go somewhere else, I'd make sure Riley was taken care of in some way or another. Even if his pride took a hit in the process. I'm not selling because I don't want to, that's all."

Hmm. Who'd have expected Reece Donovan to be *this* good of a guy? And did it change anything about her quest here?

No.

Same answer as his.

Because it couldn't.

This wasn't a game where nice guys were treated differently than non-nice guys—probably *most* of the property she'd acquired over the years had belonged to relatively nice people. This was just about business—first, last, and always.

Still, she wondered aloud, "How did you meet Riley?"

"Found him sleeping on the beach early one morning when I was out for a walk about six months ago."

"And . . . ?" There had to be more to the story, after all.

"Well, it's against the law to sleep on the beach around here," Reece explained, "so I figured I had two choices. Either call the police . . . or buy him a meal and offer him a place to stay while he gets back on his feet."

Her chest expanded with the kindness she felt radiating from him in that moment. A kindness that, again, she just thought most people wouldn't extend—out of fear or worry or lots of other perfectly reasonable emotions. And he'd stated it so simply—like it was nothing. "It was good of you," she said. Not that she liked paying him a compliment under all the circumstances. But it moved her so much that she couldn't . . . not.

And she thought maybe he'd eat that up, given the nature of their relationship so far, but instead he just shrugged it off. "Sometimes people need a hand."

Deciding maybe it would be a wise time to switch to a lighter subject, she said, "Mind if I ask you something else?"

"We'll only know if you ask it."

"Where on earth did you get that giant—"

"Dinosaur?" he interrupted.

She tried to hold back her slightly embarrassed smile, but it snuck out a little anyway. "Yes. Where did you get your giant dinosaur?"

A faint smile traced his lush lips. She realized it was yet one more thing she found attractive about him—his mouth. *But stop being ridiculous. And keep digging.* After all, the answer to convincing him to sell could come from anywhere.

"I found her on the side of the road when she was a baby," Reece replied. "She'd been dumped off by someone who didn't want her, and then hit by a car."

Camille held in her gasp, but it was like a tiny knife to her heart. And—oh crap. Did this man's decency never end? And why was she suddenly seeing Fifi in a whole new light, as this tender, needy creature who craved love the same way a kitten or a puppy might? "Was . . . was she badly hurt?" Camille asked, trying like hell not to really care.

He gave a small nod and a certain darkness passed over his face that she hadn't witnessed before. "Pretty bad," he told her. "But I took her straight to an animal hospital, and they fixed her up, and I nursed her back to health. And we've been together ever since—eight years now. What happened to her when she was young made her so she's still sensitive at times—but I can usually calm her down pretty easy."

Camille flashed back on the sounds of the iguana thrashing about in her bathtub—and of Reece soothing her. She'd thought it was silly at the time; she'd not imagined something that looked so . . . *prehistoric* could ever need to be soothed. "Times like when a woman is leaping around screaming her head off?" she inquired gently.

He looked a little amused, but unexpectedly kind, as he quietly answered, "Yeah, times like that."

Without quite considering the consequences, she said, "I'm sorry I scared her." She meant it.

And the look on Reece's face told her he believed her. "On behalf of Fifi, thank you," he said.

Although he then used the piece of shrimp currently between his fingers to point at her across the table. "But don't think going soft on Fifi changes anything. In case that's part of your evil plan."

"I don't have an evil plan," she lied. And she didn't feel bad about that because going soft on Fifi really had nothing to do with her evil plan.

She really did think Reece was a much better guy than she had an hour ago, and her reactions to the things he'd told her were sincere.

But she still had a job to do. *So I'm going to keep digging. And pray to God he doesn't keep giving me answers that make him look like an overgrown beach Boy Scout.* "So you've lived here all your life?" she asked.

"Yep, born and raised in Coral Cove."

"How long have you owned the motel?"

"Always, in a way," he told her. My grandfather built it in the late fifties. My dad was just a kid then, but he helped, too. He and his brother took the place over eventually, and then I took it over from them later."

Aha! It was a family thing. A family legacy. Finally! That explained a lot. At last she was getting somewhere, getting some insights on this situation.

"So . . . your family would be upset if you sold it, if it was torn down," she said. Digging.

"No," he said, "nothing like that."

And that was it. Nothing more.

Hmm. So much for digging. *Maybe I'm not really getting anywhere after all.*

And just as she was trying to think of another angle, a way to pry without being ridiculously obvious about it, Reece locked gazes with her, leaned slightly forward, and turned the tables on her. "So," he said pointedly, "what's *your* deal, Tinkerbell?"

She chafed inside at the stupid nickname, but tried to be cool about it. As cool as *he* was most of the time. "My deal?"

"You're from Michigan. You live in Atlanta. You work for a big conglomerate and your job is doing their dirty work. That pretty much sums up what I know about you. Well, and you have a smart mouth and fill out a bikini real nice. So tell me something else about you."

She lowered her chin, narrowed her gaze on him. "If I didn't know better, I'd think you were actually interested in me as a human being."

He offered up a typical Reece shrug. "I just thought we were playing twenty questions, that's all."

And she smiled. Because she'd just seen a tiny chink in *his* armor now—he was interested in finding out more about her and didn't like admitting it. "What would you like to know?"

"How'd you get into this line of work?" he asked.

"I studied real estate and hospitality—that's the hotel business—at Michigan State, and got a job at Vanderhook right after graduation." She stopped to take a sip of her soda. "Over time, it was discovered that I'm skilled at negotiating, and as a result, I get to travel to a lot of waterside locales. And for being only thirty-two, I'm pretty high up in the company. That answer your question?"

His gaze narrowed. "Sort of. How'd you *pick up* these negotiating skills of yours?"

She thought back. Perhaps back a little too far, too fast. To being an insecure little girl who got bossed around, who let other people's expectations define her. She could still hear her father's booming voice now, all these years later, could still feel his obvious disdain for her shriveling up her insides.

Odd that her parents' deficiencies, which she resented as much now as ever if she was honest with herself, had ultimately made her who she was, someone who she actually liked. Even if her job might not always make her seem all that likable. But for her, being tough was a lot more likable than being weak, and she was proud of all she'd overcome, all she'd achieved.

"Let's say it was a life skill born of . . . wanting to have more than I did growing up."

"Sounds like a story there," he said, baiting her.

But she wasn't biting. "Too bad it's late and I'm tired," she told him with a knowing smile. "Shall we get the check?"

He just laughed in reply. "Sure, Tink," he told her. "Whatever you say."

She'd expected him to pry a little more. But she was glad he didn't.

She'd promised him a meal, so as soon as Polly turned their bill facedown on the table, she smoothly scooped it up.

"Thanks for dinner," he said easily. And she thought the words might have come out a little grudgingly, but under all the circumstances, she appreciated any gratitude at all.

When they stepped up to the cash register, Reece excused himself to go to the bathroom. And as Camille passed a credit card across a low counter to Polly—who seemed to be a one-woman show here—she noticed the entire place was empty but for them. And only a few tables had been filled during their entire visit. A shame because the food had been good—better than she'd expected.

"*Shoo.*"

She'd been putting her card away, but looked up at the whispery sound, which she thought had come from Polly. Polly met her gaze, smiled a bit nervously. And she went back to tucking her card into the spot where it belonged.

"*Shoo.*"

Camille looked up quicker this time—fast enough to follow Polly's eyes to an orange-striped cat who sat on the floor next to the counter, as still as a statue. Camille flinched and—for the second time since coming into the Hungry Fisherman—wondered if she were seeing things. What on earth was a cat doing in a restaurant?

"I'm so sorry," Polly said then, her eyes fraught with embarrassment. "We don't condone cats hangin' around in here, honest. Just can't get rid of this one—he's a stray, ya see, and I don't have the heart to throw away scraps that make a perfectly fine meal for him. And lately he's taken to runnin' in the back door anytime one of the cooks opens it, but sometimes we don't notice right away. I'm sure you can see my dilemma."

"Polly, Polly, Polly," Reece said, stepping up to join the conversation, "another one?"

Camille blinked in surprise. "There's more than one?"

"Heavens no!" Polly assured her. "We unloaded Dinah on that sweet Christy and her hunky boyfriend, Jack, almost as soon as they moved down here—you know that, Reece."

"But this *is* still another one," he pointed out.

"Who needs a home," she said. "I think Tiger here—that's what we been callin' him, due to his stripes and all—would enjoy it at your place."

Reece slanted the waitress a look that told Camille they'd had this conversation before. "I'm not as big a pushover as Christy and Jack are. And I already have a pet. A big one. Who doesn't need a crazy cat agitating her."

"Why, he's not crazy, not at all," Polly promised him. "He just needs a place to call home, like everyone else." Then she looked to Camille. "How about you, hon? Wouldn't you like a nice cat?"

Again, Camille balked. "Who, me? I'm not from here. I live a plane ride away. And I'm not really a pet kind of person. I travel a lot for my job."

Polly just pressed her lips flatly together and nodded, disappointed but clearly used to being turned down.

"*You* have a home, you know," Reece said, putting it back on Polly. "Why can't he go live with *you*?"

"Abner's allergic to cats," she said on a sigh, "or I'd love to have him." She shook her head. "You'd think the hat thing plus his general lackluster mood would be enough for me to have to contend with in this marriage, but no—God also made him allergic to cats, too. Otherwise, I'd probably have two or three little furballs around the house."

"I bet he has seriously mixed emotions about *The Cat in the Hat*," Reece quipped.

And Polly let out a laugh. "Oh Reece, you're such a stitch." She turned to Camille. "Isn't he such a stitch? Don't you just love his sense of humor?"

Camille cast him a sideways glance and choked out, "Oh yeah. He's a laugh a minute."

"That's what we love about Reece around here," Polly said. "How, through it all, he's stayed so happy and easygoing. Not everybody could stay that way."

"Well, we need to be going," Reece interjected before either woman could utter another word. And Camille kept her eyes down, attempting to act as if she hadn't quite caught all of that, but of course she had.

So what had Reece been through? A decline of business, sure—but clearly Polly was going through the same, so she was obviously referring to something else.

Something . . . bigger.

Something with the power to destroy a lesser man's happiness—according to Polly anyway.

They said their goodbyes and Camille complimented the seafood, and as they were walking toward the front door—guarded by a life-size fisherman carved from wood, which kind of freaked Camille out and made her wonder how she'd missed it coming in—Polly called over to them proudly, "Made that myself. We call him the Fish Whisperer."

Camille forced a smile at the nice older lady. On one hand, it was truly impressive to think of Polly carving something so large from a slab of wood. Who *did* that sort of thing? On the other, though, something about the wooden fisherman was pretty creepy. His painted wooden eyes were scary, and—oh dear!—she realized suddenly that he looked exactly like Abner.

"Yeah," Reece whispered, reading her thoughts, "he's Abner. No one knows if *Polly* knows that, but everybody else does."

Camille gave a short nod—and then, from behind her, she heard a gentle, "Meow."

Turning to peek down, she spotted the yellow-orange cat padding toward them. He stopped a few feet away, and as she made eye contact with it, she thought something in its furry little face looked a bit sad, desperate. "Meow," it said again.

"He likes you," Polly told her as if it were an indisputable fact. "He's saying, 'Take me home. I'll be a good cat, I promise.'"

Camille sucked in her breath at the small stab of guilt inflicted. It was a ridiculous reaction. She didn't even particularly like cats, and had been around few. She'd had no pets growing up—cats, dogs, or otherwise.

And she was almost thankful when Reece replied—since she'd not quite managed to. "Quit trying to guilt her, Polly. Take it from me, Cami here has a heart of stone."

Then he laughed, as if he were only kidding—but she knew he really wasn't.

And that was fine. Wasn't it? After all, what did she care what he thought of her? And her job did require her to have a heart of stone—at least when it came to matters of real estate. And Vanderhook wasn't trying to cheat him—they were being way more than fair.

So why did the words stay with her as they stepped out into the warm Florida night?

It had gotten dark while they were inside, yet the salt-scented breeze reminded her the beach was but a stone's throw away. A bright moon added light to that of the neon signs in the two connected parking lots. They crossed the restaurant's craggy lot back toward the motel in silence until she said, a bit more quietly than she'd intended, "I don't, you know."

"You don't what?"

"Have a heart of stone. I'm not as bad as you make me out to be."

His look of surprise implied she was showing too much softness, that he expected better of her. "Shake it off, Tink," he said, his voice light-hearted. "You're taking it too hard. You're tougher than that."

And—God, he was right. Ugh, what on earth was this softness about? *Knock it off. Get your game face back on—and keep it there.* "You're right—I'm soulless. Happy now?"

He just laughed. "There's the Tinkerbell I've come to know and be annoyed by."

As they continued on their way, she couldn't decide if that made her happy or sad. That he thought of her as tough and heartless.

He was her opponent—and more than that, her prey—so being tough with him, *staying* tough with him, only made sense. And it should be easy because that was who she really was—a tough chick who meant business. A tough chick who was not unpleasant, but who *was* in control.

And yet . . . despite herself, she liked him.

He gave homes to injured iguanas and home-less old men. He made people laugh despite what-ever hardships he'd been through. He had values and integrity.

And he thought she didn't.

And something in that bothered her. She'd never cared that much about being liked before, but suddenly, now, she kind of did. What the hell was *that* about?

Maybe, in the end, when you get him to sell, you just don't want him to hate you for it. Because you've gotten to know him a little. Maybe it was only natural that she should want him to see her as a decent human being, the same way she had already come to see him. Maybe it was just about desiring mutual re-spect. Or wanting to be seen for the whole person she was—not just one part of herself.

Just then she tripped a little while sidestepping a raised patch of blacktop and her arm brushed against his. And they exchanged quick glances, but then both of them looked away, kept walking.

Or . . . maybe it's just that damned attraction you feel for him making you want him to like you.

But you decided that can only be about sex—if even that. Not about like.

And that goes both ways. If something more happens between you, something physical, it can't be because you like him as a person—it can only be because he's hot and you want to take advantage of the chemistry between you, and because you also think it might some-how soften him into selling.

You want to soften him.

And instead he's softening you.

Well, *that* was a good little wake-up call.

No more softness. *Get back to being normal you. The you who wouldn't waste emotion on a homeless cat who's already being completely well cared for from the way it looked. The you who would expend no compassion on a giant lizard. The you who wonders what Reece went through that was so bad only because you can use it as a tool.*

When they arrived at the door to her room, Reece stopped, waiting as she dug the crab-shaped keychain from her purse.

He gave her a speculative grin. "Any chance you're leaving tomorrow?"

"No plans to," she replied smoothly. "I'm on vacation, remember?"

When he didn't reply but their gazes stayed locked, she ventured, "You're still eager to see me go then?"

"Yes," he said. "And no."

Hmm. Interesting.

"But mainly, I needed to know so I can call the maid, Juanita, and tell her there's a room to clean."

She tipped her head back in understanding. Then held up her key, intrigued that he was being gentlemanly enough to stick around until she got inside.

As she peered up into his warm eyes, she realized there was something nice about being with him in the dark, how nighttime could seem more intimate, private, with someone you felt that kind of attraction to. She took in the strong angle of his stubble-covered jaw, the slight crinkles at the edges of his eyes that always looked so much better on a man than a woman. And before she could stop to examine it—whether it was about sex or liking him, whether it was about business or pleasure—she suffered a tiny pang of regret to know the moment was about to end as quickly as it had begun. And then she'd be alone in her room, no longer with him.

His gaze had stayed on hers the whole time, making her heart beat a little faster, until his eyes narrowed, falling half shut and looking sexy as hell. "If you were anybody else, Cami . . ." he began, but then let his voice trail off.

"What?" she asked when he didn't finish.

One corner of his mouth quirked upward in a way that made her wish she could read his thoughts, and he simply replied, "Nothing," then gave his head a short shake. "Goodnight, Tinkerbell."

> . . . the fairy Tink who is bent on mischief
> this night is looking for a tool,
> and she thinks you the most easily
> tricked of the boys.

J. M. Barrie, *Peter and Wendy*

Chapter 6

IF YOU were anybody else I might kiss you. If you were anybody else I might kiss the hell out of you. And maybe more.

But that would be insanity. Wouldn't it? To get that involved with her.

Reece turned the thoughts over in his head as he stepped into a cool shower a few minutes after leaving her at her door.

Of course, kissing the hell out of her and maybe more could take the idea of keeping your enemies close to a whole new level. And maybe that would make sense.

But on the other hand, it would probably just complicate things. And he didn't want to complicate things. As it was, their situation was fairly simple. *She wants to buy your place and you're not selling. She's trying to wait you out, but it won't work. She'll get tired of it after a while and get out of your life.* Yep, sex only stood to complicate things.

And this nice, cool shower will make all the heat inside you go away. Make all the things you want to do to her go away. Make the tightness in your groin go away.

Swiping a bar of soap across his chest, he glanced down. The tightness in his groin hadn't gone away. Not even close. He shut his eyes. Hell.

TAMRA sat next to Fletcher on the wide side porch of his cottage that looked out over the more secluded stretch of the beach they called home.

She'd come to Coral Cove seven years ago at the age of twenty-seven and the town had become more of a home to her than anyplace else she'd ever lived. Her little pastel cottage on Sea Shell Lane just across the way, good friends like Fletcher and Reece, the fact that she was able to scrape out a living—even if sometimes meager—with her art; these were the things that made her happy. And usually sitting with Fletcher watching the waves wash in and out in the distance kept her in that relaxed place in her mind. So why did she feel out of sorts today?

"What's wrong? You don't seem yourself, my friend," Fletcher asked. He was like that. Tuned in, aware. She'd gotten used to it. And though she worried about him, something about him really did make her believe he was right and that his wife would come back. She just didn't like that he was sitting around wasting time waiting for it to happen when life was so short.

"I don't know," she replied, trying to find the source of her uneasiness. And slowly her mind delivered her back to yesterday at the pool. Something about the swim outing had stayed with her in a way it usually didn't. "Maybe . . . it's that woman we met yesterday—the one bugging Reece to sell the Happy Crab."

Fletcher looked up. "Oh? What about her?"

She searched her emotions a little more and didn't resist sharing what she found there. "I didn't like her. I think she's up to no good." Tamra thought of her friends as family, so she cared about them enormously, and she didn't like the idea of someone trying to take something from Reece that he didn't want to give.

"I liked her fine," Fletcher said in reply. "I don't like her *job,* but I like *her.*"

Fletcher was a good judge of people and generally Tamra trusted his instincts on that, but she felt inclined to argue this. "Don't you feel that what someone chooses to do for a living defines them? At least partially?"

Next to her, he gave a thoughtful nod as one of the windchimes hanging from the porch awning made a tinkling noise. "Sometimes people are misguided. And sometimes they change paths. And sometimes they don't. I think there's more kindness in Camille, though, than you might be seeing. And besides, Reece is a big boy—he can take care of himself."

Something in her gut twisted slightly at that—she

didn't know why. She supposed she just wanted . . .
for Reece to feel the same way about his motel
guest as she did. She didn't want him to be taken
in. And though he'd said all the right things, at the
same time, he'd been there swimming with her, and
joking with her, and watching her. Tamra had noticed him watching her, even though she thought
he'd been trying to be a little surreptitious about it.

"You need to meet a nice guy," Fletcher said out
of the blue.

She kept her gaze on the beach. They had this
conversation often and it irritated her each and
every time. She issued her usual reply. "You need
to meet a woman."

"I *have* a woman."

She sighed. Kim had left him nearly three years
ago. He had absolutely no indication, no reason
in the world, to believe she was coming back.
And yet he believed it so strongly, with his whole
heart, his whole soul, that he'd made this temporary stop of Coral Cove—where he'd been doing
his tightrope act at the time—into his home. He'd
even bought a house here, so Kim would know
where to find him, since it was the place they'd
happened to be when she'd up and taken off, leaving him only a short, cryptic note promising him
that things would be okay.

"Where is she?" Tamra asked. She knew full
well that she was being a smart-ass, but she felt
the point had to be made, for his own good.

"Making her way back to me, bit by bit," he
answered as he always did—with so much con-
viction, and even contentment, that, again, Tamra

wanted to believe in it, too. But she thought he could do better than to wait for someone who'd abandoned him that way.

"How about *that* guy?" He pointed to a lone man walking up the beach in swim trunks. From a distance, it was hard to make out details, but he looked fit, mid-thirties, dark blond hair.

She sighed. "I prefer to meet men naturally—not have to accost them on the beach."

"I'd be happy to accost him *for* you," Fletcher offered. "I'd be subtle enough."

Fletcher had many good qualities, but subtlety wasn't one of them. Still, she understood he was being sincere, so she replied, "I know, but . . ."

"But you're in love with Reece," he said.

A soft gasp flew from her lips as her eyes darted to the bearded man next to her. Their gazes locked as she tried to take in what he'd just said, tried to wrap her mind around it.

She'd just never . . .

She wasn't certain . . .

Surely if she felt that way, she'd know it, right?

"I . . . I . . . that's crazy," she finally answered, feeling fully put on the spot. Her heart threatened to beat right through her chest. From the shock of the suggestion, of course—nothing more.

"Your eyes tell me otherwise, my friend," Fletcher said in his calm, knowing way.

She let out a breath, tried to think clearly. "Well . . . my eyes are a little shocked right now, that's all," she explained. "Because I can't believe you'd even suggest that."

She purposely looked away, back out to the

beach. She immediately located a thin woman with long, dark hair, and even while the woman wore a bikini, it had a tie-dyed design, and something gave Tamra the impression she was a little artsy, like them. "If you want to accost someone on the beach so badly, how about her?" She pointed. "She's cute, and sort of your type, don't you think?"

Next to her, Fletcher stayed silent a moment. Then ignored her attempted dodge altogether. "If you're sincerely telling me you don't have those kinds of feelings for Reece, I'll let it go. But *are* you really telling me that? Because for quite some time now . . ."

"For quite some time now, what?" she asked. She suspected her gaze was too wide on him, her response too defensive. But she *felt* defensive.

"I've just sensed there was something there," Fletcher said. "Something you weren't saying. Or pursuing. I thought maybe it scared you. So I never brought it up, thinking you'd work through it on your own. But it seems to me that time is passing and . . ."

"And . . . ?"

He gave his head a short shake. "Life is short, that's all."

She took that in, and then stated what she felt was obvious. "Everyone's is. You're wasting time, too, Fletch." She'd had that very thought regarding him only moments earlier, after all. So the irony here seemed richer by the second.

Yet he only gave her a slight, gentle smile. "It's different for me. I know how my story ends and it's good, I promise. *Your* story isn't written yet."

He tilted his head. "Do you know how you want it to turn out? Do you know what your happily ever after is about?"

Tamra's heart beat so hard now that it hurt. She simply . . . wasn't prepared for this conversation. She hadn't seen it coming and felt as if she'd been smacked in the head with a sheet of her own stained glass.

The fact was . . . maybe . . . maybe Reece was on her mind . . . a lot.

And maybe being around him made her feel . . . warm inside. And happy. Because he was funny and self-assured and easy to be with. And she'd always been aware that his eyes sparkled when he smiled and that it made her heart skip a beat.

And for a long time, she'd just told herself it was because he was just that kind of person. That he made *everyone* feel that way. Though in this moment it was suddenly hard to deny that . . . there might indeed be something there. Inside her. That she might . . . care for him. In a different way than she cared about Fletcher or other men she knew. In a way that was . . . romantic.

But Fletcher was right—she was afraid of it.

Because what if he didn't feel the same way? How much would that hurt? And how embarrassing would that be? And what if it ruined their really wonderful friendship? Some things didn't change when you got older—there were still risks involved in letting your feelings for someone show.

She bit her lip and tried to form a reply to Fletcher's question. "No, I don't know how my happily ever after goes. Or if I even get one." She shook her head, trying to explain better. "You know I'm just glad to be where I am in life, to have friends I trust and care about." She'd been raised in a commune in Arizona. Everyone there was supposed to have been her family—but *no one there* had ever really *felt* like her family. Except, that is, for the *real* family who'd willingly given up ties to her.

For Tamra, real relationships were like gold, rare and valuable. And to risk a friendship for the sake of romance . . . that was big to her, maybe even impossible. She valued her friendships deeply, more than she thought most people did—because they were all she had.

"*Of course* you get a happily ever after," Fletcher said with convincing certainty. "We all do. If we want it enough to be open to it."

Hmm. The truth was, she'd just never spent much time thinking about being open to romance; maybe she even pushed it away. In the commune, when it came to romance and sex—well, she'd ended up feeling it was all fleeting, and confusing. Everyone there talked about love and claimed their attachments to each other were deeply meaningful, but to her, the bonds formed had seemed weak, so fragile as to not count for much in the end. She'd never sorted through it all—she'd just left it behind in a quest for a simpler, more normal life. People in her commune had preached simplicity, but she'd felt they lived in a very complex sort of emotional poverty instead.

"I . . . I . . . really don't feel that way about Reece," she finally fibbed. "Maybe someone, someday, but . . . Reece is my friend, that's all."

Because what it came down to was, she valued him too much to ever let him know she might want more. Even if Fletcher had made her realize that was probably at least part of why she hadn't liked Cami, or Camille, or whatever her name was. Despite his denials, Reece had clearly felt drawn to the other woman—and maybe that had stung in a way Tamra hadn't quite wanted to recognize.

Fletcher gave her a long look before finally saying, "Okay, Tam, okay. If you say so, I'll believe you."

"Good. Because I say so." She switched her gaze back to the beach, where the artsy-looking girl had now spread out a towel and sat down on it, facing the water. "Now, about that girl in the tie-dyed bikini."

"You know what I think?" Fletcher asked, sounding a little tired.

"What?"

"That we should just quit trying to meddle in each other's romantic lives and go get some ice cream." He pointed over his shoulder in the direction of the ice cream shop up the street and around the corner.

She made an observation. "For being such a deep guy, you always seem to think ice cream is the answer to every complicated issue."

"One of the secrets to life," he informed her, "is to appreciate the little things and let everything else take care of itself."

Hmm. She wasn't sure if life's big problems really took care of themselves, but at the moment, she supposed ice cream seemed like a good enough solution to her, too. "Let's go," she said.

* * *

A KNOCK on the door of her room at the Happy Crab the next afternoon sent Camille scurrying to answer, expecting to find Reece on the other side. Instead, before her stood a twenty-something Mexican girl in jeans and a T-shirt next to a maid's cart. Her heart sank a little as she forced a smile. "Juanita, I bet."

"*Si,*" the girl said. "Mr. Reece sent me to clean your room. Is this is a good time?" She spoke with an accent, but her English was excellent.

"Sure," Camille said, still feeling the silly sting of disappointment as she stepped back to let Juanita inside.

"I'll try to be quick," Juanita said, carrying in fresh towels.

"No rush—take your time," Camille told her, then returned to the round table she'd been using as office space since her arrival. Though the bulk of her work was done face to face, in meetings, there was still email to answer and company business to keep up with. Just this morning she'd gotten an email from her boss, Phil, informing her that her expertise with new "holdouts" might soon be required at desired properties in both Key West and Myrtle Beach.

Holdouts—that was the official company term for business owners like Reece who didn't want to sell. It struck her now that it was a little dehumanizing in a way—it lumped them all into one big category and just made them sound like a nuisance, nothing more, and nothing less.

Oh crap. This is the trouble with getting to know one of them—it makes you . . . soft.

That word, *soft*, kept coming up—and she couldn't deny that little bits of softness around her usually hard emotional shell had been developing almost since the moment she'd decided to check in here.

Maybe it had been the wrong move. Maybe you should check out right now. Go home. Or move on to the next assignment—get your usual confidence back in place. Then revisit this Happy Crab situation from a distance—figure out some other way to get the job done.

As Juanita scurried around the room—scouring the sink outside the small bathroom, stripping the king size bed—Camille seriously considered doing just that. Distance, in this particular instance, might indeed make more sense than staying so near. She kept giving herself that same advice—so why hadn't she taken it yet?

Because it always came back to the same issue: She'd never left a place before closing a deal. And even if it might be wise to revisit this negotiation later, if she departed without getting the job done, it would feel like a defeat. Inside her. And it might *look* like one, too, to Phil and other higher ups.

And she really did believe that if she stuck with this, she would find out what was keeping Reece from selling, and therein lay the solution to changing his mind.

But one more self pep talk seemed in order.

Do. Not. Get. Emotionally. Involved.

The fact that she'd wanted him to be on the other side of that door wasn't a good thing. The fact that she'd suffered a disappointment that felt downright physical was even worse.

Who *were* these women who could dabble in men like they were snacks? Who could feast on one a little while and then just be done? She'd known a few of them. And she'd always assumed that if she wanted to *be* one of them, she could. She was confident, after all. And independent. And she didn't need relationships to the degree that many people seemed to. She was content in her solitude because she'd chosen it.

So why can't you just play with him a little? Like a toy? The way so many men were so adept at doing with women?

You can. You absolutely can.

After all, it's not like he's shown terribly much affection for you; it's not like you owe him any loyalty.

So time to take a new tack. Think of him like candy, or a piece of cake. Tasty for a moment in time—and then it's gone and you forget about it and move on with your life.

As Juanita was finishing up, Camille reached for her purse and gave her a healthy tip. "For coming in to do only one room. It was probably inconvenient." She was young, and pretty, and it was easy to envision her having plenty else to do with her time.

But the younger woman was gracious. "Oh, I don't mind at all. I was surprised, since it's been empty lately, but I was already cleaning Mr. Reece's house today, so I just came here after."

Camille tilted her head. "Oh, you clean his apartment next to the office?" She pointed vaguely in that direction.

But Juanita laughed. "No, though I suspect it could probably use it. Mr. Reece has a house on

Sea Shell Lane that he doesn't live in. But it has furniture, and pictures on the walls, and dishes in the cabinets, just the same as if he did. I clean it for him every two weeks."

Hmm. That was more than a little interesting. "But you don't know why he doesn't live there?"

Juanita gave her head a carefree shake that informed Camille she'd never bothered to wonder, either. "No."

"And you're sure no one else does?"

This time she nodded. "I would know. Nothing's ever moved—everything is always exactly the way I left it other than the dust that gathers. It's an easy job," she finished with a confiding grin.

As Juanita left, Camille remained intrigued by this little mystery. There was definitely more to Reece Donovan than met the eye, and this reinvigorated her determination to find out what. And to make it work for her.

Just keep playing this out, seeing where it leads.

Having renewed her resolve once more, she decided that was exactly what she was going to do. And with that, she picked up the room's phone and dialed zero to reach the front desk. It rang for a long while—and she supposed it shouldn't surprise her since Reece didn't seem overly concerned with keeping it manned—but just when she was about to give up, he answered. "You rang, Tinkerbell?"

She ignored the annoying nickname—she was getting better at that. "I'd like to get out and explore the area a little more. Are you interested in accompanying me or am I free to go by myself?"

Slight hesitation. Then, "I'll go with you. Can't have you out and about in Coral Cove on your own."

"I'm not sure what it is you're so afraid I'll do, but okay. As long as you promise to quit introducing me as, 'she's not my friend.'"

"*Are* you my friend, Cami?" There was a hint of sarcasm and amusement in his voice, but it also felt like kind of a dare. And possibly even a flirtation.

"Maybe," she said lightly. "And maybe that remains to be seen. But regardless, I'm not the enemy you make me out to be."

"Hmm," he said, sounding skeptical.

Though she didn't let that get under her skin, professionally or personally. "So do we have a deal? I'll let you hang out with me so long as you don't make me sound like a creep?"

"I might choose to think of it more as chaperoning than hanging out," he quipped, "but yeah, okay. Leave in half an hour?"

"Sounds good."

After disconnecting, Camille changed into a cute outfit of white shorts and a beaded pink tank—having packed little, she'd gone shopping earlier at Beachtique, a surprisingly pleasant shop a few establishments up from Reece's. Then she ran a curling iron through the tips of her hair to give it some bounce, and applied makeup, focusing on making her eyes stand out. And when she realized she was putting in the same effort as if she were getting ready for a date—albeit a casual, impromptu one—she let herself off the hook with: *All in a day's work.*

> . . . Perhaps it was because of the soft beauty
> of the evening . . .
>
> J. M. Barrie, *Peter and Wendy*

Chapter 7

As THEY walked past the Hungry Fisherman on Coral Street, the town's main thoroughfare, a few seagulls passed overhead and a salty sea breeze wafted past. Something in the moment delivered her back to a time when being at the beach was brand new to her, and a little magical, when she'd first had the chance to start traveling. After having been raised in Michigan and spending her college years in Lansing, getting out of the state and seeing different parts of the country had been a revelation to Camille. To discover how many different kinds of places and people and lifestyles there were out in the world had opened her eyes. It had been what she considered the real beginning of her life.

"I love the beach," she said on a reminiscent sigh. But then remembered who she was with. She glanced up at the handsome beach bum next to her. "That probably sounds silly to you, having always lived here, but . . . it's an entirely different environment from anything I knew growing up and I just had a little flashback to my first visits to the ocean."

"So how did you get from rural Michigan to the beach, Tink?" He sounded sincerely interested, not a trace of sarcasm lacing his voice.

"The usual way," she said on a light laugh. "College trip. Spring break."

Next to her, he raised his eyebrows, took on a playful look. "Didn't do anything naughty, did you?"

She wondered what he wanted the answer to be—and then was honest. "Not every college spring break trip is about sex and alcohol. Maybe it was that way for a couple of my friends, but not for me." She focused back ahead—beach to the left, small storefronts to the right—as she added, "Anything naughty I've done was not on spring break."

"Tell me more," he prodded.

Yet she replied with a coy smile, "I'm afraid that'll just have to stay a mystery."

Funny—in the beginning with Reece, confidence had come via her professional persona only, fading when more personal sides of her had shown through. But now, slowly, she was beginning to feel a softer sort of confidence with him, even when being personal. Though—yikes—*softer*. That word again.

"Fine, then back to your more distant past," he said. "What was it like growing up in Michigan?"

She cast him a glance, trying to decide how much to say. *Be careful here.* Then again, that should be easy—she'd spent most of her adult life making conversation about things like this without saying too much. She was good at it now. And yet . . . what was it about him that made it feel easy to share? "It was snowy," she replied on another gentle chuckle. "Nice in the summer, though—not usually too hot. Working in warmer climates has taken some adjustment, but I really do love being at the beach."

"I wasn't really asking about the weather," he pointed out.

Though she already knew that. "What is it you want to know about then?"

His eyes narrowed on her and she sensed him trying to see beneath the surface. And for the first time it really hit her that in the same way he was a mystery to *her*, she really *was* a bit of a mystery to him, too. *And that might just work for me. Professionally.* It was a new thing for her to be combining the professional and the personal—making the personal *part* of the professional. *But I can do it.* In fact, she liked the challenge.

"I want to know just what makes Cami Thompson tick," he finally said.

Good question. But choose your reply with care. No chinks in the armor. "My parents were . . . strict," she began. "And they expected a lot of me. And we were poor. So as I got older, I made choices that ensured I wouldn't be poor anymore. And that allowed me to take charge of my own life, be in control, make my own decisions." She peered up at him. "Is that what you were after?"

"Maybe," he said. "And . . . sorry. I mean . . . well, it doesn't sound like a great childhood."

Damn. She kind of thought she'd stated it with such strength that he'd focus on the outcome, not the start. So she blew it off as nothing. "It's fine. It's long in the past and pretty much forgotten. I'm a here-and-now kinda woman."

As they'd walked on, she'd studied the other Coral Street establishments closer than she had up to now. Other than the Beachtique boutique, which frankly felt too upscale for its surroundings, the rest had seen better days: Beachside Bakery, whose sign was sorely in need of paint; a souvenir shop in the same situation; a pizza place that might be open or closed—she couldn't tell; and a few storefronts that were vacant and appeared rundown.

She couldn't help thinking the decay of the place—of *any* place—was sad, but on the other hand, she truly believed that the arrival of a Windchime Resort would allow many of these businesses to revive or reinvent themselves. New money would come into the community and everyone would profit. Except for Reece. But he would profit in a whole different way—just not at the Happy Crab, or at least not at its current location.

"Have you ever thought of relocating?" she asked without weighing it.

"Seriously?" he asked. "You're seriously asking me that? Like I haven't made my feelings on this perfectly clear?" She wasn't looking at him, but could feel the intense widening of his eyes on her anyway.

"We never discussed relocating exactly," she calmly explained. "And there are empty stretches of land around here. I saw an out-of-business car lot on the way in. You could build a newer, better

Happy Crab and take the run-off business from the Windchime."

Glancing over at him, she found herself the recipient of a death stare.

"And quit looking at me like that. I'm making a sincere suggestion. And it's honestly the only way I can see the Happy Crab ever flourishing again. Which I'm sure you want. I'm trying to think of ways everyone can be happy."

"*I* wouldn't be happy," he said.

She held his gaze. "Tell me why not."

"If I built a new motel somewhere else, it wouldn't be the Happy Crab. The Happy Crab is staying where it is. And if you're gonna keep hammering at me about this, I might consider it a deal broken and make you look like an ogre to the next person I introduce you to."

"All right, all right," she said, rolling her eyes. "Calm down. Forget I said anything. What's next on my big tour of Coral Cove?" They'd reached the end of the string of storefronts that lined the road across from the beach.

Reece looked at his phone, apparently checking the time. "Early bird special about to start at Gino's," he said, pointing over his shoulder to the pizza place they'd passed by, which apparently *was* open and she thought should do a better job of making that apparent. "Wanna get a pizza, then head over to the Sunset Celebration? You can catch Fletcher's act. And Tamra and other vendors sell their artwork there every night."

"Sounds nice," she said, and then asked an honest question. "But where do the shoppers come from?"

"Same as the beachgoers. They drive down from the resorts up the road."

She nodded, taking that in, thinking, again, that it was a shame the older part of town had all but died. Yet time marched on and so did progress. And Reece would surely see that soon and stop standing in its way.

REECE took a lot of pride in his little town of Coral Cove—always had—and as he escorted Cami across the street and onto the sand, he found himself really wanting her to love the nightly Sunset Celebration. As they walked, though, it struck him that perhaps that was stupid. Maybe he should be trying to make her hate the place, showing her the worst—if he could find any—that Coral Cove had to offer.

Maybe he should have painted Abner as a complete nutjob and Polly as a busybody—he loved Polly, but she sometimes did stick her nose in other people's business. Maybe he should have tried to make Fletcher and Tamra out to be eccentric bordering on weird. Maybe he should have implied that the beach was just crawling with homeless people and wild iguanas on the prowl. Maybe if he made the town look bad, she'd decide it wasn't such a great place for a Windchime Resort after all.

So why hadn't he done that?

My love of this place trumps all that.

He thought of his dad, and how much he had loved Coral Cove, too. Reece thought some things like that were just passed down through the genes. And he thought his dad would be proud of him for wanting to show Cami what he loved about the place, even under these particular circumstances.

He'd checked the weather for the evening—warm and mild, his favorite kind of night on the beach. And as they approached the entrance to the pier—flanked by a small playground and a snack hut with bathrooms on the backside—music filled the air, currently Pharrell Williams singing about being happy. Little kids' laughter trilled as they played on old swings and the same metal slide Reece had as a child. In the distance, closer to the water, people flew colorful kites as the sun dipped toward the horizon and the first hints of sunset lit the clouds with a purple glow.

Just off to one side of the pier, Fletcher had erected his tightrope, same as he did each and every night. And they'd shown up just in time because that was when Fletcher's voice began to boom across the beach.

"Gather 'round, gather 'round! Come one, come all, to the most amazing show on Coral Cove Beach!" Then Fletcher held up one finger, looking to the passersby who had paused to see what was about to happen. "Ah, but it's the *only* show, you say. It's a small town—not my fault." Light giggles wafted through the amassing crowd. "And I challenge you not to be stunned and amazed by the time I'm through."

"Will I?" Cami asked Reece as they stepped closer to watch.

"Yep," Reece said. "I've seen it dozens of times and I'm *still* amazed." It was the truth.

Cami tilted her pretty head, looked up at him. "That's impressive."

He narrowed his gaze on her. "If you're thinking how much the Windchime guests will love it, don't waste your time," he couldn't help saying.

She pressed her lips together, slanting a glance skyward, clearly weighing this. "I was actually *only* thinking that it was impressive, but now that you mention it . . ." Then she smiled.

And he just shook his head and laughed. Maybe because it was easier than arguing with her. And it was his own fault for bringing it up this time anyway.

"He seems so much . . . louder than he did yesterday at the pool," she observed as Fletcher went on with his crowd-gathering schtick.

He was addressing small children now, but loudly enough for all to hear, his eyes wide and playful as he made the kids laugh. "What's the most amazing thing you've ever seen?" he asked a small boy of about seven.

"My dog, Tootles, can walk on his hind legs," the little boy said.

"Well, I've got bad news for your dog, my friend," Fletcher told him. "You are about to witness far more amazing feats than that. Though when Tootles can walk on his hind legs on that rope"—he pointed behind him and upward—"then introduce me, because I might want to offer him a job."

"It's the performer in him," Reece explained. "The guy you met yesterday is the real him. This is just part of the show."

"What about the stuff regarding his wife?" she asked. "Real? Or show?"

"Real," Reece said. "Crazy, but real."

Cami turned to him. "Crazy? So you don't think she's coming back?"

Reece looked over at Fletcher for a minute, thinking it through, then back to the woman at his side. "Ya know, I have no real reason to think she's coming back. One day they were working here, side by side—she was his assistant in the show— and the next, she'd left him with nothing but a note. But he's convinced himself she'll come back, and I think over time he's almost convinced the rest of us, too. So the answer is . . . who knows?" He shook his head lightly. "And I shouldn't call him crazy—he's my friend and a damn good guy."

He sensed Cami considering the situation. "Maybe it's better to live with hope," she suggested.

"But what if it's really just wishful thinking? What if it's just a way of not facing the truth? Guess I'm a realist," he said. "I'd rather see things the way they are, accept things I can't change."

When she stayed quiet at that, Reece could almost read her thoughts. She was wondering, if he was such a realist, why didn't he just accept the fact that Windchime Resorts intended to move in here no matter how much he tried to prevent it? And why didn't he accept that the Happy Crab was a thing of the past?

Logically, he understood her way of thinking. And he grasped exactly what he stood to gain if he'd just sell. But *his* Coral Cove didn't have a big high-rise resort sitting across from the beach, leaving the Hungry Fisherman and the Beachside Bakery to look like tiny specks in its shadow. His Coral Cove wasn't about luxury or room service or lagoon-style pools. His Coral Cove was small and quaint and friendly—and his Coral Cove had a neon smiling crab in the middle of it all to greet people. And it was going to keep right on having that as long as he had anything to say about it.

"Are you all ready to be stunned and amazed?" Fletcher asked the crowd at large. He'd drawn a sizable gathering on the beach, a reminder to Reece that it was almost summer—high season. *There'll be more business at the Crab in a month or two. Has to be. Or . . . there will be if I can figure out a way to get rid of that sign in the old snowcone lot.*

As Fletcher mounted the tightrope to the delight of his audience, Reece knew Cami was watching closely, taking it in, studying his innate sense of balance, and the way his toes seemed to curl around the rope he walked across. And it reminded him that sometimes the impossible wasn't impossible. After all, who'd think you could walk across a rope suspended above the sand like that and not fall off? Little miracles happened every day. And sometimes bigger ones.

And he supposed he kind of needed a miracle for the Happy Crab. Keeping it out of Vanderhook's hands was one thing, but Cami was right—this part of town was dying and if something didn't happen to turn things around, he'd be the proud owner of an empty shell of a motel that no one but him cared about anymore. He wasn't much of a praying dude, but he glanced skyward and said silently: *I could use a miracle down here if you have one to give.* And he wasn't sure if he was talking to God or his dad or maybe just the planets and the stars, but either way, he tried to put a little of Fletcher's faith behind it. Just for this moment anyway.

"Hey, everybody over by the snack stand!" Fletcher called then from atop the wire.

People there looked toward his voice.

"There's a guy walking on a tightrope over here and he's really good! You should come watch!" he said. The crowd around him seemed amused as usual, and a handful of people who hadn't been paying attention began to head in their direction.

"Good decision," Fletcher told them all en masse. "Because now I'm even going to juggle! Feel free to ooh and aah." The gathering obliged.

And Reece could tell that Cami was pretty awe-struck with his friend. But his mind remained on other things. "When Vanderhook gets tired of trying to buy me out," he told her, "I'll be happy to take the snowcone lot off their hands."

She glanced over. "You have the money for that?"

So she assumed he was broke. Understandable maybe, under the circumstances. But there was so much about this she didn't know. "As long as they don't ask some insane price, sure."

"What would you do with it?" She looked sincerely curious.

And he shook his head. "Not sure—I'd have to think about it. But mainly I'd keep some big company from putting a sign up in it that drives my business away."

To his surprise, she appeared a little contrite.

"Sorry about that. That truly wasn't my doing—I don't have any control over that aspect of things."

"So your sole job is wearing down people who don't want to sell?" he asked.

"Pretty much."

It struck him as a grim existence, but he didn't say so, because something potentially more interesting had entered his thoughts. "Do you spend this much time with *all* the people you're trying to convince to sell?"

She was back to watching Fletcher—who now juggled bowling pins and was about to advance to knives—but tossed him only a sideways glance to say, "No. Never."

Was there a hint of flirtation in her voice? A bit of admission that this might be about more than her job? "But never say never, right?" he quipped with a grin.

"Right," she said, returning an easy smile. "There's a first time for everything."

And maybe it was from talking about hope, or maybe it was from trying to have a little of Fletcher's boundless faith, but in that moment, Reece began to wonder for the very first time if maybe, just maybe, it might be possible to get Cami to change her mind here—if maybe there was a chance he could convince her Coral Cove was fine just the way it was and get her to call off the Vanderhook dogs. A couple of days ago, he'd have said that was impossible. But now he was beginning to wonder if maybe that kind of miracle could really somehow happen.

" . . . I feel sure she knows they have souls."

J. M. Barrie, *Peter and Wendy*

Chapter 8

AFTER FLETCHER'S show, he passed a hat for the tips that provided his income, and Reece and Cami hung back until most of the crowd had dispersed. But when they'd gone and Fletcher approached them to say hi, Reece watched as Cami extracted a twenty from her purse, folding it so that the face value wasn't obvious, and added it to Fletcher's take for the night.

When they'd parted ways with him, Reece couldn't help making the observation: "Generous."

"See, I'm really not a monster," she told him as they meandered toward the pier where vendors currently sold various types of art.

But Reece just shrugged. "Maybe the jury's still out on that one."

"What will it take to bring them in?"

He tilted his head and raised his eyebrows, thinking the answer obvious. "Surely I don't have to tell you."

She gifted him with a soft smile. "I go away?"

Peering into her eyes, he realized that while the tougher Cami was a good sparring partner, the nicer side of her actually appealed to him much more. "You don't have to go away, Tink," he informed her. "You just have to quit trying to take what I don't want to give."

They walked on slowly for a moment before she replied without looking at him, "Sometimes it's easier for other people to see what's in your best interest than it is to see it yourself."

Reece considered the argument. She was suggesting that perhaps he was blind to the reality of the situation, in denial or something. That was a new tactic. "Debatable," he rebutted reasonably. "For drug addicts, maybe. But otherwise, debatable."

"Fair enough," she countered. "But sometimes people get so set on something that they can't see the forest for the trees."

His reply was simple. "This," he said motioning all around him with his arms, "is my forest. And the Crab is my tree. I'm keeping my tree."

And with any luck you'll fall in love with Coral Cove just the way it is and realize a Windchime Resort would ruin it. And that, he fully realized, was indeed why he hadn't tried to make her hate the place. That was why he wanted to show her what was so nice about it instead of try to drive her away from it. He just hadn't completely understood that until now.

They ventured out onto the pier past Larry, an older guy who painted beach scenes on pieces of tile, and Marjorie, who sold her homemade ice cream from an old-fashioned cart—and Reece bought them both cones, surprised when Cami chose strawberry.

"Strawberry?" he asked as they walked on, cones in hand.

She gave him a look. "Yeah. What's wrong with strawberry?"

He shrugged. "Nothing wrong with it—it's just sort of . . . girly, I guess."

She flinched. "I *am* a girl."

"But a tough one, you keep trying to tell me."

"So I should have ordered a tough flavor like your butter pecan?" She raised her eyebrows challengingly.

He was mainly kidding her, but said easily, "It's a tougher flavor. It has nuts."

"Well, for your information," she said, looking up at him, "just because something has nuts doesn't mean it's tough. And it so happens I can be tough and girly at the same time." And with that, she licked a trail around her ice cream that was completely feminine, but struck him in a far different way than she'd probably intended. Because it suddenly made him think she would be good using her tongue on other things—and he was glad his cargo shorts were loose enough that the entire town didn't see his reaction.

"What?" she asked. "Why are you looking at me weird? Is there ice cream on my face or something?"

Hell. He shook his head. "No." But then he noticed a melty trail of strawberry beginning to run down her cone and said, "You've got a drip," just before he automatically reached out a finger to swipe it away—and his hand touched hers, and it felt too good.

He drew back, broke eye contact, and licked her ice cream from his finger, kind of wishing it were *her* licking it off.

"Melts fast," she said, her voice now seeming a little breathy, sexy.

"Yep," he said, trying to diffuse the heat that had built so suddenly between them.

Well, not suddenly. It was always there, all the time. Had been from the beginning. But it was just more unavoidable in some moments than others.

He was glad when his eyes fell on Tamra then— his friend provided a much safer place to focus his attention. "Hey Tam," he said, approaching, still working on his own ice cream to avoid any further drippage situations.

Her eyes lit up when she saw him. "Reece!" And her sweet smile put him at ease, as usual. But then she frowned. "Where's Fifi—you didn't bring her tonight?"

He hadn't had a chance to reply before Cami came up beside him—and though Tamra's smile stayed in place, her eyes changed. "Oh, I see. You brought someone else."

Huh. Her tone bordered on rude, and that wasn't like Tamra at all.

"Hi," Cami said anyway. "Nice to see you again."

Tamra gave a short, almost terse, nod. "You too." But not really. That was obvious.

"Your pieces are lovely," Cami complimented her, studying Tamra's stained glass suncatchers. She touched a bright yellow and orange piece in the shape of a sun, and then one in various shades of aqua and turquoise in an abstract design Reece thought was supposed to look like ocean waves.

"Thanks," Tamra said but left it at that.

Reece interjected some small talk to Tamra— "How's business tonight?" and "Think it'll rain?"—to distract from the odd tension, and when Cami let some seascape paintings displayed by the next vendor draw her away, he couldn't blame her.

"Look," he bent closer to Tamra to say quietly once Cami was out of earshot, "I know you're just trying to do the loyal friend thing here, but she's not so bad."

Tamra peered up at him, her long mane of naturally curly hair falling around her shoulders. "She's trying to take the Crab from you, right?"

Okay, fair point. Talk about not being able to see the forest for the trees. "Right."

"Then how can I really be nice to her? And how can *you*?"

"Maybe I'm . . . just trying to win her over, show her how great Coral Cove is without her big resort plopped down in the middle of it."

Tamra cast a sideways glance at Cami, now in a conversation with the seascape painter. "It won't work. Someone like her can only see dollar signs."

Reece took that in, weighed it. He didn't want to be blinded here. But on the other hand . . . "I think there's a chance. And even if I'm wrong, it doesn't matter—she can't buy the Crab unless I sell it. I'm just trying to take the high road and show her why her company's plan doesn't make sense for this part of town."

"Well . . . I just wouldn't want to see you waste your time on something not worth wasting time on, that's all."

"Don't worry—I have the situation completely under control."

And that wasn't 100 percent true—but true enough for now, especially if it calmed Tamra's worries. "So you don't have to be mean to her on my account," he added with a grin.

She tried to smile back, but like before, it didn't reach her eyes. He wondered what that was about.

"Move it—you're blockin' my way, sonny."

Reece turned to see the familiar grin of Charlie Knight, an old man he'd become friendly with in the last year or so. Charlie couldn't walk with ease and was in his wheelchair tonight, but it was nice to see him out and about from the rest home up the road where he lived. His lady friend, Susan, also from the home, was at his side, though she was more mobile, using a walker.

"They let you out? Here? In a crowd?" Reece teased him. "Don't they know what a trouble-maker you are?"

"Nope, I got 'em fooled," Charlie said. "And me and Susan talked our friend, Ron, here, into loadin' us up into the special van to bring us out. Haven't been out to the Sunset Celebration in a blue moon and weather was too nice to stay in."

The man behind him wore scrubs and Reece

deduced he must be "Ron the Nurse." Reece was good friends with Charlie's granddaughter, Christy, and her boyfriend Jack, and he'd heard them mention Ron the Nurse on many occasions.

"So you're Christy's friend, the Happy Crab owner," Ron said. He was a heavyset man with glasses, a beard, and a friendly air, and who, Reece knew from Charlie, was gay. And while it surprised Reece a little that Charlie was so fond of him—Charlie was definitely a guy's guy, even in a wheelchair—he supposed stranger things had happened. He hadn't exactly expected to get fond of Cami, either.

"And I heard I'd recognize you by the large iguana you'd be walking on a leash," Ron said, "but no iguana? I'm disappointed."

"Yeah, where is good old Fifi anyway?" Charlie asked.

But just then Cami came back up beside him. And Ron said, "Well, hello—aren't you just the prettiest thing on the pier tonight?" as Charlie asked, "Who's this?" with a conspiratorial grin.

"This is . . . Cami," Reece said. He fought the urge to add the part about her trying to buy his business, but he'd promised, so he didn't. And that made him feel like he should explain his association with her in some *other* way, but he didn't have one, so he just moved on. "Cami, meet Charlie, Susan, and Ron."

"I was lookin' forward to seein' Fifi, too," Charlie said on a laugh, "but a pretty girl's a far better companion for a walk on the beach than a scaly old iguana."

"Don't let Fifi hear you call her scaly or old," Reece joked with him. Then he said to Cami, "Charlie's granddaughter is a good friend of mine."

"And speak of the devil—there she is right now. How's that for some timin'?" Charlie said, and Reece looked over his shoulder, spotting Christy and Jack in the distance as they chatted with Larry over his painted tiles.

"Christy! Jack!" Reece called.

A moment later, the two joined them. "Hey," Christy said, as merry as usual, "looks like we found the party!" Then her eyes dropped to Charlie. "You're the last guy I expected to see here! Why didn't you text me?"

"Last minute thing and I was just about to when we ran into Reece and his new friend here."

After Christy greeted Susan, she looked to the nurse and said, "Ron, you're an angel for bringing him!" Reece knew that while Christy and Jack got Charlie out of the home as much as possible, they appreciated other people helping make his life more active, too.

"I try," Ron said kiddingly but preening a bit.

Turning her attention to Cami then, she introduced herself. "Hi, I'm Christy. And you are?"

"Camille," she answered, and Reece realized he'd nearly forgotten she chose to use that more formal version of her name. He really did think Cami suited her better, especially as he'd gotten to see the friendlier side of her.

"But I call her Cami," Reece chimed in.

"To get on my nerves," Cami added. And everyone laughed. But Reece could still feel their curiosity, too. He didn't show up at the Sunset Celebration with a woman at his side—ever. He just usually preferred his liaisons to be more private. Because it kept people from asking questions or speculating. So why had he suddenly forgotten about that and brought Cami with him tonight?

After Jack introduced himself as well, he asked, "Where's Fifi?"

That seemed to be the question of the hour. "Gave her the night off," Reece replied, and everyone laughed a little more.

"Did you know Mike and Rachel are here?" Christy asked Reece, and was then polite enough to explain to Cami, "They're old friends from my hometown—Destiny, Ohio. Mike's parents have lived here for years and Mike and Rachel are here visiting on vacation this week."

"Didn't they have a baby or something?" Reece asked, trying to remember what he'd heard from Christy—or maybe it had been from John or Nancy Romo, Mike's parents.

"Yes—this is their first trip since then! And wait 'til you see the baby! Adorable."

"I bet," Reece said. He wasn't that into babies, but he respected that other people were.

Then Christy changed the subject. "Hey, when are we going snorkeling?"

"Anytime you guys want," Reece told them.

"Well . . . then how about tomorrow?" she suggested with playfully raised eyebrows.

"We're both taking a couple of days off to unwind," Jack explained.

Only then Christy looked to Cami. And then back to Reece. "Or if this isn't a good time . . ."

"No, it's a great time," Reece replied quickly. Because it was. "Not like I have a lot of customers to be taking care of, after all. And sounds fun. So it's a date."

AFTER leaving Reece's friends, Camille and he continued perusing the wares on the pier. The old man, Charlie, had been right—it was a beautiful night out, and after checking out all the vendors' tables, Reece suggested they cross the sand toward the water to better take in the sunset. Now they sat side by side in the sand on a quieter stretch of beach looking out over a neon pink and gold sky.

"Your friends are nice," she said. Excluding Tamra—who clearly didn't like her. But she left that part out. She could understand why, after all, and that made it mostly about business, so it didn't bother her.

Unless . . . maybe it was about more than just business. She could have sworn Tamra had looked at Reece in a way that struck her as . . . romantic. She hadn't noticed that at the pool when they'd first met, but something about tonight had seemed different.

"It was easier when I was allowed to explain who you are," Reece said. "Now they all think I have a secret girlfriend."

Hmm. Something about the idea made Camille's chest warm. Maybe she *wanted* to be Reece's secret girlfriend. "So you don't? Have one?" It dawned on her that it might be a good idea to verify that.

"No, secret or otherwise," he confirmed.

Good. Maybe it wouldn't ever really matter—but on the other hand, maybe it would. Every time he touched her, she thought it would.

Still, she couldn't help wanting to find out more about that situation. "Why not? Tamra seems . . . enamored of you."

He looked surprised by the suggestion, his brow knitting. "Tamra? We're just friends. Buddies."

"Then . . . why no one else?"

He took his time answering, still peering out over the water, watching as a pelican dove for a fish. "Let's just say I'm a no-strings kinda guy," he finally replied.

Hmm. "How old are you?"

"Thirty-five." He glanced over. "Why?"

"Just curious. Though . . . that's an age when a guy usually starts wanting to settle down if he hasn't already."

He appeared completely unfazed, hands planted in the sand behind him as he leaned back onto them. "Not me. I like my life exactly the way it is."

"You don't want kids?"

He gave his usual Reece shrug. "Kids are great, but not in the cards for me."

"Why not?"

He cast a critical look in her direction. "Damn, you're a nosy woman."

Now it was she who shrugged. "I was just asking. And I've answered *your* nosy questions."

He returned his gaze to the horizon. "It's like I said, I'm happy the way things are."

"I'm starting to think *Fifi* is your girlfriend," she told him, letting the tiniest hint of dryness color her voice.

This time his look came from beneath shaded lids. "*That* was a weird thing to say."

She gave another easy shrug. "It just seems like people expect you two to be together all the time, joined at the hip."

"She doesn't really *have* a hip," he pointed out. "But any guy iguana would be lucky to have her." Then he tossed her a glance, now looking amused. "Jealous, Tink?"

She gave an exaggerated eye roll and said with a thick dose of sarcasm, "Yes, you figured me out. I'm jealous of a humongous, scaly—"

"Dinosaur," he cut her off.

Funny, a couple of days ago that would have pissed her off, but now it made her laugh. And his suggestion that she might be jealous, that there was something between her and Reece, didn't bother her. She didn't think it was any big secret that they were attracted to each other, so she decided to officially not deny it or be embarrassed by it.

As the two of them sat watching the last remnants of the sunset, a stylish-looking thirty-something couple with a baby in a stroller came into view near where the water met the sand. The broad-shouldered, dark-haired father pushed the stroller and Camille could see the couple's shoes stowed in a mesh compartment beneath the baby's seat.

"See that guy?" Reece said softly.

She nodded. "Yeah."

"I know him. That's Mike Romo and his wife, Rachel, who Christy mentioned being in town. And I like the guy—but do you know what I see right now?"

"What?" Camille asked.

"I see a guy who's given up his life, his whole identity."

Next to him, Camille balked. "*What?*"

"I've known him for years—from his visits to see his parents. And he's a cop. And he always *acted* like a cop. He used to be a pretty hard-edged dude. Kind of a tough guy, or at least a no-nonsense guy. But look at him now." Reece motioned toward where the trio had stopped to peer out over the ocean. "Wife. Baby. Pushing a pink stroller even. I barely recognize the guy—and he's definitely not who he used to be."

The good-looking dad then stooped down next to the stroller to re-tie the baby's little yellow hat under her chin. "How's my sweetheart?" Camille heard him say in one of those playful, exaggerated voices people use with babies. "Daddy loves you so, so much. What a pretty girl!"

Then he stood up and smiled into his wife's eyes to say, "Almost as beautiful as her mother."

"Flattery will get you everywhere, Officer Romeo," the wife replied.

Then he slid his arm around her waist and said, "Give your sexy husband a kiss."

As they stood exchanging a long kiss that turned Camille warmer just watching, the surf washing up near their toes, she said to Reece, "Yes, he looks absolutely miserable."

Reece just shrugged. "Different people value different things, I guess," he answered. But Camille thought he was faking it now, just sticking to his guns to be stubborn—because different people might want different things, but she thought *all* people wanted to be happy, and Mike Romo certainly looked like a man succeeding at that.

"So what about *you*?" Reece asked then. "Do you want kids? Want to be a mom?" And then he flinched. "Wait," he said. "I forgot for a second that I really don't know you very well. And that for all I know, you already have some." She thought he suddenly looked worried—whether about having made the assumption or about her possibly having kids, she didn't know. She only knew his eyes stayed wide and he now appeared uncharacteristically off his game. "Do you?"

She decided to cut him a break, put him at ease. "No, no kids—and never been married or anything like that." In case he was wondering. "And . . . I'm not sure if I want kids or not. Under the right circumstances, maybe. But my life right now is mostly about work and travel, so if kids are in the mix, it'll be down the road."

He nodded. Then told her, "I've never been married, either."

"I know."

He slowly turned his head to look at her, silently asking how. "Please tell me you didn't do some entire background check on me."

She let out a laugh. "Don't be so paranoid, Donovan. I know you've never been married because everything about you screams 'never been married.' Right down to your—"

"Dinosaur?" he asked.

"Yes," she said with a smile.

"Reece Donovan? Is that you?"

They both looked up as Mike Romo headed their way; then they got to their feet. He had to pick up the stroller to more easily transport it through the softer, hillier sand, but he didn't seem to mind.

"Hey Romo, what's up?" Reece said in return.

"Just brought my two best girls for a little vacation—and some grandma and grandpa time for this one." He pointed to the baby, then introduced her. "This is Farris."

"Cute kid," Reece said.

"Aw—how sweet," Camille chimed in, smiling down at the baby girl—and that prompted the usual introductions between them all.

"Hey, where's Fifi?" Mike asked after that, and Reece looked tired by the question, and Camille wanted to laugh but didn't.

"I left her on her own at the Crab tonight," Reece replied. "I only hope she's not throwing a wild party while I'm gone."

After a little more small talk, Reece mentioned having heard they were here from Christy. "I'm taking Christy and Jack snorkeling tomorrow if you guys want to join us."

"Sounds good to me," Mike replied.

Then Reece looked to Camille, apparently remembering he hadn't ever explained about that. "I have a couple boats docked behind the Crab.

Don't know if you've seen 'em—but I take motel guests and friends snorkeling on the catamaran."

Huh. Of course Camille *had* seen the boats docked in the slips behind the Happy Crab, but she'd continued to think it highly unlikely that any of them were *his*. Because they were *big boats*. *Nice boats*. And there were more than two of them, but no matter which two were his, they were impressive assets.

And crap—this made him a good guy all over again. To just take people snorkeling because he could. And his guests, too. Not that he'd offered that amenity to *her*—but she decided to let that go under the circumstances.

"Then it's a date," Rachel replied with a smile. "Mike's mom will watch the baby and all six of us will go snorkeling. It'll be fun to do something with other couples on vacation."

When Camille shifted her glance to Reece after that last part, he was looking back at her. Then he said, "We're not . . ." and stopped.

"Not what?" Mike asked easily.

Reece hesitated. "We're not . . . sure what time yet, but give me your number and I'll text you in the morning."

Hmm. She'd been sure he was about to correct that whole couple assumption—but then he'd changed his tune. What was that about? One more example of him just being a decent guy? Too decent to hurt her feelings? Though she wasn't sure that made sense given that he'd said plenty of things since they'd met that could have hurt her feelings.

Still, as they walked back toward the Happy Crab a little while later in the dark, a salty breeze wafting past, she decided it was only fair to let him off the hook one more time. After all, Rachel had sort of put him on the spot, even if unwittingly. "You don't have to take me snorkeling with your friends," Camille told him, "if you'd rather not. I'd understand."

He looked up, their gazes meeting dimly in the moonlight. "You don't want to go?"

"Well, you didn't really ask me—you just kind of got roped into taking me." And when he didn't immediately respond, she added, "Maybe you should bring Fifi instead since everyone loves her so much."

She'd looked away, but another quick glance over as they traversed the sand revealed the amused expression on his face.

"What?" she asked. Had she sounded terse? She hadn't meant to. Exactly.

"You really *are* jealous of a dinosaur," he said with the same smug little grin she'd seen on his handsome face when they'd first met.

She simply rolled her eyes. "I am *so* not jealous of your silly dinosaur. But you should have told them we aren't a couple."

"I started to," he explained, sounding slightly exasperated now, "but I was afraid that would be like saying you're not my friend and I'd be accused of the whole ogre thing again. It's hard reading your mind, woman."

They walked in silence once more, approaching

Coral Street, the neon Happy Crab sign smiling at them from across the way.

"Still, I don't have to go," she offered. "If you'd prefer I didn't. They're your friends, and I'm . . . *not*, as you're so fond of pointing out, so I won't be offended."

"You would be *totally* offended," he argued. But then his voice softened, deepened. "And . . . I'd like you to go. If you want to. Okay?"

Standing beneath a streetlight, she glanced over at his illumined face. And what she saw there was . . . sincerity. So she gently said, "Okay."

And as Reece walked her to her door, same as the previous night, she . . . *felt* him next to her. It was that same awareness, that same warmth—it was his very maleness. And she'd felt it all evening, as well—and okay, maybe in every single moment they'd spent together—but there was something about the solitude of night and privacy that made it grow, feel more pervasive. Her very skin seemed to ache with the simple desire to be closer to him, touching, being touched. What would it be like to kiss him?

When they reached her door and she turned to face him, she realized her heart beat too hard and her breath had grown short. Damn it. She still wasn't used to having reactions like that. To anyone. She felt like a high school girl on her first date—though it hit her that she hadn't even experienced a reaction this strongly *then*.

"It was . . . a nice night," she said. "Thanks for taking me. And for the ice cream."

"It was fun," he told her, but she could have sworn the simple words hid something; she was pretty sure he was feeling the same thing she was. That urge for more.

"Though I'm sorry to break up you and Fifi," she teased to lighten the mood.

He laughed. "You haven't broken us up, Tink—I'm headed back to her right now."

"Two-timed with a dinosaur. That's a new one."

He tilted his head, his look at once probing and sexy. "Sounds like maybe you think we're a couple, after all."

"No," she said gently, quickly. "In this equation . . . I'm the other woman."

Another deep, throaty laugh echoed from him, and she wondered if her desire showed through her iguana jokes. Would he kiss her? Did he want to? It seemed like the night—the very air—was ripe for kissing, and her chest tightened with anticipation as she met his penetrating gaze, until he said. "See you tomorrow for snorkeling, Tinkerbell."

"Goodnight, Reecie Cup," she replied.

He drew back slightly, eyebrows shooting up. "Reecie Cup?"

She kept her expression pleasant, playful. "Fun to have a nickname, isn't it?"

And he smiled. "Touché, Tink. Goodnight."

"It's only make-believe, isn't it . . ."

J. M. Barrie, *Peter and Wendy*

Chapter 9

As CAMILLE lay down to sleep a little while later she thought about Reece some more. Why hadn't he kissed her when the pull between them was so obvious?

Um, maybe because you're trying to wheedle his property from him with no real concern for his well-being?

She shook her head slightly against the pillow, trying to clear it, sorry things had to be this way. It wasn't her fault this was the reason they'd crossed paths and why she was here. It wasn't like she could just quit her job—or quit doing it—for a guy she'd just met.

No matter how nice he seemed to be.

She reflected again on the snorkeling trips. That he didn't even use them as a promotional tool—as he surely *should* be—to draw in business. But the fact that he didn't showed her he honestly did it only to be nice, that it came from the heart.

The nice just kept right on flowing from him, damn it.

Of course, that had its upside. If things ever progressed between them, she'd know she wasn't sleeping with a jerk.

But maybe sleeping with a jerk would be better—to help her stay emotionally detached.

You have to stay that way anyway. Even if he rocks your world, in the end, you will leave here—you'll go home, you'll never see him again, and he will ultimately resent you for getting him to sell his beloved motel. He will, in the big picture of your life, your history, be a blip on your radar screen. A guy who you knew for a week or so.

So he can't *mean anything to you. He just can't. If you let him, you'll only suffer for it.*

So quit focusing on how nice he is. And how funny. And how smart.

It would be a much better idea to focus on the fact that he's hot and that you want to touch him. You've wanted to touch him almost since the moment you met.

She let out a breath at the thought. Wow. She wasn't sure she'd ever met someone and wanted to touch them that fast. She just wasn't programmed that way. Her usual hard shell—the one he'd cracked so easily—extended beyond business into other areas of her life. She didn't get emotional easily. She simply didn't allow herself to. Because it made her feel weak, and why feel weak if you can feel some other, stronger way instead?

But Reece doesn't make you feel emotions of weakness. He just makes you feel . . . good.

So maybe don't overthink this too much. Don't over worry it.

And maybe he'd never proceed to touching her anyway. If tonight was any indication, that was the case. She was still technically the enemy, after all, and maybe he was doing a better job of re- membering that than she was.

Even if he did sincerely seem to want to take her on the snorkeling trip tomorrow. She'd felt that—in her skin, maybe even down to the marrow of her bones—when he'd eventually asked her so nicely. This wasn't one-sided.

And maybe she wasn't the only one who didn't know what she wanted it to be.

Maybe it would take both of them to figure it out and see where this went.

THE next morning, Camille got a call in her room from Reece, informing her that due to overcast skies and drizzle predicted to clear up around lunchtime, he'd decided the best part of the day for snorkeling would be late afternoon, with a picnic dinner on the boat afterward. Which meant she had some free time today. Which meant she should probably do some work.

Of course, it was hard to know exactly what work *was* at the moment. She dealt with some email and administrative issues via her laptop, but after that, she knew it came down to thinking about her current negotiations. With Reece. Just last night in bed she'd told herself she could keep her job and her affection for him entirely separate, so she supposed it was time to prove that to herself. She needed to start thinking outside the box about how to get him to sell.

A change of scenery often jogged a person's creativity—and this was the time where creativity came in to play in her profession. It didn't happen often, but every now and then an acquisition required an entirely new approach she'd never thought of before. And while she still held out hope that she might eventually get the solution from Reece himself, for now, it seemed wise to start coming up with some alternative plan.

So she grabbed up her cell phone and her crab-shaped keychain and, dressed in simple cotton shorts, a fitted tee, and gym shoes, she left the room seeking inspiration. Indeed a light rain fell, so she stayed under the awning that edged the building and walked toward the breezeway that led to the back of the Happy Crab.

On the way, she encountered Riley, who carried a beat-up old toolbox as he entered one of the other rooms. "Morning, miss," he greeted her with an endearing smile. Even with as few words as they'd exchanged, she could see why Reece had gravitated toward the older man and wanted to help him. A quiet sort of kindness emanated from him.

"Good morning, Riley. Keeping busy on a rainy day, I see."

The gray-haired man nodded. "Some repairs in this room I been meanin' to get to. A guest snuck

a cat in here a few months back. You wouldn't
expect a little cat could wreck things so much, but
between cat hair and torn bedspreads and smells
left behind, it made a mess for sure."

"I wouldn't have thought so, either," she mused.

"Reece wasn't happy, let me tell ya. You'd think
Fifi would do more damage to things—but nope,
not compared to what Reece says a cat or a dog
can do to a motel room."

"Well, Reece is lucky to have you," she told him.

"Oh no—I'm the lucky one there," he replied.
And she supposed she could understand his
viewpoint. But she'd meant what she said—Reece
was lucky, too.

After they told each other to have a nice day,
she meandered past the office. She glanced casually inside but saw no sign of Reece before she entered the breezeway, soon exiting near the pool
onto the planked dock area where she'd noticed
the boats tied up. The natural bay where they
floated so majestically was definitely among the
reasons Windchime wanted this spot—with private water access added to the beach's proximity,
it would stand out from the resorts up the road for
Coral Cove vacationers.

Taking a seat in an Adirondack chair that was,
fortunately, also covered with a roof overhang,
keeping it—and her—dry, she studied the boats.
She spotted the sizable catamaran they'd take out
this afternoon with ease—and she hadn't looked
closely at it before or she'd have noticed it was
named after the motel. THE HAPPY CRAB was

painted in red script on the back, which faced her in the slip it occupied, with a small, requisite smiling crab appearing alongside the words.

Four other boats were docked in a row next to it—two large sailboats, a cabin cruiser, and a sleek, attractive sloop. She was about to wonder which of those was the second he owned when Riley exited through the breezeway and ambled toward a storage shed near the pool. When he passed back by carrying a five-gallon bucket a minute later, she said, "Riley, which other boat besides the catamaran is Reece's?"

Riley glanced toward the vessels, then pointed in the general direction of the sloop. "That one. The other three belong to folks who rent the space from Reece, but *The Happy Crab* and the *Lisa Renee* are his."

The *Lisa Renee*? Straining to see them, she barely made out the name painted in very thin lettering on the stern of the sloop. "Thanks," she said. And as Riley continued on his way, her stomach went a little hollow. Who was Lisa Renee? And how important must she have been to Reece if he'd named his boat after her?

Not that it mattered. At all. No matter what else happened between them, he would ultimately be a very temporary fixture in her life, so what did *she* care who he named boats after?

Unless . . . she counted it as one small clue regarding Reece and what he was about. And as it stood, small clues were really all she had.

She tried to add up what she knew about him. He'd been born and raised in Coral Cove and held it dear, along with this motel, which had been built by his grandfather and passed down to him. He had a house he paid to keep clean but didn't reside in. He lived a modest, laid-back lifestyle, but seemed comfortable financially—comfortable enough to pass up what Vanderhook was offering and comfortable enough not to have sold off assets like these boats. He was well liked and generous. Quick-witted and smart. He adored his pet giant iguana. Oh, and he had a boat named after a mystery woman.

When she added all that up, there were definitely more secrets surrounding him than just who Lisa Renee was—but enlightening information seemed slow in coming. Which meant she was right—she needed to start thinking outside the box here.

And maybe part of her felt a little guilty about that—to still be working so hard at this. *But again, it's not like I have a choice. It's my job.* She didn't *want* to take the Happy Crab from him—she *had* to. And if *she* didn't do it, someone else would.

He knew why she was here—so anything he chose to tell her or any time he chose to spend with her was predicated on that. So there was nothing to feel guilty about.

Her contemplations flitted back to Riley, to something Reece had said about when he and Riley had met—that it was illegal to sleep on the beach. It reminded her how there were all kinds of laws on the books—pretty much everywhere, but particularly in smaller municipalities—that people didn't really know about or had long forgotten. Reece might know the law about sleeping on the beach—beach-related laws were often more widely known in a tourist community—but was there any legal way Reece could be driven to sell that he might not be aware of?

Camille had used threats of zoning changes and eminent domain to convince holdouts to sell before—but that wouldn't work here. Those instances had been for personal residences and in areas where progress and civic revitalization were already under way.

And the thought then crossed her mind that perhaps she should pay a visit to the mayor or the town council—try to garner their support and see if they could supply some legal reason that would help move things along. But no—that would be a bad idea for two reasons.

In a small place like Coral Cove, the people in charge surely knew and loved Reece and would probably want to ride her out of town on a rail. And it might do more to stir up trouble than help her cause. She didn't need the lawmakers suddenly deciding Windchime was a bad idea here and passing some law against high-rises in the older part of the community—or anything else that could prevent a building permit from being obtained. As it was, the communications between Vanderhook and the local government had been brief and non-problematic—they knew Windchime planned to build after buying the necessary properties and that was all. Vanderhook and Windchime were skilled at flying under the radar and then pushing through zoning changes as needed before some communities really knew what hit them. Let them know Reece was trying to hold on to his motel and it was very possible they'd band together on his behalf and tell Windchime to take a hike.

So if anything legal could help her out, she'd have to find it on her own.

Just then, her phone notified her of a text message. She looked down to see it was from her boss, Phil.

What's happening with the Coral Cove deal?

She replied: Still here and working on it.

A moment later, another text. Is there a problem I should be aware of?

Camille stared at the phone, a little miffed. Phil had hired her right out of college and she considered him one of the more stable, long-lasting relationships in her life. He could be short, and blunt, but behind that, he was a good enough guy. She'd spent more than one Christmas at his home, having dinner with his family. He knew she did her job well and it was unlike him to question her.

Finally, she typed back: No. Just biding my time a little. Some holdouts require more finesse than others. You know that. She hoped it would appease him.

But it didn't. There's a lot riding on this. Windchime wants to break ground by August and a lot needs to happen before then.

Hmm. *Thank you for telling me things I already*

know. There was a lot riding on *every* deal. Resorts were big money.

And she was completely aware that there were permits to get, not to mention all the work involved in developing the property for construction before actual building could begin. She knew this was taking longer than usual, but in the big picture of things, she couldn't help feeling underappreciated and disrespected. She held this position for a reason.

So she typed back: IT'S ONLY BEEN A FEW DAYS. PATIENCE IS A VIRTUE. PLEASE TRUST ME TO DO MY JOB AND REMEMBER THAT I'VE NEVER FAILED AT IT.

She sat staring at her phone, soaking in the scent of rain and the ocean combined, and feeling . . . unsettled. Maybe by everything that was happening. But having Phil act antsy on top of it, rather than supportive, had her stomach churning a bit. She only hoped she'd expressed her point clearly and that his reply would make him appear a little more contrite.

Yet again it didn't. OKAY, BUT DON'T LET ME DOWN.

Still irritated, she wished for the days of an old-fashioned phone you could slam down or even for her old flip phone that she could snap shut to expel a little aggression, but as it was, she could only press the button to make her smart phone's screen go black. And conclude that she needed another change of scenery.

The drizzle had ended and she could even see a few gaps of blue sky in the cloud cover, so she decided to walk over to the Hungry Fisherman for a soft drink to go. Making a quick stop at her room, she grabbed up her purse, then crossed the damp asphalt to the restaurant.

Her first thought as she stepped inside was that the dark woodiness of the place felt too heavy, *too much* like being on a boat—and made her begin to hum "The Wreck of the Edmund Fitzgerald" in her head. The place was in need of a remodel, something that would let in more light. It seemed to her there were things the businesses around here could be doing to help themselves that they weren't—like Reece advertising his snorkeling trips as part of the room price. She suffered the fruitless urge to remake the whole place, the same as you would redecorate a house.

Her second was that the Hungry Fisherman was even emptier than the last time she was here. Perhaps because it wasn't even lunchtime yet— but it still made her a little sad.

She spotted Polly standing behind the register in that same rust-colored waitress uniform and headed in that direction. "Hi," she said, smiling.

Polly's eyes widened dramatically and she looked a little frantic. "You are a gift from God!"

Camille blinked, utterly taken aback. "I am?"

"Yes." Only then did she realize Polly spoke in a hushed tone. "You're exactly what I need right now—a friendly face."

Camille remained confused. "What's wrong?"

"The health inspector's here," Polly whispered, pointing over her shoulder toward the kitchen.

Now Camille lowered her voice, too. "And that's a problem?"

Polly nodded emphatically.

"Why?" Camille asked.

And Polly answered by reaching beneath the counter with both hands and lifting—until Tiger the cat's head was revealed. "This," she said. Then she immediately lowered the cat back down, hiding him again.

"I see," Camille said. Though she didn't completely.

But then Polly answered Camille's next question before she could ask it. "I would just put him out the front door, but he'd only run around to the back—and that door gets opened too often, so he'll only sneak right back in. Business is already in the toilet, but if I get caught with a cat in here, they'll shut me down, and then what? That's why you're a gift from God."

Polly seemed so frazzled that Camille began to feel that way, too. But she still didn't know why she was a gift from God. "What can I do?"

Polly lifted both hands again, once more revealing the cat's furry yellow head. "You can take this cat." Then she lowered it back down.

Camille felt her eyes go wide. "Take him where?"

Polly gave her head a brisk shake. "Anywhere. Your room." Then she began nodding. "Yep, your room. Take him to your room."

"But . . . won't he do things like pee and poo?" Her mind flashed back to the fortuitous conversation she'd had with Riley about cats just a little while ago. "I was told cats are a no-no in the guest rooms."

Polly nodded profusely, looking worried. "That's true, that's very true. Reece has had problems with that. But he doesn't need to know about this. And it'll only be for a little while, until the inspection is over."

"But what about the peeing and pooing?" Camille insisted.

Polly's eyes shifted anxiously back and forth as she appeared to search her mind for an answer. "You can run up to Albertson's and get some kitty litter and a pan. I'll give ya some money from the cash drawer."

But Camille shook her head. "That's okay—I can cover it. I'm just not . . ." *Not really a cat person. I haven't spent time with cats. I'm not the girl for this particular job.*

"Not able to say no?" Polly finished for her hopefully, then rushed onward. "You got no idea how much I appreciate it. Tiger and me both. You're savin' both our hides for sure." Polly looked around then, to make sure the coast was clear, then spoke through clenched teeth. "Now are you ready for me to pass you the cat?"

"Um . . ."

"When I pass you this cat," Polly went on in the same tone a secret agent might use, "you're to turn around and head straight out the door. This cat was never here. Got it?"

"Um . . ."

"Good," Polly said. Then thrust the striped cat across the counter.

Camille had no choice but to take it—it was out

of hiding now, after all, and she had to get it out of there. She was already going to be responsible for the closing of *one* business in Coral Cove; she couldn't risk being the cause of another. So she took the cat into her arms and did as Polly had instructed—turned around and walked out the door as swiftly as possible.

She'd begun to cross the parking lot before it totally hit her that she was carrying a cat to her room. But she kept moving.

Thankfully, the cat wasn't hefty—he was more the sleek, lean variety and blessedly docile, too, so it was easy to shift him into one arm as she wrestled her key from her purse. Maneuvering them both inside, she then lowered him to the bed.

"Meow," he said, looking up at her.

"Um, yes, hi," she said uncertainly. When the cat didn't reply, she added, "Looks like you and I will be hanging out together." Though at this point, the whole situation still felt a little surreal. How had she ended up a cat sitter? Why had she allowed Polly to pawn the cat off on her so easily? Usually, *she* was the manipulator in situations. Well, at least in her job anyway.

"Meow," the cat said again.

"I need to go get you some kitty litter," she told him. "So I'm going to trust you to be good while I'm gone and not hurt anything. Promise?"

"Meow," he said yet one more time.

And that was good enough for her. Since she knew it was all she could get out of him.

As she left, shutting the cat up in the room, it dawned on her that maybe she'd taken the cat because . . . Polly had entrusted her with it. Polly knew why she was here—she knew Camille was trying to buy the Happy Crab against Reece's will—but she'd treated Camille nicely anyway, and with trust. So maybe Camille had wanted to show Polly she *was* nice, and that she *could* be trusted, that she wasn't the bad guy here.

And she really wasn't. And maybe she appreciated Polly seeing that.

Next stop: the grocery store for kitty litter.

Her stay in Coral Cove just kept getting stranger and stranger.

UPON her return from the store, Camille set up the litter box and was pleased to find that Tiger hadn't done any apparent damage while she'd been away. She waited through the afternoon to hear from Polly that it was okay to send him back, but time passed—and no Polly.

Mostly, the cat napped on the bed while Camille worked on her computer at the table. So far so good. But a few hours into their association, the cat silently bounded down from the bed and onto the floor and over to where she worked. He looked up at her. "Meow."

"Hi," she said just as uncertainly as when she'd first brought him to her room. She just didn't know what to do with a cat. What did he want?

He meowed again and this time stepped closer to her ankles and the leg of her chair.

She backed the chair out a little and—sheesh!— the cat pounced up onto her lap like he belonged there. "Oh!" she said, leaning back slightly, arms to her sides.

The cat stepped about a little on her thighs, seeming to try to get acclimated, then eventually curled into a ball, lying down. Like she was a pillow.

But . . . she discovered she kind of didn't mind. The cat was sort of warm against her. And clearly this meant he liked her and wanted to be near her. She wasn't sure why the cat felt that way, but she couldn't deny growing fonder of him in that moment. It felt a bit like when Polly had trusted her to help with a problem and to care for the cat. It was like Tiger trusted her, too.

Reaching down, she gently experimented with petting him, enjoying the feel of his thick fur. Growing up, she hadn't had pets. Her parents had been older, having had her late in life—she'd been an only child—and they just hadn't been animal people.

In fact, they hadn't been into much of *anything*—pets, their daughter, you name it. They were practical. To a fault. She supposed being poor could do that to you. And for them, life hadn't been about fun and games—something like a pet, or a birthday party, would have seemed downright frivolous compared to the business of living and dying, paying the bills, and watching the evening news so that they could complain about the general state of the world. They thought life was hard. And they made it hard. Harder than she'd ever thought it needed to be.

Before she knew it, a strange, low, motor-like

sound began to echo from the cat, and after a few seconds of confusion over it she then understood he was purring! He liked being petted by her. She smiled, pleased to know she was making the cat happy. Just sitting there, petting him, staring out the window at the rapidly brightening day as she sun shone down on the big Happy Crab sign, something came over her, something . . . peaceful. Hmm. That was new. And kind of nice.

But soon a glance at the clock revealed that it was almost time for the snorkeling trip to commence. She hated to end Tiger's contentment, but she carefully picked him up, got to her feet, and lowered him to the bed. "Sorry," she said, "but I have a hot snorkeling date. Or . . . work. Or both." She gave her head a short shake. "I'm not sure *what* it is anymore." Then went to find her bikini.

Tink was not all bad: or rather,
she was all bad just now,
but on the other hand, sometimes she was all good.

J. M. Barrie, *Peter and Wendy*

Chapter 10

*T*HE WEIRDNESS of suddenly "being a couple" with Cami weighed on Reece as he steered the catamaran out into open waters, leaving the bay. The three women on the trip lay stretched out on beach towels on the bow while Jack and Mike got drinks from the cooler Reece had packed. And he knew they weren't *really* a couple—but the other couples thought they were, so it still felt weird.

Even their *conversation* about being a couple had felt weird.

Oh hell, who was he kidding?—*everything* about his relationship with Cami was weird. How had he ended up in this situation, taking her snorkeling as his date? Her primary goal in life at the moment was getting her hot little hands on his property— no matter how much she tried to camouflage that behind "taking a vacation" and "making him a wealthy man"—and he was actually taking her on a date? Standing behind the captain's wheel near the stern, he gave his head a short shake, trying to clear it. And why did she have to look so damn hot in a bikini on top of it all?

There were moments when she seemed . . . not at all unreasonable. Even bordering on kind. Watching her now—because yes, there were three attractive scantily clad blondes stretched out before him, but only the lady in coral drew his eye—he wondered if there was any possibility she could be reasoned with. She was clearly business-minded and committed to her job—but maybe if he tried, really tried, going beyond the banter and sarcasm, he could make her understand why he wouldn't, couldn't, sell. Ever.

Maybe he could make her see that money wasn't what made someone wealthy, that it went far beyond that. Maybe he could make her understand that, at least for some people, being rich was about home, family, community—that those were the things that mattered. He didn't talk about that stuff often, but he carried it around inside him twenty-four seven.

And he didn't *like* to talk about it—just because something mattered to you didn't mean it was easy to talk about—but he wondered now . . . if he did, with her, would it be enough to make her give up and go away?

You don't want *her to go away.*

Damn. He didn't know where that little voice inside his head had just come from, but he supposed those kinds of little voices usually spoke the truth, or at least some measure of it.

On one level, hell yeah, he wanted her gone. He wanted to be left alone to run his business as best he could, whether it was crawling with a hundred guests—or none. He wanted to quit feeling hounded by Vanderhook. He wanted life to get back to normal—or at least to what had come to feel almost normal over time. Maybe things could never get *completely* back to normal again, but they could at least return to feeling relaxed.

But then there was that other level—the level that couldn't help enjoying her presence. He couldn't have dreamed that would be the case a few days ago, but life was full of surprises—some good, some bad. So far, the surprise he called Cami had held some of both, and that made it tricky. But he'd be lying to himself to deny that he'd had fun with her last night, and the night before that. He'd be lying to deny the chemistry between them, too.

Of course, he wasn't sure chemistry and fun were good enough reasons to have suddenly ended up in the happy world of coupledom with her. And he wasn't sure where things would go from here.

But maybe the thing to do was to just take the day for what it was worth—another beautiful day in paradise. The sun had come bursting out a few hours ago, he was with friends, and he knew they'd all have a nice afternoon together.

Jack and Mike had taken seats on one of the boat's built-in benches now, chatting—though Reece didn't hear their conversation because music from the radio spilled from the catamaran's speakers, Taylor Swift singing about knowing someone was trouble.

"You can say that again," he murmured under his breath with another glance at Cami. Getting close to her was like slow-dancing with a shark. Closing your eyes to danger didn't make it go away. And yet . . . she was a lot nicer to dance with than a shark. Or at least a whole lot nicer to put sunscreen on.

Just then, Christy got up from her towel and walked back to the captain's wheel. "Hey there," she said with her usual friendly smile.

"Hey," he replied.

"So . . ." She cast him a weird and sort of expectant look that made him think he was supposed to know what it was about.

But he didn't. "So . . . what?" he asked.

"So, Camille. Or Cami. Whatever her name is." She gave her head a short shake, understandably confused. But then her smile returned. "Is this something serious?"

Oh brother. *This is what comes of getting too close to people.* Because in the time since Christy and Jack had moved to Coral Cove last fall, he'd become good friends with both of them. But his friendship with Christy was different than with anyone else he knew. Because it turned out they had things in common. Losses in their past that were similar. Some of that stuff he didn't like talking about. But for some reason he'd talked about it to *her* one night after a bonfire on the beach near Sea Shell Lane, after everyone else—even Jack—had headed in for the evening. And they'd kind of bonded.

But unfortunately, it was just that kind of thing that made a female friend think it was okay to come around being nosy. So he was quick to correct her. "No, not serious at all," he informed her.

She flinched—perhaps because he'd said it so vehemently.

But he went on. "We just met a few days ago. And the fact is, she works for the company that keeps trying to buy the Crab from me."

Christy's eyes went predictably wide. "Really?"

He nodded. "Really."

She lowered her chin slightly. More understandable confusion. "But . . . then . . . why . . ."

"After I turned down their newest offer, she decided to stick around, take a beach vacation. Which I know really means she's trying to wait me out, or just keep pressuring me to sell. But . . ."

Christy tilted her head, looked curious, maybe even hopeful. "But . . . ?"

"But . . . I guess there's an attraction between us." He narrowed his gaze on her. "Not that it's going anywhere—because it really can't. She's the enemy, after all."

Christy blinked. "Then why did you bring her today?"

"The truth?" He sighed as the catamaran bounced across low ocean waves. "Because Mike and Rachel *assumed* I would and said so right in front of her when we ran into them on the beach last night."

"The beach," she repeated. "Where you were walking. With her. Willingly."

He let out another tired breath—even though

he wasn't very tired. Except maybe of thinking about all this. "I guess . . . we enjoy each other. Or enjoy fighting with each other anyway. But it was only a way to pass an evening, that's all. And a chance to maybe make her see that Coral Cove is fine the way it is, without her big, fancy resort. Another couple of days and she'll be gone. So don't go getting attached to her or anything."

She gave him a speculative look. "It's not me I'm worried about. Don't *you* go getting attached."

Now it was Reece who balked. "Me?" He shook his head. "No worries there. I don't *get* attached to women."

"Hmm," Christy said.

"Hmm what?" he asked.

"I don't know," she said with a light shrug of her shoulders. "I guess I just thought you seemed . . . really into her. Not in an obvious way. Just in a way I was seeing in your eyes."

He made sure their gazes connected as he said, "You weren't seeing anything in my eyes. Look," he said, pointing at them. "Nothing new there— just the same old stuff. Problem with you people in couples is that you want *everyone* to be a couple. You want everyone to be in love the same way you are."

A soft smile unfurled. "Is that so wrong?"

Now *he* shrugged. "Guess not. But that doesn't make it true."

"Whatever you say," she concluded with a playful and very disbelieving tilt of her head.

And then she sauntered away, back to her towel, before he could defend himself further.

* * *

CAMILLE liked Reece's friends. She liked them so much that it caught her off guard. She wasn't used to other women being so friendly to her, so welcoming.

But then it hit her why. The majority of her relationships were professional. And she was a higher-up who wore a hard shell most of the time. Which boiled down to a pretty sad notion: *You don't have many friends.*

She'd chosen to make Vanderhook her home, her family. She'd felt secure there, always, and appreciated—much more than she'd been in the home where she grew up. So while she kept in touch with a few girlfriends from college in a loose way, mostly she didn't have friends like Christy and Rachel, girls to laugh with and just hang out with. The closest she came to that most of the time was her relationship with Phil's wife, Karen, and a couple of women in the accounting department who she sometimes had drinks with.

You haven't made that a high priority. Because work was her priority. Success was her priority. So she just wasn't that used to feeling . . . liked. At least not outside of who she was professionally. But Christy and Rachel made her feel part of their circle without even trying. As if they liked her just for her personality.

How long has it been since anyone really liked me just for who I am?

She wasn't sure. But as she sat on the beach towel she'd borrowed from Reece, in between the two women, she decided that was just too maudlin of a thought to even examine. So she pushed it aside and tried to focus on the unlikely fun afternoon she'd found herself in the middle of. *So this is what people do. For fun and recreation. This is what the rest of the world comes to the seaside for.*

She'd definitely once known this, experienced it, back in college, but maybe she'd forgotten. Forgotten how to have fun. How sad was that? But again, she shook it off and tried to just be grateful she was remembering.

When the boat ceased its forward motion through the vast expanse of the gulf, she watched as Reece—with Jack's help—lowered a sizable iron anchor into the water. The town of Coral Cove on the shore in the distance appeared tiny now, the resorts up the way the only buildings she could recognize, because they were taller than the rest.

"Here we are," Christy announced. "Is everybody ready to snorkel?"

After a general chorus of yeses, Rachel asked Reece, "So how did you choose where to bring us?" And Camille liked being reminded that Rachel, although married to Mike, wasn't a resident of Coral Cove, either, or a longtime visitor like Mike was. It made her feel less "new."

"We're beside the bed of coral that gives the town its name," he said. "Great snorkeling, and the water should still be clear enough—I don't think this morning's rain was enough to cloud things up."

Camille felt a little at loose ends as she realized most of the others were helping themselves to snorkeling equipment from bins beneath padded benches—even Mike and Rachel weren't shy about looking through Reece's supplies and picking out what they wanted. And Camille would have joined them—if she'd had any clue about snorkeling.

So it was a relief when Reece appeared at her side to say, "Don't be shy, Tinkerbell. Pick out a mask and some fins."

She tried to sound less intimidated than she felt when she asked, "Are they all the same? And if not, how do I know which ones are best for me?"

He cast her a long, sideways look, the hint of a teasing grin on his face. "Been a while since you went snorkeling?"

She returned the sideways glance and made sure not to sound sheepish when she said, "You could say that. As in never."

Reece tilted his head, smile still in place, but being less arrogant than before. "Really, Tink? A worldly woman like you has never gone snorkeling?"

"There are lots of ways to be worldly," she replied smartly.

And he said, "Well, you'll add one more to your list today." Then he took her hand and said, "Come on—I'll help you with the equipment, and then I'll give you a lesson once we're in the water."

She tried not to feel the tingly awareness of having her hand in his. She tried to ignore the quickened beat of her heart. But it was there, and she couldn't deny that her heartbeat seemed to echo into other places, too, most notably her bikini bottoms. Why, oh why, did the owner of the Happy Crab have to be so sexy?

Soon enough, though, everything felt a lot *less*

sexy as Reece outfitted her with a massive pair of flippers, which he called by the nicer name, fins, along with a thin, inflatable lifevest and a clear mask attached to a snorkel tube. In fact, she felt like some sort of bizarre sea creature as she waddled toward the catamaran's built-in staircase that descended into the water.

Due to it taking a while for Reece to get everything on her, everyone else had already gone in, and now Reece waited for her in the sea, at the foot of the stairs, his mask pushed up on top of his head, now wet tendrils of dark hair curling around his face.

It wasn't easy navigating the way down in the huge flippers—it was the equivalent of maneuvering a narrow set of steps in clown shoes—but Reece told her to take her time, and said encouraging words like, "There you go—slow and easy," and she at once loved and hated how patient and helpful he was being. In the moment, she was grateful, but certain aspects of this attraction would be so much easier if there wasn't such a decent guy hiding underneath the smart-ass parts of him.

She finally went bounding into the water with a bigger splash than intended and with it came a little cry of alarm. She hadn't thought through this. She'd imagined it would feel more natural—easier. But in fact, she wasn't comfortable suddenly bouncing around in the ocean waves that lapped around her, carrying her to and fro and making her feel she had no control over it all.

Reece clearly saw the bit of panic in her eyes—he swam toward her and let his arms close around her from behind. "You're okay—I've got you," he said soothingly.

Two thoughts raced in to blend with her general discomfort: Did he do this with every slightly panicked snorkeling passenger? And oh Lord, it felt nice to have him wrapped around her, even bobbing up and down amid the waves, even in snorkeling gear, even panicked.

Of course, the panic was dying away—being in his arms made her feel instantly safe. "I—I . . ." She suffered the urge to somehow explain. "I guess I'm just . . . not very confident in the water." Though it made her feel like an idiot that everyone else seemed *perfectly* confident in the water. Mike and Rachel already swam about in the distance, faces immersed, looking at fish. And Jack and Christy were talking, hugging, laughing, off to the right, as at ease as if they were still on the boat.

"There's nothing to be afraid of, Tink, promise," Reece said near her ear. "Your lifevest will keep you afloat, and your fins will take you where you wanna go."

She'd noticed Reece didn't even *wear* a lifevest—showing exactly how confident *he* was in the ocean waters. It made her feel weak and a little envious, even if he was being nice about it. She so hated being in a position of weakness—and it seemed to keep happening over and over since her arrival in Coral Cove.

"I'm sorry," she said. "I need this thing off my face right now." And she pushed the snorkeling mask up onto her forehead, same as Reece's, to free up her nose for easier breathing at the moment.

"It's pretty choppy right here behind the boat," he told her, arms still around her waist beneath the surface. "You'll feel better out in more open water. Lean back against me and flip your fins."

She did what he said and—with the help of *his* fins too, she assumed—the movement propelled them backward through the deep water and off to one side of the boat, which now blocked them from being able to see the others. And indeed the waves were much calmer here and she began to relax more.

"Better?" he asked, his voice warm on her neck.

Reece hadn't let go of her yet. And she was glad. For more reasons than one.

She said, "Yes," but it came out low, tentative. She was still getting used to this. Being out in the open gulf. And being wrapped up in Reece Donovan's capable arms.

Then she got brave enough to ask him what she'd wondered a minute ago. "Do you do this with *all* your panicky guests?"

"This?" he asked. Calmer waters continued to lap around them.

"Wrap around them like this," she explained, her voice going lower again.

"No," he said, his breath drifting across her skin.

"Why me?" she asked.

He hesitated only slightly before saying, "Just followed an instinct, I guess. Do you mind it?" The question felt supercharged with heat.

"No," she whispered.

"Good," he said.

And that was when his hold on her tightened just a bit, and she grew even more fully aware of being enveloped by him in such a warm, sexy way that it nearly stole her breath.

But not quite. Because what *really* stole it was when he leaned in to lower the gentlest of kisses to her neck. A soft gasp escaped her and she went a little light-headed. But then the pleasure spread all through her. From just that tiny little touch of his mouth on her skin.

Now she turned her head to look at him. His face was so close, his eyes penetrating. Seeing the snorkeling mask still propped on his head and the wet locks that curled around his ears reminded her more fully where they were. And that she had a big snorkel mask on *her* head, too. This wasn't how she'd expected this to happen. But when he leaned in again, this time bringing his mouth to hers, she didn't fight it.

It had been a long time since she'd been kissed and it moved through her like molten lava, filling every crack and crevice of her being. He was a good kisser. She tried not to wonder if she measured up and instead let herself sink into the moment, following instincts of her own, even if it had been a while since they'd been activated. It wasn't a wild, passionate kiss, but a slow, thoughtful one—somehow tender but intense at the same time.

When it ended, she let out a breath, met his gaze briefly, but then glanced away. Like the kiss itself, his eyes on her were so intense that, at such close proximity, she couldn't quite keep looking. Because it was one more thing that made her feel a little weak inside.

Even still, though, she settled her arms over his where they wrapped around her beneath the life-jacket. To make it clear that she liked it. And to maybe regain a little of her composure in some small way, exhibit some control. *She* wanted this, too, and she wanted him to know it.

So it blew her mind a little when he said, "Um, we probably shouldn't do this."

Her stomach dropped and she was glad he couldn't see her face. "Why?"

"Cami . . ." he began on a sigh, "you *know* why."

"Because of my job, why I'm here."

He confirmed it with a "Yeah."

And she let out a breath, disappointment roiling thick inside her. "I can't help my job."

"I know. But it's kind of a problem between us, don't you think?"

"Yes, but . . ."

"But what?"

Her heart still beat too fast—it was too strange to be having this whole conversation with his arms still wrapped around her from behind in the water, his body still pressed warm against hers as they floated. "Well, you seem to be very no-strings-attached and all that," she pointed out. "So if there are never any strings attached, what does it matter? Couldn't this just be something we view as . . . separate from my job?"

"It would be tough," he said.

Which maybe should have put her off. If he

was fighting it so much, why should she even want it?

And yet . . . they'd come this far, carried the flirtation forward to reach this kiss—and all that seemed like a total waste if they weren't going to explore this further. "But . . . what if it's worth it?" she asked.

And it was a bold thing to say—but something made her put it out there. Maybe she wanted to be her normal, more outgoing self with him again. Or maybe she just didn't want a chance at passion like this to pass her by.

And that was when it hit her. It was the second part. Because *Camille* would have let it pass her by. *Camille* always did the sensible thing—she took care of business, she protected herself, she looked out for number one, she got the job done, she kept up walls, and hard shells, and armor.

But *Cami* . . . *Cami* wanted this. *Cami* wanted to let down her guard, just a little. Because she'd never felt this way before—she'd never felt so drawn to a man, and as he held her in his arms, their bodies rolling with the waves, she realized she was actually *terrified* of letting this pass her by.

Because what if it never came again? This kind of chemistry. This kind of want. This kind of connection. She'd truly never experienced anything quite like this *before*, so what if she never encountered that wild desire again in her entire life? She didn't want to regret not feeling this to the fullest, not having this.

She hadn't said any of that, but she knew he felt it. All of it. Through osmosis or something.

"Damn, Cami—you're tempting me," he murmured deep in her ear. Once more, she felt the words in her bikini bottoms. And it was like . . . being revived, brought back to life—in a really hot way.

"Good," she whispered. She gave him one more sideways glance, quick—because, even now, that was all she could manage.

"I . . . didn't know you felt this way," he told her.

And she could understand that. She'd been so busy doing her job, even while softening to him, that she supposed she hadn't let her desire show—or at least not very much. But she couldn't deny now that he'd drawn from her a whole new part of herself, or . . . a part of herself she'd just never really gotten to know. A gentler self. A . . . sexier self. Cami. She didn't mind the name anymore. "I've been fighting it, too," she explained. "But I'm *tired* of fighting. Aren't you?"

Ribbons of heat raced across her skin everywhere their bodies connected, even beneath the water, as she awaited his answer.

"I just don't know if it's a good idea," he finally said again. "In fact, I'm pretty sure it's *not*."

And Cami's heart fell.

This had come upon them so fast, yet now she really wanted it, wanted *him*.

And on top of that, getting rejected sucked.

"But hell," he said, "maybe what it comes down to is . . . you're just too damn hard to resist."

And before she could even fully absorb the sudden surrender, he slid one hand from around her waist down onto her thigh, then let it dip smoothly between her legs.

"Do you mean we shall both be drowned?"

J. M. Barrie, *Peter and Wendy*

Chapter 11

CAMI GASPED, stunned—by more than one thing. That he'd changed his mind so fast. That the move he'd made was so bold. And that—oh . . . it felt so amazingly good. One second he'd been telling her what a bad idea this was, and the next, he was stroking the flesh between her thighs through her bathing suit.

Without quite planning it, she let her legs part, leaned further back into him in the water. It wasn't a decision so much as a natural instinct. It felt as if she'd been waiting for this much longer than she actually had. Or . . . maybe she'd *actually* been waiting for this her entire life. Because it was so much more intoxicating than anything that had come before.

She'd had good sex in previous relationships. But she wasn't sure one solitary touch had ever echoed through her this profoundly, numbing her mind even as it intensified her body's responses.

But—wait. Despite how eager she'd grown to move forward with him, there were certain practical concerns. "Um, um . . . your friends."

Reece's warm voice came low in her ear. "They can't see us. Can't hear us." True enough—the catamaran had drifted, separating them from the others. "Close your eyes. Close your eyes. I want to make you feel good."

Oh boy. All things considered, it was hard to keep arguing. He made excellent points. And he wanted to make her feel good. A few days ago she couldn't have *dreamed* Reece Donovan would ever want to make her feel good. And that made this sort of like a miracle. And you couldn't just pull the plug on a miracle, right? Especially a miracle this . . . consuming.

He began to kiss her neck as he touched her beneath the water. Mmm—she'd forgotten how nice neck kisses were, how they could tingle all through you. The sensations seemed to vibrate inside her in sparkly little waves, amplifying what she felt in her bikini bottoms.

She moved against his hand now—again, not a decision but a primal instinct. The truth was, she couldn't have stopped if she'd tried. Her fears of just a few moments ago were being sweetly assuaged—this chemistry with Reece wasn't passing her by; it was unfolding, they were living it, breathing it, experiencing it. And even if it never came again, in her whole life, she would *have* this, this hot, electrically charged connection with him.

Every time she remembered the oddness of where they were—the swim mask on her head, the lifevest she wore, the fact that they floated in the ocean—it seemed almost surreal. And again, not the way she'd pictured it. But when she closed her eyes and forgot all that, it was just so, so hot. Hot to let herself go in his arms. Hot that he wanted her to. Hot that he was touching her where she most longed for it, needed it.

And then soon—mmm—the unmistakable hardness of his arousal pressing against her ass. Oh, yum. She wanted all of him. She wanted to be touched by him, kissed by him—but she wanted *that* part, too.

She tried to keep from emitting moans of delight lest it be heard on the opposite side of the catamaran that now seemed to tower above them nearby in the water—and instead her mounting pleasure came out in a series of breathy sighs.

Until . . . until . . . the sighs grew a little shakier, more heated, and she knew she was reaching a certain, blessed point of no return she couldn't have foreseen even a few minutes earlier. Eyes shut, she bit her lip, forgot the people on the other side of the boat, felt nothing but the sun on her face, the warm water caressing her skin, and the sexy man embracing her, stroking her, and . . . . oh God, yes . . . making her come.

The staggering orgasm moved through her more forcefully than any climax of her life—jolting her body in his arms, again, again. She clamped her mouth shut to keep from screaming out, but feared a few small whines escaped her. She gripped the arm around her waist with both hands to give her some sense of purchase in the water.

When it finally ended, she let her head drop back against his shoulder. It still felt so wonderfully right to be in his arms, to just rest there now. Warm. Somehow safe.

But maybe that's how you always feel when you're intimate with a guy. Maybe you've just forgotten.

And then another thought hit her and she voiced it aloud, although her breath came soft, tired. "You must be a really good swimmer."

"What?" he asked, clearly taken aback.

"You must be a great swimmer. To be able to . . . you know . . . just float around doing something like that."

"Salt water's buoyant," he pointed out, "and your lifejacket helps, too. But yeah, I'm a good swimmer." Though he sounded distracted, like his thoughts were really elsewhere. Which she supposed made sense and was actually a good thing.

Until a few seconds later when he said, "I'm sorry—I shouldn't have done that."

"Huh?" Tensing inside, she automatically lifted her head from his shoulder, turned it to look at him.

"I mean, like I said, probably not a good idea."

She lowered her chin, narrowed her gaze. "You're still stuck on that?"

"You're not?"

"No," she said emphatically. "And if I can let it go, why can't you?"

He let his eyes widen slightly to reply, "Uh, maybe I have more at stake."

And rather than weigh it, Cami said the first thing that popped into her head. "Maybe so, maybe not. Maybe *my job* is at stake. Maybe I'm willing to just forget all that for right now because . . . because I want you." Wow, okay, that was really putting it out there. Yet given what they'd just done together, she supposed she'd *already* sort of put it out there—just in a different way. Which was why she was getting a little offended by his attitude. "But if you don't feel the same—fine." And with that, she physically detached herself from him in the water.

Which made her feel like she was going to sink, despite the lifevest, and she began to flail around a little.

Reece just sighed and said, "Come here," and hauled her back against him, this time face to face. Her arms circled his neck and his hands cupped her bottom—in order to support her, she was pretty sure, but it still seemed oh so personal.

And even more so when he pulled her close enough that she felt his erection again—this time pressing against her in front. She bit her lip, weakened by the fresh bolt of desire racing through her, and their eyes met.

"Oh, I *want* you," he said, his voice coming out a little raspier than she'd ever heard it. "Believe me, I want you like crazy. I want to make you pant and moan and scream. And I'm pretty sure from the look on your face that you can *feel* how much I want you."

"Uh huh," she murmured, definitely feeling it. Feeling it very much.

"But . . ." he said quietly.

Oh hell. *But* again? "But . . . ?"

He shut his eyes, reopened them, and sighed. "I'm just not sure, Tink. I . . . don't want to get caught up in the heat of the moment."

She narrowed her gaze on him accusingly. "I think you just did."

"You're right," he told her, "but I mean . . . more than that. I don't want to take things further and then regret it. I . . . need some time to think."

Part of Cami was pissed off. That he'd take things as far as they'd gone and then call it to a screeching halt. She wanted to say, *Hey, maybe you should have thought of that before you got intimate with me just now.*

But she supposed women the world over felt justified taking things to a certain point and then calling it quits. And that was okay. The rule was— it was okay because it had to be.

And she supposed one reason she felt miffed— besides a little embarrassment—was that what they'd done had gotten her . . . emotionally invested. In thinking this was *on* now, happening, that they were on the same page. "You know, if I were down on one knee with a diamond ring in my hand, I might understand you needing time to think," she told him frankly. "But since I'm not, maybe you're over worrying this."

It surprised the hell out of her when he leaned his head back and laughed out loud. Then said, "My God, woman, you crack me up and I'm kinda crazy about you."

Oh. Well. Maybe that changed things. It definitely made her happier. Not to mention restoring her confidence. "You *should* be," she told him with a cool smile. "I'm actually pretty great. Once you get to know me."

He gave her a grin in reply. "I'm glad I've gotten to know you. Because you're right—you are."

Which left her a little more reassured. And she'd just decided she was going to kiss him when— "Hey, what's up over here? No canoodling when we're supposed to be looking at fish." They both glanced over to see Mike Romo flashing a teasing smile. The wind had shifted and the boat had drifted from between them and the other two couples. "Rachel and I keep seeing a big bright blue and yellow fish and she's wondering what it is."

"Few different things it could be—maybe a queen angelfish," Reece called easily. Then he looked to the woman in his embrace and said, "Come on, let's go snorkel."

And even though she appeared a little uncertain as she said, "Um, okay," Reece had made the split-second decision that it was the right thing to do. Even if she might be thinking he'd ended their conversation prematurely.

"Here, let's get your mask back into place," he said, helping her make sure it formed a tight seal around the edges to keep water from leaking in, and then he pulled his own mask back on, too. "Tell you what, Tink—why don't you just hold on to the bottom of my trunks and kick your fins a little, but I'll do most of the swimming and can point things out to you in the coral."

And within another moment or two, they were heading toward the small reef, rejoining the rest of the group. Once they reached the coral, he explained to Cami not to let her feet or legs touch it, both for *its* safety and for hers. Then he helped her practice breathing through her snorkel tube until she got the hang of it—after which they went fish-watching.

And that seemed a whole lot easier to Reece than dealing with whether or not he should get more physically involved with her. Of course, even now, as he swam with her at his side, his groin ached and he stayed uncomfortably hard.

She was way different than she'd seemed in the beginning. There was another whole side of her hidden beneath that red suit and those high heels he'd first seen her in. And turned out he kept *liking* this other side more and more. Maybe too much.

Too much because the first side still existed. And the first side still wanted to buy his motel. And just now she'd told him that if he didn't sell, it could put her job at risk? That was big—*huge*. He wasn't even sure she realized what a big thing that was to put out there between them, to make him feel he held in his hands. But the one thing it made clear was exactly how important it was to her to get what she'd come here for. A thought that was far from comforting at the moment.

And how did a woman possess two such very different sides? Was it even possible for her to be the tough, take-charge woman he'd first met *and* the sweeter, friendlier—even if still determined—woman who was afraid of his iguana and could look so innocent at moments that it made him want to kiss it right out of her? Or . . . did it mean one side wasn't real? And if so, which side?

Big questions. Big fucking questions. That was for sure.

So just snorkel. Just focus on the moment, on the coral formations below you right now. Focus on being here with the nicer Cami, and with your friends, and the things you love. Reece truly loved this place—he loved showing people not only the charm of the town but also the whole other world that existed under the water here. So just concentrating on stuff he enjoyed seemed like a good solution at the moment. It had carried him through harder things—harder times—than this, so doing it now should be easy.

Spotting a small cherubfish peeking from a clump of gray coral, he pointed it out to Cami, its vibrant blue fins whipping away through the formations a moment later. And he was pleased when a small school of glasseye snappers went swimming smoothly past, glistening orange and looking nearly electric.

When Cami pointed enthusiastically toward a queen triggerfish, the pale blue of its lower side nearly seeming to glow, it gratified Reece that she'd gotten over her initial discomfort in the water to enjoy this. Of course, she'd gotten over her initial discomfort enough to enjoy some other things, too, so maybe he shouldn't be surprised.

They'd swum into a part of the coral where the water was deeper and the ocean floor much farther below them than before, and Reece spotted a small, harmless nurse shark probably four or five fathoms down, a distance of twenty-five or thirty feet. It was too far away to make out any detail, but he knew it by shape and the regularity of seeing them in the area. As with all the other sea life they'd spotted, he stretched out his arm, pointing it out for her to see.

After which she yanked on his wrist and thrust her head up out of the water. When he followed suit, she blurted, "What the hell is that?" her eyes enormously wide through the wet lens of the mask.

"Just a little nurse shark," he began—but he didn't get to say any more because she bounded toward him, tackling him in the water and nearly drowning him before he could tell her, "Relax, Tink, relax. It's okay, not a big deal—I promise. Calm down."

Her arms were around his shoulders again—clutching him desperately now—and his circled her waist as he looked into her eyes to whisper, "Cami, you know the worst thing you can do when a shark is around?"

"What?" Her voice was quiet, too, but still panicky.

"Thrash around and draw attention to yourself."

Finally she went completely still in his loose embrace. Good. Sheesh, for a tough woman she could be antsy.

"Just so you know that as a general rule of thumb," he told her. "That little nurse shark won't hurt us, promise—but in general, if you see a shark, just act normal and swim away without panicking. Got it?"

She gave a nod, seeming calmer now, at least a little. "Got it."

And as they resumed snorkeling—heading back into the more shallow area around the reef since that suddenly seemed the safer choice with a new snorkeler—he decided he'd just given her some good advice. *Don't panic.* And that he would heed that same advice himself here, with her.

If there was one thing Reece knew, it was that whatever happened, life went on and things mellowed out. He didn't always know the reasons things happened the way they did, but most things—not all maybe, but most—worked themselves out if you didn't panic about it.

So just think this thing with her through. Could it be like she said? Could they fool around, have fun together—in bed and elsewhere—and keep it a separate thing from her job? Maybe. After all, he was holding her right now, *wanting* her right now, and that mutual attraction moving between them had nothing to do with the reason she'd come here.

And what about the no-strings-attached part? He'd always done it that way—at least since his mid-twenties, about ten years ago, when some big things had changed in his life—so surely he could do it now, too. Surely.

So just think it over. Just see where it leads you.

It was like he'd just told her. There's no reason to panic—no reason at all.

SNORKELING had been a new and interesting experience for Cami—but all in all, she was kind of relieved to return to the boat.

Of course, a lot had changed since she'd *left*

the boat—she'd swum in the vast, open ocean waters, she'd seen a shark in the wild, and she'd been stroked to orgasm by Reece Donovan when she'd least expected it. She'd had no idea snorkeling would be so . . . world-changing.

And she still didn't know where they stood, which irked her. Especially the part of her that liked to have control over things. But she was trying to be calm and cool about that. If nothing else, her entire association with Reece was teaching her the art of patience—whether she liked it or not.

Back on the catamaran, they all ditched their snorkel gear in the big netted area in the bow so that it would dry in the warm air, then they broke out coolers of drinks along with sandwiches Christy had offered to make, and bags of chips, as well as apples, bananas, and grapes Rachel and Mike had picked up for the excursion.

They made a leisurely meal of it, talking as a group about the things they'd seen snorkeling, but then the guys split off when a conversation about the boat started up, technical stuff that didn't interest any of the girls but entailed Reece showing some things to Jack and Mike.

Cami found she liked the easy rhythm of it all— the other two couples were clearly in love, clearly in comfortable, settled relationships she couldn't help envying a little. But at the same time, all were clearly cool with spending a little time apart as well.

"You and Reece seem close," Cami observed to Christy. She'd seen the two having a private conversation earlier, and even through the course of their light dinner, she'd observed exchanges between them that implied they knew each other well and shared some inside jokes.

"I guess we are," Christy replied. "I guess because he and I have kind of a big thing in common."

"Oh, what's that?" Cami asked.

"My parents died in an accident a few years ago, when I was in my early twenties—just like Reece's did."

. . . something as dark as night had come.

J. M. Barrie, *Peter and Wendy*

Chapter 12

CAMI BLINKED. And her stomach dropped. "Reece's parents died? Suddenly?"

And Christy's jaw dropped as her eyes opened wide. "Oh God, you didn't know. I'm such a bigmouth. I can't believe I said that." Now the younger woman was crushing her eyes shut and clenching her teeth over what she'd blurted out.

"It's okay," Cami said, still trying to absorb the news. And she wasn't sure if it was *really* okay or not—nothing about it sounded okay to her—but she followed the urge to try to put Christy at ease.

Now Christy was shaking her head, and still making the face of someone who felt she'd screwed up. "I didn't realize you didn't know or I wouldn't have mentioned it. He's kind of private, so now I feel bad."

"I won't tell him I know," Cami promised. Because it was the only decent thing to do.

"I guess I just thought you guys seemed so . . .

in sync or something." Christy was back to shaking her head. "So I somehow just assumed he'd told you."

Still sitting next to Christy on the same towel, Cami bit her lower lip thoughtfully. "In some ways we're in sync. In other ways not."

And Christy nodded knowingly. "I suppose you can only get so in sync with someone whose business you're trying to buy when they don't want to sell."

Cami pursed her lips, taking that in, along with everything else she was still trying to process. "He told you about that, huh?"

"Today, when we were chatting earlier."

"Do you have any idea why he won't? Sell?" She realized as the question left her that she was asking as much from a personal perspective as a professional one. The more she got to know him, the more she truly wanted to understand him.

"Yes," Christy replied. "But . . . I've already said too much."

Cami nodded. "That's okay, I get it. And I don't mean to pry. I care in a way that's . . . about more than business."

"If he wants to tell you, he will," she said. "And I hope he does. It . . . it would make you understand. It would make you not want to press him on it anymore."

One more thing to wrap her head around: Was that possible? That whatever his reason, it would truly make her ready to throw in the towel for the first time ever and go trotting back to Phil telling him Windchime needed to let this one go? It was difficult to fathom. What reason could be that powerful?

And then it hit her that she'd been so shocked to hear about Reece's parents that she'd completely ignored Christy's own loss. "I'm sorry—about your mom and dad," she said.

But Christy offered up a small, tight smile. The smile of someone who'd struggled a lot to be able to do that and was maybe *still* struggling. But it also struck Cami as strong. "Thank you. As time passes, it gets better. And having Jack helps a lot. He's my family now. We're getting married in the fall!" she added, now breaking out into a *real* smile that lifted Cami's heart. Her joy felt a little contagious.

"Really? How wonderful!"

"It'll be a small wedding, on the beach. But I'd love for you to come."

The kind invitation caught Cami off guard—and warmed her soul. She barely knew this girl, and yet Christy acted like they were old friends. She'd never experienced anything like that before.

Of course, the particular bit of her life she'd lived the past few days here in Coral Cove was . . . fleeting at best, and at worst seemed almost . . . not even real, imaginary. "I wish I could," she explained, "but I live in Atlanta and I'm only here temporarily." *I'll be long gone by then. Back in my real life.*

Which suddenly felt a little cold and empty to her, for the first time ever. It was a *good* life, after all. Wasn't it? Good job, good income, townhouse in Buckhead. Of course it was good—great, in fact. Far better than she'd once even been able to dream.

"I'm sorry to hear that," Christy replied, sounding sincere. And it made Cami feel . . . valued. Just for her company. Not for her job skills or her wardrobe or her address or anything else—just as a person. *Do I not* usually *feel valued that way?* Yikes, what a scary thought.

"A beach wedding sounds lovely. And I'm sure you two will be very happy."

Christy nodded, smiled. "I'm sure of that, too. I'm very lucky that way."

And Cami did think Christy was lucky. Did she even envy her a little? For having a dependable love, dependable friends, for seeming so happy and content? She wasn't used to that feeling—she wasn't used to *yearning*, at all, for anything she didn't have. She'd thought she had everything she wanted; she'd thought she'd figured that out a long time ago and had gone out and made it happen.

But as the catamaran named *The Happy Crab* started back toward the shore, she had no choice but to acknowledge that maybe there was a little more to a happy life than she'd chosen to recognize up to now.

SHE stayed aware of Reece the whole ride back, even though they didn't talk. Music played on the boat, and the sun set on the horizon in dazzling slashes of orange and pink. Sipping on a glass of pinot grigio from a bottle someone opened, she exchanged casual conversation with others in the group.

After a little discussion about Mike and Rachel's baby, Rachel announced that she considered herself a horrible mother. "Oh my God, this is so embarrassing, but last week I found her on the kitchen floor trying to eat cat food! Which is bad enough on its own, but she's lucky Shakespeare— that's our cat—didn't take a swipe at her for that." Rachel pressed her hand to her chest, clearly reliving the horror of it.

Yet Cami instantly said, "Things happen. But that doesn't mean you're a bad mom. You seem like a *great* mom!"

And Rachel seemed sincerely touched by the sentiment.

"I don't care if she eats a little cat food," Mike chimed in to say. "Just as long as she never grows up and never wants to go on a date. Ever."

Rachel just shook her head and informed them all, "Someone has some overprotective tendencies that he's going to have to get under control pretty soon."

"I've heard about that from Anna," Christy said. Cami had gathered that Anna was Mike's sister and a friend of Christy's from Destiny, the small town in Ohio where Mike and Rachel still lived and Christy had been raised. "And if I know Anna, she won't let Mike be *too* controlling of his little girl."

"I'm counting on that," Rachel said. "Hopefully between the both of us we can teach him not to be so overbearing. Or we can at least hold him down long enough to muzzle him when boys start coming around."

"Boys," Mike groused, rolling his eyes. "I *know* boys. I *was* boys. Boys are no good."

Reece had told Cami that Christy made jewelry for a living, so she inquired about that, learning that Christy consigned her work—repurposed vintage costume jewelry—at various boutiques and resorts and was making a healthy living at it. Jack, she found out, was also a successful entrepreneur, providing online investment advisory services. She told Christy she'd love to see some of her jewelry and they agreed to get together tomorrow at Christy and Jack's cottage on Sea Shell Lane.

Through it all, though, she stayed aware of the man steering the boat, aware of the magnetic pull still connecting them even in this moment. She thought about the fact that his parents had died in some tragic way. She thought about how he'd touched her in the water earlier, and how connected she'd felt to him, how connected she'd continued to feel as they'd snorkeled together, as he'd helped her and guided her. And she thought about how, despite all that, she truly had no idea where they stood now.

As he skillfully maneuvered the large catamaran into its slip behind the motel just as dusk began to fall, the girls putting on their bathing suit cover-ups and everyone gathering their belongings as they thanked Reece for a great time, Cami had no idea what came next between them. When the group began exiting the boat a few minutes later, she grabbed up her beach bag and followed the rest down the little extendable plank to the wooden dock, aware Reece was behind her.

After they all crossed the dock and passed the pool, then entered the breezeway that led to the front of the Crab, goodbyes were said and Cami started toward her room. And, walking past the office a few seconds later, she became aware that Reece was accompanying her.

In one way she liked that, of course, but in another, it left her disgruntled. She'd never liked guys who sent mixed messages, and things were feeling pretty mixed with him right now. As close as she'd felt to him in the water earlier, she couldn't forget that he'd left things very abruptly up in the air. So she said casually, over her shoulder, "You don't have to walk me to my room."

"I know I don't *have* to," he told her. "But maybe I *want* to."

Hmm. "I'm a big girl," she said anyway.

"And I'm a gentleman."

"Debatable," she retorted, glancing over at him.

His scrunched lips told her he was weighing her response. "Fair," he agreed then, "but here we are." And indeed, they'd just reached Room 11.

She shrugged, then dug to find the crab keychain in her bag. Holding it up, she let her eyes go sarcastically wide as if to say, *Got it, so guess we're done here.* "Well, goodnight," she told him.

She turned her attention to the door lock, but in

her peripheral vision thought he appeared a little confused. "You seem . . . pissed."

"Pissed would be a strong word. More like . . . just ending the evening." Then she gave him a sizing up look, trying to read him—what was he expecting here? "You weren't . . . planning on a goodnight kiss or anything, were you?"

He tilted his head, narrowed his gaze. "It had crossed my mind."

"Are you still thinking? About us? About whether it's worth it?"

"Yep."

"I'm not interested in kissing while you're thinking," she said. "And about that thinking, I wouldn't take too long on that if I were you."

He raised his eyebrows. "Why? Checking out soon?" He'd asked with the same hopeful tone he'd have used a couple of days ago, but she was at least *pretty* sure he was kidding about that part now.

"No," she said. "But I may withdraw the option."

He smiled teasingly. "Is that a threat, Tinker-bell?"

She met his gaze, returned the small, confident smile, and gave the obvious answer. "No—a promise."

He emitted a light chuckle at their banter and she went on. "If you don't think I'm worth whatever risk you feel is involved, then *I* don't think *you're* worth getting any closer to. That simple."

He raised his eyebrows. "Is there a deadline?"

"Yes."

"When is it?"

"Soon," she said.

He balked. "Soon? That's all I get?"

"Yes." She shoved her key in the lock and turned it. "Goodnight, Reecie Cup." Then she opened the door, went inside, and shut it behind her.

ONCE inside, she leaned her back against the door and let out an emotional breath. She didn't really like issuing an ultimatum, because she still really, really wanted him. But on the other hand, a girl had to have standards and had to know what she was worth.

Yes, this was a powerful chemistry that the soft, girly part of her wanted so, so badly to bring to fruition. But the other her, the tougher her she'd always known, demanded a guy's respect. And didn't want to be yanked around.

So she didn't regret the ultimatum—but for some reason it had stolen her breath, much more than, say, a high-power negotiation on which millions of dollars rode.

Maybe you're just a little more confident about your career than your personal life.

But Reece doesn't have to know what.

She flipped on a light—then gasped at the sight of a yellow cat standing silently at her feet.

"Oh my gosh—I forgot about you!"

"Meow," he replied.

Then she added, "Sorry—it's nothing personal. Just a lot on my mind." And she supposed now that she probably should have left a light on for the cat, but how would a non-cat person know such a thing, so she tried not to feel bad about it.

"Anyway, time to take you home. Well—home to the restaurant." She tried not to *feel* the cat's homelessness. He was a cat, after all—he wasn't Riley.

Bending to scoop him up in her arms, she opened the door and glanced out, looking in both directions to make sure Reece was gone from the dimly lit sidewalk that lined the rooms. No sign of him, so she took a few steps out—only to see that the Hungry Fisherman was dark, closed up for the night. "Damn," she whispered.

Then she peered down at the cat who seemed so content in her grasp. She supposed she could just set him outside the restaurant's back door. There were probably nice fish scraps in the garbage cans there. And it was plenty warm out, and dry, too.

And yet . . . she'd gotten him from Polly, so she decided it wouldn't feel right not to just officially return him to Polly. Not that she liked the idea of keeping the cat overnight. But . . . he really wasn't any trouble.

So as she stepped back into her room, she peered once more down into his eyes—which she suddenly noticed were a wide and vibrant blue—and said quietly, "Guess we're roommates for the night. But don't get too comfortable here."

Of course, maybe she should tell *herself* that, too.

She lowered the cat to the bed, then headed for the shower, her thoughts returning to Reece—and the secret she'd learned from Christy. She'd only been able to examine the news in a scattered way so far, in the midst of everything else going on.

The taking-care-of-business part of her wished she could just ask him about it, find out the facts. But she couldn't let on she knew—she wouldn't betray Christy like that. Still . . . what on earth had happened? And was that what not selling was all about—preserving something that his family had created? If she knew the whole story, *would* it make her abandon this acquisition? It remained hard to imagine *anything* could make her want to do that. As she'd told Reece today in the water, it could very well cost her job.

Not that she thought Phil would fire her over it—but he'd be enormously displeased and she could very well be demoted. It would change everything about how she was regarded at Vanderhook, the only place she'd ever worked outside of a Dairy Queen in her hometown and a drugstore in Lansing during college, and the only connection in her life that felt like home or family to her.

You shouldn't have to be afraid that someone you consider family will demote you.

But then, she supposed she didn't know as much about family as most people did.

Maybe finding out about *Reece's* family wouldn't affect her at all when she thought about it like that. Maybe it would only remind her how disconnected she usually was from people, places, emotions.

After the quick shower, she put on a ribbed tank and cotton drawstring pants, then ran some fresh water in a glass from the bathroom and set it on the floor for Tiger, along with a crumbled up peanut butter cookie on a napkin—the only food she had in the room at the moment. After saying goodnight to the cat, she turned out the lights and climbed into bed.

In one sense, she liked how quiet it was here at night—it wasn't nearly so peaceful at this hour in Buckhead, even in the residential area where she lived. It was part of a city, and that just made it different.

Will it be so quiet in this spot when a twenty-story Windchime Resort is sitting here?

She shook her head against the pillow. What did it matter?

Then she rolled over in bed. *What is wrong with you? Worrying about how quiet someplace you really have no connection to is at night? Examining all these emotions? Worrying about a guy you don't even know that well? Worrying about a cat, for God's sake? Do you even know yourself anymore?*

There's nothing wrong with being tough inside—it's a good thing.

And maybe she should just get back to being that way. Once and for all.

Like her ultimatum to Reece. That had felt more like her old self. Even if underneath it, she'd been secretly wishing he'd just kiss her anyway.

But still, tough is good. Tough is good. Tough is good.

When a warm pressure met her hip, she gasped, then figured out it was the cat. "Wh–what are you doing?" she whispered.

Then she sensed him curling against her, settling into the curve of her waist. And she couldn't deny that something about that, about just knowing the cat wanted to be next to her, was . . . unexpectedly nice.

Tentatively, she reached down, her arm atop the covers, and let her palm gently come to rest on the cat, in his thick fur. Like earlier, he began to purr, and despite herself, she liked feeling that silent but sure connection.

Then it hit her all over again.

Oh God—who am I?

I don't even know anymore.

All are keeping a sharp look-out in front,
but none suspects that the danger may be
creeping up from behind.

J. M. Barrie, *Peter and Wendy*

Chapter 13

THE NEXT morning, she got dressed and made the short walk to the bakery up the way. She bought three glazed donuts, two for her, one for Tiger. She didn't know if cats *liked* glazed donuts, but she supposed she'd soon find out. "If only there were *fish*-flavored donuts," she told her feline friend upon her return, "then I'd know exactly what to get you."

Tearing one of the donuts into small, cat-bite-sized pieces in a small glass bowl designed to look like a seashell from the bedside table, she lowered it to the floor. She'd also bought a small carton of milk, so she poured a little of that over the donut bites for good measure. She didn't know much about cats, but she at least knew they liked milk.

Tiger lapped at the milk like a maniac, then nosed at the donut bits, then resumed lapping the milk, so she nudged his little orangy face aside long enough to pour in a bit more. And as she ate her own breakfast, she kept glancing down to see that eventually the cat experimented with eating the soggy donut bits and that by the time she finished her breakfast, he had too—his bowl was empty and had literally been licked clean.

She smiled down at him. "You *are* a donut eater!" Maybe being a cat person wasn't so hard. Maybe, like many things in life, it was just a little trial and error.

"But . . . I guess it's time for you to go back to Polly."

She felt a little bad about that in a way. *I shouldn't, though. It's not like I have a good place to keep the cat.* He was an illegal boarder at the Happy Crab, after all. And surely he'd find a nice home somewhere, with someone Polly just hadn't asked yet. And he had a much better chance of finding that home back at the Hungry Fisherman where Polly could keep right on asking people.

Scooping Tiger up into her arms, she suffered a tiny jolt of melancholy, but looked down at the cat and said, "You'll be fine."

"Meow," he said. And it sounded like a plea.

"You will," she insisted. "Because you have to be and that's all there is to it. Got it?"

He didn't reply—*but that's okay, because he's a cat and they don't really reply*—and she stuffed her room key in the pocket of her shorts and, with a quick look up and down the sidewalk outside her door, she set out for the restaurant across the blacktop.

It was early, only a couple of cars parked off to one side, and she assumed those belonged to restaurant staff, so she figured it would be safe enough to carry Tiger in the front door.

So it came as a surprise when she strolled in to see Polly standing with a man in khakis and a button-down shirt holding a clipboard.

Polly's eyes nearly leapt out of her head as they met with Cami's. "I'm very sorry," she said rather forcefully, "but we can't have animals inside our restaurant. You'll have to leave your cat outside!"

Cami blinked. Then tried to get hold of herself. "Um, okay."

Then she turned around and walked right back out the door, Tiger still clutched in one arm.

She stood outside, trying to wrap her head around this. Taking the cat from Polly yesterday was beginning to seem like a bigger favor than it had appeared to be at the time. What was she supposed to do with a contraband cat?

As she pondered this, the restaurant's plate glass door swung open behind her, and out came Polly in her waitress uniform and beehive hairdo. "Good gravy, I'm sorry, hon," she said, her tone of voice closer to the one Cami was familiar with. "The health inspector came back again today! That was him standin' there. He found a few discrepancies and gave us a chance to fix 'em after he left, but he's still examinin' other things. Kind of a stickler. So when I saw Tiger, I didn't know what else to do." She shook her head, glanced down at the cat. "Sorry, Tiger." Then she lifted her gaze back to Cami's. "He saw you out here lookin' bewildered and suggested I might want to make sure you were okay."

"I'd be *more* okay," Cami said, attempting a smile that probably didn't come off quite right, "if I knew what to do with this cat."

"I know, I know," Polly said, regret filling her voice. Then she gritted her teeth slightly, and asked with wide, hopeful, bordering-on-begging eyes, "Can you just keep him today, too?"

Cami let out a sigh. She supposed it wasn't that inconvenient, but . . . "What if Reece finds out? I've told him I don't need maid service every morning, but for all I know, the maid will come back today."

"If he finds out, I'll take full responsibility," Polly promised.

So Cami looked down at the cat, informing him, "Looks like we're still roommates."

"Meow," he answered.

"I think he really likes you," Polly said.

AFTER Cami met Christy for lunch at a small deli and ice cream shop near Christy's home, the two proceeded to Christy's cottage on picturesque Sea Shell Lane. Both sides of the small street were lined with modest but well-kept pastel cottages of pale blue, warm peach, butter yellow, and sea green. The lane came to a dead end at the beach, where a weathered wooden staircase nestled amid beach shrubs led down to the sand.

"This is so lovely," Cami said as Christy led her up the walk to the little green cottage she shared with Jack. The homes were small, far less sizable than Cami's Atlanta townhouse, but they oozed with a charm that called to her.

"We love it here," Christy said. "The beach access is wonderful, and the neighbors are friendly." She pointed across the street to a home painted a soft shade of blue with a wide porch facing the ocean and said, "I think you know Fletcher, right? That's where he lives, and Tamra, the artist, is next door to us." She motioned to the right.

Just as Cami was looking, Tamra walked around the side of her home to the well-manicured front yard. Her long, curly hair was pulled back in a low ponytail and she wore gardening gloves and carried a trowel. Then Cami noticed the tray of nursery flowers near the porch and other signs of Tamra being in the midst of a gardening project.

Christy waved to her neighbor, so Cami did, too. But if she wasn't mistaken, Tamra's return wave felt a lot more friendly when her eyes were on Christy than when they shifted briefly to Cami. *But that's okay.* She was sure the other woman was just being protective of Reece. Really, she was lucky so many people in Coral Cove had been so kind to her given how much they loved Reece and that most of them knew why she was here.

And that was when it hit her. Hadn't Juanita, the maid, said the house she cleaned for Reece was on Sea Shell Lane? If she was right, she of course wondered which one it was—not that it mattered, but it was difficult not to be curious. And she was tempted to ask Christy, but thought better of it under all the weird circumstances. She didn't want to make the younger woman feel any worse than she already did over giving away something personal about Reece he hadn't chosen to share.

Once inside the cute green cottage, Christy showed Cami a collection of the jewelry she'd made using old pieces she picked up at thrift stores and flea markets. She melded pieces together to make chunkier necklaces, bracelets, and broaches that nearly took Cami's breath away. "Exquisite," she exclaimed, truly impressed with Christy's skill and talent.

"I've never been creative in tactile ways," Cami said, "so I admire people who are."

"I've always loved working with jewelry," Christy told her. "And Jack does a lot of carpentry and home repair stuff, both for us and for friends, so it's nice that we both have that 'working with our hands' thing in common. It's kind of what brought us together, actually," she concluded. And Cami thought of her and Reece. And that what had brought *them* together sounded way less romantic.

But then, we aren't really together.

And maybe we won't be. Because maybe he'll decide it's not worth it to him. Or maybe I'll let his indecision make the decision for us. Still, no matter how she sliced it, it left her a little sad inside to realize that, in comparison to Christy and Jack, her life definitely lacked romance.

But we all make choices—and you've always been perfectly happy with yours.

Up to now anyway.

In an effort to quit thinking so hard and quit feeling so much, Cami focused on studying Christy's jewelry, piece by piece, and before the afternoon was done, she bought a beautiful bracelet constructed of thick pearls of white and pale pink, with little silver heart-shaped charms mixed in. It was very different than any other jewelry she owned, and like the cottages on Sea Shell Lane, it somehow spoke to her. She thought it looked . . . romantic.

And when they parted, Cami felt surprisingly energized—by the gorgeous day, by Christy's friendly company, by the salty scent of the sea breeze, the call of seagulls in the distance, and the quaint splendor of the pastel cottages.

Of course, when she waved at Tamra while getting in her rental car—and Tamra lifted only the stiffest, smallest wave in return—that brought her down a little. And as she drove back toward the Happy Crab, she felt a bit . . . empty inside.

Maybe it was Reece's indecision. Or maybe it was about envy; she'd never been around people—around *lives*—like the one Christy was leading, and it seemed unexpectedly appealing, even special.

But you have a good life, too—don't forget that. God knows you could have a worse one.

Just keep reminding yourself of that and everything will be okay.

AN hour after she'd finished planting flowers, Tamra sat on Fletcher's porch with him sipping iced tea in the shade.

"Did you know there's a new lifeguard work-

ing the beach at the lifeguard tower across from
Reece's place?" Fletcher asked her.

"No," Tamra answered. "Why?"

"Met him after my show at the Sunset Celebration last night. Seemed like a nice guy—mid-
thirties, I'd guess. Handsome muscular blond
type of dude."

She tossed him a sideways glance from the
white wicker chair next to the one he sat in. "And
you're telling me this for what reason?" she asked
dryly.

He returned the sideways look. "Came up
that he was new here, just moved down from the
Panhandle, and he's single. Seemed interested in
meeting people. That's all."

She rolled her eyes. "When you describe someone to me as handsome and muscular, that's *not*
all."

The ponytailed man beside her just shrugged.

"Remember that girl in the tie-dyed bikini I
pointed out to you a few days ago?" she asked.
Because two could play at that game.

"Mmm hmm." Though his answer sounded
absent—he appeared far more interested in looking out across the now-empty sand toward the
water.

"I saw *her* at the Sunset Celebration and struck
up a conversation. She works at Sunnymeade, the
nursing home where Christy's grandfather lives,
as an art therapist. Seemed nice. And *also* single."

"Still not interested," he said.

And she let out a sigh. "Well, sounds like we
should fix the tie-dyed bikini up with the life-

guard since they'd probably be more interested in each other than either of us are."

He let out a laugh. "Now that's an idea. We could start a Coral Cove matchmaking service."

"Because we're both such shining examples of romantic bliss," she said—and Fletcher laughed again.

Then more quietly said, "Don't worry—I will be. Soon enough."

She studied him long and hard, trying to really see the man behind the ponytail and beard, the man behind the bravado on the tightrope. "I don't understand how you're truly so sure," she said, honestly trying to grasp it.

He squarely met her gaze in response. "If I doubted it," he said, "then I'd worry. And what good does worry ever do? For anybody?"

"Sometimes worry makes you . . . prepare. Or take precautions. Develop a backup plan. What's wrong with having a backup plan?"

"What's wrong with having a backup plan," he said, "is that it makes you . . . prepared to settle. For the thing you don't really want. And then that's what you end up doing. But I don't want that. And I know she's coming back, so I don't need that anyway." He ended with a smile that, as usual, almost made her believe his wife really *would* just suddenly reappear one of these days. "So that's why I'm not interested in the tie-dyed bikini," he went on. "But why aren't you interested in the lifeguard?"

Now it was she who peered out over the sea, weighing her answer. Fletcher was her friend.

Probably her *best* friend. And if you can't tell your best friend the truth, who could you tell?

Even though something about *this* truth felt . . . scary. Because it would change things. It would make her . . . vulnerable. So much more vulnerable than she wanted to be, even with him.

Still, something urged her to quietly say, "Maybe you were right the other day," her eyes still on the ocean. She found a sailboat on the horizon to fasten her gaze on. It made the confession easier. "Maybe I do have feelings—*those* kinds of feelings—for Reece. But I just don't think it would work."

"Why?" Fletcher asked calmly, not sounding the least bit taken aback.

Tamra's stomach churned. "Because I doubt he feels the same way."

"How do you know until you put it out there?" The question sounded so well-reasoned and sensible.

Though she thought *her* answer was full of good sense, too. "I guess I really don't. But once you put it out there, you can't take it back. It's kind of sink or swim. And if it's sink, I lose his friendship. And that's huge to me."

"Look," he said, leaning forward, "I understand your worries. But like I just said, worrying is just borrowing trouble, creating a worst case scenario that doesn't even exist."

She bit her lip, let out a sigh, finally met his gaze. "But I still have to consider the consequences, don't I?"

And Fletcher shrugged. "There are consequences if you *never* tell him, too." And as those words were worming their way into her soul, he took it even further. "If you go after what you want, you might not get it. But if you don't, you guarantee it."

She drew in her breath and promised him she'd think about it.

Then they sipped on their tea in silence for a minute, and she found herself watching him again, tilting her head slightly, and . . . trying to see him through fresh eyes. She tried to see him in a whole different way. Just to . . . try it on for size.

Because the truth was, they had a lot in common. They got along well. They appreciated each other. They enjoyed each other's company.

And, squinting lightly, she said, "You know, there are probably people who would say *you and I* should get together."

In response, Fletcher narrowed his gaze on her and she could feel him doing the same thing as her, trying to weigh the idea she'd just tossed out, trying to see her in a new light.

After a few quiet seconds, the only sound that of the waves rolling up onto the sand in the distance, he leaned slightly toward her, and so she leaned toward him, too . . . until their mouths met in a tentative kiss.

Which made them both immediately back away from each other as they both said, "Nahhhh."

REECE attached the pink collar and leash Tamra had bought for Fifi a few years ago. "At least if you're going to have that thing, we can make her look a little more like a girl," Tamra had said. Reece remembered being surprised and amused when a Christmas gift had turned up at a holiday gathering at the Hungry Fisherman with the Feefster's name on the tag. He let her have the run of the Happy Crab and the dock area behind—she wasn't one to wander off—but when he took her off the premises, he used the leash, more to keep from scaring the shit out of tourists than anything else.

As they ambled slowly—slow ambling was Fifi's usual pace—down the walk that led past the motel rooms, he was caught off guard by a faint sound. Sort of like a . . . mew. He stopped, confused. And so, then, did Fifi. "Did you hear a cat?"

He knew the iguana couldn't answer, of course, but he tended to talk to her anyway.

He could have sworn the noise came from his right, from one of the rooms. But other than Riley's, near the office, the only room occupied was number 11, and he knew Cami didn't have a cat.

Then again, Fifi had managed to get trapped in Cami's room before she checked in, so he made a mental note to ask Riley to inspect all the vacant rooms to make sure a cat hadn't snuck in while maintenance was being done. He was an easygoing guy, but a cat or dog in a motel room not equipped for them was trouble and he didn't need any messes right now. Well, not any additional ones anyway— even if most of the messes in his life at the moment were more figurative than literal.

Cami—*she* was a figurative mess for him. As

he and Fifi went on past her room, he wondered what she was up to in there. Or maybe she was out and about—it was a nice day. He hadn't seen her since last night after the snorkeling trip.

And that was good. Wasn't it?

Part of him couldn't believe what he'd let happen in the water with her. He couldn't recall a time when being attracted to a woman—*or hell, let's just call it lust*—had gotten the best of him that way. He'd never fooled around in snorkel gear before—it wasn't exactly the sexiest situation in the world. But apparently the pull between him and Cami was that strong—strong enough to override fins and a mask and an inflatable lifejacket all at once.

Of course, now that had him thinking about how it had felt. To kiss her soft mouth. To wrap around her warmth beneath the water. To touch between her legs. And . . . to feel her response.

Even now, as he and Fifi crossed the road to the beach, remembering made him a little hard in his khaki cargo shorts.

Taking things that far with her had been foolish, ill thought out. Or actually, not thought out at all—he sure as hell hadn't left for the snorkeling excursion planning to get any closer to her than they'd already been. But then she'd grown unexpectedly panicky in the water. Which—unlike when she'd been screaming bloody murder at his iguana—had given him the urge to take care of her a little. And so he'd followed that instinct. And the next thing he'd known, things were happening. The touching. The kissing.

And then her coming in his arms. His heartbeat kicked up now, and he got a little harder still.

And then he'd told her he wasn't sure they should go any further. Maybe it made him a jerk to fool around that way and then put on the brakes—but he'd been as honest about the situation as he *could* be. And if he didn't protect himself, who would? Given what she'd come here to do, going to bed with her still sounded like a mistake, despite her claims of keeping business and pleasure separate.

So it's good you're resisting her charms.

It's good you haven't seen her today.

It's good you're walking your iguana instead of knocking on her door to say hi.

And still, how long would he *successfully* resist those charms? She was a clever, quick-witted smart-ass who, underneath it all, showed a sort of sweetness and vulnerability that kept surprising him.

She's your perfect match.

Except, wait, where had *that* voice in his head come from? He was seriously hearing weird things lately, or letting his thoughts get away from him. And he seldom did the latter. Things had happened in his life that he couldn't control, but when it came to his thoughts, his mind, that he usually kept in check.

As he and Fifi zigzagged around towels, umbrellas, and beach blankets toward the water, then turned to meander up the shore, he perused the beachgoers, keeping an eye out for bikinis, or more specifically for bikinis unaccompanied by swim trunks or kids. Single women, or groups of them. It was easy to meet girls on the beach, and though he'd never have guessed it in the beginning, Fifi was often more of a chick magnet than a baby or a puppy would be. She was unique, interesting, something to ask questions about—a natural conversation starter. Young women on vacation thought it was fun to take a picture with Fifi for their Facebook page or to text to their friends back home. He wasn't much of a social media guy himself, but he had a feeling Fifi was probably famous there by now.

But he didn't see any bikinis that interested him in that way today. And he supposed it was because a particular *coral* bikini stayed on his mind the entire time.

He walked Fifi to the pier, then turned back. White seagulls with gray wings flapped about nearby, terrorizing tourists who didn't know better than to let their snacks be seen from above. Two little kids digging in the wet sand near the tideline seemed both terrified and fascinated by Fifi, so Reece stopped to let them look at her. Their dad came out from under the family umbrella to take a few pictures.

The whole while, though, questions about Cami flitted through his head. How long was she planning to stay? And what was she hoping to accomplish and how? Did she really think anything would convince him to sell at this point? Or was staying about . . . him, about pursuing this thing between them? And did she think ending up in bed with him could affect the situation? Surely not.

Cami was a lot of things, but he didn't think she was fake, or manipulative in an underhanded way. No, she kept all her manipulations on the surface. A thought which made him laugh out loud as he padded up the beach in a well-worn pair of flip-flops. He actually admired the tough, determined way she did her job, even if he was glad to have discovered the rest of her personality, too.

He didn't know the answers to his questions. But he did know he needed to figure out what he was going to do about her. He didn't want to lead her on, didn't want to get them heated up only to decide again that it was a bad idea. Either it was a bad idea completely, in a hands-off kinda way— or he had to decide he was going to go there, completely, and let go of any doubts.

As he and Fifi meandered slowly back past Room 11 a few minutes later, he considered stopping, knocking. Doing the letting go thing. Thinking about her still had him a little hard, and it wasn't just about the way her curves looked in a bikini or how it had felt to touch her—everything about her drew him like a magnet. That was what it felt like—that strong, that intense, that forceful.

But as his chest tightened, he thought better of it—didn't knock, kept walking.

He hadn't reached that letting go point, that no doubts point, quite yet . . . and maybe he never would.

*   *   *

Iᴛ was late that afternoon when Reece went out to clean the pool—one nice thing about no guests was being able to do that sort of stuff whenever you felt like it—and found Cami sitting next to it. Of course, she again wore the same coral bikini he'd come to know so well now. And damn— everything inside him tightened when he saw her. In a good way, a hot way. With her hair piled up on top of her head, a few messy tendrils falling down around her face, her cheeks sunkissed, she looked fucking beautiful.

She lay stretched out on a lounge chair, eyes closed, and as he walked past, headed toward the pool shed where he kept supplies, he said, "Got your sunscreen on, Tinkerbell?"

He glanced over in time to see her eyes bolt open in surprise. "Um—yes."

He was pretty sure a seductive expression snuck out, even as he said, "Cheeks looking a little pink there, honey—might be time to reapply."

She reached up to touch her right cheek, appearing at once sleepy and slightly alarmed. Again, it brought out a strange innocence in a woman he still found it hard to believe he could see that in. And as he went on about his business, grabbing the stuff he needed from the shed, he began to ask himself a *new* question about her. What would she be like in bed? Take-charge, determined, controlling? Or would he find some hint of innocence there, too? And he didn't even care what the answer was—he only knew he wanted to find out.

"Is it bad?" she asked.

He looked up from what he was doing, distracted by his own thoughts. "Is what bad?"

"My sunburn—my cheeks."

"Ah." He tipped his head back in understanding. He'd almost thought she'd been reading his mind and was reprimanding him. "No, not bad. Just need to . . . be careful."

Sounded like good advice. But somehow he feared he was getting closer to tossing caution to the wind every moment.

AROUND ten that night, Cami found herself padding in flip-flops toward the office of the Happy Crab. Having declined Reece's most recent offer of maid service in order to protect a certain kitty, she needed fresh towels. She should have mentioned it to him earlier, at the pool, but had forgotten. She'd been more wrapped up in what it felt like to be near him, remembering him stroking her to orgasm, and her awareness that they weren't talking about it, or about much of anything.

It had left her wanting and perturbed. The truth was, she'd have never let him touch her that way if she'd known it wouldn't go further than that. She just wouldn't have wanted to, well, go racing to third base without rounding it for home.

And she knew she could have called the office and he would have brought her some towels. But hey, if he wanted to not talk about where things stood between them, fine—yet that resulted in making *her* not want to be around him or con-

verse with him about anything at all right now.
Take that, Donovan.

She entered the now dimly lit office quietly,
pleased to find it still unlocked at this hour. She
had no idea where towels might be, but thought the
large cabinets behind the check-in desk seemed a
likely spot. Only . . . a door lay open—the one she
knew led to Reece's apartment, and she could hear
the sound of a TV.

*Well, just be quiet and he won't even know you're
here. Find some towels, then head back to your room
and Tiger.* Who she had, for some reason, not bothered to return to Polly today. And Polly hadn't
come for him, either. Maybe he was okay to have
around. He didn't cause any trouble, and he used
his litter box like a champ, and coming back to the
room to be greeted by him continued to just be
kind of . . . pleasant. So why put him out just yet?
She decided to think of it as a little vacation for
him, too. And she'd even picked up a little catfood
at a nearby convenience store.

She moved stealthily toward the wooden cabinets, but then gasped slightly when she realized
she'd nearly stepped on Fifi, who lay stretched
out in the floor like a huge three-dimensional and
very scaly rug.

Unfortunately, she couldn't reach the cabinet
overtop of Fifi's wide girth, and she couldn't easily
step over her, either. Hmm—what to do.

Only then she found herself studying the
iguana in the pale shaft of light beaming through
the open doorway, thinking it was sort of amaz-

ing that she wasn't afraid of Fifi anymore. Slightly startled at first sight maybe—but already she felt calm in her presence.

And for some reason then, she stooped down, looking into Fifi's eyes, trying to see in them what Reece did.

"Don't supposed you'd want to move?" she whispered to Fifi.

"Do you want to touch my iguana?"

She gasped louder this time, darting her gaze upward to find Reece peering down at her. Then, despite herself, she let out a laugh. "I needed towels," she said, "and didn't want to bother you." It was hard to stay mad at him.

He gave her a grin, that typical Reece grin that now kind of buried her. "I'll get you some," he said. "But you didn't answer my question."

She smiled back, feeling the warm flirtation move between them. "I'm . . . not sure if I want to or not."

"She likes to be petted," he told her, crouching down next to Cami. "Don't you, girl?" Then he proceeded to demonstrate, stroking his hand along the enormous iguana's neck.

"So she really likes that, huh?" Cami asked.

"Yep. Try it. Her skin is softer than you think."

Cami tentatively reached out her hand. Reece was right—the iguana was much softer to the touch, so much more pliable, than she'd anticipated. Slowly, she began to pet Fifi, gradually getting comfortable with it.

"See?" Reece said. "Not so bad, right?"

She glanced back up at him, into those gorgeous brown eyes, which were now only inches from hers. "Right," she agreed gently. "But . . . how do you know she likes it?"

He flashed another disarming grin. "By the way she smiles when you do it."

Cami continued gingerly petting the reptile, but after a moment said, "I don't see her smiling."

"I do," he replied. "A matter of perspective, I guess."

As Reece stood back upright, Cami did, too. Which was when she fully realized he wasn't wearing a shirt. He smiled gently as he pointed to a small utility sink inside the open storage closet. "You should wash your hands."

"Is your iguana dirty?" she teased gently.

He arched one eyebrow. "Don't get me wrong—sometimes dirty is good," he said. "But you should still wash your hands." He ended with a wink.

And so she did, using the antibacterial soap on the sink's edge—but all the while she stayed more aware of Reece than anything else. Was he watching her? She could almost feel his eyes touching her, and as she lathered her hands, then rinsed them beneath the faucet, an almost electrical current rippled up and down her arms.

After she stepped aside, Reece took her place in front of the sink and washed up, too. She took in the muscles in his back, his arms, the tan skin that covered them and looked so touchable she could almost feel it beneath her fingertips even from a few feet away. Touching Fifi wasn't bad, but touching Reece sounded a lot more fun.

And it was only as he turned off the water, dried his hands on a towel hanging from a metal ring on the wall, and pivoted to face her that she noticed what he did wear—only a pair of thin gym shorts like the ones he'd greeted her in that first morning at the pool. And the reason she noticed was . . . undeniable. It made her heart beat faster as the spot between her thighs tingled with heat.

So she followed her instincts and said, "Um, is that a bottle of sunscreen in your pocket or are you just happy to see me?"

He locked her in place with a gaze that came from beneath shaded eyelids and said, "It's not sunscreen, Tinkerbell."

His careless manner had gone at last,
his eyes were sparkling . . .

J. M. Barrie, *Peter and Wendy*

Chapter 14

SHE DIDN'T even mind being called Tinkerbell anymore. Maybe because his tone held far more affection than malice. And the words drew her gaze from his shorts up to his face—probably a safer place to be looking at the moment.

Or maybe not. Those eyes. The heat in them melted her.

"Am I too late?" he asked.

"Um . . ." Oh God—she wasn't mentally prepared for this. And was he saying what she thought he was saying? "Are you too late for what?"

He lowered his chin, pinned her with a sexy look that burned right though her soul. And when he didn't reply, she got the idea he thought that look was an answer—but it really wasn't, all things considered.

"Because just being glad to see me doesn't mean

much, you know. You were glad to see me in the water the other day—*really* glad to see me—but you still put on the brakes. So I just need to understand where we stand here."

"Okay," he told her, nodding slowly and, if she was reading him correctly, appearing seriously intent on seduction. "I decided you're right. It's worth it."

Something blossomed in Cami's chest. Maybe it was excitement. Or maybe it was fear. A part of her had already concluded that this probably wasn't going to happen—so in a way it was catching her entirely off guard. "Maybe I should be offended," she pointed out politely, "that you had to think about it."

He tilted his head and spoke with full, persuasive confidence. "Or maybe you should be flattered. That I didn't just follow my urges and let my dick do the thinking. That I'm in this with my head, too. Truth is, this might be the first time I've ever thought about the pros and cons of sleeping with someone after the opportunity presented itself. And it's the first time I've had a real reason not to go there. But what it comes down to is—you're impossible to resist." And then he lifted his hand to cup her jaw, his fingertips grazing the tender skin just below her ear. "Are you flattered yet?"

More than being flattered, she was also nearly too aroused to breathe. "Maybe."

"Let me convince you," he said deeply. And then he leaned in, slid his palm warmly behind her neck, and kissed her.

Their last kiss had been very nice—but this one

was better. They weren't wearing snorkeling gear or free-floating in the Gulf of Mexico for starters. And for finishers—mmm, he was a really good kisser. That lush mouth of his moved over hers with absolute sureness and skill. Without quite planning to, she found herself lifting her hands to his chest, bare and warm, and a slight shift in how they stood then brought other body parts into contact below.

Pressing that neediest spot between her legs against the rock-hard proof of his desire made her moan into his mouth. And as both his hands dropped to her ass, pulling her in tighter, snugger, her entire being dissolved in his strong arms.

Thought faded away, leaving behind only sensation, urges, instinct. There was nothing to do but give herself over to it. It wasn't like her—that kind of surrender. But then, nothing that had happened since she'd met Reece Donovan was really like her. So why would she have expected this to be any different?

The only thing that drew her from her complete abandon was when she heard a heavy shift behind her. It reminded her there was a giant reptile on the floor—something she could scarcely believe she'd managed to forget, actually. She broke the kiss, but remained glued to Reece as she glanced over her shoulder.

"Um, I think your iguana is watching us."

He quirked a slight grin. "And . . . you're afraid she'll post it on Facebook?"

"Uh . . ." It wasn't that, of course—but it was hard to transform thoughts into words at the moment. A rare occurrence for her.

"Trust me, she won't tell," Reece rasped with a sexy wink. "But if it'll make you feel better, we can go in my bedroom and shut the door."

" 'Kay," was all she managed. God, it was like her brain had just vanished.

"Wrap your arms around me," he instructed, so she slid them around his neck and he tightened his grip on her bottom, hoisting her upward until she was curving her legs around his body, too, and he was carrying her through the open door to his apartment.

She took in only scant details—modest surroundings, retro furniture she suspected had been here since it was new, the only modern-feeling object in the room being the flat-screen TV on the wall. He carried her past it and through another open door to a bedroom, after which he threw her to her back onto what turned out to be a waterbed. She gasped—stunned and wholly excited.

Something about it felt primal, hot—suddenly finding herself in his private space gave her the sensation of having been carried off by some roguish beast, back to his hidden lair. She felt fully immersed into his world when she'd least expected it.

But of course her surroundings weren't her real focus—all that lay in her periphery. Her attention centered on the man towering over her now, his look suddenly that of a fierce, hungry animal. She'd had no idea Reece could look that way. And she'd never have suspected how much she'd like it.

She met his gaze unabashedly.

And as more of that invisible heat flowed between them, she realized that gazing into his determined eyes right now was an act of . . . laying herself bare. Before she even got that way. It was stark, intimate. Something about it felt more intimate than *some* sex she'd had with men she'd known much better and been in committed relationships with.

But she didn't have any more time to examine that before he was climbing onto the foot of the bed on his knees and sliding his tan, leanly muscled body up over her curves—until he lay atop her, locking the fingers of both his hands with hers, gently pinning her beneath him.

She could have felt trapped—trapped by this man who *she* had been trying to trap in another way. But instead she fell into the joy of . . . surrender. To all of it.

She didn't surrender to much in life, and she'd never truly surrendered herself to a man—in this way or any other—but to him, now, she surrendered completely. Even as her legs instinctively wrapped around his hips to pull him down onto her.

A soft groan left him when his erection pressed so solidly between her parted legs.

"Baby, I'm so ready for this," he murmured deep in her ear. The take-charge lust in his voice moved all through her like a liquid thing.

"Me, too," she breathed up at him. Every cell of her body seemed to pulse.

"I'm so damn glad I stopped waiting," he told her.

"Uh huh," was all she managed to reply.

A soft, low laugh left him as he suggested,

"Maybe I should just shut up and have my way with you."

And she whispered, "Yes. Have your way with me."

And at last, he resumed kissing her, firm and deep—and soon, without thought, she found herself bringing her tongue into the mix, pressing it into his mouth, and he met it with his own. While she'd unexpectedly liked the sense of surrender, she also relished this little bit of returned boldness on her part, too.

Soon his fingers unlocked from hers and his hands found their way to her breasts, beginning to mold and massage them through her tank top and bra. Oh God, yes—she loved him touching her there, loved the firm caress on her sensitive flesh.

She'd already been moving against him below—she couldn't help it, her body had taken over—but now her pelvis worked more vigorously, rhythmically, against the erection that had her on the verge of exploding that fast.

Had any foreplay ever felt this good? Maybe she was blowing it out of proportion because it had been awhile, but she didn't think so. Her body felt malleable in his arms, and as if it had a mind of its own. She couldn't have stopped its responses if her life had depended on it. And letting herself go like this felt . . . real, and honest, and right, and . . . mmm, as if their bodies were in perfect sync.

Soon he was pushing up her top, over her breasts, then slowly but deliberately using both hands to extract them from the cups of the pale pink bra she wore. She felt sexy, wholly *sexual*, to have that part of herself revealed to him now, especially when he looked down to study them, then whispered the word, "Beautiful," against her skin just as he lowered a kiss to one beaded nipple.

She shivered as the kiss rippled through her in waves. And when his tongue began tracing circles around the taut peak, tender but jagged cries left her throat. Below, she moved in still deeper gyrations against his perfect erection.

Finally, he closed his mouth fully over her breast, suckling, and she found her fingers threading through his dark hair, heard her pleasure leave her in guttural moans that grew from the recesses of her soul.

Through this, he'd rubbed and teased and played with her other breast, but now, as he continued sucking firmly, his hand grazed ever-so-tantalizingly down over her stomach—and into the elastic waistband of the cotton shorts she wore.

And as much as she missed his hard-on when he shifted it toward her hip, she also loved the sensation of his fingers dipping between her thighs. Where he'd touched her in the water, but overtop her bikini then. This was different. Flesh to flesh. Fingers to wetness.

Eyes shut, her surrender grew more complete as she threw her arms up over her head, thrusting her breast a little deeper into his mouth, and grinding against his fingers where they stroked through her moisture. She felt so alive, so free, and so . . . ready for more.

"Please," she murmured breathily. "Oh God, please."

It was all Reece could do not to erupt in his pants. And so when he said, "Please what, honey?" and she said, "In me. I want to feel you in me," she didn't have to ask twice.

Things moved faster then. He rose slightly, enough to pull her shorts down and off, along with her panties. She pushed at his shorts and underwear, as well, as he reached toward the bedside table, toward a drawer where he prayed there was a condom or two. Relief flooded him when his fingers closed around a square packet—thank God. He should have planned for this, but he hadn't. He hadn't seen it coming this quickly. He'd thought he was biding his time, being careful and thinking it through. But then there she'd been, touching his iguana, her face, body, right next to his—so, so close—and he simply hadn't wanted to fight it anymore.

He helped her get his shorts off, then ripped into the condom. He liked that she was watching, liked seeing her tongue come out to gently touch her upper lip as he rolled the condom down over his hard and ready cock. He could hear them both breathing, panting, impatient and wanting. His heart threatened to beat through his chest.

Part of him wanted to strip away her top and bra, too—but another part of him liked how in disarray she looked, top pushed up, breasts on display. And besides, he didn't want to waste the time right now. He ached to fill her.

So he simply parted her legs, looked down on her naughty, welcoming loveliness, and then thrust slow and firm into her sweet, hot flesh.

She closed her eyes beneath him, let out a series

of heated little cries, then gazed up at him to say, "Oh my God, you feel *so* good."

He raised his eyebrows at her and managed through labored breath, "Yeah?"

She nodded. "Big."

His face flushed with warmth and he gave her a grin. "That's what I like to hear."

Beneath him, she let out a trill of laughter that echoed down into his erection—until he emitted a low groan. "Damn, Tink," he rasped, "you feel pretty good yourself."

She answered by biting her lower lip, flashing a heated look, and lifting herself against him. Ah, he felt that where it counted, and began to move in her, driving, taking on a hot, hard rhythm that made her breasts shudder with each plunge. Her eyes fell shut again, her head dropping back into the pillow, and he rained a few kisses onto her pretty neck before thrusting into her body even deeper.

"Oh God, I want on top of you," she said after a while.

And Reece fell for her a little harder. "See why I like you?" he asked, casting a lusty grin as he gripped her hips and began to roll with her so that he'd end up on his back.

Her eyes went wide as their bodies shifted. "Because I like it on top?"

He laughed. "Because you know what you want and don't hesitate to go for it. And you're a little bit of everything. A little bit hard, a little bit soft. A little bit sweet and a little bit wicked." As she ended up atop him, rising upright, he took in the fact that her long, loose hair had gotten messy and her breasts were just as gorgeous from underneath. He gave her a wink. "And I'm ready for you to show me some more wicked now."

If he wasn't mistaken, her eyes sparkled with amusement—and maybe even a hint of lechery. "And what's wicked?" she asked, beginning to move on him in sexy circular motions.

He glanced down at where their bodies met, then back up at her eyes. "*That's* a little wicked," he breathed deeply. At that, her movements intensified and her expression grew more animalistic. Oh yeah, he liked a messy-haired, animalistic Cami. A lot. "Aw baby," he bit off amid rising pleasure, "ride me."

As she did, she looked lost in a trance—until she bent over him in a way he read as a silent demand for him to kiss and suck on her breasts some more. "Looks like you're having *your* way with *me* now," he told her.

"Do you like it?" she purred.

"Do your worst," he challenged. And then he opened his mouth, happy to slip it back around one pretty, pointed pink nipple.

He sucked and she moaned. Her movements grew harder, rougher. He pumped up into her, matching her rhythm. And then finally, she began to grind on him slower, deeper, her body straining with the heat of being on the brink. It brought *him* to the brink, too. He suckled her harder, harder, sensing that was what she wanted, needed.

And then she came, crying out, rocking roughly on him, and he felt it racing through her whole body, jolting her, consuming her for those few seconds in time. And though he took pride in being a generous lover, he couldn't remember a time when a woman's climax had been enough to make him come, too—but it did. With no means to control it, and no wish to, either, Reece pounded his orgasm into her sweet body, again, again, again, letting it all spill out of him.

Afterward, she gently collapsed onto him, her breasts and tummy warm and moist with the perspiration they'd generated. His arms closed around her, fulfillment dropping over him like a blanket.

They lay together quietly that way, their bodies still connected, until she asked softly, "So were you right? Was it worth it?"

"Oh my God, are you kidding?" he murmured, still weakened from it all. "Let's do it again."

THEY slept. The lights and TV were still on, and the office door still unlocked, so when Reece awakened about an hour later, he got up and walked around, making things quieter and darker, and locking up.

When he re-entered the bedroom, he saw by the dim lighting of a lamp still on beside the bed that Cami had at some point shed her bra and tank top and lay completely naked now, stretched out amid tangled sheets.

Had it been worth it, she'd wanted to know. Hell yes. He wasn't sorry. How could he be?

He'd truly not left his living room earlier ready to dive headlong into this with her—he'd only been heading out to lock the front door before going to bed. But when he'd seen her there, bent down over Fifi, she'd looked so casual, natural, her hair shoved unthinkingly back behind her ears. And she'd been studying the iguana as if . . . she were really trying to know her, maybe trying to understand why Reece cared about her. Her expression had held a sense of searching . . . and innocence. And a beauty that defied description.

So . . . no regrets about what they'd just done, none at all.

It would be like she said—it wouldn't affect their business dealings.

And hell, for the first time it hit him that, at worst, maybe it would work in his favor—maybe she'd be into him enough that she'd give up on buying the Happy Crab and let him live here in peace.

That wasn't a motive, not at all—he'd accepted that by sleeping with her, he was sleeping with all of her, including the piranha part—but he wouldn't mind getting a happy by-product out of it.

God, she really was beautiful. He liked her hair tousled. Of course, he guessed he'd seen it that way before—on the boat, and even mussed from the constant sea breeze blowing in off the gulf. But maybe seeing it messy from sex, messy spread across his pillow, was something he felt deeper, in his gut.

And her medium breasts were perfect. Of course, he was a guy—he liked *most* breasts—but hers were among the prettiest he'd ever seen, her nipples erect even in sleep.

In fact, just studying her now began to turn him on again. Fast. A glance down revealed a massively growing hard-on.

And in one way, he hated to wake her up. He hated to wake up anyone sleeping. It was just a thing with him—he'd gone through a period about ten years ago where sleep had been hard to come by, so he respected it.

And yet . . . he had no idea how long she would stay in his life. For all he knew, she could be gone tomorrow—literally. And knowing that her exit, in some aspects, would actually be a good thing and lift a heavy weight from his life, gnawed at his stomach. Because how could he want her gone? He liked her, a lot. And now they'd connected in a whole new, intense way.

And so he decided waking her, gently, would be okay.

She lay on her side, one arm curled under the pillow, so he eased into bed behind her, sliding his palm onto her bare hip, loosely spooning her.

She shifted, just enough to press herself back into his warmth. And into something else, too— which made her gasp ever-so-lightly before she murmured a pleased-sounding, "Oh."

"Find something you like, Tinkerbell?" he whispered throatily in her ear.

"Uh huh," she breathed, and pressed further.

A low groan escaped him and he wanted nothing more than to ease his rock-hard erection into her soft warmth—but he stopped, took the time to find another condom and put it on. When he leaned back against her there afterward, she let out a hot sigh and whispered, "Please." Damn, he liked when she did that.

So he wasted no time entering her sweet heat again, both of them moaning as he slid slowly deeper, deepest. He began to move in her, and maybe it was a lack of inhibition from doing this fresh out of sleep, but in mere seconds, their bodies were rocking together with what felt like the power of a locomotive, until at some point, she moved onto her hands and knees as he plunged into her from the back, both of them panting and groaning their pleasure.

At some point, Reece looked down, took in the slender curves of her body before him, the fall of her hair, the newly acquired tan lines stretching across the middle of her back and low on her hips. But soon he closed his eyes and just got lost in the sensations. Not just what it felt like to thrust into such snug warmth over and over again, but the sounds she made, and the very smells in the air: sea and sand, the kind that permeated even walls over time when you lived at the beach, and the faint scent of a blueberry bagel he'd put in the toaster for a late night snack right before all this had started.

He'd liked it earlier when she'd taken control in bed, but he also liked now, liked having taken it back. He liked the heated push and pull of it. The exchange. The rhythm their sex had already taken on reminded him of Cami herself—sometimes hot and hard, other times sweeter and softer.

"Aw—baby, I'm gonna come, I'm gonna come

in you," he warned her—because it snuck up on him fast and, like before, there was no stopping it.

And she said, "Yes, oh yes—come. I want to make you come."

And holy hell—that pushed him right over the edge.

Afterward, when he'd collapsed atop her, kissing her neck, aware that sleep would probably grab him even quicker this time, he said, "I'm sorry, Tink," near her ear.

"Sorry?" She sounded perplexed, turning to meet his eyes.

He gave her a sleepy, self-deprecating grin. "That one got away from me. I didn't mean to finish before you."

"I don't mind," she told him. "Don't get me wrong, but for me . . . orgasm can be overrated. I'm more about all of it. Just how it feels. To have you inside me. To move together."

"Damn, that's generous." And kind of hot, he thought.

A soft trill of laughter spilled from her, light and carefree. "Who knows, maybe I'll change my mind tomorrow, but for tonight, that's what I liked best. Just all the heat of it, you know?"

Reece drifted off into post-climax slumber, two thoughts floating through his brain. Who'd have thought this woman would turn out to be his perfect lover? And why, of all the women in the world, did his perfect lover have to be also trying to end his life as he knew it?

"But who is he, my pet?"

J. M. Barrie, *Peter and Wendy*

Chapter 15

CAMI MOVED quietly through Reece's apartment, naked, still surprised by it all, and a little startled to discover she liked feeling so immersed in his world. The lights were mostly out, so she was careful to watch for Fifi, who she figured could be anywhere. Fortunately, windows admitted a glow from the neon signs and streetlamps outside.

After passing through the living room, she entered a small kitchen done in what she couldn't help thinking of as "Happy Crab red"—it sported circa 1950s appliances and cabinetry, all in shockingly good shape, and even a red Formica table. Spotting a bagel in the toaster, and an open jar of jelly, she wrapped the bagel in some paper towels on the counter and put the jelly back in the small but tidy fridge.

Turning back, she soon came upon a little bathroom, also done in the Happy Crab's signature color, complete with the popular tiling of the era—in red and white—around the sink and shower. She found herself both intrigued and a little astonished to discover such classic vintage interior elements tucked away in a place you might least expect to—a failing row motel whose glory days were long past.

It was the bathroom she'd been seeking in the first place before indulging the urge to wander, so she proceeded to wash up a bit before heading back to Reece and bed.

A dim lamp remained lit in the bedroom, letting her see how sexy he looked lying there asleep with his mussed hair and scruffy face. She'd just had the best sex of her life with him. Had she really only met him less than a week ago? That didn't seem possible. But sometimes the world worked in mysterious ways.

She reexamined her own thought then: best sex. There was no doubt of that in her mind but . . . what made it the best? Because there were pretty major intimate things they hadn't even done yet. And it was the very first time, so it should have lacked the comfort that grows with familiarity. She barely knew him, in fact, now that she really thought about it, and they had so little in common.

Maybe it was the best because of how something in him had begun to soften something in her. Or . . . maybe those parts of her were there all the time, but she didn't let them show—only Reece had seen them early on and after that she just hadn't bothered hiding them.

Was there something about this place, the

people here, that made it . . . easier to be softer? Maybe the town and people themselves held a certain kindness, openness, which life up to now had mostly taught her to keep hidden. Maybe Coral Cove somehow drew it out of her. Even if it had originally been revealed by the unlikelihood of finding a "dinosaur" in her bathtub.

Regardless, she knew Reece had seen sides of her usually kept private. And she supposed in bed it had been the same. And it had happened so naturally, without a thought.

He knows me better now than . . . well, than most people, in ways.

How strange that seemed. Reece already knew sides of her that she hadn't shown, ever, to people she'd worked with for nearly a dozen years, people she considered the closest thing she had to family.

She found her gaze drifting from the man who'd just brought her so much pleasure to other things in the room—pictures on the walls. Mostly of people she didn't know. She walked around the bed to study them anyway.

In one, of a family, she figured out she was actually looking at a young Reece, as a teenager, standing next to his parents, and maybe a sister? Predictably, he'd been cute then, too.

"Yep, it's me, Tink."

She turned to study the man in bed. Odd how comfortable she was being naked with him already. "Your family?" she asked.

He gave a lazy nod against a pillow.

And she suffered the burning urge to ask other simple questions, the kind that would be entirely normal if she didn't know his parents had died: *Where are they now? Do they still live nearby? Do you see them often?* But even as the inquiries lay on the tip of her tongue, she couldn't bring herself to do it, to put him through it. She wasn't sure why. *You are going way too soft here.* So instead she just said, "You look like your dad." Because he did.

"Yeah, before he lost his hair," he said on a light laugh. In the picture, Reece's father still had pretty much. "And Lisa took after my mom."

Cami's heart skipped a beat. "Lisa? As in the *Lisa Renee*?" The boat out back. Though they'd never discussed it.

"Yeah," Reece said easily. "Dad bought the boat right after she was born. I was four and pissed as hell they were naming the boat after her. But he explained about boats being named for girls and bought me a puppy and I got over it." He ended on another gentle laugh that perhaps held a hint of wistfulness. Or maybe she was reading too much into it.

And why was she actually relieved to learn the boat was named after his sister? Why did she even care?

Because deep inside, you wondered what woman was dear enough for Reece to name his boat for. You felt jealous of someone who Reece loved that much, who Reece shone his particular brand of light down on so brightly. You wanted to know how that felt.

She bit her lip, pushing back such troubling re-alizations. And she wanted to ask more about his family, but she didn't. Though it was hard to be-lieve he hadn't used this opportunity to mention his parents were no longer alive. The reference to his dad's hair almost implied that he was still . . . somewhere. This was the perfect time to tell her— and most people would have—so why hadn't *he*?

She began to wonder exactly how long ago the tragic loss of his parents had taken place. Was he not over it yet?

Then again, if you had parents you loved and they died young, how long *did* it take to get over it? Or did you ever? She didn't know—she couldn't fathom such a thing. For many reasons, one of them being that she'd never felt close to her mom and dad.

"Tell me about the boat," she said, finally climbing back under the sheets with him. It seemed a less personal thing to ask about.

"Just a boat," he said, rolling to his back in bed next to her, not meeting her eyes.

A beautiful boat, in fact. So not just a boat. "Take it out much?" she asked, propping on one elbow to peer down at him.

"No," he said with a slight shake of his head, his hands cupped behind it.

"Why not?"

He shrugged. "No reason."

He seemed completely disinterested in the conversation at this point, yet she felt the need to give him her unasked for opinion anyway. "Seems like it would be nice for sunset cruises—you could offer that to your guests in addition to snorkeling trips."

Hands still behind his head, he tossed her a matter-of-fact glance, eyes shaded. "You're giving me business ideas now? For a business you want to see razed to the ground."

Now she tried to shrug it off, too. "It was just an idea. You could make good money with those boats. You could draw more motel guests by advertising excursions as part of the stay, or you could make them a whole separate earner."

Now he looked at her more directly, one eyebrow lifting suspiciously. "Trying to find me a new business to get into, Tinkerbell?"

"Not really." And she honestly wasn't. Trying to make the most of things just came naturally to her. "I'm more talking about capitalizing on what's already here. This town could use some businesses like that—snorkeling trips, sunset wine and cheese cruises. With all the resort business up the road, you could make a killing on that alone."

Yet he still eyed her critically.

So she widened her gaze on him. "And seriously, I'm just thinking out loud here. About things that would help the town. You love it so much, maybe you should pay attention to me— I'm smart about stuff like that."

He still appeared doubtful, though. His voice wasn't harsh but just probing when he said, "I still don't get why you'd be trying to help me here when it's at odds with your goal."

She pursed her lips, thinking that over. "I'm not sure I agree. Replacing the Happy Crab with more modern accommodations and wanting to be helpful to you aren't mutually exclusive." Though then she let out a sigh, adding, "But I guess from your vantage point, they would be."

"And besides," he said, "I thought we agreed that if we ended up here together like this"—he then moved his finger back and forth between them, indicating their nakedness—"that it would be a nice little no-strings arrangement, separate from business."

"It is," she assured him easily. "I guess I just can't stop my brain from spinning ways to make things better." Though why did the reminder about there being no strings sting a little?

Now, finally, his eyes changed—they suddenly held sex in them again as he said, "Well, afraid you'll have to forgive me if I'm appreciating other parts of you besides your brain while you're lying here next to me with no clothes on."

It made her forget her reaction to what he'd just said, forcing her focus wholly into the present moment. "Um, which parts?"

His eyes dropped to her breasts, visible above covers pulled only to their waists, and he reached out to trace a circle around one nipple with his fingertip before moving his touch to the other to repeat the motion. "These," he said as the effects of the ever-so-light caresses trickled straight to the juncture of her thighs.

"And this one," he added, sliding his hand beneath the sheets to smoothly dip his fingers between her legs.

A soft gasp escaped her as the pleasure spread through her.

And she breathily managed to inform him, "Um, it's safe to say that they appreciate you, too." Then, as he leaned in to kiss her, she wrapped her legs around his hips in order to appreciate him a little more.

CAMI didn't know how to feel when she woke up to daylight and a scrawled note from Reece.

Headed out for morning walk on the beach.
Help yourself to anything you want and I'll see
you later.

She noticed he hadn't invited *her* for a walk on the beach. So maybe this was how he politely gave a woman the old heave-ho. Or at least made it clear that he wasn't suddenly crazy about her or anything.

So she toasted another of the blueberry bagels she found in a twist-tie bag atop the fridge, then headed back to her room.

She also didn't know how to feel when she caught herself scanning the part of the beach within view as she made the "walk of shame" back to Room 11. She didn't *feel* shamed—she just knew that if anyone saw her coming out of Reece's apartment this early in the morning she would probably be embarrassed. Camille wouldn't have. But Cami . . . well, undoubtedly there were disadvantages to the softer sides of her personality that Reece and this place seemed to draw out of her. But she didn't see Reece or anyone else, so maybe it didn't matter.

She didn't know how to feel when she walked into her room to find a yellow cat curled up on her bed and realized that she was, again, actually happy to see him. The room would have felt empty otherwise, and maybe a little lonely under the circumstances of feeling so uncertain about Reece.

"Hi," she said to the cat.

"Meow." He stood up on the bed.

So she leaned down to pet him, assuming his standing was an invitation for her to do that. He pressed his head against her touch in a way that indicated he liked it, and it was strange how nice that continued to feel, to make the cat happy through such a simple gesture.

"I guess I should probably take you back to Polly," she said to Tiger. She honestly wasn't sure why she hadn't yet. Maybe because . . . it still seemed more like taking him back to being homeless than taking him back to Polly. The more time she spent with Tiger, the more the idea of his homelessness bothered her. Everyone should have a place where they felt loved, a place they felt they belonged. "Or . . . maybe I won't. Just yet anyway."

She'd had the curtains in her room closed when she'd left last night, but now she decided to open them and let the sun in. And she needed to map out a plan for her day so she wouldn't just sit around and mope.

But why would you mope? You got what you wanted, after all—you got to experience sex with him; the opportunity, and the powerful chemistry, didn't pass you by. And it was the best sex of your life.

As she pulled back the drapes, though, and again caught herself peering out as far as she could, across the street, toward the beach, she understood all too well.

It's easy to say no-strings-attached . . . before you feel attached. And it's easy to say a little good sex with someone you want badly is better than *no* sex with someone you want badly . . . until it's over. But it was over and she felt attached. Damn it. How had that happened?

Ugh, another downside of this being more open thing. You accidentally let down some sort of wall or barrier that usually holds any vulnerability or risky emotions at bay.

And the truth was, even having gotten what she'd wanted, she'd somehow come out of it feeling rejected all over again. And it was her own damn fault, every bit of it. She'd agreed to the no-strings thing. And in reality, she couldn't have a strings thing with him anyway, for so many reasons. But the fact that he was so absolutely happy to get up and leave her in his bed to go do something as completely everyday and mundane as take a walk sent a clear message: *It was fun, but I'm done.*

And that should be fine with her. It shouldn't hurt. Even a little. She was a grown-up, and sometimes grown-ups had sex without it meaning anything or forging some intense bond.

Only . . . she'd woken up a time or two in the night and it had never even crossed her mind to leave, to cut it short, to make *sure* it meant nothing. She'd liked being in his bed, liked knowing he was next to her. She supposed, deep down, she'd hoped there'd be more.

But there wasn't. *And that's okay.* She swallowed back the slight lump in her throat and told herself she'd just learned something valuable: One night stands didn't work for her. It was probably why she'd never had one. She just had too much respect for herself and thought she was worth more than that, and wanted any guy she slept with to think it, too.

Okay—lesson learned. Now move on with your life. Quit thinking about Reece. Quit thinking about last night. Quit thinking about all the sexiness, all the naughtiness, all the heat, all the sense of . . . connection. It's over—no need to dwell on it and let it make you feel bad or like you're missing out on something by not having more.

So she took a shower and freshened up and it felt a little like . . . washing last night away. Or at least washing away the vague feeling of loss it had left behind inside her.

And in the spirit of toughening back up, she mentally dug in her heels and reminded herself why she was here. She had a job to do and it would be a good time to get back to doing it.

Good Lord, if Phil knew you just slept with the holdout, he'd have a cow.

Or . . . maybe he'd ask you how you were using that to leverage Vanderhook's position.

But either way, she'd just keep that her little secret, put it behind her, and get back to figuring out how to acquire the Happy Crab the old-fashioned way—which meant, if you can't convince them, find a way to force it.

And so as she dried her hair, then put on clean

khaki shorts and a fitted tee, her mind turned back toward legal routes. Were there any laws that Reece or the Happy Crab might be unwittingly breaking?

Opening her laptop, she sat in the chair near the window and propped her feet up on the sill, ankles crossed, getting comfortable for doing some online searching. It didn't take long before she'd accessed the City of Coral Cove's website, and soon after that, she came across a lengthy document containing all the town's laws and ordinances.

Since she didn't know what she was looking for, she simply began to read. It was dry, stale reading at best, but it was all she had to go on right now, so she stuck with it, meticulously wading through it for over an hour.

There were lots of laws about things like water and sewer and easements, and for all she knew, Reece wasn't within regulation on one or more of those things, but it would take some serious investigation to figure that out. *So keep looking.*

And that was when she stumbled upon something that had never crossed her mind—some laws concerning animals and reptiles.

No EXOTIC OR WILD ANIMALS CAN BE KEPT, LOOSE OR CAGED, AT A RESIDENCE OR BUSINESS. No EXOTIC OR WILD ANIMALS CAN BE SHOWN OR DISPLAYED FOR PROFIT WITHIN CITY LIMITS. No WILD REPTILES CAN BE KEPT, LOOSE, ON THE PREMISES OF A BUSINESS.

She stopped. Reread that last one.

And then her cell phone rang, startling her, and she nearly threw her laptop up in the air.

Getting hold of herself, she snatched the phone from the table next to her to see that—speak, or think, of the devil—it was Phil himself.

"Hi Phil," she answered, trying to sound friendly as she picked up.

"I hope you're making some serious progress on the Coral Cove property because Windchime is breathing down my fucking neck. I just got an earful from them on the phone."

She winced. Clearly he was paying it forward. But she tried to make light of it and change the tone. "Well, hello to you, too," she joked.

"This isn't funny, Camille. What have you got for me?"

Her stomach dropped a little. Had he ever sounded so downright disrespectful toward her? Or . . . maybe he *always* had and she'd just never noticed before. Strange—looking at the world through softer eyes made her notice things that she wondered if, in the past, had just escaped her.

"I'm still working on wearing the owner down." Which wasn't *exactly* true, but she had to say *something*.

On the other end came a dissatisfied sigh that cut through her heart like a knife. "That's not good enough. And I don't know what the problem is or what's taking so much time, but let me make this very clear—you need to acquire this property, one way or another. If the seller won't sell, find another way. And you need to do it fast. Got it?"

Camille sucked in her breath. This was the closest Phil had ever come to yelling at her and it hurt. Even though she supposed she shouldn't take it personally. "Or what?" she asked sharply, now letting her own anger show.

"Or I'll find somebody who will."

Oh. Wow. He was threatening her. Threatening her job. Threatening the core of her life, the thing she held dearest. And all over one slow-moving acquisition. She felt like the A student bringing home a C and being treated like a delinquent for it. Her stomach churned.

She couldn't lose her job. She *couldn't*. It was all she had. Everything. Without it, who would she be? She didn't even know.

Her gut response: *Give him something—anything*.

"I'm looking through laws and ordinances," she heard herself say. To show she was working at this constructively. And maybe she even felt a little guilty since a lot of her intended work *had*, along the way, definitely turned to pleasure.

"Anything there?" For the first time, he sounded hopeful.

"I'm not sure, maybe. I need to learn more about what some of the laws regarding water and sewer entail. And there's one about reptiles loose on the premises that he might be breaking because he has a giant iguana."

"Hmm . . ." Phil didn't sound impressed.

But then, she supposed an iguana and vague

possibilities concerning water didn't exactly seem promising. So she added, "I just found this stuff within the last few minutes, so I haven't gotten to dig into any of it yet—give me a few more days. I need to tiptoe around it. People here love the property owner and would get behind him if they knew the whole situation."

"A few more days, huh?" Phil asked, back to sounding doubtful.

"Yeah," she said simply. But she delivered that one word trying to sound as professional and determined and capable as she usually was.

"Don't let me down on this, Camille," he told her. And then he hung up.

> . . . and above all, you lost the certainty
> that you would win.
>
> J. M. Barrie, *Peter and Wendy*

Chapter 16

"Asshole!" she bit off—so sharply that the cat curled in the chair opposite her flinched.

"Not you," she said. "Him."

And then she set both phone and laptop aside—because she felt the urge to pull the kitty over into her lap. Like maybe the companionship would be a bigger help in thinking it all through than continuing to hold on to cold, hard pieces of technology.

"Besides being homeless," she said to Tiger wistfully, "you really have it pretty good. No job or overbearing boss to deal with. No pesky relationship problems. Okay, yeah, food and shelter are significant issues, but . . . at least you have those for now, right?"

She sighed, though, knowing that wouldn't last, either. And a part of her thought she should consider taking Tiger home to Atlanta with her, but . . . she wasn't sure if he would like being a strictly indoor cat who never saw the light of day in her condo. Something about him fit here, at the beach. Or maybe she was just using that as some sort of excuse, a reason not to get any further attached. Attachments only seemed to hurt, after all. Old ones, new ones—all of them.

"You're a nice cat," she told him, and he responded by rolling to his back in her lap and she knew he wanted her to scratch his tummy, so she did.

"But you look practically obscene like that, you know," she added on a laugh.

And then she noticed something else. She hadn't seen a lot—okay, not any—cat genitalia, but . . . something about the glimpse she'd just caught didn't seem quite right to her. So she reached overtop the cat and Googled on her laptop until she found some photos that confirmed it.

"Oh my God!" she said, peering down at the cat. "You're not a Tiger at all! You're a . . . Tiger Lily!" Tiger, it turned out, was actually a girl!

She was still absorbing that when a knock came on the door. She flinched and peered down at the cat—who now suddenly felt like a girlfriend and confidante. "Who could that be?" she whispered. Then she lowered the kitty to the floor, got up, and checked the peephole.

"It's Reece!" she said on a soft gasp, suffering a blend of shock, joy, and horror all at once. After which she sent a panicky look to Tiger Lily. "Hide!"

When the cat did not immediately scamper out of sight under the bed, she remembered cats

don't speak English, so rushed to scoop up her
furry orangy-yellow friend and rush her into the
bathroom. "Be quiet," she gently admonished her.
"It's for your own good." Then shut the door and
rushed back to open the other one.

The man on the other side gave her his usual
laid-back, sexy smile. "Hey."

And last night came rushing back to her. Apparently she hadn't washed it away at all. In fact,
the fresh memories, heightened by his presence,
made her warm all over, in some places more than
others. "Hey," she said, that giddy sort of elation
moving all through her now.

"I was thinking of hitting the beach."

"I thought you already hit it this morning."

"I mean for swimming. It's a beautiful day.
Thought you might want to join me."

Oh. So . . . no heave-ho. She'd misread that.
There was . . . more.

And maybe how much that thrilled her should
have scared her, too, warned her she was getting
in too deep here—but it made her too happy to
even examine that part. In fact, no less than pure
jubilation rushed through her veins. And it was
so uplifting to no longer feel rejected! Not to mention a nice distraction from what had happened
between her and Phil.

"Okay," she said nonchalantly. She didn't want
to show her hand, after all.

And he looked pleased. "Great. Toss on your
suit and we can go."

But her thoughts flew to the cat, who she didn't
want to leave trapped in a windowless bathroom

all day. "Tell you what," she said. "Give me ten minutes and I'll meet you at the office."

He nodded. "Cool."

Just then, she heard a slight mewing sound. Just one. But crap.

She watched as Reece squinted in confusion. "Did you just hear a sound like a cat?"

She shook her head definitively. "No."

Yet his expression grew more perplexed. "I keep thinking I hear a cat somewhere. I've had Riley check all the rooms, though—so I don't know what the hell I'm hearing." He gave his head a light shake, as if to clear it.

"I don't know either," she said, then began ushering him toward the door. "But tick tock on that ten minutes. Gotta get ready."

Which was precisely when she heard a slightly louder meow, which she instinctively tried to cover with her own voice, and what came out was a sudden and long sort of, "Wowwwwww."

Reece had just turned to go, but now he stopped to give her a weird look. "Huh?"

She blinked and tried to act natural. "I just said wow."

He lowered his chin, widened his eyes in question. "About?"

"Like . . . wow, I love swimming at the beach. And I haven't done that in a while, so I'm excited." She smiled and attempted to look that way.

"Okay, Tink, whatever you say," he told her, sounding a little skeptical—but then headed for the door again.

When it finally closed behind him a few sec-

onds later, Cami let out a sigh of relief. Then went
to release the captive in the bathroom.

As Tiger Lily came trotting out, Cami informed
the cat, "Um, bad job on the staying quiet. You seriously need to work on that or you'll get us both
in big trouble."

REECE hadn't exactly planned to end up at the
beach with Cami this afternoon, but here they
were. As he glanced at the woman next to him, all
stretched out in the sun, eyes shut, skin glistening
as it tanned, he thought through his day.

This morning he'd wanted to escape. It had
seemed wise. As it always did. It was how he
usually handled any overnight visitors to his
bed—he left a friendly note and took an early
morning walk. It wasn't about dumping her—or
anyone else. It was about just . . . putting some
healthy distance between them. Reminding them
both that this wasn't a big, serious, joined-at-the-
hip kind of thing. A little distance was usually a
good idea.

There was always something a little other-
worldly about being out on the beach just after
sunrise, when it was empty and felt . . . new, like it
had been somehow reborn overnight. There was
just something pure and . . . raw about it at the
same time. And then the sun rose a little higher
and more people started to arrive, and eventually
it turned into another normal day—and that was
when he'd headed back.

He'd returned to his apartment hoping she'd

be gone—yet sorry when she was. For reasons he couldn't explain. From what he could tell, she'd eaten something and drunk a small glass of juice, then vacated the premises. No return note. No clue of whether she was happy or sad or mad or anything else.

And normally that would have suited him fine, but for some reason she'd stayed on his mind. So he'd taken a shower and found some productive stuff to do.

He'd gone to the grocery and bought the raw veggies that made up Fifi's diet, and spent some time cutting them into meal-sized portions for the coming week. Then he'd cleaned her habitat next to the office, watering the plants there and dusting the heat lamps that kept her warm when the Florida temps dropped to less than tropical. After that, he'd filled a bucket with some soapy water and taken to washing his boats, then hosing them down. They were due for it, especially the sloop.

As he'd worked, he'd thought about his discussion with Cami about the *Lisa Renee*. And how they weren't going to mix work and pleasure, but she sort of had anyway with that conversation. It was confusing to him and he still wasn't sure whether she'd really been trying to be helpful—or manipulate him.

"Gettin' her ready for a voyage?"

He'd stopped spraying down the sloop's bow at the sound of Riley's voice and looked up to see the good-natured old man approaching on the dock. "Nah," Reece said. "Just figured she was due for a washing."

"Maybe you should take her out soon," Riley suggested.

That was probably true. But he'd explained to Riley why he didn't. "You know every time I do it just brings up bad memories for me."

Riley had nodded in understanding. But then he'd said, "Oughta take the lady in room eleven out for a ride and build some *better* memories."

Reece hadn't responded to that, just changing the subject with his older friend.

But then, damn, somehow or another he'd soon found himself finished with the boats and meandering down to Cami's room to see what she was up to. The idea about the beach had just popped out of his mouth.

And here they were. And he wasn't sorry. Now they basked in the sun, but a little while ago he'd found himself playing in the breaking waves with her, laughing with her, kissing her. It had been . . . nice. Fun. And shockingly easy considering where they'd been a few short days ago.

You like her too much.

And that should worry you like hell.

Because you never *like girls too much. You always keep a pretty firm control over that.*

But maybe Riley was right. Maybe it was time to try building some new, better memories. Maybe.

Still, it shocked him to hear the next words that came unexpectedly out of his mouth a few minutes later as they left their towels to go get some drinks at the snack shack by the pier. "You have any plans tonight?" he heard himself ask.

"No. Why?"

"Don't know if you'd be interested, but . . . *Mutiny on the Bounty*'s on cable and Riley and I are gonna order a pizza from Gino's and watch at my place. If you'd want to join us."

Nope, he definitely hadn't planned that. And maybe it wouldn't even be her kind of thing. A simple night of pizza and a movie on TV. And with an old man she didn't know, too.

So it made him happier than he could easily understand when she smiled and said, "A date with you, Riley, and Clark Gable? How can I resist?"

TAMRA sat on a bench by the pier, staring out over the water, her heart beating too fast. She'd been doing a lot of serious thinking lately, and a lot of deciding that maybe Fletcher was right. She was thirty-four years old. And while she was satisfied in some ways, maybe in others she was letting life pass her by, too content to be a spectator rather than someone who's out there really going for the whole enchilada of things.

"Most of the things we really want in life," Fletcher had told her just yesterday, "lie just on the other side of our fears."

And so this morning she'd gathered her courage and called Reece and asked if he wanted to go for a walk on the beach with her. They did that from time to time—it was nothing unusual—but this time, for her, it was different. This time, she was going to let him know how she felt. About *him*. She was going to face that fear. Come what may.

"Hey."

She flinched, lost in her own thoughts and more than a little startled to look up and see that he was here, already, and this was it. She'd met him for walks dozens of times, but this, now, suddenly felt downright surreal. Planning to do something brave and then actually managing to do it were two different things, and this had been a lot easier when it had lain in the future.

"Hey," she said, forcing a smile. And then taking in his. He had such a *great* smile. It kind of turned her inside out.

"Ready to walk?" he asked.

She nodded, got to her feet. Then looked around for the thing that was missing. "No Fifi again?"

"I left her in charge of the front desk today." He winked. And it melted her.

And as they began to head down toward the water, both of them barefoot and carrying their shoes, Reece said, "So what's up? You sounded . . . kind of intense on the phone last night. Anything I should know about?"

Oh crap. She'd sounded intense? This wasn't the opening she'd hoped for. Things were supposed to be relaxed, mellow, easy. It was supposed to come out naturally—somehow. That was how she'd envisioned it anyway. She hadn't planned out a worst case scenario—because Fletcher had advised against that. "Planning out a worst case scenario is just inviting it to happen. Expect it to go the way you want," he'd said. But already, it wasn't going that way.

So she said, "No, not really—just felt like taking a walk, catching up. What's new with you?"

"A lot, actually."

Huh. That was new. Reece was such a carefree guy that questions like that usually met with a shrug and, "Same old, same old," or something pithy like, "Fifi got a clean bill of health at the vet's and she's in the mood to party." So she said, "Really?"

He replied with a nod. "It's about Cami," he told her.

And Tamra bit her lower lip and looked at the horizon stretched out ahead of them without really seeing it, praying her emotions didn't show as her stomach plummeted. Already, she knew. In her heart. She was too late; she'd waited too long. "Oh?" she said. But it came out stiffer, her voice higher, than intended.

And Reece stopped for a second and gave her a funny look before they walked on. "You don't seem to like her. How come?"

She pulled in a breath, let it back out. "I'd think it's obvious. She's trying to wheedle the Crab from you. Isn't that enough?"

"I see where you're coming from," he said, "and I appreciate your concern, but . . . the thing is, there's something between us, her and me."

"Something?" she asked quickly. Her chest contracted, aching more with each step they took.

"Something like . . . romance, I guess. Even though that's not a word I usually get into using. But I don't know what else to call it. And it feels . . . real. Realer than anything I guess I've let myself feel in a long time."

Another deep breath—in, out. *Just keep breath-*

ing. Get through this. Even if he just shattered your heart into a million pieces.

"Sooo . . . you're not saying, 'That's great, Reece—I'm really happy for you!'" He glanced in her direction again. "You really hate her that bad?"

Breathe. Just breathe. She wished she were anywhere else in the world now, wished she could run away from this conversation. "Hate is a strong word," she managed, trying her very best to sound reasonable, "but I just . . . worry for you. I mean . . . of all the women to fall for, Reece—this one?"

"I know it seems weird," he said. "I know it didn't come about in the normal way."

She forged ahead with her next thought. "I hate to say this but what if . . . what if she's just using you to try to get the Happy Crab?"

He answered with a shake of his head. "I worried about that, too, at first, but I don't think that's what's going on. Mostly, talk about the Crab and things between *us* have been completely separate. And she mentions trying to get me to sell less and less.

"God knows I never expected this to happen. And I'm still not a hundred percent sure of how I feel, but . . . I just like being around her. A lot." He laughed. "I mean, I can't even explain how good and kind of . . . filled up I feel just hanging out with her, arguing, or talking about nothing, or not even talking at all.

"I don't know where it'll go—maybe nowhere, maybe somewhere. But for now, it's . . . good."

"Well," she said softly, having taken all that in, "I'm . . . happy for you." And although it was hard to say that without letting a certain amount of sorrow leak through, she meant it. His happiness mattered to her. And in that strange moment, she realized exactly *how* profoundly she cared for him—enough that she truly wanted him to be happy even if it was with someone else, even if she could never have what she wanted with him, even if she would always be on the outside looking in, wondering what that felt like and wishing she could know. *Oh God, how did I deny my feelings for so long? And why?* Her chest felt like it was caving in now as she said, "I truly mean that."

"Thanks, Tam," he said, and then he reached out to squeeze her hand in his. As the innocent touch moved all through her, her heart broke a little more.

"Just . . . promise me you'll be careful, Reece," she insisted then. "I wouldn't want you to get hurt. Or lose something you value." *The way I just lost my heart.*

As Cami drove back toward the Happy Crab after a short shopping expedition, new purchase in the passenger seat next to her, she thought back over the previous night and subsequent morning.

After *Mutiny on the Bounty* ended, Riley had kindly excused himself, claiming sleepiness, though she'd seen a glint in his eye that made her think he just wanted to give them privacy. And privacy was nice, because it had been mere moments after his departure that she and Reece started making out on the vintage sofa they'd sat on to watch the movie.

As he'd lain her down on the nubby fabric, she followed the instinct to say, "Um, should we be doing this here?"

"Here?" he'd asked with raised eyebrows, looking more than a little surprised that she might be the one putting on the brakes now.

Even though that wasn't what she'd been doing at all. "On this couch," she explained. "It's in such good shape. How does a couch that I'm guessing is at least fifty or sixty years old even look this good?"

His warmth pressed against hers as he let out a light laugh. "Guess they don't make 'em like they used to. Or maybe it's because this one belonged to my uncle Barry. He never got married, or dated much that I know of, so I'm guessing it didn't see this kinda action much." He ended with a cute, sexy wink that made her feel fluttery inside.

"Well," she said, "I don't want to be the one to mess it up after all this time, so . . . why don't we take this back to your waterbed?"

"My waterbed can take whatever you want to dish out, baby," he teased some more.

And his waterbed had indeed taken it. And like the previous night, it had been unbelievably intense. There was something about the connection between them when he was inside her, when they were looking into each other's eyes, that stole her breath in a way no other sex ever had. Her whole body seemed to vibrate with the invisible way it fused them together. Or fused her to him anyway. She had no idea if *he* was experiencing such fusing with *her*—or maybe *all* his sex was this way. A thought that had made her sad, so she'd pushed it away as soon as it had come.

This morning, when she'd awoken, he was still beside her—no empty pillow, no note about walking on the beach. And after indulging in a hot morning quickie, he'd made them scrambled eggs and toast.

Across the little Formica table from him, she'd asked if she could use his washer and dryer—even with the shopping she'd done since her arrival, she needed to do some laundry. So he'd shown her the laundry room, which she could tell served the whole motel, and it had felt oddly intimate for him to see her dirty undies and bras—even if he'd taken a couple of them off her himself now.

"Want me to call Juanita, have her come clean your room this morning?" he asked as they worked on the laundry.

Some fresh sheets would have been nice, so she was about to say yes—when she remembered her furry roommate. "Um, if you can just give me some sheets, I'm happy to change them myself."

He'd drawn back slightly, the move implying that her virtuousness was throwing him. Little did he know it wasn't virtuousness at all. "I don't mind calling her," he said.

But Cami shook her head—and realized she should probably go soon. Because she did indeed have a kitty to check on. Hot sex fogged her brain a little—but now she was remembering she had certain things to take care of. So as she pulled the last couple of items from the dryer, dropping them into a laundry basket Reece had loaned her, she shook her head. "I'm fine with doing it myself—honest. And I'd better head to my room anyway—email to check, things to keep up with at the office."

And when he raised one eyebrow, looking suspicious, she added coyly, "Yours isn't the only property I'm in charge of convincing someone to sell, you know."

"Well, Tink," he said, "I hope you do a better job with everybody else than you've done with me," and they both laughed lightly.

How strange that it had actually become a joke between them now. Even though she still needed to acquire the Happy Crab. In some way or another.

Since leaving him, she'd fed Tiger Lily and put out fresh water, and she'd changed the sheets and added newly washed sea green towels to the bathroom. After that, she'd searched online to find a nearby pet store out on Route 19, the big, busy road further inland that ran parallel to the beach and the beach towns that lined this area of the Florida Gulf Coast.

Now pulling into the Happy Crab's lot after her trip out, she grabbed up the bag from the store and went into her room, happy to see the cat again. She wasn't quite sure when she'd officially become a cat person, but when it hit her what she'd just done—what she'd just bought, for heaven's sake—she knew that a serious change had come over her.

She said to Tiger Lily, "Look what I got for you," and withdrew from the bag a pretty lavender collar and matching leash, as well as a little heart-shaped silver tag that said "Tiger Lily" in a pretty script. "No one will mistake you for a boy now," she added with a succinct nod.

Reece had told her he had plans to help Fletcher do some work at his house this afternoon, so she knew it was safe to take the cat out for a walk. Which was good, since she'd decided the cat was probably tired of being cooped up in such a small space. She realized there were plenty of indoor cats in the world, but knowing Tiger Lily had been living outside until just a few days ago, she felt compelled to offer the cat an excursion.

Good-natured as she was, Tiger Lily calmly allowed Cami to put the new collar on her. She smiled down at the kitty afterward, saying, "The tag looks like a little necklace on you. Very stylish." Indeed, the orange cat appeared infinitely more feminine now, and as Cami had hoped, the lavender was a good color against her fur.

Then it hit her that if a homeless cat didn't mind wearing a collar . . . maybe that meant she'd had a collar before. And a home. Which made Cami feel even more protective of her, and happy to perhaps be returning her to some of the things to which she'd once been accustomed.

Clicking the leash in place, she said, "All right, let's take you for a walk, young lady cat."

Of course, she knew good and well that she should probably be doing exactly what she'd told Reece she would be—working. But her heart just wasn't in it these days. Which was strange—since her heart had *always* been in it up to now. One more way in which she barely recognized herself.

Was it really possible . . . that her heart was no longer in taking the Happy Crab from Reece, even if she truly thought it best for the community? The place had so much odd, quirky charm. It was such a throwback to a simpler time that she'd never really experienced herself and had only seen in pictures, on old beach postcards.

And *would* a big resort, right here, on this spot, change that charm too much? Now that she was examining it from this particular angle, the truth was . . . maybe.

The resorts up the road—they fit. They were like islands unto themselves—they'd been built on previously empty stretches of marshland no one had ever developed before and little else sat around them. But would a lavish Windchime Resort really increase the appeal of the Hungry Fisherman? The Beachside Bakery? Gino's Pizza? Would there be a quaint sunwashed dock out back where the pelicans hung out and boat owners could rent a slip? She had avoided facing this, but . . . the more she got to know the area, the more she had to question the wisdom of putting a high-rise here.

And yet, at the same time, another fact remained: This part of town simply couldn't survive as it was. It was dying. And why let it die when a brand new hotel could bring it back to life? Wouldn't a *new* sort of Coral Cove be better than a *dead* Coral Cove?

It took a slight bit of coaxing with the leash to get the cat out the door, but after a moment she followed, and as they set out up the walkway that lined the motel, Tiger Lily began to get more comfortable and trot out ahead of Cami at a nice, easy pace.

"Great day in the mornin'! Do my eyes deceive me or is that cat wearin' a purple collar?"

Cami glanced up to see Polly in her usual rust-colored dress heading toward her across the parking lot. She looked more aghast than Cami could have imagined.

"Guess what?" Cami said. "This cat is not a boy. So I've renamed her Tiger *Lily*. And I'm doing what I can to help her regain her femininity."

"Huh," Polly said, appearing even more surprised as she met up with them on the blacktop. "Well, I'll be." Then she shook her head. "But I still don't know why you'd walk a cat on a purple leash. Or walk a cat at all. That's really more of a dog thing."

"Is it?" Cami tilted her head to ask. She didn't know, not having any background in pet ownership. "They had cat leashes, so I bought one. And . . . I've decided I can keep her with me at least until I go back to Atlanta. After that . . . I don't know." She didn't even really want to think about that, in fact. So she'd just decided not to, for now. "But for as long as I'm here, she's out of your hair and in mine."

"That's music to my restaurant-operatin' ears," Polly said, seeming relieved.

Cami smiled. "Well, we're off to take a walk on the beach."

Though Polly still looked like she found the concept odd. "You'll likely be the only cat-walker there. Can't say I've ever seen a cat bein' walked on the beach before, not in all my years."

And as Cami and Tiger Lily proceeded across the street and onto the sand, Cami thought: What kind of place considers it more normal to walk a giant iguana on a leash than a cat? The unique little town of Coral Cove, that was where.

THE next day found Cami by the pool, Reece in the chair next to her, both of them soaking up the sun, listening to music echoing from speakers mounted on the back wall of the motel. "When there are more guests, I have colored umbrellas and tables I put out," he told her, "so it looks a lot more . . . fun then."

She glanced over at him, a little surprised, a little touched, that he seemed to care about her knowing that, that he took pride in how she perceived his business, even under the weird circumstances. "I can see where that would add a lot. But it's nice enough as is," she assured him, which was true. It was a simple rectangular pool that had clearly been here a while, but a few palm trees lined the perimeter on one side, and the dock and boats on another made it feel . . . not fancy—but pleasant in an old-time Florida way.

A few minutes later, they both waded down the steps and into the water, rippling with light beneath the sun. Ah, so cool on her hot skin, and a sensual sigh left her as she leaned back to float with her face toward the clear blue sky.

What felt even better on her skin, though, was when Reece ran his sure hands up her outstretched legs. She lowered her feet to the bottom of the pool and stood upright in the water, moving into his loose embrace for a kiss as heated as the air around them.

"What is it with you and water?" she asked on a laugh, her arms resting around his shoulders.

"Hmm?" he murmured, now kissing her neck, clearly only half hearing her.

"I can't be in the water without you making a move on me," she teased, then kissed him again.

He arched one brow. "You complaining?"

"Not at all," she replied, giving him a smile. "Just starting to think you have a water fetish or something."

"Maybe it's not the water," he suggested. "Maybe it's the bikini." He dropped an appreciative gaze toward her cleavage. "With no offense to your mind, Tink, it's hard to look at you in this without appreciating all those other body parts." And he ended with one of those sexy little winks she felt between her thighs. He was the most sexual man she'd ever encountered. Or . . . maybe it was just the reactions he inspired in her that made her feel that way.

"How exactly are you appreciating them?" she asked flirtatiously. It was so easy to be drawn in by him.

He released her from his grasp to point to his eyes with one hand, his brain with the other.

"Ah," she said, tipping her head back.

Then he pointed to his sexy mouth and added, "But I was thinking about appreciating them with *this*, too."

When he clamped his hands firmly on her hips, his fingers curling possessively over her flesh, she oozed with want for him. "Um, um . . ." she mumbled, so caught up in her own desire now that she couldn't summon words as he gently backed her toward the edge of the pool, then lifted her up and sat her down on the tile at the edge.

After which his fingertips dipped smoothly into the elastic of her bikini bottoms. "Let me take these off, honey," he rasped near her ear.

Oh my. She tingled in the whole general area where his hands were. "But . . . what if someone comes?"

"No one's going to come but you and me," he assured her. Wow. She felt *that* between her thighs, too. Enough that she lifted from the concrete just enough to let him begin pulling her bikini down.

Even as she continued expressing certain valid concerns like, "What if Riley shows up?"

"I sent him in my car on some errands. Won't be back for hours." Now Reece was tugging the coral Lycra bottoms over her outstretched ankles and off, looping them over his wrist. And she couldn't believe she was sitting there, naked from the waist down next to the Happy Crab's pool.

"Wh-what about your friends?" she persisted. This seemed ridiculously risky; she felt way too exposed.

But as he skillfully parted her legs, his palms pressed to her inner thighs, he only whispered, "Shhh. Close your eyes. Let me make you feel good."

So they lay there in the sun,
and their bodies glistened in it . . .

J. M. Barrie, *Peter and Wendy*

Chapter 17

ONCE SHE shut her eyes as instructed, it changed things. It made her let go. Of fears. Doubts. Everything but pleasure. And what pleasure it was.

With the sun warming her, she leaned back on her elbows and basked in the sensual joys Reece's ministrations delivered. She ceased thinking, leaving room only for feeling, absorbing, and letting her body respond.

Before long, though, she opened her eyes back up again, aroused to meet his gaze as he pleasured her, licking and kissing her most sensitive spot, and soon pushing two fingers up into her.

When jagged little whimpers began erupting from her throat, she bit her lip to stifle them. But she stayed connected with that penetrating gaze of his, fully immersed in what they shared.

Until orgasm became imminent, and that made her eyes fall shut again, made her sink deeper into herself, made her give herself over to that place of getting closer, closer—and then the sweet release. Despite her best efforts, a few whimpers of pleasure escaped her—she simply couldn't hold it in—and she rocked against his mouth, riding out what was unquestionably one of the most powerful climaxes she'd ever experienced.

Afterward, she lay back on the ground for a few seconds, exhausted by it—but she wanted to be close to him at the same time, so she soon eased back down into the water, sliding her arms around his neck.

As they exchanged slow, heated kisses, their bodies coming together beneath the surface, she murmured, "I'm guessing that's not a bottle of sunscreen in your pocket, right?"

"No way, baby—that's all for you," he promised, their foreheads touching. "If you want it."

"Oh, I want it," she assured him.

And as the heat amped back up into flames, he closed his palms over her hips and turned her to face away from him in the water, and then covered her hands with his as he planted them on the edge of the pool. After that came the marvelous hardness—first, it pressed into the center of her ass, and she arched instinctively against it. And then he was slowly, surely sliding it up into her, filling her completely. She let out a low, impassioned, "Oh . . ."

"Aw baby," he rasped behind her. "You're so warm, so snug."

And she arched even deeper now, wanting still more—and he took the hint, beginning to thrust.

Yes, yes, yes—somehow she always forgot how good this felt; it was never any less than magnificent to have him plunging into her over and over.

She wasn't sure how long they moved like that together—only that her legs grew weak and his arm soon circled her waist, holding her up, anchoring her to him. And that every thrust stole her thoughts, leaving her only to absorb the consuming sensations. And when he came, she knew a certain wholeness, a deep satisfaction, from having taken him there. She liked making him feel good, too.

So it was surprising to her when his first words after that were, "Aw shit."

She looked over her shoulder as he pulled out of her. "Kind of a mood killer," she informed him.

He just shook his head, ran one wet hand back through his thick hair. "I'm sorry, Tink. I just realized I forgot a condom."

"Oh." The word left her high and light and slightly alarmed.

"But you don't have to worry," he rushed to promise. "I'm always careful. That's why it caught me so off guard. I don't *ever* forget." Then he narrowed his gaze on her just slightly. "Are *you* always careful? And God, please, tell me you're on the pill."

She nodded. "I am, for health reasons. And otherwise . . . I haven't had to be careful in quite a while. In case that adds to your assurance."

He looked surprised, in a way that made her feel flattered. "Really? Why not?"

She shrugged. "Color me picky."

And he tilted his head. "How'd *I* get so lucky?"

"Guess I'm just hot for dinosaurs and neon crab signs."

He let out a laugh that warmed her heart as she closed her arms back around him.

"So," she asked, "you really *are* always careful? Except for now?"

A nod from him, too. "Cross my heart."

"So you really haven't done it with anyone else in the water like this? Because seriously, you seem to have a thing for water. Or bikinis. Or whatever. But it still comes back to water. Where it's pretty hard to use a condom."

And he appeared to think back through it until he finally said, "Now that you mention it, I don't think I've *ever* done it with anyone in the water before." Then he made a slight face. "Which is almost weird considering I've lived at the beach my whole life."

And something in that pleased her immensely when she'd least expected it. She *liked* hearing he'd done something with her that he'd never done with anyone else. Even if—maybe *especially* if—it was a little surprising.

"Guess you'd better get busy and make up for lost time on the water sex," she teased him.

"You volunteering to help?"

She smiled. "Maybe." And tried really hard not to think about leaving or this being temporary and her having no idea how it would end. Or when.

She'd never been in a relationship anything like this one before. She'd never been with anyone so fun or carefree. She wasn't sure she *herself* had ever been so fun or carefree. She'd never felt so deep into anything she knew had to be short term. And she wasn't sure how to deal with any of that—other than to just push it from her mind.

After that, she got her bikini bottoms back on, and they soon lay next to the pool just listening to music and talking. When he went in to get drinks and snacks, he returned with Fifi, who Cami was truly starting to feel a little more friendly toward.

"Hi, Fifi," she said as the big iguana lumbered toward their lounge chairs.

"I think she just smiled," Reece said—but when Cami lifted her gaze to his handsome face, it was *his* grin that stole her attention. And maybe even her heart if she was honest with herself.

"Afraid I still can't see it," she told him regretfully about the iguana's smile.

"Stick around long enough and you will eventually," he promised her easily. *Too* easily. Like maybe he didn't even realize what he'd just said. *Stick around. Eventually.* She found herself wishing she could. She wished she could just somehow freeze time, right now, and that nothing would have to change.

They stayed together until the day began to wane, then Cami got bold enough to ask Reece if he'd like to walk over to the Sunset Celebration with her. They parted ways only long enough to shower and get ready, then dined on a funnel cake and ice cream at the pier. They watched Fletcher's act and checked out what the vendors were selling, and Cami even bought another stained glass suncatcher from Tamra, this one in the shape of a cat, perhaps hoping it would make Reece's friend finally warm up to her. But when it didn't seem to, she let it go, reminding herself that, in the long run, whether Reece's friends liked her didn't really matter.

The sun set in streaks of neon pinks and warm, mysterious purples as they walked along the shore, and when Reece casually held her hand as they strolled, she realized how much she liked it. And that she felt far more from such a simple touch than she probably should. *But that ship has sailed—nothing to do but ride it now.*

When he walked her back to her room, stopping at her door and waiting as she dug out her key, he said, "I had a nice day with you, Tink."

His dark eyes shone warm on her and her voice came out sounding a little more girlish than usual as she said, "I had a nice day with you, too."

He tilted his head to one side—hair messy from the sea breeze as usual. "Want to do something tomorrow?"

She bit her lip. "Like what?"

"Anything you want," he told her. "As long as it doesn't involve me signing a contract."

They both laughed, and it struck her again how odd it was that the topic had become a source of amusement between them.

She said, "Could we take out the boat? The other boat, the one named after your sister?"

Then watched as his expression changed, drooping a little. Why did he act weird sometimes when she brought up that boat?

"Or not," she added quickly. "It was just a thought. It's a pretty boat."

Reece swallowed visibly then, and slowly he began to nod, and to look more like his normal, easygoing self—until finally he said, "Okay. Yeah."

But she still winced. "Are you sure? Because we don't have to. We could—"

"No, I'm sure," he cut her off. "It's a good idea."

And that was when a light but clear and distinct "Mew" could be heard from inside her room.

"Atchoo." She quickly pretended to sneeze to cover the sound.

But Reece arched one eyebrow in her direction, his expression practically saying, *Are you serious about that sneeze?* so she lowered her eyes, feeling caught.

Then a longer, louder mewing sound met her ears, and when Reece glanced over to her window, she did, too—to see a cat's round little face peering back at them from where it stood on the table looking out. Uh oh. The jig was up.

When she dared peek back at Reece, his gaze had narrowed accusingly. "So—either a cat broke into your room while we were away or you're harboring a fugitive. Which is it?"

"I'm harboring a fugitive," she admitted—mainly only because she was pretty sure he wouldn't buy the other answer. She gritted her teeth slightly and gave him a please-don't-kill-me look. "But it was for Polly. The health inspector was there—two days in a row even—and Tiger Lily is extremely well behaved. She uses her litter box like a pro and is very tidy with her food. You'll never even know she was there."

He lowered his chin. "Tiger Lily?"

"Polly was calling her Tiger when she thought she was a boy—but turns out she's a girl, so I added the Lily part. Cute, don't you think?"

"Cats shed," he replied dryly.

"But I figured you'd want me to help your Hungry Fisherman friends—your neighbors. I was trying to do the right thing, the *nice* thing. And besides, Polly didn't give me much choice."

"That I can believe," he said, shifting his weight from one flip-flop to the other, "but I'm betting the health inspector is gone now. Because I've been hearing this incessant meowing for days and was starting to think I was losing my mind."

Cami bit her lip and took in another quick glimpse of the cat in the window. "I'm not proud of this," she admitted to Reece, "but . . . I guess I got attached to her."

"But I have a no pets rule."

"But what about Fifi?"

"Fifi doesn't shed."

"No, what I mean is . . . I've never really had a pet before, but I'm guessing the attachment I feel to Tiger Lily is something like what you felt for Fifi that made you bring her home."

His look grew irritated then—like she'd hit a soft spot. Bingo! It was gratifying to see she still possessed some of her good negotiating skills, even if this was a far different thing than she'd ever negotiated before and she was coming at it from a far different angle than she was familiar with. He drew in a breath, let it back out—heavily. "Well, what's going to become of this cat? If I let it stay, I mean."

Cami had no choice but to be honest with him. "I'm not sure. I'm taking that one day at a time. There's . . . a lot I'm taking one day at a time right now." That last part made her drop her gaze again, though. It felt like admitting weakness—toward him and what they shared, and also toward his business and the reason she'd come. Even if she was no longer sure how to deal with *any* of this anymore, she didn't need to let *him* know that.

But oh well—what's one more chink in the armor?

In fact, she wasn't even sure she was *wearing* armor anymore. Maybe it had all fallen off somewhere along the way, piece by piece.

"I promise I'll clean up her hair or any mess she makes." And as the words left her, it struck her that normally she'd have told him it didn't really matter since soon his motel would be torn down anyway—but had she actually begun to doubt that now? "She's really very clean, like I said. She's a very nice cat. I even bought her a lavender leash."

At this, his eyebrows shot up. "You bought the cat a leash?"

"Fifi's leash kind of inspired me, I guess."

Now Reece just gave her a sizing-up look and shook his head as he said, "You really are a very confusing woman in ways, Tinkerbell."

"I'd prefer to think of it as . . . multi-faceted and complex."

Which made him lean his head back and let out the deep, hearty laugh she'd come to love—just before their gazes connected, something caught fire, and he gave her a deep, passionate kiss that took her breath away.

When it was done, her lips felt a little swollen—her whole body, in fact, seemed a little lighter than it had just a minute before.

"We'll take out the *Lisa Renee* tomorrow," he told her. "Goodnight, Tink." And then he turned to walk away.

And as she stood there, watching him go, it hit her. *I guess I get to keep the cat in my room.* Then she smiled down at the furry face still peering out through the glass, and in that moment anyway, all felt right with the world.

As bright sunlight slanted in through Reece's bedroom window, he rolled over, somehow expecting to find Cami's warm, naked body next to him. Only—shit—she wasn't there. And then he remembered that they hadn't spent the night together, and that it was probably wise. Habits like spending the night seemed like a bad idea for many reasons.

And then he remembered what he'd agreed to do with her today. He wasn't sure taking out the *Lisa Renee* was a good idea, either, but he was trying to believe it was. Maybe Riley was right—maybe making new memories on the *Lisa Renee* would help blot out the old. And maybe enough time had finally passed—maybe it wouldn't take him back to that dark day. And hell—if he wasn't ever gonna use the boat, he should sell it, honor his family's memory by at least letting someone else enjoy it; it had been his dad's pride and joy, after all. And if he *hadn't* sold it, that must mean he wanted to keep it, use it. He hadn't *yet, much,* but maybe that changed today.

He also wasn't sure it was a good idea to have a cat in Room 11. But something about the look in Cami's eyes had talked him into it. Damn, she could be persuasive when she was sweet.

Just don't let her persuade you into anything else you don't want to do. A cat was one thing. So was taking out a boat. Even sex had turned out to be . . . um, pretty damn great, and so far he couldn't see a downside to the decision.

And as long as she didn't go back to trying to convince him to sell the Happy Crab, they'd be just fine. For . . . however long this lasted. But he wasn't gonna think about that. Or how it would end. He honestly had no idea at this point what tomorrow held with Cami, let alone the day after, and next week sounded like an eternity away.

The truth was—he'd spent a lot of time with her now and he was feeling pretty . . . involved. And even . . . surprisingly okay about that. And when she left, he'd miss her.

But you're in it now, and you're a big boy—you can take care of yourself. So just enjoy the day and quit thinking so damn much.

SUN swept across the water, making it sparkle as the white sloop named the *Lisa Renee* cut a swath through the sea.

As Reece had navigated their way through the small bay behind the Happy Crab, he'd shown Cami a spot where dolphins often played near a bridge that led to the open gulf. And as they'd passed under it just moments ago, he pointed out the Sunnymeade Retirement Center and its sprawling grounds as being where Christy's Grandpa Charlie resided. "Took him and some of his friends from there out on the catamaran for dolphin watching a couple months ago," he mentioned.

She thought about how much such an excursion had probably meant to the older people, even if Reece's casual tone implied that it was just another boat trip. "It's nice that you're so giving in ways like that," she told him.

He replied by glancing over from his spot behind the captain's wheel, one eyebrow lifted. "What, you aren't going to tell me I should be charging them for it?" Amusement glimmered in his gaze, but she also understood that he was really asking.

"Well, not with elderly people who are probably subsisting on a small, fixed income," she said, eyes widened to remind him that he should understand by now that she wasn't heartless. "And I suppose it's none of my concern what you charge anyone for anything anyway." Wow, she really was mellowing the past few days. What was it? Reece? The cat? Coral Cove in general? She wasn't sure but went on to say, "I was just thinking like a businessperson because that's how my brain works. But if you don't want to make your boats a business, who am I to shove it down your throat?"

Now his eyes narrowed on her in full suspicion. "Who *are* you and what have you done with Camille Thompson?"

She threw her head back in laughter, then informed him, "I guess I'm just starting to look at some things from a different perspective."

Although he still appeared playfully wary, his expression softened as he said, "Well, that's refreshing to hear. And speaking of getting new perspectives . . ." He lowered his chin slightly, his gaze inquisitive. "Do you still hate when I call you Cami?"

She shook her head and answered honestly. "I guess . . . it grew on me or something."

His response was a sexy grin that moved all through her, making her heart beat faster.

Wow? Still? He can affect me that way just with a smile? As his attention shifted back to the waters before them, she watched him, felt that invisible connection flowing between them even now, and couldn't help thinking how many unanticipated surprises had awaited her in this little town.

"Want to help me put the sails up?" he asked, rising from his seat. Until now, he'd used the boat's motor, explaining to Cami it was easier that way until they were out in open water.

"Sure," she said. "Just tell me what to do."

Reece unfurled a white sail, instructing her, "Okay, grab on to that line to your right and pull it tight—and hold it until I can walk over and show you how to tie it."

And as she knotted it the way Reece taught her a minute later, ending with a small sense of accomplishment, she thought: *God, he's right—who am I?* The woman who'd marched into the Happy Crab in her red power suit a week and a half ago would never have been interested in learning to raise a sail or tie a sailor's knot. She wouldn't have loved the wind whipping through her hair and she would have found the burst of sea spray that misted over her face just then downright offensive.

This place—this man—has broadened your horizons, expanded who you are when you least expected it. She found herself smiling over at him, thinking he'd given her an enormous gift—one she hadn't even known she wanted.

Once the sails were hoisted, Reece turned off the boat's motor and informed her they were officially sailing. After that, they drifted up the coastline, Reece pointing out other towns and landmarks along the way.

When he turned the boat directly out into the vast gulf waters, pointing the bow toward the horizon, he told her they'd soon come upon a tiny uninhabited island he knew of. She'd had no idea islands like that really existed, but Reece said, "Sometimes they pop up after a hurricane and disappear after the next. Or sometimes they last a while. This one's been here as long as I can remember, but there's a lot more vegetation now than when I was a kid."

As the little island came into view, Cami spotted a small, sandy beach flanked by palm trees and low-lying brush. "Palm trees grow that tall that fast?" she asked, surprised.

Reece nodded. "Some species grow one to two feet a year."

"Can we visit it?" she wondered out loud. "Walk around?"

Flashing another of his intoxicating grins, Reece said, "You read my mind, Tink. Thought we'd have lunch there and go for a swim."

Although she couldn't pinpoint exactly what was different than before, the next couple of hours felt more romantic than anything Cami had experienced in a long while—maybe ever. Reece had brought a blanket and a picnic basket with sandwiches, some fruit, and a bottle of wine complete with two wineglasses. Somehow even taking the sloop's inflatable dinghy from the boat to the beach was fun. The beach wasn't as tidy as Coral Cove's—sprinkled with bits of shell and driftwood and other sea things—but she liked how natural it was, liked being someplace she figured not many other feet had tread.

She'd worn her bathing suit under her shorts and tank top, so as Reece had suggested, after they ate, they ventured hand-in-hand into the relatively calm water to cool off. Soon they went in deeper, playing and splashing and leaping over the waves.

Before long, Cami found herself with her arms wrapped around his neck and her legs wrapped around his waist—and that was when he carried her back into the more shallow, calmer waters near the shore until he stood about waist deep. And when he began to kiss her. And when he began going hard against the tender spot between her legs.

"Oh . . ." she breathed between kisses, loving the way he felt. Loving being held completely aloft in the water that way, so that she couldn't have drawn back from his body even if she'd tried.

"Just when you thought this day couldn't get any better," he said with a teasing arrogance.

And she laughed. "You and the water again," she pointed out.

"Maybe it's *you* and water again," he countered. "Seems like you've brought out some new water-sex-loving side of me or something."

An idea that turned her on even a little more than she already was. So rather than continue playing around, she leaned near his ear and murmured, "I want you."

His hands cupped her ass already, and now he squeezed, the sensation it created echoing all through her, just as he promised, low and raspy, "You're about to have me, honey."

A moment later, her bikini bottoms were pulled aside and he was entering her, making her feel wonderfully full with him beneath the mid-day sun in their private little paradise. "Oh God," she breathed as the pleasure expanded through her, and then she followed the instinct to grind against him, find her rhythm, something primitive and wild. And she let herself go completely in his arms because he made her feel safe that way, like she could release all her inhibitions and let every ounce of herself flow freely without any fears.

Almost as soon as she came, he followed, and as he drove up into her in gloriously hard thrusts, she leaned her head back and drank in the relentless heat and passion he spilled into her.

Afterward, they kissed, and he whispered, "You make water more fun, Tink."

And she said, "So do you, Reecie Cup."

He laughed at the silly name, and they proceeded, hand in hand, back up onto the beach, where they stretched out on the blanket to soak up some sun.

They left the little island around two in the afternoon but agreed they weren't yet ready to venture back. Cami didn't know if Reece was feeling the same as her, but she liked being alone with him like this, feeling a little isolated, secluded, like they were the only two people in the world. Although she'd brought her cell phone out of habit, she'd realized earlier that they were out of range, and while that would normally make her feel cut off from civilization, right now it suited her just fine. Reece was all she needed to fill her day.

When she first noticed she hadn't seen any land in a while, she suffered a twinge of uneasiness, but quickly let it go, deciding that just made it all the more a grand adventure. And if Reece was unfazed by the distance between the boat and the shore, then so was she.

After a while, he let the boat just drift, stretching out to relax with her on the deck in the sun, listening to music on the radio. Eventually, she was so relaxed she fell asleep.

And when she awoke a while later, she found herself staring up at the tall white sails looming overhead—and at Reece, now on his feet.

Only . . . did he look worried? She squinted, then sat up to better see his expression. "Something wrong?" she asked, still trying to get fully awake.

Reece struck her as more serious than usual,

peering slowly to the right and then to the left out over the ocean. "Not really," he said. "Just seems like we're becalmed now."

"Becalmed?"

"No wind," he explained, adding, "but no biggie," as he walked toward the boat's stern. "That's why we have a motor."

Getting to her feet, she watched as Reece turned a key near the captain's wheel, then pressed a button—same as he'd done to start the boat earlier. The engine behind the *Lisa Renee* began to crank . . . slowly—very slowly. But . . . maybe that was normal? Though she thought his expression still held too much concern.

"Then why do you look so grim?" she asked.

And it was then that the motor ceased cranking at all, going completely silent.

And Reece said, "Because now something's wrong."

Sometimes, though not often, he had dreams,
and they were more painful than the dreams of
the other boys.

J. M. Barrie, *Peter and Wendy*

Chapter 18

REECE'S STOMACH dropped like a stone. Part of him was trying not to overreact, not to treat this like some unsolvable tragedy, but . . . Jesus Christ. Had he really not checked the wind report? Had he not tested the motor? Sure, he'd used it to depart the dock and it had seemed fine then, but clearly he should have run it longer after letting the boat sit unused. Had he really brought Cami out here into the middle of the ocean without taking some simple precautions to ensure getting her back? How the hell had he let something like this happen?

His natural instinct was not to let his distress show. And he was pretty well-practiced at staying calm, not letting the bad shit leak out through his eyes. As his gut tightened, he ran a hand back through his hair, wrapping his mind around the situation, and then stated the obvious. "Engine's dead."

Cami looked uncertain—like she was trying not to panic. "What could cause that?" But he heard what she was really asking: *How big of a deal is it and can we fix it and get home?*

Reece thought through possibilities. "Could be any number of things. Bad battery. Corroded wiring. Starter gone bad. No way to know for sure until I can have some tests run on the engine. Not gas, though. I filled the tank this morning." For good measure, he pressed the start button again and this time the sloop's diesel engine made no noise at all.

"The wind might pick up," he informed Cami. "But in case it doesn't, I'll radio for help."

Relief washed over her face at his words and he was glad he could put her at ease. But it didn't make him like this situation any better. And though a lot of sailors might wait patiently for the wind to return—because it very well might, any moment now—he instead headed straight for the boat's small cabin, which held the same two-way radio it had when his dad bought the boat.

The truth was, remembering how to operate it would be guesswork. His dad had kept them all well-versed on it back in the day, but it had been a damn long time now. And then an awful thought hit him—what if it doesn't work? What if it's too old or something? He frequently made sure the radio on the catamaran was in good working order, even though he seldom had to use it, either, but he hadn't looked at this one in a very long time.

He glanced over his shoulder to see that Cami had stayed on deck. Good. Less pressure to look like he had this situation completely under control.

Strange—usually he felt like he did have situations under control. But maybe it was this boat, its history—maybe he'd been right in the first place and taking it out had been a bad idea. Had he really not performed more thorough checks? When it hadn't been on the water in ages? What the hell had he been thinking?

You were thinking about Cami and her coral bikini and about what to pack for lunch, and you were busy finding a bottle of wine and making sure you brought a corkscrew and decent glasses. You were busy trying to impress a woman.

He shook his head at the inanity of it. Especially since, on one hand, he still didn't know if he should be *trying* to impress her—because he still wasn't 100 percent certain what her motives were with him. And on the other hand, if she was completely sincere in terms of their relationship, he didn't think he *needed* to impress her—he thought she liked him for who he was. He couldn't remember, in fact, the last time he'd done something to impress a girl. Which must mean—*you're really into this one. You're* really, really *into her.*

Damn. How had that happened so fast?

But he didn't have time to examine that question right now.

Turning on the radio, he was happy to hear it buzz to life. And after picking up the handheld microphone, he let himself think back, feel his way through it, turn the knobs and dials that made it connect to someone out there.

"Hail Tow Boat U.S.," he said, calling for the national towing company. "Hail Tow Boat U.S. This is the *Lisa Renee* hailing Tow Boat U.S."

He went quiet then, waiting for a reply, aware of his own heartbeat.

And just when he'd begun to fear a reply wasn't coming—it did. The towing company answered, and he explained his situation. And he was told they'd be happy to tow them in, but that unfortunately it might take a while. "Whole area's becalmed," the man on the other end informed him in a Texan accent. "Lotta calls for help all along the coast. You good with food and water?"

Hell—it was gonna take so long that they were worried about his food and water supply? "Good for how long?" he asked.

"Unless the winds pick up, probably morning."

Damn it, he hadn't expected that. And this made things . . . a little more serious. They wouldn't starve or anything, but they might actually get hungry. "Good on water," he said, because he'd packed a cooler with plenty, thank God. "Less good on food, though." There were some snack chips they hadn't eaten and a couple of bananas.

"We'll get to ya as fast as we can, partner," the voice on the radio said. "Just stay hydrated and hold tight."

"Will do," Reece said. Trying to sound cool about it. Not so much for himself, but for Cami.

Because she'd trusted him to take care of her today, trusted him to know how, and he'd done a shitty job. And it just brought back too many bad memories. Apparently making *better* memories on this boat was easier said than done.

He took a deep breath as he exited the cabin back out into the bright, hot sun and met her expectant gaze. He tried to appear calmer than he felt when he said, "Good news and bad news. The good is that the towing company will come if the wind doesn't pick up before they get here. The bad is that we're not the only stranded boaters and they probably can't reach us 'til morning."

"Oh," she said, and he saw her trying to be calm, too. But he still felt shitty.

"We have plenty of water," he informed her, "but less food. Dinner will be bananas and Fritos. Breakfast will be more Fritos."

"I . . . like Fritos," she offered softly, hopefully.

And he appreciated that, but . . . hell. "I'm sorry, Tink," he told her. "So damn sorry." He shook his head, shut his eyes. "I screwed up and now we're both paying for it."

"It's all right, Reece," she told him, her voice so gentle—so different than the woman he'd first met—that he thought she must sense his anger at the situation. And indeed it was building inside him, like a bubble filled with something toxic, expanding, growing bigger and bigger.

Until it burst and he punched his fist into the padded captain's seat to let some of it out.

Then he looked over at her, a little embarrassed that he'd done that right in front of her. Maybe he wasn't so good at hiding his emotions after all.

"Sorry," he said again—then ran both hands

back through his hair. After which he stalked away from her, toward the front of the boat, just because he didn't want to keep letting her see how distraught he was, and the only way he knew right now was to get out of her direct line of vision.

Reaching the bow, he sat down on the deck, against the railing, looked up at the blue sky now dotted with flat, white clouds, and felt how hot it was without the usual wind at sea. He planted his feet out in front of him, knees bent, legs spread slightly, and leaned his head into his hands. *Just stay cool, man. Quit remembering. Don't go back there. This isn't that. This is so fucking far from that that it's stupid to even let one remind you of the other.*

And yet . . . it *was* reminding him. And his heart beat too fast. And he could almost feel the shock of it again, the horrific loss, taking over his body, shutting him down.

"Reece, I don't see how this is your fault. Why are you so upset about this?"

He looked up. Shit, she'd followed him. And it struck him anew how beautiful she was. And how he wished they were safe and sound, back on dry ground, and that he'd never let her down. He hated letting anyone down.

"I mean, I know it's far from ideal," she said, "but it'll be fine, won't it? They'll come for us, even if it's not until tomorrow. It's not that big of a thing."

"Maybe I just don't like the idea of floating around out here helplessly," he snapped at her. "Maybe I don't like feeling I can't take care of myself, or you. A person shouldn't be on the water if they can't be a responsible sailor." He knew he'd spoken the words with too much vehemence, but there was no calling them back.

Cami had never seen Reece like this before. What had happened to her slightly arrogant but easygoing beach bum? What had happened to her sexy, playful lover?

"I'll be fine, I promise," she told him, wanting to make him feel better. "And you're perfectly responsible. Sometimes things just happen, that's all."

He looked up at her. "I should have checked the motor, I should have checked the wind report. I *always* check the weather before I go out on the ocean—*always*. It's completely irresponsible not to."

With that, he pushed to his feet, turned to face the water, and wrapped his hands around the white railing, appearing more distressed than she would've even believed he could. He seemed to get lost in the view then, looking as if he were suddenly somewhere far away. And when he spoke, it came out so low that she wasn't sure he'd actually meant to say the words out loud. "I thought maybe this would fix things. But maybe some things just can't be fixed."

"What are you talking about?" she asked gently. "What are you trying to fix?"

He let out a sigh, didn't look at her as he murmured, "Nothing." Then shook his head.

Cami couldn't help feeling suddenly uncomfortable. This wasn't the Reece she knew. She'd seen different sides of him—the friendly, laid-back side; the cocky, confident side; the seductive and even surprisingly romantic side—but she'd never seen a dark side, and what had fallen over him now struck her as so dark that it conflicted with the bright sun shining down on them as it began to dip slowly toward the horizon.

What is so very wrong, Reece? Because yeah, she knew this situation was troubling—she wouldn't even deny that it really sucked—but his eyes right now . . . his eyes conveyed something far worse than what they were experiencing.

She had a feeling this had something to do with the loss of his parents, but she wasn't sure how it all fit together. And she wanted to know. But not because she wanted to use the information to get him to sell the Happy Crab—she wanted to know because she cared about him. And she wondered what he'd been through. She sincerely wondered what kept him holding on to a place that was dying. And what else he might be holding on to too tight. Upon meeting Reece Donovan, she'd have thought he was the last man who'd be harboring secrets, and yet she had a feeling there were even more of them than she'd realized up to now.

So finally she decided to say what she was thinking. "You know, I'm not the only complex one here. For a guy who's usually so relaxed, there's a lot more happening inside you underneath the surface."

At this, he looked up, clearly snapping out of his malaise—or trying to anyway, trying to act normal. "Not really," he said. "I'm an open book—what you see is what you get."

But she wasn't buying that. And she supposed her eyes said so, because after they exchanged a long, almost uncomfortable look, he tried to excuse his reaction. "I'm just worried about Fifi," he claimed.

She raised her eyebrows emphatically, silently expressing her skepticism.

But he argued, "There's more to owning a giant iguana than you'd think. I'm just hoping Riley realizes we're not back and feeds her and makes sure she's in for the night and cleans up after her. It's important."

She tilted her head. "Why?"

"Most iguanas can carry a strain of salmonella," he explained. "I get her tested a lot, and she's being doing fine lately, but I still have to be sanitary with her. I'm pretty careful about it—I just don't make a big deal of it because I don't want people to worry needlessly."

"That's why you made sure I washed my hands after I petted her," she realized.

He nodded.

Finding out there was more to being an iguana parent than met the eye, and that it sounded like a lot of work, made her remember, "She really is lucky to have you."

"Thanks," he said quietly, but she could see that his thoughts had already turned back to their predicament—and despite having learned something interesting about Fifi, hers now came back to his overreaction to it all. And to what she really wanted to find out, what she really wanted him to *want* to tell her.

So she carefully considered her next move for a long moment before saying pleasantly, "Tell me about your family."

"Didn't we already have that conversation?"

"Yes," she said. "But I mean . . . the parts you didn't say. There's more to know about your family than your dad losing his hair and you getting a puppy."

She could sense him weighing *his* words, too—looking into his warm eyes, she could practically see the thoughts and memories flying around behind them. Finally, he told her, "Okay, you want to know more—here's some more. We loved the beach. We lived in a little house on Sea Shell Lane—and it was small, but perfect for us because we didn't need much. We ran the Crab with my uncle and it was like my second home growing up. The beach was, too.

"We loved to go sailing, all four of us, even though my mom never learned much about it— she just liked to come along for the ride, and she always said it was the one time when she let the rest of us do all the work and take care of *her*, not the other way around. My mom and dad were great parents, and my sister and I were close. It was . . . a pretty great life." He concluded with an affirming nod. And she'd noticed that while he'd started out sounding terse, the longer he'd spoken, the more sincere and . . . perhaps reverent he'd become.

Even so, though, all Cami could hear was one word, the one he'd said over and over again. *Was, was, was.* Everything in past tense. And she knew his parents were gone now, so maybe the past tense made perfect sense—but why wouldn't he just tell her? "Was?" she asked.

"What about *your* family?" he shot at her instead of responding to what she'd said. "You haven't exactly told me much, either, you know." Now he'd resumed sounding tense, defensive, and it was an obvious attempt to change the subject.

But that was fine. Maybe if she opened up to him, maybe if she told him the hard parts of *her* life . . . he'd tell her the hard parts of his. And she wasn't even sure why she wanted to *put* them through anything hard, but when you cared for someone, she was coming to realize, it just made sense to share your life with them, to share your-*self* with them—the ups and downs, the good and the bad.

"I don't talk about this a lot," she said, "but okay, I'll tell you about my family."

Then she sat back down on the blanket where she'd been sunning and sleeping only a little while ago, and she again lay back on it and closed her eyes. Because this *was* hard, and it was the kind of hard she didn't consider herself very good at, so shutting her eyes made it a little easier.

"I told you I was raised in Michigan," she started, "but the stuff I didn't tell you is . . . my parents were . . . unhappy people. My father worked at the same factory as his father, and his father before him, scraping to get by, being fairly miserable and bitter, feeling that life is just a thing you struggle to get through.

"And that's what they taught me, he and my

mom both. That no matter how hard you work, you never have enough. That life is about money, and that if you don't have it, you can't be happy. I think my mother actually had higher hopes at one point, when she was young—she wanted to go to college and become a teacher—but then she married my dad and I guess she became resigned to living a hard, thankless sort of life, too.

"They spent twenty years together thinking they couldn't have children, but then they did—me. All in all, though, I'm pretty sure I was a disappointment to my dad because I wasn't a boy. And like I said, there was never any money to spare—no fancy presents, no dresses for school dances, no money to go see a movie with my friends. At least until I turned sixteen and was able to get a job. And to be honest, I don't know why they even wanted kids—they were already very set in their ways by the time I came along, and . . . content to be discontent, I guess would be a good way to describe them."

She stopped for a moment, realizing how quickly thinking back on her girlhood could deliver her back there, even still. She was so different now, so evolved from that life—and yet she supposed some things never left you and were actually as near as just closing your eyes.

So now she opened them, peering up at the blue sky and white clouds above the boat. She would tell him the rest, but maybe it was easier to do so remembering that it was in the past, that she wasn't there anymore, and that being stranded on a boat with a guy she was crazy about was far preferable to being stranded in a disheartening life you couldn't escape.

"They weren't people who . . . celebrated anything in life," she went on. "We never had a birthday party—barely even a birthday cake. We never had a dog or a cat, and I didn't have friends over. And again, I think my mother would have been a different person, a happier person, without him, but he wore her down, made her *be* like him.

"My dad always pressed me to work very hard, but in a way that made me feel like I owed him, like I was supposed to make a lot of money someday so he could finally rest, like I was supposed to pay him back for supporting me or something. So there was a lot of pressure to make good grades and never have too much fun or take life too lightly.

"Going away to college freed me, showed me how much more hope life could hold. Or . . . maybe I always knew deep down and was just glad to find out I was right. I was convinced that if I worked hard and worked smart that I could get a good job, but one that would be about *more* than just money—one that would let me be *happier* than they were, too.

"And so I did that. And I moved far away. And I found a new sort of family at Vanderhook. And if it seems like I take my job pretty seriously, it's because . . . because it's important to me to have financial security, and also because . . . it's really all I have. And . . ." She still stared up into a wide blue sky and took in the hugeness of it. "And this isn't so bad, Reece. Being stuck on a boat, even if we get a little hungry, even if it takes a little while to get rescued—it's just not so bad. I mean, look at the sky. It's incredible. And it looks far more incredible from this spot, right here, than it ever did from my front yard growing up. I just couldn't *see* anything there. Not clearly. But now . . . now I'm able to see the beauty in things."

Oh boy. Had she really just gotten that maudlin about her past? Had she really just completely spilled her guts that way? Once she'd gotten started, it was like having turned on a faucet she couldn't turn off. *I went way, way too far there. Ugh, I'm pathetic.*

That's when Reece's handsome, unshaven face appeared above her, blocking out the blue. But she didn't mind—he was the one thing that looked better to her right now than a beautiful swath of sky. "I'm sorry, Tink," he said.

She blinked up at him, a little dazed from her confession combined with the late day heat. "Sorry? But you didn't—"

He interrupted her. "I'm sorry you had to go through that, sorry you didn't have a great family, sorry you didn't have a great life growing up." He took her hand, squeezed gently, sweetly. "I'm just . . . sorry. Because it sounds really shitty. And you didn't deserve that. And . . . I guess it makes me see how far you've come, and how really amazing you are."

She blinked again, this time as she absorbed the unexpected compliment, and then tried to reclaim a little of the dignity she feared she'd let get away from her these last few minutes. "I . . . I'm not one to feel sorry for myself—it *was* what it *was*, nothing more, nothing less. I just . . . wanted to make sure you know that I'm not upset to be stuck out here. In the big picture of my life, it's . . . nothing. It's truly fine. And . . ." She managed a small laugh for him as she added, "I really do like Fritos. So it's all okay."

Reece peered down on her. From the moment they'd met, he'd thought she was beautiful. But right now, he thought her so much more beautiful than ever before. It was one thing to have a pretty face, a rockin' body. It was nice to be likable and fun and funny and sweet. And it was admirable to take your job seriously and do it with passion. But it was another to have all those qualities when you were set up for failure, when life could have more easily made you cold and angry and heartless. So to know she'd responded to that situation by becoming the person she was just made him all the more in awe of her.

And God—she'd really . . . told him stuff. Serious stuff. And he had a feeling if he asked her more, she'd answer—openly. She'd laid herself bare before him—in a different way than previously, in a way that went way beyond the nakedness of sex.

And maybe that meant . . . it would be okay. To tell her *his* stuff. To tell her the real reason getting stranded at sea was eating into his soul. God knew he didn't want to think about it, of course. But the fact was . . . she probably hadn't wanted to think about the stuff *she* just had, either. And since it was already boring into his gut, it wasn't like he hadn't already gone there in his head.

He'd let her see there was something wrong, reactions he usually kept buried deep—so he supposed it only made sense that she'd asked him about it. Maybe he should just appreciate the fact that she cared. Enough that she'd just shown him maybe she wasn't always quite as strong as she liked to act in certain ways.

And yeah, he'd seen her softer sides before, but this . . . this was different. This was openness. This was trust. This was . . . being real.

But . . . he didn't even know how to begin. She might not talk about her past much, but he was betting she did it more often than him. Around Coral Cove, people *knew* his past and they were polite enough not to bring it up. And the women in his life since then had all been transient, never around long enough to get into this stuff—and hell, maybe that was why he liked it that way; vacation flings didn't ask big questions.

His heartbeat had slowed as he'd listened to her talk, but now it picked up again. So he stood up and walked to the rear of the boat where the rest of the food and water was stashed. He opened the cooler and took out two bottles of water, then grabbed up the large bag of Fritos he'd brought along but which they hadn't yet opened.

Returning, he tossed the bag down on the blanket next to her, then handed her one of the waters. "Since you like these so much, figured we'd have dinner." He tried to say it in his usual jocular way, tried to give her a grin, but wasn't sure either effort succeeded.

She was still nice enough to reward him with

a small smile anyway. "Thanks," she said quietly, opening the water and taking a drink.

"I . . . appreciate you being so cool about this," he told her, sitting down across from her on the blanket.

She just shook her head, fluffing it off. "It's really fine. Like I said, I'd rather be stuck on a boat all night with you and some corn chips than stuck back in Nowheresville, Michigan—trust me."

He managed a little chuckle this time, a sincere one, as he said to her, "Nowheresville—that's the official name of your hometown?"

She smiled in response. "Yeah—ever heard of it?"

And they laughed a bit, and their eyes met, and he got a little crazier about her than he already was.

He wordlessly tore into the Fritos bag and held it out for her to reach in, and they both began to feast on the chips. And without warning or prelude the words left him. "My family is gone."

"Gone," she repeated, her eyes calm but wide and intense on him.

"Dead," he clarified. It was a harsh word—he felt a little stabbing sensation in his chest to say it, even now—but it was the fact. They'd been dead a long time now.

He sensed her tensing slightly. "I'm sorry," she said quickly, softly.

And he could almost feel the sweetness and care in her eyes, but he didn't dare look there, not right now. "It's . . . it's okay. It was a long time ago."

"Your . . . whole family?" she asked. "Even your sister?"

He nodded. And the very air around them seemed to hold a weight it hadn't before. Their silence was thick with the reality he'd just laid out between them.

"But . . ." she began slowly, "it's not . . . really okay, is it?"

He drew in his breath, tried not to react to that. "Like I said, it was a long time ago. Ten years."

Cami pulled in her breath. Something about hearing him tell her even this much made her begin to feel his heartbreak. "But if it was okay," she told him gently, "it wouldn't be so difficult to talk about. And . . . I'd like to know about it if you want to tell me, but if you'd rather not, Reece, I won't press. I don't want to make anything worse."

"No, it's all right," he insisted again quickly. And he wasn't even sure where the words came from or why they'd tumbled from him so instantaneously.

Maybe it was a gut reaction, a defense mechanism—maybe he didn't want to appear weak before her. Or . . . maybe deep inside, there was some part of him that just wanted to be real with her, too.

"The thing is," he began, aware that the sky was changing now, that the first hints of twilight were upon them, "it happened here, on this boat."

She sat up a little straighter at the news. "Oh. Wow. Now I get why you don't bring it out much." Then she cringed. "And I'm sorry if I twisted your arm on that."

But he shook his head. "No—you didn't. I decided it was a good thing to do." Then he stopped, rolled his eyes. "Maybe not the best decision I ever made, but it was mine."

"What happened? To your family, Reece?"

He met her concerned gaze only briefly, then had to look down. The truth was—he didn't mind telling her, didn't mind her knowing. He supposed he trusted her now. But none of that made it easy to talk about, and the more time had passed, the less he'd been required to do that with anyone. Once upon a time he'd had set, simple, rehearsed things to say about it, things he could spit out by rote. Only now he'd gotten rusty.

So all he could really do was . . . tell her. As best he could.

"I was twenty-five. Lisa was twenty-one and had just come home after graduating from the University of Florida. She wanted to take the boat out to celebrate. Both of us were dating people seriously at the time, but she wanted it to be just the four of us, the family. I remember joking with them . . ." His mind drifted back and he could hear them all laughing together in the kitchen of the cottage on Sea Shell Lane. "I was saying, 'It's always Lisa, Lisa, Lisa.' But I really didn't feel that way at all. I was proud of her.

"Anyway, my uncle Barry had just died about six months earlier—heart attack at forty-nine. I'd moved into his old apartment at the Crab to officially take over as manager—but we were all still getting over *that* loss and she thought the outing would be good for us, as a family. It was the first time since he'd died that things were starting to feel kind of normal and happy again."

He let his gaze drop to the blanket they sat on, to the fabric that stretched between them. "But it didn't turn out very happy after all." Then he took a deep breath. Damn, this sucked to remember. Why wasn't he used to it now? Why wasn't he immune to it after all this time? "Because I let them down."

Her voice came in a whisper, like it pained her to ask him. "How?"

It still shamed him, even now. "I forgot. I just fucking forgot. *Everything.* First off, I was supposed to check the weather. It was my job when we sailed, always—I checked it to make sure it was okay. But I forgot and didn't do it, and they assumed it was fine. And then I even . . ." he stopped, shook his head " . . . actually forgot to show up. Just plain forgot we were going. I was with my girlfriend, having fun, not paying attention to the time. And so Lisa left a note telling me they'd waited for an hour and were going without me since I obviously didn't care enough to be there. I was . . . a little less responsible back then. And if I'd shown up on time, they wouldn't have died."

"But . . ." It was clear that last part had thrown her—she wasn't sure what to ask now.

And since he'd started this, he owed it to her to tell her the rest without making her any more uncomfortable. "A storm came. A bad storm. They might have known about it from the weather radio on the boat, but the Coast Guard thinks they just couldn't outrun it. They were capable enough sailors—they had the safety equipment. All three of them were found wearing their lifejackets and Lisa's safety line had even been attached, but had broken." He stopped then, shook his head. Still, after all this time, it was hard to believe they'd died. His dad and Lisa had both been good sailors. And storms in the gulf weren't usually that big, or deadly.

"But my dad had a bad knee from an old injury," he explained, "and he was walking with a limp at the time—he'd twisted it somehow the week before. And Mom, like I said . . ." He shook his head again. "She'd never learned anything about sailing.

"And as for Dad and Lisa . . . I'm not sure, they might have just panicked. When you head out on the boat on a sunny day, the same as dozens of times before, you don't think about freak storms. You're not ready for it mentally. We'd seldom gotten caught out in storms, and never a really bad one. I've spent a lot of time imagining what that might have been like, thinking about how freaking powerful nature can be." His heartbeat increased again just remembering the sobering horror of how helpless they'd surely felt, how frightened.

Only then did he raise his eyes back to Cami.

"We'd been on the water our whole lives—and so this shouldn't have happened. But it did." His stomach went hollow as he sank a little deeper into the memories. And he had to pull in another deep breath and let it back out to go on. He let his eyes drop away from hers again, let himself peer blankly past her, past the boat's railings, out to sea. "And if I'd remembered, if I'd been on time, if I'd been out there with them, they wouldn't have died." His chest tightened as he sank a little deeper into guilt.

"But . . . why are you so sure of that? Why are you so sure you could've saved them all?"

Another deep breath, in, out. "I wouldn't have panicked. I could've reacted quicker. I knew exactly where the safety lines were and could have gotten everyone hooked to the boat."

"But you said Lisa's was broken," she interrupted.

"I would have saved her anyway," he insisted too forcefully. "I would have saved them all!"

Reece met Cami's gaze just briefly then, but pulled it back down. There was something about sharing this—sharing it so completely—that left him unable to look into her pretty eyes. So he let his fall shut again—like some sort of defense mechanism that made it all seem a little more like a dream, a little more like he was alone just thinking through it than actually telling someone. Telling someone, seeing their reaction . . . now he remembered why he didn't do it often. Telling it made it so real. Telling it made it happen all over again.

And yet he went on. He was almost done. And deep down he knew there was some value to purging it from his soul a little more, even if it wasn't easy.

"When they weren't back by dark, I knew

something bad had happened. I remember sitting on the dock behind the Crab, watching, waiting, my stomach tied in knots because I knew they hadn't planned to be out that long. I'd checked the weather by then—I knew there'd been storms offshore. But I still kept waiting to see the boat's lights coming in to the bay. I waited and I waited. Only they never came."

Letting out another breath, he ran a hand back through his hair. The water was so calm now, the surface as close to glass as the sea ever got. Hard to believe it was the same ocean that had swallowed up his parents and sister in some unpredictable fit of rage that had served no purpose.

That was it—the end of his story, all he wanted to say about it. The aftermath didn't matter. Seeing the boat towed in with broken rigging and a tattered sail . . . the outpouring of compassion and love from the community . . . the empty months that followed where he hadn't quite known what to do with himself and couldn't even fall asleep to escape the reality . . . the fact that slowly, somehow, life had gone on and he'd pulled himself together and just started acting normal again, like the guy he'd been before it had all happened. And he *was* that guy—he just had a lot less now than he'd started out with.

Cami reached out to touch his hand. "You know, don't you," she began, "that there's no way to know if you could have made a difference."

"I was young, strong, able-bodied, quick-thinking."

"But you can't know how bad that storm was.

You can't know exactly what happened. You can't be sure. So you should stop blaming yourself."

"I could have at least checked the fucking weather. And I'm still pretty sure if I'd been there that—"

"Reece, sometimes things just happen," she cut him off. "And it's nobody's fault. Just like that engine not starting. You couldn't have predicted it. You couldn't have changed it. It's not your fault. The motor not starting isn't your fault, and what happened back then, that wasn't your fault either. And your family wouldn't want you to blame yourself."

He stayed silent for a long moment . . . because he felt the truth in her words. A little anyway. "Probably not," he replied, his voice so low it was barely audible.

"Reece, I really am so sorry about asking you to take me on the boat," she burst out then. And she looked so remorseful that he felt compelled to put a stop to it. He didn't mind a slight change of subject, either.

"No, seriously—if I'm gonna *keep* the boat, I should *use* the boat. Otherwise, I should get rid of it. I went to the trouble of getting it repaired back then, I've kept up with the maintenance on it, and I should take it out."

"But you . . ."

He met her gaze. "I what?"

She hesitated, then spoke more softly. "You kept your family's house, too, didn't you?"

When he didn't answer right away, she looked a little guilty and said, "Juanita mentioned she cleans a house for you that no one lives in, that's all."

He felt . . . caught at something. But that was ridiculous. "I just . . . never decided for sure what to do with it. For a while thought I might want to move back in." He shook his head. "But then I just kind of stopped thinking about it."

Her eyes stayed locked with his. And he could almost read her unspoken thoughts. *You've paid someone to clean it for ten years but you stopped thinking about it?*

"Maybe you . . . just don't want to let go of the past, leave it behind," she said gently. "I can understand not wanting to give it up. I mean . . . it sounds like such a *good* past."

He nodded, just a bit. About the last part, not the first. "It *was* a good past." Then he really thought through what she'd said. "I guess it's just that . . . it was their *lives*. Their lives are in that house. And in the motel. And in this boat, and the catamaran, too. I guess it just feels . . . wrong—disrespectful or something—to . . . go dismantling their lives that way."

"I get it," she said. "I guess . . . if you leave everything the way it was, it's kind of like . . . things haven't changed completely. Kind of like your own . . . Never-Never Land."

Cami couldn't tell how he'd taken that. She was still reeling from the horrible story he'd shared with her, and she wasn't sure she was doing, saying, the right things. She was trying, though. So she added more—her *own* truth. "Loss is hard. I get wanting to hold on to all the left-over pieces. There are things . . . things I wouldn't know how to let go of, either."

He tilted his head. "Like what?"

She pursed her lips, felt a little weird saying it, comparing the two things. "My job." She shook her head. "I know a job isn't like a family, but . . . like I said, it's the closest thing I have to that—it's pretty much everything to me because I left my family behind. I mean, we keep in touch, but not closely. And I send them some money—paying my dad back, you know." She grimaced slightly, admitting that. "But . . . I guess everybody has to care about *something*, so my job became the thing I care about, the place where I put all my emotional marbles."

And now, now that she'd said it, she felt kind of pathetic. And maybe it would be different if her job was something meaningful. But it wasn't—not really. Not enough for the loyalty she'd invested in it, the importance she'd placed on it.

"I'm sorry," Reece said then, squinting a little from the sun. It was setting now, sending bright blasts of orangy rays across the boat.

She tilted her head. "Sorry?"

"Don't take this the wrong way, Tink," he told her, "but I guess that just sounds kind of sad to me."

Yep, she was pathetic. But she tried to explain by saying, "No, my life before—*that* was sad."

Now he peered at her from beneath shaded lids. "I don't like to think of you being sad."

She tried to lighten the moment. "What will be sad is if I lose my job over you not selling." But then she immediately shook her head. "God, I'm sorry—I didn't say that to try to make you cave or anything. It's because I feel so comfortable with you now—I think I just forgot who I was talking to for a second."

"I'm sorry my decision affects you so much, Tink, I truly am—but I really can't sell. You know why now."

"Can I say something honest," she asked him, "without you thinking it's about my job? Something I really mean from the heart?"

He hesitated slightly, and it made her think—*hell, maybe I shouldn't go there*—but then he said, "Okay." And she felt she had no choice but to follow through with what she'd started.

"I understand now why the Happy Crab is special, but . . . I'm not sure it *stays* special if it's not serving the purpose it was supposed to. And it's none of my business but . . . it seems like you're not moving on. If you keep holding on to the past, you're holding on to the bad parts just as tight as the good. And I promise that I'm not saying that to try to get you to sell, Reece. I'm saying it because you're a pretty incredible guy. And I think you could be living a better, happier life. You deserve a life as wonderful as *you* are."

She touched his hand again, but she couldn't read his expression. And she worried about the things she'd just said. Maybe they hadn't come out right. There was nothing wrong with the life he was living—she just didn't want him to make big decisions for the wrong reasons. She didn't want his past, his loss, to hold him back in any way. "I just see . . . so much light in you," she went on, trying to get closer to the truth of what she'd intended. "I wouldn't want anything to keep it from shining as brightly as possible."

She squeezed his hand in hers then—and when he squeezed it back, her heart lurched with relief and affection and a whole other host of happy emotions. And when he looked into her eyes now, she realized his were glassy with emotion. "I appreciate that, Tink—I really do. But the thing is . . . I'm not ready for that. I'm not sure I ever *will* be. Because the motel is . . . the cornerstone of my life, the foundation. All the other cornerstones are gone—they died. So without it . . . I don't know who I'd be anymore." He stopped, sighed, and she felt how much he was opening up to her. "Can you understand that at all?"

She bit her lip, thinking of cornerstones, foundations. And yes—she *could* understand. Because that was how she felt about her job. That was the cornerstone of *her* life. And maybe that sounded shallow to people who had great families or close, lasting friendships, but for her, her job was her life, her job was her family, her job was her security, her job was the thing her existence revolved around.

So in that moment she understood, in a way she hadn't before, even after the story of his family's deaths, exactly how much the Happy Crab meant to him, and that it was a part of him, and that it was the thing that held his life together and gave it meaning and purpose. She understood it to the marrow of her bones, to the core of her soul.

And she understood it so wholly, so deeply, that she knew . . . she knew she had to let it go.

No matter what it meant for her, no matter what the loss might cost her. Whether or not she thought it was practical, or in Reece's ultimate best interest, or anything else—she had to let it go.

And she heard herself whisper the words. "I'll stop now."

He looked up. "What?"

"I'll stop trying to buy the motel. I'm done trying to take it from you."

At that, his face took on a confused look, pure puzzlement, and she knew why. She'd wavered in certain ways with him—she'd let him see sides of her that detracted from her strength, and she'd made herself vulnerable with him over and over without that ever being part of the plan—but she'd never wavered on intending to purchase the Happy Crab. She'd never wavered on being sure she'd find a way to make him sell. Until now.

"I mean it," she told him. "You love it too much. I get that now, really get it, in a way I didn't before. I'm giving in, backing down. Because it's the right thing to do. And because I want you to be happy."

His eyes narrowed slightly then as he leaned a little closer. "But what about you, Tink? What does this mean for your job?"

She blinked, thought, blew out a breath as the reality hit her, a whole *new* reality. "I'm not sure yet. I might lose it." She suffered a sense of uneasiness then, because it made certain things—like her feelings for him—startlingly clear.

"You'd do that for me?" he asked.

And she pursed her lips, gathered another bit of courage, and whispered, "Looks that way."

She glanced down, feeling oddly bashful now, until he reached out, using one bent finger to lift her chin. When their gazes met again, his face close to hers, he said, "That's the biggest, nicest gift anyone's ever given me."

She was having trouble breathing now. Because he was right—it was an *enormous* gift. And it was from her heart. Which she felt like she'd just reached into her chest and pulled out to hold in her palm between them, for him to do with whatever he would. Talk about feeling vulnerable. But she tried for a smile, and said softly, "Do I get a thank-you?"

His eyes warmed on her and he leaned in to give her a slow, tingly hot kiss that reverberated all through her body. "How's that?" he asked deeply.

"It's a good start," she said. "Now keep going."

" . . . I mean to keep you."

J. M. Barrie, *Peter and Wendy*

Chapter 19

As REECE smoothly laid her back on the blanket, she glanced toward the horizon, now ablaze with streaks of pink and a dusky, darkening sky above, and said absently, "We missed the sunset."

"Doesn't matter—the sun sets every night." And hovering over her, he pointed a finger up and down her body to say, "Right now I'm a little more interested in what's going on over here."

"Oh . . ." she breathed, liking the sound of that, just before his mouth melded back to hers, setting off a fresh flare of desire in her bikini bottoms.

Of course, when his palm covered her breast and his thumb began to stroke its way across her nipple through her top, pleasure erupted there, too. And oh Lord, she wanted him. She'd *always* wanted him, and God knows every time they'd done it she'd wanted him, but something about *this time, now,* surpassed all that. *Maybe it's because of what you just gave him. Maybe it's about surrender.*

Maybe surrender and the way you want him are the exact same thing.

She threaded her fingers through his hair, then ran her hands over his shoulders, arms, as she kissed him back with all the passion inside her. She let her fingernails scrape lightly across his skin and loved the hot, low groan it drew from his throat. And when he untied her bikini top behind her neck and drew it down, baring her breasts to the evening air, she felt . . . free.

She knew no one would see them; she knew the vastness of the gulf was as private as any bedroom and that doing it in the pool behind the Happy Crab had definitely been much more risky—but something about being with him like this, here, made her feel even wilder and more impassioned. She felt the depth and the breadth of the ocean all around them, and as he kissed his way down onto one breast, then closed his mouth over the beaded tip, it seemed almost as if they were a part of it, a part of nature—and a much better, sweeter part than that which had stolen so much from him.

Soon Reece rained sweet, hot kisses down over her neck, her shoulders, her breasts. And nothing else in the world mattered to Cami but the moment, the connection they shared. Yesterday's hardships, tomorrow's losses—they didn't exist right now. The only thing that existed was being with him, touching him and being touched by him, surrendering the last parts of herself she'd held back until now.

As a bolt of electric energy shot through her, she clamped her hands onto his bare, tan shoulders and pushed hard, rolling him onto his back on the blanket. Even in the dusky air, she saw his eyes go wide and wild at her forceful move. And she loved that. She loved that whatever she chose to do in bed he liked. And fed. And appreciated. Whether she was docile and compliant or taking charge, she could always feel him soaking that up, letting her know in his responses that he was with her, all the way.

Despite the short time they'd spent together, he made her feel more secure in bed than any man she'd ever been with, all of whom she'd known much longer and better than she knew Reece.

But then, maybe knowing someone wasn't always about time. Maybe sometimes two people just connected, and the connection could happen as easily over a few days as over a few months or years.

And the connection she experienced with him now went *way* beyond having anything to do with time. What it lacked in length it made up for in other more important ways. And she wanted to show him the depth of her emotion in this moment, how much she cared, how much she wanted to make him feel good, how strongly she'd realized his happiness and sense of security was more important to her than . . . well, than her own, she supposed.

Biting her lip as she sat upright next to him, she reached down and pulled at the tie on his swim trunks. It would have been impossible not to feel how big and hard he was underneath just from the incidental contact, and she followed the urge to run the flat of her hand down the stiff column beneath the fabric.

The low moan that left him made her every cell tingle with desire. So she didn't waste any time before tugging at his waistband, and as he lifted up, pulling his trunks down and off.

And Lord, he was beautiful naked. She'd seen him that way before, of course, but maybe not in situations where she could easily stop for a minute and study him. "Mmm . . ." The sound rose from her throat without planning, and her hand found him again—this time it circled his thickness and began to caress.

"Aw . . ." he sighed and his eyes fell shut in the deepening night air as she stroked and massaged him. "Aw, that's nice, baby."

But she wanted to give him something even nicer, and it was something that came from her very soul.

Leaning over him, she lifted his erection in her fist, then licked lightly over the tip. A thready moan echoed from him, fueling her hunger, so next she kissed him there, light, gentle, getting acclimated to being that close to this part of him in a new way. Soon enough, though, instinct and heat led her to lower her mouth down onto him, slowly but thoroughly taking as much of his length between her lips as she comfortably could.

As she moved on him that way, his hot sighs and groans made her feel both a power and a pleasure, like both the giver and the taker, and she got lost in the ministrations, loving the feel of his hands in her hair, his heated whispers and moans; all of it wrapped around her, the same way she felt the sky and ocean wrapping around them right now, too.

After a while, though, she was ready for a different kind of pleasure, ready to be filled by him in a different way. So she eased him from her mouth, then rushed out of her bikini bottoms and shed her top entirely.

As she straddled his torso, he reached for her hips, pulling her down until her most sensitive spot pressed on his most rigid. She hissed in her breath at the sweet pressure, surging with wetness. Then she lifted herself, balancing atop him, and let his hands guide her as she sank down, taking him inside inch by filling inch. She didn't attempt to stifle her deep sob of pleasure as she sheathed him entirely.

"Oh God," she murmured.

"You can call me Reece," he said.

And she laughed at a moment when she'd least expected to—but things got heated again fast, because she felt him so profoundly in this position, and because she was too aroused to keep from grinding on him in the primitive rhythm that gripped her body.

After that, no more thought. Only a consuming pleasure, a place she was sweetly drowning. And then a precipice, something she was mounting, getting closer and closer to—until came that instance of blissful release, a powerful explosion that spread mind-numbing ecstasy all the way to the tips of her fingers and toes.

And then she let herself descend onto his

warmth to rest, his arms closing around her like a safety net catching her when she fell.

The only sounds for a few restful moments of recovery were her labored breath and low music on the radio that had played, forgotten, through all of this—something by Jackson Browne.

But then Reece was the one rolling them, resituating them, until she lay flat on her back on their blanket, him still buried warm and snug inside her, his handsome face and sexy eyes above her.

His slow, deep, deliberate strokes took over her senses. And then there were sweet kisses on her mouth, his fingers twining in her hair. And plaintive notes from a piano seemed to punctuate the moment, and she recognized the old song, "Hold On Hold Out," and Jackson Browne was speaking through part of it, talking to whoever the song was about, it seemed, and saying, "I love you."

Just hearing that, so heartfelt, so real, as she and Reece moved together, made her chest tighten, her heartbeat increase. And as she gazed up into his dark eyes then, she experienced a strange jolt of fear, out of the blue, and she realized it was fear that . . . even as connected as she felt to him right now, what if they weren't feeling the same thing?

Guys could so easily detach from sex, it seemed. She was sinking deeper and deeper into this, but what if she'd sunk too far? She almost knew she had, in fact. Because she was as deep as you could go here. And whether or not he really understood this, by giving up on buying the Happy Crab, she was sacrificing *everything* for him.

Everything.

And that was when he softly said, "It's true."

"What's true?" she whispered.

"What he said."

She lay there beneath him, trying to interpret that, silence beginning to stretch between them—until he added, "In the song. I think I'm in love with you, Tink."

She tried to hold in her gasp, but a wisp of it snuck out anyway. "Really?"

"I didn't mean for it to happen," he said, shaking his head slightly.

"Me neither," she told him.

"You neither?" he asked.

She shook her head.

And he blinked. "Are you saying . . . ?"

"Yeah. I'm kind of in love with you, too."

"Oh . . . oh God," he said, and then he began to pump more powerfully into her again, his eyes falling shut.

She cried out with each hard thrust he delivered now—until he was coming inside her, telling her so, and telling her she was beautiful and amazing as he gently collapsed atop her.

AFTER sleeping a bit, Cami awoke to find them in full darkness. Her head rested on Reece's chest and his arm curled around her. A kiss on her forehead told her he was awake, too—and that was when she glanced up to find herself utterly awed by what she saw.

"Look at the stars," she said. There had to be

millions of them, right in plain view. "I've never seen so many before."

"Even in Nowheresville, Michigan?" he asked.

"Yeah. It's just different out here. Magnificent," she said, still looking up, basking in it. "And it's so quiet."

"Cave quiet," he said.

"Huh?"

"Once my family went on a trip north to see some relatives, and we took a tour of Mammoth Cave in Kentucky. There's one spot on the tour where they tell you to be quiet and turn out the lights, and it's the blackest, most soundless place you've ever been." They both gazed silently upward for a minute, still taking it all in, until he added, "Even if you're becalmed, there are usually still small waves, a little movement. But right now, right this second, this is . . . true stillness."

A few minutes later, Reece untangled from her and got up, quieting the radio and turning on the mast light to ensure no other boats would collide with them now that it was dark. The glow it cast was soft and low enough that Cami could still see the stars.

When he returned, she said, "It's getting chilly," and together they wrapped up in the blanket they'd already used in so many other ways today. And once they were snuggled up in it together, she smiled up at him and said, "See, this isn't so bad."

"No—it's not," he agreed. Then murmured something about building better memories.

"Huh?" she asked, not quite able to hear.

"Riley told me I should make new, better memories on the boat," he explained. "For a while there earlier, seemed like that wasn't working out too well, but . . . maybe things have swung back in the other direction."

"Sometimes," she began, thinking aloud, "life's little gifts show up in mysterious ways—like . . . finding a dinosaur in your bathroom." They both laughed. "Or an engine that won't start."

"Sorry, though," he said. "We didn't get around to eating much earlier. And after I promised you a delicious dinner of Fritos and bananas, too."

They exchanged grins in the dim glow of the mast light, and she was surprised at how clearly she could see his face, but she supposed her eyes had adjusted. And she thought it a nice reminder that sometimes life required some adjustments and then suddenly things that hadn't seemed to make sense suddenly did. And in response, she reached under the blanket, to what lay between his legs, and said, "Forget the Fritos. This was much more satisfying."

"Mmm . . . keep that up, baby, and it will be again."

She did. And it was.

WHEN the sun woke them the next morning, the breeze lifted Cami's hair, blowing some long locks onto Reece's chest.

"Your hair tickles," he said sleepily.

"Need a hairband," she said, still half asleep herself. "There's one in my beach bag, but that's all the way at the back of the boat."

And then Reece said, "Wait a minute."

"Huh?"

"Your hair is blowing."

"Uh huh."

Then he sat up next to her, looking around. "The wind is back," he said. And she could almost feel the smile in his voice before she glanced up to see it on his face.

Talk about injecting early morning energy— they both immediately started putting their bathing suits back on, and Reece wasted no time preparing to sail. Part of Cami couldn't help being a little sorry the strange, calm interlude was ending—because so much had changed in the hours since the wind had died—but she liked seeing Reece so happy. And even if they'd shared some pretty great moments out here, she understood why being stranded on this particular vessel in the middle of the Gulf of Mexico remained a situation he was ready to bring to an end.

The return of the wind was brisk, so they sailed quickly. They ate Fritos and bananas on the way, and rehydrated with water, and at one point, Cami walked up behind Reece, where he sat at the captain's wheel, and wrapped her arms around him from behind.

And she didn't want to act like some insecure little girl . . . but she still found herself saying near his ear, "So . . . what you said last night . . ."

"The thing you said back?" he asked.

"Mmm hmm."

He gave her a sexy, playful sideways glance. "It still holds, if that's what you're wondering.

It wasn't some stranded-at-sea delirium or any-thing."

"Good," she said, pleased. "For me, too." Then she kissed his neck, and he turned to kiss her lips, and as it echoed all through her, potent as ever, now it felt . . . less temporary, and more like a thing she could feel safe holding on to.

She wasn't sure what would happen next, with Vanderhook or anything else, but she was okay with that, because she had Reece now, and they were in love, and this was real, and even if she was a little scared in some ways, she was excited in others, and she just knew everything would work out okay.

WHEN the shore came into sight it felt like return-ing after a long voyage, and when Reece steered the boat into the bay that led up behind the Happy Crab, Cami couldn't quite believe her eyes. There, standing on the dock at the rear of the motel, waited all of Reece's friends, cheering when they saw the *Lisa Renee*.

"You're a popular guy," she said to Reece.

He just laughed, yet appeared gratified. "Must have heard we didn't make it in last night."

As wind carried them closer to the Crab, Cami could make out Christy and Jack, Fletcher and Tamra, Riley, and the telltale rust-colored dress and beehive made Polly's presence the most dis-tinguishable of all.

"Looks like a big party at my place," Reece called as he began to maneuver the boat into its slip.

"Almost a rescue party," Jack replied.

Fletcher and Jack were already busy tying the boat up to the dock as soon as it glided into place, and Polly added, "Riley came over to the restaurant last night, worried when you two didn't come home, so I called up a customer who works for the Coast Guard. He put me in touch with the towin' place and I got the skinny. Riley was ready to take the catamaran out to find ya, but then we remembered none of us really know how to operate the darn thing."

Light laughter wafted through the crowd.

And Polly went on to say, "We were about to set out to find somebody with a boat to drive a couple of us out there this mornin', but I called the towin' fella back up and he said you'd radioed in and were on your way back."

"You guys are great," Reece said. "And I'm just glad to have gotten us both back in one piece." As he said it, he threw an arm casually around Cami's shoulder and pulled her snug to his side, and she knew the secure warmth of "being a couple," for real now, pleased that he wasn't trying to hide it. They'd come a long way since, "She's not my friend."

When they stepped on to the dock, Christy and Polly hugged Cami like she was a long-time member of their community, and she found herself hugging them back. "I'm so relieved," Christy was saying. And Polly told her, "I hardly slept at all knowin' you two were stuck out there." In the past, Cami hadn't traditionally been a very touchy-feely person—her parents just hadn't cultivated that kind of affection in her—but these particular people made it easy to reciprocate their kind, caring ways.

Meanwhile, the guys were sharing more manly forms of greetings—slapping Reece on the back, helping him get the boat further secured—and then Riley lifted the lid on a big box of donuts Cami hadn't noticed him holding until now. "We got breakfast at the bakery—thought ya might be hungry." And despite having just eaten their unusual breakfast of corn chips and bananas, Reece and Cami simply exchanged *oh wow* looks before both practically diving on the donuts.

The group migrated to an old picnic table behind the motel, where Cami and Reece discovered they'd also brought orange juice and drink cups, and they all made a mini-feast of the donuts while Reece and Cami told of their adventure at sea. They left out all the actual good parts, of course—the sex, the talking, the declarations of love—but everyone seemed riveted just the same. And Cami assumed all of Reece's friends knew about the tragedy in his past and silently understood why this might be traumatic for him—even though he did a great job of playing it off light.

When the story was done, Christy said, "I'm sure you guys want to get some rest today, but tomorrow, Jack and I are taking you two to lunch."

And Polly chimed in, "Free seafood buffet on me tonight."

Fletcher added, "And . . . I'll treat you to a free tightrope show at the Sunset Celebration," concluding with a wink, and everyone laughed.

It was nearly noon by the time the party dispersed, and Cami realized she indeed was exhausted. As she and Reece walked in the rear door of the Happy Crab's office, he said, "I actually have a lot of stuff I want to do today, but . . . you can hang out if you want. If you don't mind me working at the same time."

She couldn't help being curious. "What kind of stuff?"

"I need to clean out the boat. And, uh, call somebody to check out that engine," he said on a slightly sheepish laugh.

"You get now that there was nothing you could have done to make that engine start, right?" she asked, pointedly meeting his gaze. "Or to have known it wouldn't. You get that sometimes things just happen that are out of our control and it's not your fault?"

He gave her a quick, brief nod. She supposed such understanding might be easier from a distance, when you weren't the one in the middle of a situation—but she hoped that maybe, just maybe, the events of the past day would begin to help him let go of the guilt he'd suffered all these years about his family.

Even if he went right on talking, making it clear he didn't want to get into discussing it again right now. "And I want to order some pool supplies and give the pool a good cleaning, and I should place an order for some new guest towels, too. To tell you the truth . . ." He paused then, shifting his weight from one flip-flop to the other and raising his eyes back to hers, "I've kinda been holding off on that stuff, just in case I somehow ended up losing the Crab—but now that I know that's not an issue anymore, I can get back to normal."

She smiled, felt his relief all over again, and quietly said, "Good." And inside, she couldn't help thinking about the fact that Phil, Vanderhook, and Windchime weren't going to take this well, but she was too tired to think about how she was going to cast it in the best possible light. Maybe she could find reasons why another spot in the area would actually be more favorable. A big part of her job was spinning things the right way, so surely she could figure out how to do it in this situation, too.

"And with any luck, that damn Windchime sign will come down soon and I can get back some of my business, too."

She offered a nod of agreement, then realized exactly how sleepy she was. "Would you mind," she asked, "if I head back to my room to grab a few more hours' sleep? I'm more wiped out than I thought—and I should really check on the cat, too."

"Oh yeah," he said, his voice teasing. "I forgot the Happy Crab has a resident cat now."

But he said it as if the cat could stay—*would* stay—and she couldn't help thinking it implied she would stay, too. And the truth was, as strange a suggestion as that would've sounded like a week ago, now she was beginning to imagine it could be so; she was beginning to imagine a whole, new simpler way of life. She wasn't entirely sure of her role in it yet, other than being with Reece, but . . .

well, don't worry about that right now. You have a nap to take, a cat to tend to, and Vanderhook to deal with.

So she kissed Reece goodbye—a long, passionate kiss she felt all the way to her toes—and they agreed to meet up later.

REECE greeted Fifi—to whom Riley had given great care in his absence—then started in on the tasks he'd told Cami he wanted to accomplish today. As he spent time cleaning the boat, it struck him what a beautiful day it was, even with the heat and some humidity thickening the air. The bold blue of the sky seemed more vibrant than usual, and the clouds floating past appeared . . . softer somehow.

After that, he called in an order to replenish his pool chemicals. And that got him in the mood to clean the pool—which was a job that took some muscle, but once he got going, he realized he had a lot more energy than he might have expected after yesterday.

And then it hit him that especially blue skies and extra energy might just be because he was . . . hell, he was happy. Really happy. Relieved the drama was over with Vanderhook, and . . . in love. Damn, he hadn't seen that coming.

When his family had died, he'd broken up with his girlfriend, Stacy, soon after, mostly because he'd decided he hadn't wanted to be in a relationship. Even then, he'd realized that most people would cling to the only other important relationship left in their life—but he'd been so lost at the time that he'd ultimately turned inward, told himself he didn't want something serious, didn't want to feel obligated to someone. Now he wondered why.

Maybe I was just afraid to lose her, too. Maybe having no ties felt safer.

He'd been twenty-five at the time, and he hadn't had an official "girlfriend" since, by choice. Until now. Today.

Seemed Cami brought out all *kinds* of new sides of him—first water sex, and now this. He laughed as he dragged a big sponge along the side of the pool. Or . . . maybe he'd just grown up a lot since then. Maybe he'd finally started to heal from the loss.

Although he didn't like it, he couldn't deny something she'd said to him last night—that he'd worked hard to keep everything the same since they'd died. And it was true. It was true that he hadn't wanted anything else to change, or fade away, or stop being the way it was. The house where they'd lived, the Happy Crab, the *Lisa Renee*.

But suddenly he felt as if . . . well, as if change might be okay. *Some* change. Would he ever be ready to give up the Happy Crab? Nope, probably never. Would he be willing to let go of the house? He wasn't sure, but . . . maybe. Either that or he really would move back into it eventually. And if he did that, he'd . . . make changes *there*. And that might not be easy, but he'd do it, because he *could* now.

Letting himself love somebody . . . hell, that was a pretty big change to start with. From here, maybe it would just be a matter of baby steps, and of . . . letting himself feel secure in new ways. In ways that would help him let go of the past because the present and future looked brighter to him than they had in a long time.

Not that he'd been leading a bad life. He thought he'd coped pretty damn well with his losses. But maybe it was time to start coping *better*, moving forward instead of just standing still.

"You need any help with this, padre?"

He looked up to see Riley exit the office, Fifi meandering out along with him, and smiled. "No—thanks, but I'm good."

Riley smiled back. "I've never seen a fella so chipper about cleanin' a pool."

And Reece decided to confide in his friend a little. "Guess I'm chipper for other reasons."

"Did you make some better memories on that boat ride?"

Reece let his smile widen. "You could say that."

"That makes my heart happy, my friend."

"And not only that," Reece told him, "but Cami's not trying to buy the Crab anymore. So it's a big relief to know I've heard the last from Vanderhook, too."

Riley and Fifi kept him company as he finished the job, and he informed Riley they had a cat now. "I'm not thrilled about it, but Cami seems attached to it already. And considering my own attachment to the Feefster here, I figure I gotta be understanding, right?"

"Exactly right," Riley said in his quiet way.

And then it hit Reece that he'd let the cat thing

go from the moment he'd found out about it, like it was nothing. Which kind of proved right there how crazy about her he was. And reminded him how damn good it was to feel that way about someone, and to have someone feel the same way about him.

After he finished the job and had put his cleaning stuff away, Reece lay back on a lounge chair for a few minutes to just bask in the sun—and in the brand new happiness he found himself floating in. He'd loved Stacy, and he'd been in love once when he was a teenager, too, with his high school sweetheart, Heather. But this, with Cami . . . it felt like a grown-up sort of love, something he simply hadn't been capable of . . . before right now. And he knew they'd only known each other a short time and that this had come about in a pretty freaking unlikely way, but it still felt *solid* to him. *She* felt solid.

He couldn't wait to see her again in a few hours. He couldn't remember a time when he'd looked more forward to the seafood buffet next door or the Sunset Celebration. Because Cami made everything new.

Heading indoors, Fifi at his side, he took a shower, put on clean shorts and a T-shirt, then settled on the couch with his laptop, ready to place that new towel order online. Unlike most people these days, he wasn't a guy who lived and died by technology, and he didn't have email on his phone, so he decided to check his email while on the computer as well.

He clicked to open his mail program and his

eyes fell on—whoa—an email from Vanderhook. His stomach tightened. The message had arrived only an hour ago.

> Dear Mr. Donovan,
> As you know, Vanderhook, Inc. would like to acquire your property in Coral Cove, Florida, although you have declined our very generous offers. It has come to our attention, however, that you are in violation of Coral Cove Health Code Ordinance 354.76 which states that no reptile shall be kept loose on the premises of a business. We would like to offer you another opportunity to accept our most recent offer before we are compelled to report the infraction to the city health department, which we feel certain would result in the closure of your business, not to mention the potential for hefty fines.

The letter went on, but Reece stopped reading. The words on the screen before him seemed to blur as certain facts raced through his brain. But he could barely process most of them, because the biggest one roared through his head—and heart—like a freight train.

Cami had betrayed him.

And everything they'd shared last night was a lie.

"Now we have him," Hook shouted.

J. M. Barrie, *Peter and Wendy*

Chapter 20

Taking a deep breath, Reece tried to calm down. But how could he? He'd trusted her. He'd trusted her when he'd opened up to her about his family, his past. He'd trusted her when she'd told him she'd let go of trying to buy the Happy Crab. And—damn . . . he'd trusted her when he'd said he loved her. And when she'd said it back.

Sitting there still staring at the computer, his heart shriveled into a tight little ball inside his chest.

He'd trusted her—and instead of going back to her room and taking a nap, she'd instead taken what he'd told her about Fifi on the boat and used it to dig up information to strong-arm him into selling, then promptly turned that damning information over to her bloodsucking bosses.

He slammed the laptop shut, thrust it aside on the couch, and ran his hands back through his hair, still trying to process it.

How could she? How could she be so fucking cold? So heartless?

Was it all an act? Was every ounce of softness she'd ever shown him all pretend—all designed to wear him down, lure him in, garner his trust?

Well, he supposed everything she'd told him about her life in Michigan *was* true—it would *take* that kind of cold, unloving upbringing to create such a ruthless person.

A million more questions raced through his head. How calculated was it all? Had she been gunning for Fifi all along—had the health department's visit to the Hungry Fisherman given her the idea to find some way to bring them down on the Crab, too? Or had the nugget of insight he'd shared on the boat about Fifi's care provided fresh inspiration on how to win her ugly game? And if he hadn't told her that, what was the next step in her plan? How else had she been conspiring to get her way through lies and deception?

He'd had no idea Coral Cove had a law on the books about reptiles—it was probably old, one of those laws people had long forgotten about, because most people in town knew Fifi. Hell, her picture had been in the *Coral Cove Weekly Sun* before.

But the fact that iguanas were known to carry harmful bacteria could definitely make her a target, no matter how careful he was, no matter that the simple procedures he followed took care of the issue. If someone complained about her, he could *easily* see the health department shutting him down. Not just warning him to remove the iguana, but shutting him down and making it very hard—and probably time-consuming and expensive—to reopen.

Still, it was hard to process all that in his brain—because it just hurt so fucking much.

And the longer he sat there absorbing it, the deeper it stung.

This was what it felt like to be betrayed. She'd made him into a fool. And she'd ripped his heart out in the process. He shut his eyes. *God, to think how happy I was all damn day today, to think how good she made me feel, how ready I was to dive headlong into this thing with her.* It had felt so real.

And that she'd gotten to him through Fifi, the one thing she knew he really loved in this world—he shook his head—that was about the lowest blow he could imagine.

It was difficult for him to understand that some-one would do such a thing for money, for a job. But when he thought back to the Cami—*Camille*—he'd first met in his office not even two weeks ago . . . well, maybe it wasn't so hard, after all. *That* woman had seemed capable of being morally bankrupt. *That* woman seemed like someone who would stab you in the back. He'd thought of her as a piranha—and now he only wished he'd *kept* thinking of her that way. That was the real Ca-mille Thompson. And the rest was just pretend.

But maybe it wasn't all pretend.

Screaming when Fifi had been in her bathtub—that had been real.

He knew in his heart certain other moments had been real, too. He might be a fool for her, but he wasn't an idiot.

So he amended his thought. Maybe it hadn't all been pretend—but the important parts were. And the most important part of all was that, in the end, she'd betrayed him, she'd screwed him over, and now he'd lose his family's business, one way or another. Whether he gave in and took the money or whether he waited here until the health department came and shut him down, he'd lost.

He'd lost the Happy Crab.

He'd lost the love he'd thought he'd found.

And hell, right now, this minute, he finally lost . . . hope.

"ARE you hungry?" Cami asked Tiger Lily.

"Meow."

She smiled down at the cat. "I'll take that as a yes." Then she fixed the kitty a bowl of food and refreshed her water. Watching the cat practically dive on it when she returned the bowls to the floor, she couldn't help feeling good inside that Tiger Lily no longer had to scrounge and beg for something to eat.

And she felt good in other ways, too. She'd slept sweetly, thinking of Reece. Then she'd showered and gotten ready for their date tonight—going to the Hungry Fisherman and the Sunset Celebration suddenly sounded more romantic than she ever could have dreamed.

That was when a loud *bang—bang—bang* came on her door. She flinched, and so did the cat. What the hell?

Tensing sharply, her first instinct was to go

for the phone, call for help—only then she heard Reece's voice. "Open up in there! Open the door, Cami! Now!"

Her spine went ramrod straight. She'd never heard Reece sound so angry. What was going on? She rushed to the door, turned the lock, yanked it open. "What's wrong?"

"I guess you think I'm pretty fucking stupid." His eyes were narrow slits.

"What?" she asked, completely disoriented.

"I heard from your bosses," he snapped. "Got a nice, threatening message from them."

She blinked, drew back, all the more confused. *"What?"* she asked again.

"Yeah, they let me know about the ordinance you found. That was pretty damn quick work. And wow, using my pet against me—that's . . ." He shook his head. "That's downright brutal. But at least I totally get it now, totally get who you are and what you're about." His eyes burned through her with pure contempt.

It was all so shocking that she couldn't even come up with how to respond. "I—I . . . what are you talking about? You heard from them how?"

"In an email," he said impatiently. Then gave his head a pointed tilt. "Look, you don't need to keep on acting innocent—it's all out in the open now. I was a big enough fool to feed you vital information that could get the Happy Crab shut down—and you ran with it. Just like the vulture you are."

She blinked again, let out the breath she hadn't

quite realized she was holding until she'd begun to feel dizzy. "I have no idea what you're talking about, Reece. Can you calm down and explain to me what happened?"

He lowered his chin, his expression scornful. "Are you claiming you didn't find some law about reptiles? That you didn't tell people at Vanderhook about it?"

"Well . . . I did, but . . ." She swallowed nervously. *Crap, I shouldn't have said that. I need to fix this somehow.* "I—"

"*Stop*," he said forcefully, then held up his hand. "I never should have trusted you." He was shaking his head again, his eyes spewing venom at her. "I guess I just forgot people like you even exist. Because, see, most people I know are pretty nice. And I guess I took that for granted. I forgot there were bloodsucking assholes out there who'll do whatever it takes to make big money—even if it means lying and pretending and doing whatever else is necessary to get what they want."

"Reece, I didn't do this." It was the only defense she could come up with amid her shock. "Not really."

His eyebrows shot up in mock amusement. "Not really? That kinda sounds like you did. And I'd respect you more—a little anyway—if you just told the truth now and quit acting like someone you're not."

"But I—"

"And another thing—pack your bags. Get out of my motel. Now."

Cami blinked yet again, even more stunned now. Was this really happening? Everything suddenly felt surreal.

"Meow."

They both looked to Tiger Lily, who stood across the room peering over at them.

"The cat can stay, though," he said. "It's not *her* fault you're a horrible person without a conscience." And with that, he turned to go—and Cami's heart sank.

It was more desperate impulse than decision that made her reach out, grab his arm. "Reece, wait."

He jerked his head in her direction, glaring.

"You aren't even going to let me try to explain?" she asked. Her voice shook now.

And his expression dripped sarcasm when he coldly replied, "There's nothing you could say that I'd believe, so why waste my time?" Then he yanked his arm away and turned to leave again.

Only he stopped just outside the open door and sent her one last scowl. "This is why I don't get close to people anymore. In the end, you always end up alone, and the only question is—how bad does it hurt getting there? Thanks for reminding me of that. It's a mistake I won't make again."

"Listen, Tinkerbell," he cried,
"I am your friend no more.
Be gone from me forever."

J. M. Barrie, *Peter and Wendy*

Chapter 21

CAMI FELT numb. She felt numb as she pulled out her suitcase and packed up her clothes and toiletries and zipped it shut. She felt numb as she looked down at her cat—Tiger Lily felt like hers now—and said, "I don't know what to do with you right now. I . . . don't know what to do about *anything.*"

She couldn't think straight. It took a lot to throw her off her game, and Reece Donovan had done it more than once. But this time . . . this time was a doozie. She hadn't seen it coming. And she still didn't completely understand it.

Well, she did, sort of. Clearly, Phil had set someone to digging and found that law she'd told him about. *Oh God, I never should have mentioned that.* But at the time she'd felt under such pressure to appease Phil in some way and it was all she'd had. And it was before she really understood exactly why Reece couldn't part with the Happy Crab. Things had already been changing then, but they'd only changed *totally and completely* out on that boat with him last night. If only she could go back in time and not send Phil that text.

But . . . why had Reece been so mean, refusing to even listen, assuming the worst of her?

Because you look guilty. Of course it seemed like you were responsible for this. And, at least in part, you actually were. You wish you were innocent here, but you're not. He's probably going to lose his motel now and there's nothing you or anyone else can do to fix it.

When she'd returned to her room earlier, it had crossed her mind to check her email, but she'd opted to go straight to bed instead. Now, she went to the laptop still on the table, not yet packed, and opened it up to see if there was any further information inside.

She found three emails from Phil—the first two demanding that she call him, the last a terse message saying that since she hadn't responded and obviously wasn't interested in doing her job, he'd taken matters into his own hands, getting his administrative assistant to locate the ordinance about reptiles, and informing "Mr. Donovan" that he would be reported to the health department if he didn't accept their most recent offer. The message closed with: WE'LL DISCUSS YOUR LACKLUSTER PERFORMANCE ON THIS ACQUISITION WHEN YOU RETURN TO THE OFFICE. WHICH SHOULD BE NOW, BY THE WAY, IF YOU WANT TO REMAIN EMPLOYED BY VANDERHOOK.

Wow. Just wow. She couldn't believe him.

But . . . on the other hand, maybe she could. Maybe he was . . . only doing his job, the same as he'd expected her to do hers. It wasn't unreasonable for him to be upset with her for the way things had gone here.

And then, for the first time since her return, it occurred to her to check her cell phone. She'd turned it off when they were at sea, out of range, to save the battery, and simply hadn't thought to turn it back on until now. Strange. She supposed she'd quit living and dying by her electronic communications. Other things had begun to feel more important. Coral Cove had shifted her into a slower, sweeter mode of living.

On the phone, she found five texts from Phil, the most recent a couple of hours ago, telling her to check her email and haranguing her for not answering him. The truth was, under the circumstances, his anger was fair.

And she honestly didn't know if she'd have a job when she got back to Atlanta.

And she wasn't sure if she *wanted* a job—at least the job she currently had. Again, she didn't know *anything* for certain right now. Everything felt foggy and confusing.

Okay, what do I know for sure here?

Reece has demanded I leave the Happy Crab. Reece was a total jerk to me. I am at fault for part of the reason he's mad, but not all of it, and he didn't even care enough to let me explain my side of things. And so even if he's justified in one way . . . well, maybe he's not the totally great guy I thought he was. I mean, I opened myself to him last night in so many ways. I put my heart on the line, and my job on the line—for him, because his happiness felt more vital to me than my own.

I gave him . . . the most precious thing I could, all I had to give, and he just repaid me by believing the worst of me, not letting me defend myself, and throwing me out of his motel.

She glanced in the general direction of the office. "Fine, you scumball," she said under her breath, "I'll go." And God, her heart hurt. It felt like he'd just crushed it under his heel, like it was made of paper—but she had to ignore that right now. She just had to. Because she had to figure out what to do with Tiger Lily and . . . also what to do with herself.

Go back to Atlanta? Or stay here, in Coral Cove?

Making a few short term decisions, she scooped the orange-striped kitty up into her arms and cuddled her to her chest. The cat purred and her body felt warm and cozy next to Cami's skin. *I wish I could just stay here, like this, right now. I wish Reece had never come to my door, and that we were getting together for dinner and a walk over to the pier to see our friends, and watch Fletcher's show, and maybe I'd even buy another suncatcher from Tamra to try to make her see I'm not so bad, and then we'd walk on the beach and hold hands and I'd still feel safe.* But none of that could be. Everything had changed. She shut her eyes for a few seconds, allowing herself to absorb the pain, then bolstered her courage to try to push beyond it as best she could.

She hugged Tiger Lily to her once more and

said softly, "I have to go. But I'll make sure you're taken care of."

And it broke her heart to lower the cat on the bed and begin to leave. But Reece had given her no choice, and so she began operating on auto-pilot to get some necessary tasks accomplished. That was what much of her life had been like as a girl—when her father was harsh with her, or when her parents hurt her by denying her some simple thing other kids had like money for a movie or something new to wear—and she reverted back to that now. Moving forward, ignoring emotions for as long as it took to get through what needed to happen.

She packed her laptop in its bag and wheeled her suitcase out to her rental car.

Then she went to Riley's room, bracing herself and knocked, hoping he'd be inside. A moment later, he answered, wearing his usual gentle smile. "Well, Miss Cami. What can I do for ya?"

His smile and cheerful attitude nearly buried her, but she did her best not to let emotion leak out. She took his hand, squeezed it, and hoped she could get through this. "Riley, Reece and I have had a disagreement and I have to go. There's a cat in my room—Reece said she could stay. Will you take care of her for me?" She swallowed back the lump in her throat as she finished, making the mistake of meeting the old man's kind, worried eyes.

He blinked repeatedly, looking upset, caught off guard. "Of course I will, but . . . surely you're not really leavin'. Surely whatever this is can be worked out. You . . . you make him happy."

Oh shit. She had to shut her eyes, crush back the tears. *Be strong. Get back in autopilot.*

So then she opened her eyes back up, pressed her lips together, and squeezed Riley's hand once more. And tried to keep it simple. "It's Reece's choice that I go. Thank you. About the cat. And for being so nice to me."

She didn't wait for him to reply because she couldn't. She turned and walked away, her heart beating painfully in her chest, her brain still filled with the fog of all of this, of everything good turning so irreparably bad.

She got in her car, started it, tried not to see the Hungry Fisherman in the distance, tried not to feel the warmth of Coral Cove crowding in around her, somehow reminding her that . . . it wasn't hers to feel right now. It was suddenly as if it belonged to Reece and could only come to her through him, and that if he didn't want her here, she didn't belong here, wasn't a part of it anymore.

Still moving automatically, she drove up the road, out of town, past Sunnymeade and toward the big resorts beyond. She drove up beneath the wide awning of the first she reached, called the Sand Dollar, where a bellman rushed over to her window to ask with a smile, "Checking in?"

"Yes," she said.

And then she did.

Even the resort's simplest room was lavish, especially compared to the Happy Crab, but it felt . . . plastic to her in some way—a little too perfect, a little too fancy. It simply didn't feel like where she was supposed to be. But neither did the Happy

Crab at the moment. And neither did Atlanta. She missed her cat already.

This . . . this is a place to sleep tonight. A place to think. A place to figure out what I want. From life, going forward.

She sat down in a plush chair, the drapes drawn, letting in only a scant amount of late daylight. She didn't turn on the TV; she didn't want to take a walk or explore the grounds; she didn't want to call Phil or answer her email. She felt entirely . . . directionless. For perhaps the first time since she'd left her hometown in Michigan all those years ago.

How did Reece Donovan drain the direction, the drive, the determination right out of me that easily?

And she was so, so angry at him. That quickly, he hadn't believed in her, and it made her feel like . . . like the person she *used* to be, the person who had put her job first above all else. But she *wasn't* that person anymore, and why didn't he know that—why couldn't he see and feel that? She punched a throw pillow as hard as she could. Then she flung it across the room.

She found herself thinking back on when they'd first met. She'd wanted to go to bed with him. She'd wanted not to pass up experiencing the fiery chemistry that burned between them. She'd felt it was better to experience it than not, no matter what— that it was some sort of gift in life that shouldn't be squandered lest it never come again.

And she'd gotten what she'd wanted. But of course, she'd learned along the way that she wasn't a casual sex sort of girl. From the start of

their physical relationship, she'd felt an attachment she couldn't deny or push down and she'd
had no choice but to roll with it. She'd already
been in too deep to get out. And she'd trusted that
it would all just be okay in the end somehow.

But it wasn't okay in the end. It wasn't okay at
all.

*Are you sorry you went down that road? If you
could go back in time, rebuff his advances, not put forth
your own, ignore the desire between you—would you?
If it would have avoided all this hurt, guilt, and every
other horrible thing you're suffering, would you have
passed up what you had with him?*

Then came the answer. *No way. How could I?*

And then something big hit her. *This wouldn't
hurt so much if what was between us hadn't felt so
incredible—so positively amazing.* So maybe the
profound pain she was experiencing right now
simply . . . validated it, proved it had been worth
it. Maybe the pain was a way to measure how
much good had been there, how much joy it had
filled her with.

The only thing she would really take back
was . . . hurting Reece. In so many ways.

Making it so he'd lose the motel. And doing it
through Fifi. And making him feel betrayed. And
making him believe she'd faked her feelings for
him.

She wanted to scream out loud that it was an
accident, all just an ugly, random accident, completely out of her control—but she'd lit the fire.
She'd supplied all the ammunition. She was the

bad guy here—no matter how she looked at it.

Now he was going to lose his home, his business, all because of her. She felt like an idiot never to have realized how much that would wound *her* in the end, too. *You've always been the bad guy, a bully, in your job. Always. It was just easier when you didn't see the aftermath. When it didn't hurt someone you love.*

It struck her then what a horrible job it was. How many people had she hurt? How many lives were worse off because of her? How many people resented what she'd done, what she'd taken from them? God, how did she even sleep at night?

She'd just never seen it before—she'd never let herself.

I don't know how to fix this. Any of it.

I don't know who I am anymore.

So what the hell do I do now?

Sitting in the chair, she finally broke down and cried. She didn't indulge in tears often, but hell—if she was ever going to cry, this seemed like a pretty good time for it. As she sobbed into her hands, and then a tissue—and before she knew it a whole overflowing *handful* of wadded tissues— visions darted through her mind.

Reece. Their sex. The picture of his family on the wall. Everything that was at once typical and unique about the Happy Crab.

Polly's beehive. Riley's gentle eyes. Tiger Lily's warmth. Fifi's . . . smile. Which she thought maybe she'd see now if she only had the chance to look again.

The smell of a Florida drizzle. Reece rubbing sunscreen on her back beneath the hot, tropical sun. The million stars they'd lain beneath last night that had made her feel she was seeing something wondrous for the first time.

For all she knew, maybe she *had* seen that many stars back in rural Michigan. Maybe it had taken being with Reece, observing the world through his eyes, to make her really *see* them.

She wasn't sure how long she let herself cry, but finally she made herself stop. She could cry forever and it wouldn't repair anything. Only . . . maybe this *had* actually helped a little. The things she'd thought about as she'd shed those tears had reminded her all over again just how many changes she'd gone through since meeting Reece.

And I might not know who I am anymore, but . . . at least maybe I'm figuring out who I'm not. And who I'd like to be.

And that seemed like a starting point. A weak one. Yet all she had right now, so she supposed it would have to do.

Pulling herself together, she opened the curtains, ordered room service, and tried to start piecing together a few decisions, about what to do tomorrow. At this point, one day at a time was all she could handle.

TAMRA sat on Fletcher's back porch with Fletcher and Reece, looking out over the sea. Funny, usually peering out over the beach gave her a sense of peace, just from witnessing the beauty and massive scope of it all—but today she found herself seeing something closer to starkness. The wind was up, making the waves choppy, and the sky overcast, more white than blue. But she supposed her perception might have as much to do with the horrible story Reece had just told them as it did with the actual state of the weather.

He'd explained all they'd missed over the last couple of days—including the deepened connection he'd experienced with Cami on the boat, making it so he had a lot more to mourn than just the impending loss of the Happy Crab.

It hurt like hell to hear it—all of it. It hurt because she knew how much the place meant to him and why. And it hurt to hear how Cami had treated him—because Tamra understood romantic pain now so much better than she had just a few months ago. And to be betrayed like that, by someone he'd put trust in . . . well, one could argue that he'd trusted too soon, too fast, especially given what had brought her here in the first place—but none of that really mattered.

What mattered was that she couldn't imagine what that particular agony was like. It was one thing when the other person just didn't feel the same way as you—but it was another altogether when they earned your trust and then shit all over your feelings for them. Which, from what she could tell, was exactly what Cami had done.

"What are you going to do?" Tamra asked him. "About the Crab."

Poor Reece looked exhausted and overwrought as he raked a hand back through his messier-than-usual hair. She'd never seen him this way before. And she could truly *feel* just how invested he'd been in all this, and how deeply it was affecting him. But she was glad he'd at least gotten out of his apartment, that he'd come to them to talk about it.

"I haven't decided," he said. "I know it would be smart to take the money. Like Cami's been telling me from the start, I could do whatever I wanted with that kind of money. I mean, I've always been comfortable—I have life insurance from my family, and until that sign went up in the lot next door, I've had at least a little income from the Crab. But if I took the deal, I could start something brand new, or I could invest it all, retire at thirty-five, and live off the interest."

When he ended on a sigh, though, Fletcher stated the obvious. "Only you don't *want* to start something new, and you don't really want to retire at thirty-five."

At which Reece let out an almost cynical laugh. "Sounds crazy hearing you say it, but it's true. And so there's also a stubborn part of me that wants to just sit there and wait and make them come shut me down. Only . . ." Another heavy sigh. "That isn't very satisfying, either. Vanderhook wouldn't even be the ones to lower the ax. All *they* need to do is make a call to the health department. And sure, I could still sit on that property forever and not sell it, but if the Crab isn't open, I'm not sure what the point is. My family built a friendly little motel, the first in Coral Cove and the last that's still standing since the resorts moved in. So if it just ends up a vacant piece of property that isn't used or enjoyed by anybody, that's not exactly in keeping with my vision. Or my dad's or uncle's or grandfather's."

"Could you just move Fifi up the street?" Tamra motioned over her shoulder in the direction of the little house Reece owned two doors down from hers but hadn't lived in since before she moved here.

"I thought of that," he said. "I thought of moving her, and moving myself. But I don't think it would fix the problem. There's plenty of evidence, right down to pictures in the newspaper, of Fifi having lived there. And I'm pretty sure the whole issue behind the ordinance is the idea that she might carry germs that would make the whole place be deemed unclean—even if that's not true—so I think they'd enforce it whether she was still there or not. And I'm not even sure what hoops they'd make me jump through to reopen."

He slumped over slightly, blew out a big breath. "And I guess I'm just tired. Of fighting. I'm one guy with a little motel. They're a massive corporation. And I have a feeling that even if I found a way to get out of this problem with Fifi, they'd just come up with something else. So maybe it's just time to cut my losses and throw in the towel. I hate losing my family's business—but now that I know Vanderhook isn't above playing dirty, I'm not sure I can save it."

After a long, somber moment of silence, Reece looked at Fletcher. "I don't know how you do it, man."

"How I do what, my friend?" Fletcher asked in his usual, calm way.

"How you . . . forgive your wife so easily for

hurting you. How you don't feel angry about it every freaking day. How you reconcile it all. Because to find out that what I thought I had going with Cami wasn't real . . . Damn. I don't even understand how she could have faked some of that stuff." He shut his eyes, clearly in pain, and then reopened them. "But I guess she did."

Fletcher said, "I'm able to see the futility in anger. I can forgive my wife because I know, in the end, when she comes back, that I'll be filled with such happiness that it won't matter. So I just . . . skip ahead to already feeling that way. It saves a lot of pain, I promise you." Then he gave his head an inquisitive tilt. "Do we know for certain, though, that everything you experienced with Cami was fake?"

Reece blinked, clearly thinking it over, and for some reason Tamra's heart rose to her throat waiting for the answer.

"If she ran back to her room," Reece replied, "and used information I'd given her on the boat to get what her company wanted, almost as soon as we got back, doesn't that mean it *had* to be fake?"

Fletcher's gaze narrowed. "One thing doesn't necessarily equal the other. And from what I can tell, your conversation with her afterward wasn't really a fact-finding mission."

"I figured anything she'd say would just be a lie," Reece shot back.

"Maybe so, maybe not," Fletcher reasoned. "But regardless, the one fact *I* see is that you're making assumptions based on what happened, when in fact, many roads could have led to this outcome. You believe you know what Cami did or said, what her intent was, but I'm not sure your email from Vanderhook, or even her admission that she communicated with them about that ordinance, is proof that everything you shared with her wasn't real. As I say, doing the job she was sent here to do and having sincere feelings for you aren't mutually exclusive."

As Reece silently took that in and mulled it over, Tamra did, too. And after a moment, she asked Reece a question, one that felt important to her. She reached over, touched his arm, and said, "Did you really believe her on the boat? Did you really feel like she loved you?"

In the wicker chair next to hers, Reece gazed out over the sea, thought it over for a minute, and said quietly, "Yeah. I did. I really did. Next to the loss of my family, it was . . . the realest thing I've ever felt."

Tamra thought Reece a good judge of people—while he usually faced life in an easygoing, optimistic way, he wasn't the sort of guy who wore rose-colored glasses or imagined things to be something they weren't. And while part of her wanted to be a different sort of person, a person who would use this time to swoop in and try to make some big, romantic play for him, the bigger part of her just wanted his true happiness—perhaps more than she wanted her own—and so she knew what she had to do.

* * *

CAMI had hoped her sincere resolve would allow
her to wake up with some new sense of direction, or hope, or a way to somehow correct some
of what she'd messed up. Unfortunately, however,
she opened her eyes to find herself on the tenth
floor of a fancy resort that felt strange and distant
and sort of cookie cutter to her, and everything
still felt wrong. She wanted desperately to do the
right thing here, but she didn't even know what
that would be.

And the very thought of Reece was like a knife
to her heart. She loved him, but . . . had he really
loved *her*? She found it hard to believe anyone
who really cared about her wouldn't even listen
to her side of the story, and would be so very cold
and heartless, sending her away like that. Maybe
Reece had more in common with Peter Pan than
living in his own personal Never-Never Land.
Maybe he'd never grown up. Maybe he didn't
know how to love.

A directionless hour or two in her room finally
led her outside—and she found herself heading
to her car, and then driving to the Hungry Fisherman. She couldn't fix *much* here, but she could at
least ask Polly to check on the cat and tell her that
if she or Riley could just look after the kitty for
now, once she got settled and got some direction
back in her life, she'd be happy to adopt Tiger Lily
permanently.

"I'm still not sure life in my place in Atlanta
would be very exciting for her," she said across
a table to Polly in the empty restaurant, "but . . ."

"But cats don't need a lot of excitement," Polly

explained to her, swiping her hand down through the air. "And that kitty couldn't be luckier to find somebody who cares as much as you do. She belongs with ya, plain and simple."

"Well," Cami said with a conceding tilt of her head, "it's more like *you* found me for her. So thank you."

"Nothin' to thank me for, honey—I just wish things hadn't turned out like this." She'd told Polly the main gist of what had come down yesterday afternoon.

"Me, too," she said on a sigh. "I know I haven't exactly handled everything here wonderfully myself, but . . . don't I deserve a guy who would at least hear my side, who wouldn't jump to conclusions and assume the worst about me?"

Polly patted Cami's hand where it sat on the table, curled lightly around a soda glass. "You do, and I'm surprised at Reece. But . . . well, he's had a rough way to go over the years, and I guess maybe he had a kneejerk reaction that . . . wasn't only about you. If that helps at all."

Cami took that in. Now that she knew Reece's past, she could easily understand that. But at the same time, it still hurt. "I guess," she began, "what it comes down to is—there's the part of this that's about me and him, and the part that's about his business. And even if I'm upset over the me-and-him part, I feel a lot of responsibility about the Happy Crab. And I just wish I could fix that for him."

Polly took a sip of her soft drink, and Cami thought she looked surprisingly hopeful as she said, "There must be a way."

"I can't imagine what it is," Cami told her. Because it seemed impossible at this point.

And yet . . . something in Polly's voice made her begin to at least wish, to wonder . . . *was* there any conceivable thing she could do that would somehow reverse all this and make things right?

When Cami left the restaurant, she considered venturing across the parking lot to knock on Riley's door and say hi to Tiger Lily, but she thought better of it. She was persona non grata at the Happy Crab and she wouldn't want a nasty run-in with Reece.

But instead of getting back in her car, though, her flip-flops led her across the street to the beach. Maybe seeing people out having fun would lift her spirits. And maybe a walk along the shore would do something to inspire her next move. She wasn't sure why she was even still *in* Coral Cove, but by the same token, she couldn't quite bring herself to go home. Right now, Atlanta and Vanderhook didn't *feel* much like home.

She carried her flip-flops in one hand as she walked up the packed, wet sand along the water. The sound of the surf rushing in and out was indeed calming, and so she tried to focus on it and let it still her mind. The one big asset she'd always had in life was her belief in herself. She always believed in her ability to succeed, to solve problems, to do whatever it took to accomplish her goals. And so if there was an answer to this, it must lie inside her—and that meant she just had to relax and let it come to her.

Just then, her phone buzzed—she had a text.

THIS IS REECE'S FRIEND, TAMRA. CAN YOU MEET ME? IT'S IMPORTANT.

Whoa.

Was Tamra going to tell her off? Defend Reece's honor? And had she lifted Cami's phone number from Reece's phone when he wasn't looking? Or maybe she'd gotten it from Christy, who also had it. Regardless, it seemed like a lot of trouble to go to—but what else could Tamra really want with her, all things considered?

Though she'd said it was important. What if it was? What if Tamra actually had something constructive to say?

All she'd felt from Tamra so far was judgment, resentment, and a general sense of disdain . . . so maybe agreeing to meet her wasn't wise, but following her gut instinct, which was really all she had to go on these days, she texted back:

I'M ON THE BEACH. MEET UNDER THE PIER IN FIFTEEN MINUTES?

Tamra agreed. And Cami was nervous—but too curious, she supposed, to do anything but follow through, so she headed toward the pier.

When she saw Tamra approaching from the direction of Sea Shell Lane, her chest tightened. *Please don't let this be a mistake.* She really wasn't up for another ugly confrontation—with anyone.

"Hi," she said when Tamra was just a few feet away.

"I only came to say one thing," Tamra told her.

Wow, talk about getting straight to the point. "Okay."

"I sat around wasting time with Reece, never telling him I had feelings for him."

Oh. Yikes. Well, already this explained a lot. Like why Tamra had taken such an instant dislike to her. She'd been an unwitting rival.

"But if I had another chance to let him know how I feel, I would take it. So if you really love him, if you really want him, you should do something to fix this. Because *he* really loves *you*. And I know he has some issues, but that doesn't change how amazing he is. And I just want to see him happy.

"I think people act like love, real love, is something you can find around every corner. But I haven't found it too often myself. I know plenty of people who haven't. So if you find it, you shouldn't let it just slip away. Because what if it never comes again? If I were in your shoes, I wouldn't give up on something good just because some bad things happened. If you truly love him, if you truly never meant to hurt him, you need to dig down deep and find a way to show him."

And with that, the other woman started to walk away—but then she stopped, looking back pointedly. "And if I'm wrong here—if you really did use him and really don't give a damn, then please do the decent thing and go the hell away."

Then she turned around and trod back up the beach away from Cami.

On the one hand, it was hardly a miracle solution. She still didn't know how to fix any of this.

But it was . . . a reminder. That love counted for something and shouldn't just be thrown away over a misunderstanding or a mistake, no matter how big. And that Reece *was* a great guy. And yeah, he *was* flawed. *We all are.* But maybe his re-action yesterday was forgivable. If he *wanted* her to forgive him.

No, Tamra hadn't given her any answers. But she had perhaps . . . shone a light where there hadn't been one before. And maybe that was enough, enough to inspire Cami, enough to show her what direction to look in.

Toward Reece, not away from him.

"I don't see how it can have a happy ending."

J. M. Barrie, *Peter and Wendy*

Chapter 22

$\mathcal{W}$HEN CAMI lay down to bed that night in her resort hotel room, she still didn't have any practical answers on how to do what Tamra had said—figure out a way to fix things with Reece, and *for* Reece. But Tamra's confrontation had made Cami remember: All her adult life she'd been a woman of action, and this seemed like a good time to get back to that old taking-care-of-business side of herself—only this time she needed to focus on what she could do for *other* people. She felt more determined than discouraged now, and just hearing that Reece loved her helped *a lot*—it was like a salve on her wounds.

And so when she woke up the next morning, it was with an idea in her head.

And as she showered, that idea led to another, and another.

And the truth was—she had no idea if *any* of them would work. Because if fixing all the Happy Crab's troubles were as simple as the plans now filling her brain, why hadn't she thought of them before?

But then . . . sometimes inspiration was simple. And sometimes it just took a little hope to nudge it into being. And maybe that was why all this was coming to her now.

So it was with a fresh new sense of resolve to get what she wanted that she put on her red power suit and pumps one more time—and set off for the Coral Cove City Building.

REECE tried to feel like his old self as he put Fifi's leash on her and walked her across the street to the beach. But he didn't.

He tried to feel like the same old laid-back, carefree guy he'd been a few weeks ago as two attractive twenty-something female tourists approached him in bikinis to ask about his giant iguana and have the usual photos taken with her. But he didn't pull that off, either. In fact, despite that one of the girls was flirty as hell and had a tattoo on her lower back that said Easy Come Easy Go, he wasn't interested. At all. He even ended up making an excuse for why he couldn't get together with them later that night.

This'll get better, though. It just takes a little time. Wasn't that what people said about breakups anyway? He'd had so few relationships that he barely knew how to deal with his emotions at the moment—he only knew he didn't like them.

But hey, if that old saying was true—if it took half the length of a relationship to get over someone—he'd be over Cami in a flash. Because at least this had all happened fast. At least he hadn't had the chance to get used to having her around, used to depending on her, used to what it felt like to love her and have her in his life.

Even if it felt, oddly, as if he *had*, as if she'd been a part of his world for much longer than just a couple of short weeks.

Funny, he'd never have believed a woman could have such an impact on him that quickly.

And he knew he had some stuff to deal with, some big decisions to make about how exactly he was going to respond to Vanderhook's underhanded threat. All he'd managed to do so far was spend time thinking about the Tinkerbell who'd flitted in and out of his existence nearly faster than he could blink—but who had still changed . . . everything.

THREE days later, wearing the shorts and flip-flops that now felt much more normal to her than her suits, Cami once again got in her rental car—but this time she made the short drive to the Happy Crab.

It was nearly dusk—the sun would set soon—and she hoped Reece wouldn't be at the Sunset Celebration tonight; she hoped he'd just be hanging out at home. She hadn't seen Polly or any of her other new Coral Cove friends in the last few days—she'd been too busy; nor had she responded to any of Phil's texts or emails. Only as she parked her car in the Happy Crab lot did she finally decide to send him a quick text. She kept it simple, vague.

I KNOW I'VE BEEN OUT OF CONTACT. IT'S COM-
PLICATED, BUT I'M HANDLING THINGS.

If Phil knew what that actually meant, it could
spur him to action that could risk counteracting
some of her recent progress. That's why she'd
stayed silent until now. And this text, she supposed, was intended simply to keep him a little
confused, off balance. She didn't expect it to
regain his trust or anything, but she figured it
couldn't hurt if he thought they were still on the
same side, working with the same goals. Though
she'd kept it distant and unspecific because if this
were, say, a trial, she would officially be considered a hostile witness by now. She'd jumped ship,
joined the other team.

Even so, she was nervous as hell getting out of
the car. She needed to talk to Reece, but if he was
still as angry with her as he'd been the last time
she'd seen him, she wasn't sure she could handle
it. Her heart still reeled from those last few painful moments between them—and only focusing on
the other tasks at hand had held her together and
kept her functioning like a normal human being.

She took a deep breath as she approached the
office door. When she pulled it open and stepped
inside, she suffered both disappointment and
relief to find Reece wasn't behind the counter. But
she smiled when she saw Fifi stretched out on the
floor behind it.

"Hi," she whispered, walking back toward the
huge iguana. She wasn't sure why she was whis-
pering, but maybe having no idea where Reece

was kept her uneasy. She was dying to see him, yet also afraid to—both ready and not.

Without weighing it, she stooped down to get more up-close and personal with Fifi. "I owe you an apology, Fifi," she said, voice still low. And maybe it was stupid to be apologizing to a reptile who couldn't understand her, but perhaps it was like talking to Tiger Lily—there was a certain comfort in it, and even if the cat couldn't make actual sense of her words, Cami felt that on some level she absorbed the sentiment and feelings within them.

"I never meant to use you to hurt Reece. I never meant to hurt Reece at all." She shook her head. "I still don't know how all this really happened. I guess the main thing is—I never meant to fall in love, but I did, and that made everything confusing.

"And I don't know if he'll ever forgive me, if he could ever trust in me again or believe how much I really love him, but I think I've at least found some ways to fix some pretty big things. And I hope I can fix more of them. Fortunately, when it comes to real estate, I'm pretty good at fixing things. At having vision and seeing what needs to be done. So that part I'm feeling pretty confident about. It's the other part—about Reece and me—that I'm not as good at."

"Do you want to touch my iguana?"

Reece watched as Cami flinched, then stood up and turned to face him. Her eyes were wide and beautiful, but she looked full of fear. He'd heard a lot of what she'd said. And it was almost enough to give him some sort of hope—about everything—but even so, his heart felt hard in his chest. It almost seemed to whisper to him: *Don't trust so easy this time. Be more careful than before.*

"Hi," she said softly.

"Hi." He met her gaze but tried to follow his heart's sound advice.

"I . . . I think I fixed the problem," she said again.

"How? And which one?"

She blinked, still looking nervous. "I talked to the mayor. About the ordinance. And about how Vanderhook was planning to use it against you. He wasn't even aware of the ordinance and when I explained what was at stake, he called an emergency meeting of the town council yesterday and they abolished it. He said he could understand the possible need for the law, and that it could always be reinstated at some point if necessary, but that since your family was responsible for making Coral Cove a tourist destination, it was the least he could do. He doesn't want to lose the Happy Crab, either."

Reece's heart lifted. Yeah, this was a *big* problem averted. Freaking enormous!

And he was pretty amazed—both that she'd gone so far to repair the situation, and also that it had never occurred to him to throw himself on the mercy of the town because of his family history in Coral Cove. "But . . . as much as I appreciate that," he told her, "don't you think Vanderhook will just find some other way, dig up some other meaningless infraction?"

"Actually, no," she said, sounding far more hopeful than *he'd* felt in days. "Now that the mayor has a firm understanding of the situation, he and the town council are prepared to back you up. As luck would have it, one member of the council is the manager of the Sand Dollar Resort and was very on board, for obvious reasons, with preventing Windchime from coming here. The mayor has proposed a zoning law for this stretch of Coral Street—no buildings over two stories. They're voting on it tomorrow morning and he expects it to pass easily. And after that, Windchime won't even be a possibility here."

"That—that's incredible," he said. Because it really was. Damn, a zoning change. Why the hell had it never occurred to him to be more pro-active about this in bigger ways? He'd just sat here digging in his heels since all this had started, hoping they'd give up and go away—and what Cami had done made so much sense. He shook his head. "I should have thought of that."

"Not necessarily," she reassured him. "You run a motel—not the whole town. This kind of stuff is *my* business—I'm *trained* to think of it."

He narrowed his gaze on her. "But you're thinking of it for *me* now, and not Vanderhook? Really?"

She nodded, looking as sweet and earnest as he'd ever seen her. "I never meant to hurt you, Reece, I promise. I told my boss about that ordinance before we ever went out on the *Lisa Renee*, and even then I did only because he was pressuring me and I'd just run across it. And that was before I realized I didn't want to take the Crab from you anymore, that I didn't want to take *any-one's* property from them anymore if they weren't willing to part with it gladly."

Despite himself, Reece was still afraid to believe. Believing had felt so simple on the boat. And he'd ended up feeling so foolish and hurt for his easy trust. "Are you saying you no longer work for Vanderhook?" he asked, needing more information.

"I haven't quit *yet*," she told him. "Because I want to throw them off the trail and not give them time to do anything sneaky before that zoning law is passed. I'm pretty sure there's nothing they really *could* do at this point now that the town is on your side, but still, I'm learning that it's better to be safe than sorry."

He nodded. And found himself *wanting* to believe in her again.

Because he was crazy in love with her.

But he wasn't sure how. How do you wipe out pain and distrust? It had taken him so long to open up and feel that way for anyone. And she'd made it seem like such a big mistake.

"There's more," she volunteered, "if you'd like to hear it."

"Sure," he replied. "Go ahead."

"I've talked with the mayor a lot over the last few days—I've shared with him my preliminary ideas for ways to reshape Coral Cove in the coming years to revitalize the older part of town, to increase the flow of business here while maintaining its charm. And . . . I'm not sure how you'll feel about this, but . . . he's offered me a job and I've accepted it.

"It's on a trial basis for now—I'll present a more detailed plan to the town council, and if they're on board, I'm Coral Cove's first town planner and

I'll head up a planning commission. It doesn't pay much, but I've come to realize I don't need much—at least not as much as I thought I did for a while. So . . . I'll be staying on here, as long as the job becomes permanent. And I'm sure I'll be working with you some, so I hope that's not a problem."

Reece just blinked. It was a lot to take in.

She was staying. In Coral Cove. He'd be seeing her—maybe a lot. It changed things.

In one way, it made him unbelievably happy—because despite himself, just seeing her right now was filling his soul with something incredibly good, something he'd definitely been missing ever since he'd sent her away.

But in another way . . . was he ready for this? What would they be to each other? Could he really have faith in her? Everything about this conversation said yes. But after the blows of the other day . . . how could he be sure?

"It's not a problem," he finally said, exercising some caution. "And the idea of fixing up this part of town is . . . great. I've wished for a long time something like that would happen, but I wouldn't know how to begin."

She flashed a slightly self-deprecating smile. "Then I guess it's lucky I came along. In a roundabout way, I mean."

"In . . . *other* ways, too, Tink," he said gently.

"Reece," she said then, seeming at once a little bolder but also brimming with emotion, "I just need to tell you that . . . you made me a better person. Something about you, and this place, made me . . . different than I was when I got here.

And I know it probably makes no difference after what happened the other day, but . . . I really do love you. In a way that I'm not sure I've ever loved a man before. And I can't believe I managed to screw it up." Her eyes fell briefly shut.

Reece said nothing. Part of him wanted to tell her it was all okay, that they'd find a way to work things out, that he'd figure out how to trust her again. But another part of him feared that was too big right now, too big a promise to make to her—or to himself. He just wasn't good at that—trusting. And now he wasn't sure it was the right road for him to take, the life he wanted to live. Because it was huge, that kind of faith. And he just wasn't sure he had it in him anymore.

And she must have sensed all that, because she seemed unable to meet his gaze then, and she sounded much more subdued when she said, "Anyway, I just wanted you to know that. I'll be looking for a place to live in the next few days, and after that, I'll be heading back to Atlanta to part ways with Vanderhook, put my townhouse on the market, and start packing."

"That'll be hard for you," he acknowledged, remembering how dear she'd held her job.

"Yeah," she said softly. "But . . . it's time." She still didn't meet his eyes as she added, "I'll get Tiger Lily as soon as I can, and I hope you and Riley won't mind looking out for her until then. And please thank him for me."

"Sure," he said shortly.

Then watched as she headed toward the office door.

He let her walk out. Let the door close behind her. Felt his chest tighten.

He glanced down at Fifi. He could have sworn she gave him a critical look.

"Stop taking her side," he scolded the iguana. "Even if . . . it seems like she's done about everything humanly possible to make things better here."

Uncertain, he walked to the plate glass door and looked out, saw her getting in her car.

And then his heart rose to his throat.

And he pushed through the door.

"Cami!"

She was inside the car but hadn't closed the door yet. Now she stopped, looked up, got back out.

"I . . . I know a place you could live," he told her.

Her voice sounded nervous, too high-pitched, as she said, "Oh?"

"My cottage. On Sea Shell Lane. It's small but nice. Beach access. And you'd already know your neighbors."

"That's . . . amazingly generous," she said. "But . . . I know you've always kept it the way it was before—"

"It's time for some changes," he said, feeling suddenly like maybe it really *was* time to move on from the past once and for all. "And I'm sure any changes you'd make would be good for the place."

"Well . . . if . . . if you're sure, that would be great. I'd really love that."

"I am," he said.

And she looked hopeful but maybe a little confused, which he could understand. She wanted more from him.

And . . . he wanted more from him, too.

"Tink," he said.

"Yeah?"

"Maybe . . . maybe after we see how things go for a little while, maybe . . . we can start to . . . work our way back to where we were, back to how things were out on the boat."

Her eyes went wide, her mouth forming the shape of an "o." She pressed her palm, fingers splayed, to her chest. "Really? Are you saying . . . ?" She shook her head. "Can you possibly forgive me, Reece?"

"I'm . . . starting to," he said. "Because . . . I love you. And because I guess I'm just starting to see . . . how much you've sacrificed for me. And . . . how many people do that? How many people would give up their whole lives, their careers, for somebody else?" He stepped toward her. "That's pretty amazing."

She tilted her head, and though her eyes brimmed with emotion, he also thought he saw just a hint of the saucy Tinkerbell he'd first fallen for. "You know," she said cautiously, "I didn't want to say anything, but you're right—I did kind of sacrifice everything for you."

"How can I thank you, Tink?" he asked with an indulgent grin.

And she said, "Kissing me would be a good place to start."

So Reece complied, kissing her beneath the late day neon glow of the large smiling red crab sign. And all was well at the Happy Crab Motel once again.

> " . . . and he found her, and they lived
> happily ever after."
>
> J. M. Barrie, *Peter and Wendy*

Epilogue

6 months later

CAMI FLOATED on a blow-up raft in the pool behind the Happy Crab, late day sun warming her skin. There wasn't much time for floating in pools these days, or many occasions when the pool was empty and quiet like this, for that matter. But autumn had fallen over Coral Cove, bringing an end to high tourist season, and that suited her fine because there were a lot of plans to implement over the winter.

Of course, there'd already been a lot of wonderful changes. It hadn't taken long before Reece had moved in to the cottage on Sea Shell Lane with her, along with Tiger Lily, who Reece had soon admitted was an extremely easy cat to live with once he got over the fact that she shed a little. Fifi had stayed on at the Crab because the cottage was just too small for a "dinosaur," and she was well-acclimated to her home at the motel. Reece had experienced a little separation anxiety at first, but he saw her every day and it turned out fine.

Now Riley lived in Reece's old apartment, happy to be gainfully employed as the "assistant manager, maintenance expert, and head iguana caretaker" at the Happy Crab. Much of the vintage 1950s furniture had been moved to the cottage—simply because Reece and Cami both liked it—and into the motel's apartment they'd moved Reece's family's furniture from the house. Reece had embraced the spirit of change, finding ways to simultaneously let go of certain things even while holding on to them a little bit, too.

Cami had promptly quit her job at Vanderhook, and though Phil's nasty and dismissive attitude had hurt, she'd gotten through it by focusing on the future and on all her new friends in Coral Cove. Leaving Atlanta behind so easily had shown her how little of substance she'd really had there—and she knew in her heart that fate had led her to where she was meant to be.

She loved her new multi-faceted job of revitalizing Coral Cove. Some days it meant putting on her old business suits and wooing investors she knew from her association with Vanderhook, or working to get state or federal funding, or arranging advertising to draw people back to the older part of Coral Cove. Most days, though, it was denim shorts and flip-flops while she worked to revive the town, one inch at a time.

Just last month an island of soil, grass, and shrubbery had been dug and planted in between the Crab and the Hungry Fisherman, breaking up the sea of asphalt that had stretched between them. It was little touches, little bits of warmth and beautification, that would bring back Coral Cove's quaint appeal. The Beachside Bakery was getting a new façade next week, and she almost had Jack DuVall talked into investing in a miniature golf course she hoped to put on an empty lot beyond Gino's Pizzeria. A lot of her work these days was talking small business owners into spending a little money to spruce things up, and in the cases where they simply couldn't, finding other ways to get the needed funds.

And she was further gratified to feel it all becoming a mass labor of love for the community. Fletcher donated time on a regular basis to whatever project someone needed help with. Even Tamra had finally gotten friendly with Cami once she and Reece had worked out their troubles. And as Tamra was an avid gardener in addition to being an artist, she had volunteered when it was time to do some planting in front of the Happy Crab a few weeks back, and seemed eager to help out on any occasion she could.

Business had returned to the Happy Crab when Windchime's sign had come down in the adjoining lot, and Cami had gone so far as to buy the little chunk of land herself. She planned to convert the old snowcone shack into a mini-tourist center and was already talking to the local businesses about investing in flyers and coupons to distribute.

Reece had gotten on board with her idea to make

better use of the boats, and he now advertised a free snorkeling trip or sunset cruise with a three night stay at the Happy Crab, and also sold tickets for the same cruises independent of that. Cami had ideas about building additional dock space behind the Crab, stretching up behind her tourist-center-to-be and was working on attracting additional boating businesses to the area. She was also in talks with the local marina about space for larger tourist-based boats she hoped to draw in.

She'd told Reece over a picnic dinner on the beach last night that she almost had her first day-trip fishing boat "hooked."

And he'd said, "That's very punny, honey."

Just now, a light touch at her ankle made her draw in her breath and open her eyes—to find the handsome man she lived with standing next to her in the pool, grazing his hand up her thigh.

"You're very quiet and sneaky," she said, tingling from the touch in all the right places.

"I learned it from my dinosaur," he told her.

And then he came closer, leaning down to give her a scintillating kiss she felt all the way to her toes. The best part of her life in Coral Cove was that every time Reece kissed her, she forgot about everything else. Rebuilding the town, giant iguanas, Tiger Lily, the rocky road they'd taken to get here—it all faded to the background when Reece pressed his mouth to hers. Or to anyplace else on her body as well, for that matter.

A moment later, she abandoned the raft and soon stood making out with her sexy beach bum in the pool. And when certain delicious sensations began to occur below, she couldn't resist smiling into his eyes to ask, "Is that—"

But he read her mind and cut her off. "Nope, it's still not sunscreen, Tinkerbell."

And she said, "I'm glad you're still happy to see me, Reecie Cup."